Acknowledgments

As an author, I find it more challenging to write a genuine heartfelt acknowledgment than the first fictional sentence of this book, which you are about to start reading in just a few seconds.

First and foremost, I want to express my gratitude to you for choosing to engage with this book, whether by purchasing, borrowing or discovering it. It's truly a remarkable feeling to see something that began as a fleeting idea in 2018, a mere tangle of thoughts and a single badly written sentence, now transformed into a 400-page reality that you hold in your hands ready to be explored.

Of course, I must also thank my partner, who managed to endure my creative phases, which can last a very long time. I know sharing your life with a creative person is difficult. So, thank you, Linda; I love you.

And of course, I must also thank everyone else who provided invaluable input, making the book what it is today.
Thank you, Davide, for the truly remarkable and unique cover.
After all these years of knowing each other, it's always a pleasure to create something with you. Thank you to the many test readers and the
"Book Club" who provided critical feedback in corrections, thought experiments, or criticism. My brother, who first introduced me to books.
Marius, Dave, and Davide also contributed.
Thank you also, to Alice for reading, correcting, and providing feedback on the English version of this book.
And now, the time has come. There are only three blank pages (in case you want to take notes or just doodle), a Map of Seattle and two obligatory pages separating you from diving into the world of 2066. Enjoy, and see you in the next book.

Imprint

Fragment

Author: J.L. Litschko
Publisher English Version: Amazon KDP
First published: 2024

All rights reserved. No part of this publication may be reproduced, stored in a retrieval system, or transmitted in any form or by any means, electronic, mechanical, photocopying, recording, or otherwise, without the publisher's prior written permission.

Disclaimer:
The information in this book is provided for informational purposes only.
The publisher and author are not liable for any damages or
negative consequences of any action based on this information.

© 2024 J. L. Litschko
Cover Illustration: Davide Di Donna — davidedidonna.com
Logo Design: LeechTM — Leechtm.com

Table of Contents

One. *The Inheritance of the Past*
Two. *Fragments of Yesterday*
Three. *Lost innocence*
Four. *On the Edge of the Abyss*
Five. *Flight into the Unknown*
Six. *Dangerous Connections*
Seven. *Amithayus*
Eight. *Forgotten faces, forgotten Places*
Nine. *The Flower of the Night*
Ten. *The Echo of Time*
Eleven. *The Way of the Sword*
Twelve. *The Last Spark*
Thirteen. *On a Knife's Edge*
Fourteen. *The Last Bastion*
Fifteen. *A Single Life*
Sixteen. *Between Two Fronts*
Seventeen. *Collapse of Conformity*
Eighteen. *Implants and Intrigues*
Nineteen. *Underground Movements*
Twenty. *Breakdown*
Twenty-one. *War Zone*
Twenty-Two. *Fragments*
Epilogue. *Allies*

SEATTLE

- AMITHAYUS
- OLD MEDICAL
- BEACON HILL
- PINEHILL
- NOMAD DISTRICT
- CARPENTERIA

ONE.
THE INHERITANCE OF THE PAST

Seattle, 2066 11:17 AM — Old Medical District

The first encounter with Death always ends in red and black, behind your eyelids, when you emerge as the first loser from your first last situation.

And believe me, ten minutes of being dead feel like an eternity when you are actually dead.

I was once asked, what's the final perceivable color? What a silly question. You're dead. You don't care anymore. Even though I knew the answer. I had experienced it 6 times before.

But what I can tell you is this. After your Death, there are only shades of brown: light woody browns, dark earthy browns, and leathery skin-dried, mostly crusted browns. It all reminded me strongly of a painting by Anselm Kiefer that I had seen only once, many decades ago.
And yet, it stayed with me. And now, in 2066, it probably hung alone on a wall in an old museum, rotting away with the other paintings—The same faith as most people I have dealt with.

I rarely invite visitors to my Day Job, which remain in my Head. And if they do, it's for a maximum of ten minutes.

A fleeting thought entered my mind. Everything lying before me was someone's eternal Pain.

It gave me a twisted sense of peace. But as with all the previous times, that would change quickly. I entered the room quietly.

Someone might still be home.

I took off my glove, and the fingertip of my left hand touched the iron door handle. A feeling like an old friend I hadn't seen in a long time. A familiar feeling. One I had tried to lock out for many years.

But an addiction is always there, even if it is hidden.

I enjoyed every single bit of it. It wasn't painful.

"Of course, I can bring it to you in another glass if you're afraid of getting hurt by that little crack; I love serving you all day long." the irony in her voice was unmistakable.

I saw an older male arguing with a female, probably his wife, in the living room. He looked pretty drunk.

"No, thanks," the male replied, extra dry. The red wine in his hand and bloodstream did the rest as he tried to sit down, failing hilariously.

I released the door handle. My eyes glimpsed over the shattered wine glass on the floor. Next to it, two half-empty bottles of extra dry, extra cheap American wine.
A plastic fruit bowl with the obligatory worm. And an eLetter that caught my attention.

"Dear Mr. Serpentine, We are writing to inform you that your loan request for 250,000 new dollars from Bank of America cannot be approved due to your current US-ID credit limit with us. We hope you remain loyal to us, and we look forward to a personal appointment with you…"

My eyes rolled back until they hit the far end of my skull. I knew the rest of the platitudes from my
own' ,invitations. 'Debt was almost the only thing you could get everywhere, quick and easy these days.

Next to a small Teardrop shaped ball of iron or graphite, delivered primarily free of charge, straight through your Head.

"They definitely weren't blessed with much money," my partner Simmons murmured from the next room. He had pushed through the door behind me, walked down the hall, and examined the Serpentine's bedroom without me noticing him.

"Not much money," I muttered to myself. I had already guessed that when I turned off the six-lane highway onto Berington Road. The Old Medical District, where Berington Road was located, had long ceased to be a destination for wealthy clients. The middle class had disappeared in the last ten to fifteen years, taking significant new dollars with them.
As far as I heard from rumors spreading throughout the streets of Seattle, those who could afford it and were of Asian descent settled in the 'Amithayus' district, not far from the Old Medical Center. This enclave was established on an island about three decades ago—a massive, 60-foot-high, walled-off area in the heart of Seattle.

With a generous interpretation, one might call it a gated community. According to my poor knowledge of Asian languages, the name Amithayus meant something like 'the immeasurable life.'

It was immeasurably densely populated, with around 24,600 inhabitants per square kilometer, and it was complicated to cross the district border into Amithayus. From what I gathered talking to witnesses, it was very hard for People like me, working in a job paid for by the government, to cross into Amithayus. Unless you were of Asian descent or on good business terms with the local Crime Syndicates or bringing some convincing arguments with you. Suitcases full of new dollars or the severed Head of one of the local rival clan members were a welcome currency — among regular money by merchants and other people selling or buying goods. Free trade in the newly Unified America.

USA. USA.

Not so much for the 'Amis,' as the inhabitants called themselves. It gave them the same feeling as the Roman Catholic Church felt shortly after it became known that the Pope elected in 2030 was neither male nor female.
A sacrilege. Blasphemy.

Off with his Head.

At least it was safe there. However, simple anarchic chaos reigned in the Old Medical District on the outskirts of Seattle, as there were neither border controls nor armed security patrols.

At least not anymore. There's nothing of value left to guard.

Consequently, the hospitals and medical bio-faculties established there decades ago were rundown. They experienced a brief influx of patients willing to pay cash or electronic money to improve their natural abilities. About seven or eight years after the opening of the Old Medical District, the last patient who could or wanted to pay for their treatment came and went.

No one who can tell the story survived.

Over time, the hospitals became collection points and shelters for drug addicts and other lost souls of modern society. Most of the once-expensive renovated apartments from the early twentieth century deteriorated within a few years into transit stations for drug and human trafficking, mainly from the middle and southern parts of New America, such as Salt Lake

City and New Las Vegas. Gambling and holographic video booths completed the picture.

"This hole is simply no place for a couple trying to maintain a bit of normalit.. The Serpentines didn't break free from their past in time," I murmured while still searching their Apartment for clues on what happened.

No matter what, they no longer had problems with any debt collectors.

"That was at least a caliber nine or ten from a very short distance, maybe a meter or less. "Simmons pulled me out of my thoughts. "It definitely surprised both of them; they hadn't been home very long, maybe an hour, maybe two?" Simmons continued to look around the bedroom. "So if you ask me, it was clearly a mistake. Someone searched for money, found nothing, and then unexpectedly stumbled upon the couple. Probably shot them out of frustration because they had nothing valuable. People get maimed, beaten or shot daily over trivialities. Sometimes, it's about something to eat, then it's for a new dollar or two, and at the bottom of the barrel, it's always: ‚Hey, mister, got a vial of synth-crocodile? "Simmons said slightly resigned, while putting on a glove to avoid destroying any evidence while searching the Apartment.

"Synth-crocodile," I mused. One of the nastiest concocted drugs originated in early 21st-century Russia and spread to America by the late 2020s.

It's cheaper than Opioids and hits harder.

Even after a single use, the injection site showed a greenish skin change and a leathery surface texture. It was simply disgusting to look at, and most croc addicts didn't live longer than six months.

It's cheaper. And hits harder! Thanks for explaining it twice, Junkie. I understood the first time that you've just injected your death warrant.

"What should we do with them now?" Simmons asked me again in his deliberately rough manner. "Should we call the guys from the precinct or summon the plastinators to come and seal them up?" He took a synthetic cigarette from one of the many boxes in his pocket. Then he waited for my answer, though he already knew what would happen next.

"A mistake, you said? "I let those two words run through my mind multiple times as I walked into the bedroom. I stood before Mrs. Serpentine, who lay on the floor unnaturally and twisted. After removing my glove again, I hesitated for a second before touching her shoulder with the fingertips of my left hand. The Pain I hadn't felt for years immediately returned, as it shot through my Arm and intensified in my Head. Cold sweat ran down my forehead. Excruciating Pain swallowed me whole as her last moments took over behind my eyes.

From now on, I had ten minutes. A painful eternity.

"You talked to George, didn't you? You know how strange he's been acting since his partner moved out. He is your brother, after all, not just some stranger…"

"He's not my brother anymore!" Martin catapulted out of his seat. The half-full glass of red wine shattered before me on the floor. "A nobody, that's what he is! And don't call him my brother! Just because we have the same father. His face turned the same color as the wine stain spreading on the light carpet. He was now yelling directly at me. I was sure he meant me, as I was the only person with him in our Apartment.

"He simply didn't deserve any better, that damn son of a bitch. That child molester! And as for that whore Jenn he was involved with, I was suspicious of her from the beginning."
I looked at Martin with pity.

I truly felt sorry for him. The last moments of a life should never end in a quarrel. But few people adhered to that.

Why did I mention his brother anyway? I knew how much the topic affected him.

Did I really know?

"What would such a rich young slut want with an asshole like George?" It was a rhetorical question, and I was sure he wanted to answer it himself.

That I knew for a fact!

"The damn family is so filthy rich. She can amuse herself with a different guy every day and doesn't even give me, her brother-in-law, a small loan, even though we desperately need it right now..."

I watched Martin stop speaking and gesticulating in the middle of the sentence. His gaze had turned toward the door during the last sentence. His facial expression still showed a slight hint of anger but slowly gave way to astonishment. Did I see a trace of confusion in his eyes?

Or was it a realization?

Time slowed down rapidly inside my Head as I tried to overcome the Pain I felt.

I was out of practice. But I wanted to know what was happening, so I also tried to turn my Head. At that moment, I felt a tearing pain in my left cheek, which abruptly reversed the direction of my Head against my will. The Pain shot through my whole body, and it took a fraction of a second for me to refocus on the sound of the splintering wooden door behind me. I heard Martin's scream, transitioning from a howl to a gurgle as he collapsed in front of me. The Pain in my left cheek overwhelmed me, and I lost the strength to form a clear thought.

It had been five years since I last invited a dead person to switch places with me. Meanwhile, I had forgotten it wasn't just pictures, sounds, and noises.

Damn feelings.

Joy and compassion. Laughter and crying. Happiness and contentment. I liked that. And then, there was Pain.

Endless Pain. My old friend.

I had invited you back; somehow, it felt like you'd never truly been gone.

As I fell, I managed to turn my upper body towards Martin. I focused under excruciating Pain on recognizing what else, besides the rest of the door and the table, was flying past and into me.

"Some exotic type of bullet," I pressed out of the corner of my mouth toward Simmons while staring at him with wide eyes. He just raised his right eyebrow and took another drag from his cigarette. Something with a rifled extraction groove. Bullets are designed for a single purpose. Precise shooting with lethal outcomes on the first shot. "You don't see those often any more."

And even more rarely feel them!

"Especially not at crime scenes, where everything is just accidental." He heard my little jab and responded with a snort. That was a real advantage of ballistic killing methods. It was much cheaper and could be bought in much larger quantities almost everywhere.

But here, in this moment, it was about precision over mass.

I experienced it firsthand as, under screams and the loss of motor control in all my limbs, I crashed headfirst into the door frame and then onto the floor with a cracking sound. The second shot that entered our Apartment had pierced my spinal cord.

I didn't know such a small woman could hold so much blood.

I must breathe. Slowly. Lay Still. Even though each breath becomes a burden. In and out.

I recognized the approaching calm enveloping me. I had experienced it before. And although it had frightened me more than anything else in the world the first time, it was the most beautiful thing ever given to me by another human being.

She shared his last moment with me!

Keep breathing. I feel the cold. Left and right.

I can't move my arms.

I need to breathe. My field of vision narrows, and the surrounding sounds become muffled.

Life is always red and black when you close your eyes for the last time. Always.

I breathe.

"I'm afraid!" Mom was the most beautiful woman I had ever seen. "Everything will be fine, and you will wake up again after the surgery, my little angel. Just be as strong as you were the first time you fell and scraped your knee.
"Do you remember? It didn't hurt too long. "Don't forget, we will always love you, Mona! Don't forget that."

No, how could I ever forget that? Our last shared thought. Another fragment of a memory.

A dull, popping sound right next to my ear.

Simmons continued to look at me with the same bored expression. Meanwhile, I took a deep breath. Then I opened my eyes and reached for my black, oxidized knife. I rolled my sleeve up above my elbow.

"Oh, you still do that," Simmons said, slightly surprised.
"Again," I replied, making an extended cut just below the elbow. I put the knife back in its sheath and felt my Arm acknowledging it with a brief, intense pain.

> *I was back here.*
> *And with me, the memory of Mona's Death.*
> *The seventh scar on my Arm.*

TWO.
FRAGMENTS OF YESTERDAY

Downtown Seattle, Beacon Hill, 2066 08:12 AM - Holster Skyward Tower

Neele clicked her tongue as the elevator doors closed around her. For two years, she had grown to despise the forced smile she had to wear every morning when she entered the building of her employer in Downtown Beacon Hill. The building was an ostentatious display of wealth, visible miles away along South Orcas Street as you approached from the sea.

In the early 2020s, the area was filled with homes where picturesque families barbecued, their scents wafting for miles. But after Columbia City was purchased by Holster Skyway Inc., under the then-living Thornej A. Holster Sr.—God rest his soul—the idyllic family life disappeared.

Five years into construction, life was a sea of concrete and steel frames bathed in the sparse glow of construction lights and displays promising a bright future. Ten years in, the first champagne bottles were popped, and hands were shaken for two reasons. Most buildings were ready for occupancy and could be admired by the gawking public; the press attended each of the 104 openings, outdoing themselves with superlatives about the technological marvels, limitless possibilities, and the greatness of living in a futuristic city like Seattle.

A small but influential part of the population raised their gold-plated glasses to toast the death of the thinker and leader, who, as the press would have us believe in numerous special and breaking news segments, had passed away peacefully from natural causes just weeks after the final complex's opening.

That same evening in 2052, as is customary with family conglomerates, Thornej A. Holster Jr. took the helm of the global corporation and promptly dropped the "Jr." from his name. Under his leadership, the company grew and solidified its market-leading position in biotechnology and other vital industries, including semiconductors, kinetics, and robotics, and less publicly, of course, in the arms trade.

Moreover, he acquired the aerospace industry of Boeing Corporation right across the street. Calling Holster Skyway Inc. a global player would be an understatement. Talents from all fields were sucked in and packed into the newly completed Skyward Tower—a pool of creatives and intellectuals building an empire of flesh and metal, all under the glow of the latest scientific advancements.

But as we know, where there is light, there is also shadow.

Neele was acutely aware of all this as she exited the elevator, which had played the same four-bar tune with bongos and ukuleles for years. She was tired of it. The nagging feeling of having made some mistake whenever she had to present a breakthrough in some scientific field to the board, heralding a revolutionary new era in this or that.

It was always about money and prestige. Four years ago, when Neele joined Holster Skyway Labs, she had imagined it differently, probably like everyone else, idealizing her employer. The beeping sound pulled her out of her thoughts, and she lifted her finger from the door opener that granted her access to the locker room. She stripped down to her underwear and slipped into the black and light-gray shimmering HELPS Mark IV (Hazardous Environment Laboratory Protection Suit). It was one of the first prototypes of an AI in a protective suit that could process and combine all the data around the user. She had designed and built it two years ago with her then-mentor. And now it was on the verge of being mass-produced by Holster Skyways. "Another thing taken out of my hands, "she thought after turning, clicking, and closing the last of the six security latches. HELPS announced itself as ready with a gentle male voice:

"Hello, Dr. Neele; it's good to see you again. Have a very safe day."

"Thanks, HELPS. I'm sure I will." Neele opened her calendar as she walked towards the airlock, scanning the day's tasks, greeting two long-time colleagues, and sharing a quick joke with Dr. Caldwell, a brilliant scientist who had been with Holster Skyway for over a decade. His expertise in advanced quantum entanglement and biomechanical implants was indispensable to the company, and he was also her boss.

So, be friendly, smile, and quickly move towards the airlock leading to the lab's center. Once there, she observed the busy bees diligently buzzing around their apparatuses. She mused a dance of worker drones as she walked towards her cell. A long white corridor stretched before her, with small rooms branching off to the left and right, separated by airlock doors, waiting for their diligent workers every minute, every day. It was always the same.

But today was different. The airlock to Neele's little domain closed behind her, and Neele noticed something had changed in her lab. She was momentarily confused. This wasn't how she had left it last night when she was one of the last to leave. She had met up with two old friends afterwards, resurrecting the good old times for a few hours, maybe indulging too much. But she was confident that what she saw now was not how it was yesterday.

On her first day, she brought a Thermoflex-wrapped picture and a few other items to make the sterile, white environment of the lab complex feel a bit more like home. These usually sat in one of the many white cabinets in her section alongside the vials and other essential research items. But now, they were all gone.

To put it less scientifically, the room was empty. All the instruments, devices, machines, measurement stations, cabinets, chairs, tables, shelves, and materials Neele and her colleagues had worked with for the past two years were gone.

"HELPS, what the hell is going on here?" she heard herself say as she incredulously surveyed the lab.

"It is Thursday, August 26, 2066, 08:12 AM. You are slightly earlier than usual, Dr. Neele. Have a very safe day."

"That's not what I meant." She rolled her eyes as she took a few steps forward, thinking, earlier? I'm 15 minutes late. "What happened to my lab and my research?

She was almost there. Her project had finally stabilized in metaphase, and they had managed to maintain stable cell division. She and her team could now determine which types of cells could reproduce how many times in what form. They were ready to move to anaphase. It was another medical breakthrough, perhaps even a tiny revolution in biogenetics. They were so close to the final step—maybe another month or two—then they would have been ready to commission the first prototype. And now everything was gone.

Everything except for a white, tiled container about two meters long, embedded in the floor in the middle of the room. How could she have missed that? Was it there when she entered the lab? Or last night? Or always? What is that?

"Your research is always in your lab, Dr. Neele. Have a very safe day."

"What do you mean, HELPS?" she thought as she approached the container. It was covered with pentagonal white tiles that extended in a semicircle about a meter to a meter and a half along the floor. As she stepped into the semicircle, Neele felt a strange sensation of light moving through her suit. The container emitted a faint hum as Neele placed her hand on it. She felt a pulsating energy traveling from her fingertips through her body, ending at her spine. It sounded like the hiss of a wildcat in her head, and with that sound, the container's lid split open where her hand had been. She stumbled back, taking seconds to comprehend what had just happened.

The unknown container had opened at her touch, revealing its contents.

Was it placed there precisely for me? Could anyone open it? Or just me? Who had placed it there? And why?

So many questions still needed answers. What was the purpose of all this?

She moved closer to look inside and froze as her brain registered what she saw. "What the hell…"

"Your pulse has increased rapidly, Dr. Neele. Please have a very safe day," Helps said, but she could not focus on anything else but what lay before her. She stared into a small child's face, looking back at her with a cold, icy gaze. Adrenaline shot through Neele's veins, her thoughts racing.

This can't be real. This is impossible.

Neele stumbled back from the container, the lightness she felt moments ago becoming nauseous. It was as if someone had punched her in the ribs.

With her last coherent thought, she commanded her hand to press the button that opened the airlock, allowing her to escape the lab. Her left hand obeyed with difficulty, and she crawled out of the lab more than walked. The long white emptiness of the corridor greeted her. But her mind was fixated on one thing. She was sure. The face staring back at her from the white container was one she had last seen precisely 16 years ago.

She could never forget it. It was the face of her little brother. And 16 years ago, that day was the worst day of her life.

Carpenteria, Seattle 2066 4:21 PM - ECLE Station

Subconsciously, I hoped it was just a coincidence, that it was just some random junkie who had stumbled into the Serpentines' apartment looking for some new dollars or something to sell for his next fix.

But it didn't look that way when Martin hit the floor in front of me, and it certainly didn't feel that way when the bullet struck my spinal court.

I looked up from my computer, where I had typed the preliminary report and reached for my cold coffee. Six hours had passed since Simmons and I had been at the Serpentines' appartment, and typically, I would have already pushed the experience out of my consciousness, but this time, it just wouldn't go away. Something about the whole situation unsettled me. If only I had turned my head more, I could have seen the shooter.

I spat the coffee out—a mouthful across my completely disorganized desk and all the old case files.
"Ugh, that was disgusting." I had no problem with cold coffee —quite the opposite. It was refreshing in the sweltering heat

that had lasted for years. I had also gotten used to the taste of oat, soy, and palm fiber milk.
But the stuff Simmons had poured into my coffee with a mischievous grin after we arrived was revolting.

"And isn't it great? It tastes almost like real synthetic milk, but it's made from a subspecies of horchata crossed with something like beetroot. This stuff is amazing," he said, peeking expectantly from behind his monitor.

"Yeah, 'amazing' is one way to put it," I muttered, frantically wiping the spilled beetroot coffee from my computer. The old tissue didn't make much of a difference.
"Hey, Simmons, doesn't this whole thing seem off to you?" I looked at him over the edge of my screen. "We're constantly reopening old cases, some over 40 years old. We've been doing this almost non-stop for two years. And honestly, our success rate is... modest."

"So what?" Simmons murmured, slightly offended, from behind his desk. "I'm not exactly the youngest anymore," I heard him say, followed by more keyboard clatter.
"What's so strange about it?" he whispered.

"That's what I'm getting to: I can't for the life of me figure out why someone would kill these two middle-aged people. They weren't rich, they weren't famous, and from what I sensed, they were still in love with each other. So, it wasn't a crime of passion, and I'm ruling out a domestic dispute for now. But you know what's stuck in my mind, Simmons?"

"No, I don't, but you're going to tell me," he grumbled, still slightly miffed.

"Martin Serpentine mentioned the word 'pedophile' in connection with his brother while he was upset. I can't stop thinking about whether there's any connection between the murderer, his brother, or..."

Simmons jumped up from behind his monitor.

"Or the super rare ammunition. It could all be connected," Simmons finished my sentence. That was one of the reasons I loved working with him. He might seem disinterested and absent, but deep down, he was always alert, with his brain only ever outpaced by his mouth.

I grabbed another tissue with my left hand while yanking my jacket—which could be better described as a trench coat—off the table with my right hand, almost pulling myself down. I tried to clean the stains while shoving everything necessary I wanted to take with me into my pockets: my slightly older Beretta Quantum service weapon and my synthetic Nanoflex-Polymer gloves that shielded me from the ability to perceive fragments.

"What is that thing you do with your left hand?" I had been asked so many times throughout my life.

The Answer I gave, was always filled with scientific jargon, it's called CTRS or Chrono-Tactile-Recollection-Syndrom. When I first encountered it as a little boy, I found the word 'fragment' more descriptive, and most people understand it better when you try to explain it to them.

I took my black oxidized knife, which I always carried.
I had it custom-made and sewn into my trench coat by my trusted cutter a few years ago with a convenient holder.

And yes, you can take the word 'cutter' here literally. My Guy was a mix between a Master Tailor and a Weapon smith.

Then, my ECLE-ID badge (Emerald-City-Law-Enforcement), a few new American dollars, and the most persuasive argument of all time in the history of police work. Then, a few extra new dollars for the next snack machine. And finally, for the immediate little hunger on the way to the snack machine, a few mint candies from Sergeant Mitchell's desk, which his wife Nancy made herself at home, by hand, without an automated cooking robot, using only 80 percent synthetic ingredients. They were the best mint candies this side of the Duwamish River.

"Oh," I exclaimed as I stopped in the hallway. I had forgotten the keys to our service vehicle. Just as I was about to turn around, I heard a soft jingle from the end of the hallway. It was Simmons, holding the elevator door open with one hand and softly jingling the car keys with the other.

"Are you going to keep talking to yourself? I've been standing here for almost two minutes, waiting for us to finally get moving." He said impatiently. "I've even contacted my guy in the Old Medical District to ask about the rare bullets you mentioned. And I also asked him about a pedophile, but I think he misunderstood."

As the elevator door closed, I remebered why, despite all the other colleagues at Emerald City Station, I had insisted on working exclusively with Simmons in the future. I had read his files. Every single line. And some of them more than once.

Only some people can make the right decision at the right time in the right place. But at least he tries.

THREE.
LOST INNOCENCE

Seattle, August 26, 2050, 6:55 AM - Snoqualmie Ridge

After waking up, Neele loved spending the weekend mornings outside on the little hill behind her parents' house. Watching the forest and listening to the sounds of nature was one of her favorite morning activities. She thought summer vacation was the best. Sipping her cocoa and tearing pieces off her blueberry muffin to throw to the songbirds competing for the best bits of muffin and the most complex melodies.

Neele lost herself in thoughts and anticipation of the day ahead. As she mused, she whistled the tune her little brother Peet had taught her a few days ago. It was some odd children's song, but she liked the rhythm. It was as beautiful as the day that lay ahead.

For months, they had planned to visit the new amusement park on the edge of the Boeing complex in Seattle. Popcorn, caramel apples, and all the fantastic unknown sweets were Peet's primary motivation for relentlessly badgering their parents: "Is the amusement park opening next week? When is next week? Can we go now? How about now?"

Neele, on the other hand, was more interested in the big attractions. She wanted to see how Boeing had merged
nature and technology into a fever dream of fantasy and
adrenaline. She was most excited about the exhibit celebrating "150 Years of Boeing: Innovation Soaring into the Future." Humans and nature are harmoniously connected by metal and science. Flying and falling. And then rising again. The rides were the closest thing to the feeling of flying she had first

experienced at six years old. And she had loved it from the start.

"Hey, Neele," her father called from the porch door. "We're leaving in five to ten minutes. Can you grab your backpack and Peet's from his room if he left it there? He's so excited he keeps forgetting it. We're packing everything else into the car," he shouted, disappearing back into the house.

"Coming, Dad, just finishing my muffin!" Neele jumped up, stuffing the last bits of muffin into her mouth and washing them down with the rest of her cocoa. She checked her watch and saw it was 6:55 AM. Dad had mentioned leaving around 7:00 AM. He was always punctual, especially when it came to avoiding crowds. That is probably why they moved to Snoqualmie Ridge shortly after Neele was born.

It was much quieter here than in Seattle. Neele was about to dash down the hill when she paused. "What was that noise?" she asked aloud, turning towards the forest. That didn't sound like birds, she thought.

She stepped a few paces from the house towards the forest about 15 meters ahead. Dense century-old trees stood watch, observing everything. "Just like me." Mid-giggle, she froze.

There it was again. This time, Neele heard it clearly. A dull metallic clanging followed by a faint humming. She moved closer to the forest, which seemed to loom more prominent with each step. She opened the small gate in the metal fence separating her yard from the forest and stepped through. The further she moved from the house, the more precise the noise became. Rhythmic clanging, like something hitting time and time again, interrupted by an occasional hissing and a faint humming. Or was it whimpering? She wasn't sure. There it was again. A whimpering. Like an injured animal. But it sounded deeper. More human. Was someone there?

"Hello, is someone there?" Neele called softly, more to herself. No answer. The clanging and hissing grew louder, but she still couldn't see anything, and every fiber of her being told her to turn back.

Yet, she took a few more steps towards the forest, almost to the edge of the clearing. She was now about 30 meters from her house. There it was again. Metallic clanging, then a loud hissing. And then a distinct, very loud human whimpering, followed by the snapping of branches and a heavy thud, followed by a muffled cry of pain.

"Hello, is someone there? Do you need help?" Neele called into the forest, and an unexpected reply came: "I'm sorry, but you're the one who needs help."

At that moment, all hell broke loose. First, she heard a deep, menacing rumble that seemed to come from the depths of the earth. Seconds later, the world exploded in a blinding flash of light. Time seemed to stand still before brutal reality hit her full force. She was lifted off her feet and thrown several meters, landing hard on the ground with her left arm, taking the brunt of the impact. Everything around her spun, and her entire body convulsed in pain.

She heard the voice say, "Close your eyes," and the pain was so intense she couldn't do anything but obey. The world around her became hazy and indistinct. She could only see the peaceful morning scene torn apart in a blinding flash. Branches snapped loudly and flew like projectiles through the air. Birds that had been happily singing moments ago burst into feathered fragments before her eyes. Rocks and dirt erupted around her, and she heard windows shattering in the distance as a shockwave ripped through her house and the surrounding area. The Neighbors roofs lifted briefly into the sky before crashing in a thunderous collapse, disappearing in an ever-growing cloud of dust. The ordeal lasted no more than twenty seconds, but when Neele woke up, almost 30 minutes had passed.

A biting smell of smoke and burning wood mixed with the fresh morning air, burnt her nose. She lay under a metal plate covered in debris, dirt, and ash. The heat of the explosion was so intense that even from behind what was once a hill, she could tell something terrible had happened. Neele felt paralyzed. She tried to sit up, but when she put weight on her left arm, a searing pain shot through her. She screamed and collapsed back down. Her left arm was, medically speaking, wholly wrecked. She writhed in pain and tried to move her right arm. It hurt, but she could move it. After another minute, she tried again. She rolled onto her right arm and, using all her strength, pushed herself up, the metal plates that shielded her from the blast clanging to the ground in front of her. She knelt and looked towards where the hill had been moments ago. "What is going on?" she asked as her eyes reflected the devastation. Her heart pounded like a hammer, her hands shook. She felt the cold, hard ground beneath her knees, and warm blood trickled down her forehead. Her mind was a chaotic jumble of fear, confusion, and the urgent need to find her family.

Her family. "Oh my God. Mom, Dad, Peeti. Where are you?" Neele screamed, dragging herself towards where the house should have been. But all she saw was a mix of shattered and melted metal, splintered glass, and wood mingled with other debris. The couch she loved reading on in the evenings lay broken at the far end of what was once the yard.

"Mom! Dad! Where are you?" Neele called, but there was no answer. In pain, she struggled through the wreckage, calling for her family. All she heard was the crackling of burning wood, the occasional collapse of debris, and a constant dull buzzing in her ears. Her parents were nowhere to be seen. It took minutes to fight through the remains of her house. She remembered her dad saying they should meet in the car. But the car wasn't where it usually was. Several meters down the street, it was lying on its side, a grotesque distortion of its former shape. The body of the car was crumpled by the blast, looking like a discarded piece of paper. The once shiny gray paint was soot-blackened, covered in deep scratches and dents. Smoke rose from the engine bay, and a sharp smell of burnt rubber and molten metal filled the air. Various colored streams leaked from the vehicle's wounds onto the black asphalt.

She could see inside the car through the broken rear window, which was just as devastated. And there she saw something inside. It was small and yellow, entirely made of fabric. She moved as quickly as she could towards the car and looked inside. There he was. The little yellow backpack, filled with toys, was next to a small motionless body, half covered in soot and blood, one hand on the backpack, the other resting against the body. The body was still strapped inside the car.

"Peet, Peet! No, please, no!" Neele gently pulled at his arm. His body was cold and lifeless, and when she pulled a second time, the backpack fell from his hand and hit the ground. Its contents spilled out: candies and some of his favorite toys, including several small metal cars, a model Boeing airplane, some crayons, and a picture he had drawn. Neele recognized the image immediately. Peet had started it for her a few days ago. It was supposed to be a surprise for her, a homemade ticket to the park. But Peet always forgot to put his things away, so Neele had found it earlier. On the ticket, he had drawn two people, both wearing helmets and capes, standing in front of a tall tower. Around them were many small buildings and people. Now, Neele couldn't hold back her tears and started sobbing uncontrollably. "Peeti, please wake up. Please… you can't leave me." Her tears mixed with the blood from her wound, streaming down her face as she clutched her little brother with her working arm. She remained motionless for several minutes, unable to comprehend what had happened. The world around her blurred, and the pain and despair threatened to overwhelm her.

After what felt like an eternity, she faintly heard the sirens of fire trucks and emergency services approaching. It took another ten minutes for Neele to finally put the picture in her pocket. Tears streamed down her face as she hugged her little brother one last time. Then she stood up and slowly walked towards the sirens on the horizon. The reality of the situation hit her with full force.

Her family was gone, and for the first time, she was alone.

OLD MEDICAL DISTRICT

FOUR.
ON THE EDGE OF THE ABYSS

Seattle, 8:39 PM - Somewhere on a Highway - Old Medical District

When the Chevrolet Glide hit the market in 2045, it was known for its efficiency, luxurious interior, and speed. But now, almost 20 years after many years of service,
having taken bullets, other bumpers, and countless miles, the Glide is more of a modern classic. Some would call it
nostalgic charm, but Simmons and I saw it more as an
unreliable piece of junk with solar panels on the roof that worked only ten percent of the time.

Simmons and I drove through the narrow streets of the Old Medical District. The desolation and decay of the area stood in stark contrast to the glittering skyscrapers in the center of the Pacific Commonwealth, which had formed in 2066 from the former states of Washington, Oregon, and parts of California. The political upheavals of the past decades had necessitated a new federal structure, and the Pacific Commonwealth was the answer to these challenges. Seattle had become the center of power, with the industrial giant Holster Skyway Inc. extending its tentacles across the entire Free Trade Zone of Unified America.

Our meeting point was the Main Street Pharmacy, a rundown store perfect for an inconspicuous meeting with an informant. The area was notorious for violence, drugs, and other illegal activities, making our visit non the less risky.

"I can't remember the last time it was pleasant to drive into this shithole," I muttered to Simmons as we turned off the highway, and the modern LED streetlights gave way to the flickering light of old sodium lamps.

"Me neither," Simmons replied, lighting his fourth synthetic cigarette since we left. "No idea why we're stupid enough to show up here twice in one day."

"Something about this case won't let me go. The way the Serpentines were murdered doesn't fit a simple burglary. There's more to it," I said, thinking about the precise shots I had witnessed. "And I don't believe it was some 'Crok-drug-induced Satan told me to kill them' thing. Everything was too smooth."

Simmons glanced up briefly as the ash from his cigarette flew into the back of the Chevrolet Glide. "You think it might have something to do with all the experiments conducted in the Old Medical? The whole district was full of illegal bio-implants and forbidden research a couple of years ago."

I thought for a moment. It was indeed a possibility. I had yet to get any information about Mrs. Serpentine's professional background during my last encounter, except that Martin Serpentine wanted to borrow money for something urgent.

"We should not overlook Martin Serpentine's sister-in-law. According to him, she had a penchant for criminal activities. Check with the department and see if you can find out who she is, her name, and where she is now."

"Got it, boss," said Simmons, hammering away at his communicator's screen. The colorful screens he rapidly worked through blinked in pretty colors and reflected off the windshield.

At least some color in this dreary area.

"Do you think the Serpentines saw or knew something they shouldn't have? Or maybe they were just in the wrong place at the wrong time, and that's why someone visited them?" Simmons asked, pausing five seconds from using the screen as an anger management tool.

"Well, I mean, this communicator here says Martin Serpentine was still an employee of the month at the Holster Biotech Research Facility until a few hours before his death, and his wife Mona was an archive assistant at Holster Skyway Inc., the main company of the vast empire that Thornej A. Holster built over the last ten years since his father, God rest his soul, handed the name over to him."

"Maybe now's the perfect time, as we drive the rundown streets of Seattle, to break down the Holster Skyway Inc. conglomerate a bit more," said Simmons, starting to absorb the information on his communicator.

"So, we have the already mentioned Holster Skyway Inc., the parent company controlling numerous subsidiaries and stakes in various industries, which one could safely call an all-consuming monster if one thinks ill of them. Then there's the Holster Biotech Research Facility (HBRF), which revolutionized biotechnology with its advanced implants and genetic breakthroughs within a few decades. Next, we have Skyward Tower Industries (STI), which spends all day building skyscrapers that define the skyline of Seattle and beyond, casting more shadows than light. Then there's Holster Kinetics and Robotics (HKR), which merged a few years ago with the defense department and now operates under the name Holster Defense Systems (HDS).

"Aren't we lucky," said Simmons, "to have such great internal synergies at Holster. Two newlyweds meet, and nine months later, a new baby that can conquer the world if it grows big enough. And if there are complications at birth, Holster

Pharmaceuticals (HP) helps with a load of pills right after birth. How lucky we are to have been born in the Free Trade Zone of United America. And speaking of Pills, turn up ahead, and we'll be at our meeting point."

The Glide rolled slowly into the parking lot of the Main Street Pharmacy, and I could already see Simmons' informant standing in one of the darker corners of the poorly lit lot, nervously looking around. I blinked and thought hard.

„I think the Serpentines stumbled upon something they shouldn't have. We have to dig deeper," I said as I parked the car, and the lights automatically turned off.

"Yeah, sounds like the beginning of a good plan," said Simmons. "But let me talk to him. Maybe I can get more out of him since he knows me. And maybe I can explain the child molester thing to him."

"Let's get this over with as quickly as possible; I don't like this area," I said, touching my service weapon to ensure I had packed it. I was finally ready to get some answers, no matter the cost.

BEACON HILL

FIVE.
FLIGHT INTO THE UNKNOWN

Downtown Seattle, 2066 08:35 AM - Holster Skyward Tower

The cold neon lights of the lab flickered as Neele panicked and stumbled out barely keeping her footing. Her hurried steps echoed unevenly on the metallic floor, her heart pounding in rhythm as she frantically hit the elevator button.

"Come on, come on," she commanded the door, glancing around in panic. Seconds felt like minutes until the relieving "ping" sounded, and the elevator door opened. Neele rushed in, repeatedly pressing the button for the basement and the door close mechanism.

The elevator moved slowly, and Neele pressed herself into the corner, watching the floor indicator closely. 103, 102, 101... it would take at least 50 seconds to reach the bottom, then another 30 seconds past security, 13.5 seconds through the corridor, 5 through the security door, and then she would be outside. "And then what?" Neele said aloud, her mind already two steps ahead. She wasn't a renowned researcher with a quick mind for nothing and was also equipped with a HELPS suit. Still, she couldn't suppress the rising panic.

HELPS had suggested she control her breathing for the third time to manage her racing heart, but she couldn't stop thinking about Peet's face in that metallic sarcophagus. Neele felt cold sweat on her forehead, slowly trickling down her back inside the HELPS suit. She pressed the visor of her helmet against the wall, checked the floor indicator, now showing 76, and lowered her head slightly to relieve her shoulders. *Breathe in and out. In and out.* Neele closed her eyes for a few seconds.

"Think," she told herself. "It makes no sense that your brother who was killed 16 years ago, was lying there with open eyes, staring at you."

Dead people, no matter how much you miss them, don't just reappear. Especially not when you held their burnt body in your arms for ten minutes. "So, think." Neele opened her eyes, and her brother Peet's face was directly in front of her, reflected on the HELPS suit's display. She gasped, unsure how to react. Then he opened his eyes. Panic gripped her as she hammered the stop button. The elevator jerked to a halt, throwing Neele off balance. The display showed floor 42. The door opened with a dull sound, and Neele stumbled into a part of Holster Skyway Central Research Facility she had never been to. The room was about 30 meters long with very high ceilings, at least four meters. It had no windows or openings to the outside; as far as she could see, everything was cast in darkness.

There was only sparse emergency lighting on the sides, partially obscured by large black machines reminiscent of old servers. These machines all played the same rhythmic pattern over and over, drawing her deeper into the room.

"HELPS, where are we?" Neele whispered into her suit as she walked down the dark corridor, watching the machines. It took a few seconds for HELPS to respond.

"Apologies, Dr. Neele, my connection to the HELPS network is disrupted in this room. We are on the 42nd floor of the Tower. The 42nd floor was closed eight years ago after an accident and subsequent fire. After a thorough inspection by engineers, structural analysts, and other inspectors, it was declared uninhabitable and closed to personnel. We shouldn't be here. Have a safe day."

Neele didn't know what to say. A fire in the building she had worked in for four years, and no one had told her? Not even her lab neighbor Ann, who always wanted to know everything during lunch breaks and shared unasked information. "This will be an exciting topic for the next lunch gossip if I get out of here," Neele murmured to herself, continuing towards what she hoped was the end of the room. The further she moved from the elevator door, the louder the room seemed to get. Each step had increased the noise level from a gentle hum at the elevator door to a deafening, chaotic noise, making it hard for her to think. She was about ten meters from the end of the room when the noise level nearly drove her mad. "HELPS, help me, I can't understand my own thoughts. Can you deactivate the surrounding noises?"

"**Apologies, Dr. Neele, but I cannot. I don't know their source or what is emitting them.**" "Damn it," Neele screamed inside her helmet, unsure if she said it out loud. "**But I can configure the HELPS Mark IV to block external noises inside the suit. Should I do that for you?**"

"Yes, damn it, do it, HELPS. Hurry up," she yelled against her chaotic, loud thoughts.

"**Done, Dr. Neele. Have a safe day.**"

Silence. Neele knelt, both hands over her non-existent ears in the HELPS suit. It hadn't helped, but now it was quiet. Really quiet. Neele stood up. Her body and the suit, usually creaky and squeaky, were silent. Interesting, she thought, finally hearing herself think again. The room had taken away her two most important senses, sight and hearing, and the HELPS suit took the remaining three. No smell, taste, or touch.

Neele swallowed hard and moved further into the dark room. About four meters from the end, a small light and a button below lit up. Then another and another.
She recognized the basic shape of an old, wall-mounted control console with unfamiliar architecture. The console was clearly

old, the oldest thing in the building. Carefully, Neele approached the console and touched the cold, smooth metal. It seemed familiar somehow. She looked around and saw the console was about three meters long and two meters high, but only the three lights were active. She pressed the first button gently. The first light went out, and the other two grew brighter. Neele turned around, hoping something had changed in the room, but it was still engulfed in darkness.

She pressed the second button, and it went out; the third light now glowed alone. "Okay," Neele said aloud, raising her hand pressing the third button. The light went out… and nothing happened. Neele looked around. The console was still in darkness, the room unlit. "Okay?" she said again, less enthusiastically. "I expected something else. I thought a door would open, the lights would come on, or the noise would stop. Although…"

"Hey, HELPS, is it still unbearably loud around me?" she asked, and after a few seconds, HELPS responded.

"It is still deafening around you, Dr. Neele. Aside from a small electrical pulse and a vibration through the console, I detected no change."

"Thanks, HELPS," Neele said thoughtfully. "But I must have activated something," she murmured, running her hand over the console's buttons and metal. There. In the middle, something was different. About ten centimeters into the console was a small opening. She leaned closer, using her helmet lights to see better. She turned left and right to get a better view but couldn't identify what she saw.

"HELPS, any idea what I'm looking at?"

It took a moment for HELPS to respond, during which Neele ran her fingers over the opening.

"With limited access to the HELPS network, this answer may be incorrect, Dr. Neele. I compared the opening to thousands in our archives and am 85 percent sure it's an old data transfer interface. It appears to be a General-Purpose Interface Bus developed in the early 1960s for connecting and controlling scientific and industrial instruments. Likely the oldest variant, allowing data transfer up to eight MB/s."

"Okay!" Neele said, pleased. "And, uh, HELPS, can you connect to it?"

After several seconds, HELPS responded. The data transfer in this room must have been severely disrupted; usually, HELPS responds in milliseconds.

"I can connect to the interface, Dr. Neele, but you must authorize it."

"Uh, okay," said Dr. Neele, "then, uh, do it, please." She felt a slight vibration under her right arm and, lifting it, found a small red cable with a strange connector. She took the plug in her left hand and approached the old interface. She pressed the unfamiliar connector into the console's slot, and after a second, a holographic interface appeared inside her helmet. A small command line filled with asterisks appeared before her eyes. "A password prompt," she murmured. She hadn't seen one in years since most systems switched to retina scans or biometric data for higher security.

"HELPS, can you do anything?"

"I've activated my universal protocol translator and I am checking thousands of passwords per second, Dr. Neele. It may take up to 96.7 hours to find the correct password. Have a patient day."

Great, now HELPS was being sarcastic. Just what she needed. But at least they were closer to decrypting this room and hopefully some of her questions. Neele sat on the floor, knees to her chest, hugging her legs with her left arm, extending her right arm to maintain the connection. She stared into the room's darkness, slowly closing her eyes as the words on the display grew more minor and less significant. About ten minutes passed, listening only to her breathing, the only sound she could hear. Then, with a PING, HELPS alerted her:

"Data structure analysis complete. Access code decrypted. You may proceed, Dr. Neele."

"Wow, thanks, HELPS, that was faster than we expected."

Neele took a deep breath and stood up. She began sorting through a massive pile of folders, subfolders, entries, and records. The earliest entries were from 1984; the latest was just two months ago. There had to be about 100,000 pages of data.

"Phew," Neele said. "How am I supposed to find anything relevant in this? HELPS, can you organize this logically so I can understand what I'm looking at?"

"I can assist in searching for specific entries, Dr. Neele. Do you have a keyword for me to search?"

Neele knew immediately what she needed to know.
"Search for 'Snoqualmie Ridge.'"

HELPS whirred cheerfully, and the number of subfolders shrank to 900.

"Okay, load all that into the suit's memory, HELPS," Neele said, swiping through the first entries. She vividly remembered Snoqualmie Ridge. It was where she had spent the first 16 years of her life until that fateful day.

Most entries included images, newspaper articles, photos of burnt and demolished houses, and numerous diagrams. She swiped further until she found a file marked with Dr. Caldwell's name. The file was encrypted and couldn't be opened.

"Huh," Neele said. "What did Dr. Caldwell have to do with the Snoqualmie Ridge disaster? That was sixteen years ago. The lab didn't even exist back then."

"HELPS, can you load this file into memory and help me decrypt it?"

It took a few seconds for HELPS to respond. What it said was different from what Neele expected.

"Warning, Dr. Neele. Unauthorized access to my systems was detected. It will take approximately two minutes to complete the download. While reviewing the files, I scanned the room and detected vibrations in the ceiling and floor panels, indicating we will have visitors soon. Something in the data must have triggered a security protocol. Please have a safe day."

Neele swallowed hard, her heart racing. "How long until they arrive?"

"Approximately 90 seconds, Dr. Neele."

The response came much later than needed. "We don't have 90 seconds!" Neele shouted as she saw the elevator door slowly open at the other end of the hall, the light from the security guards' suits piercing through the widening gap.

Neele looked around frantically for an escape route. It felt like the download took forever when HELPS spoke again:

"Download almost complete. Security forces are in proximity. Please have a safe day."

"Shit!" Neele whispered, even though she knew the approaching guards couldn't hear her. Then it struck her—this was one of her advantages. She couldn't hear the guards, and they couldn't hear her as well. It was still loud on the outside, but as HELPS cut the outside noises, the Guards must have done the same in with their Suits. Neele grabbed the UDMI plug and yanked it out of the console mid-download. The display in her helmet stopped at 47 percent. It wasn't everything, but at least she had something that could hopefully provide answers. She could escape the room, evade the guards, and exit the building.

"HELPS, turn off the helmet light and find an alternative exit. And hurry up this time!" Neele said, crouching past the console towards the black server wall. The light in her helmet went out, and aside from the natural reflection of her suit under light sources, she was now one with the darkness. The room was divided into five corridors with servers and machines, each aligned with the old console. Neele moved along the outer wall towards the elevator.

"During the room scan, I found two potential escape routes. The nearest is about 15 meters ahead on the right. Please have a cautious day, Dr. Neele."

"Okay, I'll try to make it there, HELPS," sneaking along the wall. She moved meter by meter towards the supposed exit.

So far, the guards hadn't seen her, and she had only spotted one. She saw him slowly trying to discern something in the darkness with a fixed gaze. The only light came from the electric shock baton he held. A shiver ran down Neele's spine, but fortunately, he passed without seeing her.

Neele hurried to the side door, pressing her body weight against it. The door opened slowly and squeakily, but she didn't care. She needed to get out. Once through the narrow side door, she forced it shut with all her might. "HELPS, now what?"

"Run ten meters down this narrow corridor, turn left, then another three meters, and you'll reach a grate. You'll need to remove it. It may be dangerous there, Dr. Neele. Have a cautious day."

The corridor Neele was in not only grew more narrow but also lower, forcing her to kneel to continue. After about a minute, she turned left and saw a grate flooded with artificial light. She hit it with all her strength, and on the third try, the mounting broke, and the grate crashed loudly inside. She could hear again.

"I took the liberty of re-enabling ambient sound, Dr. Neele. Please have an especially cautious day now."

Neele looked up and then down. "Damn it," she shouted into the abyss, realizing she was at the edge of an elevator shaft on the 42nd floor. "Are we in an action movie? Do you expect me to rappel down or something? I'm not doing that!"

HELPS responded immediately, giving her an unwelcome answer.

"No, Dr. Neele. I don't expect you to jump to your death. My calculations show our best chance is to jump onto one of the descending elevators as it passes. We'll have exactly 28 seconds to enter the elevator before it stops. If we miss it, we'll lose the opportunity to escape the guards before the building locks down in less than 90 seconds."

Neele heard a loud screeching noise at the end of the corridor she had just come from.

"You have seven seconds until the next elevator. Prepare to have a safe day."

Neele tensed her muscles, pressing her arms against the shaft walls. She had no choice. Guards behind her and a 42-floor drop in front. With a deafening whoosh, the air was sucked around her as the elevator raced past.
"Now, Dr. Neele," HELPS urged.

Neele pushed off the wall and leaped into the void.

"Damn it," was all she could say as she landed roughly on the elevator roof three seconds later. She lay on the rapidly descending elevator roof. There. That looked like an opening. HELPS counted down the remaining floors. 30, 29, 28. Neele fumbled with the latch, trying every direction.

Why wasn't there a universal direction for opening or closing things? No, its always turn or lift and sometimes a push-squeeze mechanism.

"Aah," she exclaimed. It was a slide-push hybrid mechanism. It clicked as HELPS counted floor 20. The latch gave way, and the hatch opened. Neele kicked it open, grabbed the side handles, and swung into the elevator with all her strength. She dropped about three meters, landing hard on her right arm. As she got up, she stared into the wide eyes of two people in business suits. They stared back, bewildered, as HELPS counted the final floors.
"We have 60 seconds until the building locks down. Have a safe day, Dr. Neele."

As the doors opened on the ground floor, Neele had no better idea than to wave goodbye to the two people.

Then she bolted out of the metal box into the vast lobby.

She tried not to draw attention and didn't look back to see if the two people followed her. Neele crossed the lobby quickly until she reached the security scan systems near the exit. Then it hit her. She had never left the building in a HELPS suit.

Was that even allowed? Would the guards stop her? Damn. She hadn't thought of that.
Her heart raced, unable to calm after the elevator jump. She moved forward, and as she passed through the biometric scan system, there were no signs of anything unusual.

Apparently, walking in a HELPS suit was normal.

Than she stepped outside.

Her heart pounded, and her lungs burned. She moved quickly a few meters from the entrance and stood behind a tree, its generous shadow hiding her. Neele removed the HELPS helmet, tucked it under her arm, and breathed deeply in the clear morning air. Only an hour had passed since she entered the lab, yet so much had happened. Neele fought back tears that suddenly flowed. She didn't understand why her little brother was in that white box in her lab, she didn't understand what that room was, and she didn't understand what Dr. Caldwell had to do with the Snoqualmie Ridge explosion. But she knew she needed answers. She fumbled in one of the HELPS suit's equipment pouches until she found her communicator.

Her fingers trembled as she dialed a number.

It took a few seconds for the line to connect.

"Hey, it's me. Neele. Sorry for not calling earlier, but I urgently need your help. I found files I don't understand, which somehow relate to my past."

The female voice on the other end said just four words, but they were what Neele had hoped for. "Come to me, ganjin."

Neele hung up and threw her communicator into the nearest trash can. It was convenient that trash was now compressed on the spot. At least it gave her a head start, she thought, as she ran down the street, trying to blend into the crowd.

The red cable dangling from her right arm constantly reminded her that she had to do something. These files in her suit might cost her life. But she had no choice. She had to find the truth—for her little brother, for herself, and for all those who lost their lives on August 26, 2050.

OLD MEDICAL DISTRICT

SIX.
DANGEROUS CONNECTIONS

Seattle, 9:10 PM - Old Medical District

The area was so bleak and rundown that trash on the street looked old and weathered. Simmons and I got out and looked around. The usual figures loitered in the dark corners, their eyes constantly moving, searching for the next hit or victim, whichever seemed more lucrative. And right now we looked like the perfect next thing. Old, coffee-stained, and like tourists who had lost their way.

Who even comes here after 6 PM?

A small, nervous man named Lenny, who was in his late fifties, was already waiting at the corner. He saw us and waved frantically as if afraid we might miss him. "Hey, here, Simmons, come here!" I heard him shout.

"Hey, Lenny, you old corpse mouth," Simmons yelled as we approached. "Do you have what we need?" I looked puzzled at Simmons.

The story behind that nickname would need explaining back at the station.

Lenny nodded hastily. "Yeah, yeah. I've got the information you want, but it's unsafe here. We should go somewhere else. There's a small diner nearby with good WonderBread burgers and a quiet corner for us."

Simmons and I exchanged a glance and then I nodded.

"Fine," Simmons said as we sat on the metal chairs and I began studying the Wonder Diner menu. The diner, like almost everything in the area, had seen better days, though judging by the variety of synthetic meat products in different WonderBread variations, it was difficult to imagine that it was better before.

We sat in a back corner far from the few other customers who looked surprisingly normal for this place.

What was normal in the Old Medical District, anyway?

A young waitress, maybe in her early twenties, skated over to our table and cheerfully took our orders. For me, it was the synthetic WonderBread Special Synthloaf, with half-synthetic chips and pickle relish that was basically just flavor and color liquid. Simmons ordered a classic Wonder Grilled Deluxe, synthetic American cheese between two slices of WonderBread.

Plastic with plastic, delicious.

And Lenny, after insisting that the department cover the bill, ordered the WonderBread French Toast Special, richly soaked in Wonder-Egg and fried golden brown with milk substitute. It came with the best smoky bacon imitation in all of Seattle, as Nancy the waitress assured us as she rolled away, happily whistling. Simmons began grilling Lenny while I took a quick look at all of the differnt WonderSauces on the table.

I never knew they now also came in Can Form. It was probably cheaper to manufacture.

"So, Lenny, what do you have on the ammo?" he growled with a suddenly deep voice over the table, taking a sip of hot WonderCoffee Ultra-Plus.

With an extra shot of beet milk... The thought made me shudder.

"The rifled one?? That's rare stuff, man," Lenny said, looking nervously around.

"Yeah, we know that already. What else do you have?"

"Okay, okay, so. Only a few dealers in the whole Pacific Commonwealth still deal with ithem. It's almost impossible to get these days unless you have direct connections to the arms industry. Maybe one or two small intermediaries in Seattle still trade with them."

"Okay," Simmons said. "That's not bad. And you know the two from kindergarten or were you old school friends?"

I couldn't help but twitch my lip.

"No, man. You know I have nothing to do with those people anymore. I'm done with that crap. Always 'Lenny, pick this guy up,' 'Lenny, take care of this.' Lenny, Lenny, Lenny. I'm clean now. At least when it comes to that kind of business."

From my experience, I knew Lenny was partly right, though no one who spent their life in the Old Medical District was clean. Even if it was just on the outside.

I suspected it could have wide-reaching implications, but the rarity of the ammunition played into our hands. Fewer players at the table increased the chances of hitting the jackpot. And who didn't always want to win?

"Stop beating around the bush and tell us what you know."

"Yeah, man, okay. Don't yell, Simmons," Lenny said, slightly intimidated, licking his lips. "So, the two intermediaries here in

Old Medical. I only know their names. The smaller dealer is Rico Sanchez, also called 'Rocket Rico,' he runs his business out of a small pharmacy near 6th Avenue, opposite the old, abandoned St. Augustine General Hospital. I don't know why he's called that, but I'm pretty sure he's not the person you're looking for."

"Okay, and how do you know it's probably the other dealer?" Simmons asked in his not-so-subtle tone.

"Because you know the second dealer personally, Simmons. Or should I say 'dealeress'?" I looked at Simmons, then at Lenny, and back at Simmons, seeing his eyes widen.

"Not Maddie?" Simmons whispered.

"Yes, exactly her. Maddie Turner, also known as 'Maddog.'

"My Maddie is active again?"

I took a moment to process the "my" in Simmons' last sentence. But after a few seconds of consideration, I believed I could piece together what I had just heard. I recalled what I had read in Simmons' files, even though 70 percent of them were redacted. Before his almost eight-year career at the Emerald City Department, he had done something as an undercover investigator. I couldn't find out precisely what it was, but it probably had something to do with the local clans and possibly weapons. And with Maddog. I didn't know much about Maddie' Maddog' Turner, but what I knew was enough to have respect for her and Simmons. Maddog was one of the few female criminals in Seattle who had made it into the higher echelons without too much sex appeal. Instead, it was her, let's call it aggressive way of turning negotiations in her favor. You could call it blind rage when she tore chunks of flesh from her opponent with her mouth. At least that's what the files said. But, of course only after she had slowly crushed every little finger on both hands of the person. She seemed to handle arguments well.

A lovely woman, this Miss Turner.

"Where is she now?" Simmons said, snapping me out of my thoughts.

"Ah, I knew you'd still be interested," Lenny said. "I asked around after your call earlier if anyone knew more, and as luck would have it, someone did. And now I know, and soon you will, too. But first, I need to eat this WonderBread French Toast Deluxe coming my way."

Simmons and I turned around and saw Nancy approaching the corner with a tray far too big for her delicate hands. Struggling to keep her balance and almost losing it, she finally did. She crashed face-first into the now dropped WonderBread assortment on the floor. At that exact moment I heard a crack behind me and a gurgling sound.

I turned around as Simmons jumped up and rushed to Nancy. Lenny had clutched his left arm to his mouth, from which a massive fountain of blood sprayed onto the table, while he had tried to hold on to the table with his right hand. The impact was so strong that his head was jerked backward. The bullet had passed through the tissue in his mouth, creating a gaping hole where there was alreadyone. His head, or what was left of it, was flung back against the stone wall. With the second crack, Lenny's entire body went limp. He slumped forward onto the table, then his liveless body carried by his own blood, slid to the floor.

It took me a second to realize what happened while Simmons, was already two rows away almost at Nancy's location crouching on the floor. "Get down, you idiot!" He yelled. So I did. I threw myself to the ground. And thanks to Lenny's blood

I slid further than I had planned. Just in the nick of time, as more bullets riddled the surrounding furniture.

I heard some of the guests in the front part of the diner squeal and scream as they ran over each other in panic. But I also recognized the unmistakable sound of weapons drawn from their holsters or other protective coverings.

Metal and leather. As far as I know, that usually results in a nasty surprise.

We weren't alone in the diner, and somewhere out there, someone was sitting in an elevated position, turning Lenny into a literal corpse mouth. Amid the screams and panic, I could hear Lenny taking his last breaths. I raised my left arm and activated the red button on my ComUhr strapped around my wrist.

It gave a soft ping, and I knew we had to survive the next four minutes for everything to be okay.

I grabbed my service weapon and pulled it from the holster. After quickly checking the magazine, I noted I had 18 rounds left. I slid to the edge of the diner chair and peeked out. I saw Nancy's body being dragged behind the massive seat with XXL chairs for particularly hungry customers. I waited for Simmons to give me a signal. He was the one who always came up with a plan in hopeless situations. And this wasn't the first time we had both ended up in a shootout. I knew he was about to do something stupid and I would support him. That's how it had always gone so far. I turned and crawled to the other side of the diner chair and looked around the corner. There, on the floor, I saw something brilliant. Simmons had somehow managed to arrange six Wonderfries on the floor in a plan. So there were six shooters. Probably five in the diner. I hadn't noticed the first shot. So there was perhaps one outside, likely with a silenced weapon. In any case, six people within 100 meters wanted us dead.

„Not bad for the Old Medical after 6pm."
Next to the six Wonderfries, there was a clear line of spilt Wondercola, forming a semicircle. And then there was a piece of synthetic sour pickle, likely representing me.

Hilarious, Simmons.

And to the left of it all, leaning against a chair, was a large piece of Synthloaf, probably Simmons. I guessed he was planning to flank them.

A good plan, I thought.

But first, I had to listen carefully. By now, the screams in the diner had nearly stopped and I could hear footsteps approaching my position. I estimated they were about ten meters away.

I looked at my ComUhr; we had three minutes and twenty seconds to go.

"Now or never," I shouted, diving out from behind cover with a half-roll and firing two shots in the direction where I thought at least one opponent stood. Slightly off. It was three completely black-clad figures who were caught off guard and jumped into cover while opening fire with their automatic weapons. Around me, fabric and dirt flew as I dived behind the next cover. A shower of splinters and sparks rained down on me. I fired two more shots blindly from cover in their general direction, and then waited. I heard a groan, then a loud crash, like splintering wood, followed by a thud. One down, now two directly ahead, and three for Simmons to handle. I leaned against the chair, thinking. I had fourteen rounds left in my weapon and two opponents in front of me. If I jumped out

I might hit one but the other would tear me apart. I needed something to distract at least one of them.

I looked around the floor. On my left there was only destroyed furniture, a few broken plates, and a pile of dented Wonder sauce cans in various flavors. More destroyed inventory, forks, torn napkins, and food debris scattered across the floor to my right.

"Bah," I said, "**this place looks like a cafeteria after a childrens birthday party got wild. At least I won't have to clean this up when it's over.**"
I shouted to show the two opponents I was still there and that they should focus on me. Because in the corner, I saw something that could help me.

"Come here, little friend," I whispered as I crawled to the cleaning drone that had just tumbled out of the corner where its electric charging station was. It was about half the size of a standard cleaning robot from the 20s and moved towards the most enormous mess in front of it. I gently grabbed it and lifted it off the ground; it responded with a soft beep. I picked up two dented Wonder sauces with my other hand and held them before the drone's sensors.

"Okay," I said softly. "This is your next cleaning target. Got it. This is your final boss. It's making everything dirty, and you can't stand that. Ignore everything around you and go to where this stuff will be everywhere. Got it?" The drone stared unblinkingly at the two cans and beeped more wildly. I took that as a sign that it understood.

I set it down but still held it as its little wheels spun. With my other hand, I hurled the two Wonder sauces toward my enemies. One can landed against one of the tables as it rolled behind them. Damn. The other can, however, hit one of the diner sofas a few inches from the armed guy on the left side as its Chlorofluorocarbons inside rapidly expanded outwards, exploding in a spray of cocktail sauce.

My little robot friend beeped more energetically and I let it go. It shot straight towards the new pink splotches it couldn't stand. The two men, confused by the sounds and movement, stepped out of cover and opened fire on the little guy.

I took advantage of this distraction. Grabbing the diner seat in front of me with my right hand, I pulled myself over the edge with the synthetic arm's strength and launched forward toward the two men, who continued spraying bullets down the aisle.

With my left hand, I fired two precise shots towards the man on the right. One bullet hit his left arm and the second tore through his chest, sending a spray of blood over the furniture. He collapsed, firing a few parting shots at his comrade, which missed. The second enemy realized he had only shot a cleaning drone, turning his full fire on me. I landed about three meters from my last cover, crashing into another row of diner chairs. They were the XXL chairs I had seen earlier. Looking around, I saw Nancy on the floor curled up with a deep bleeding wound on her shoulder. She was still breathing. She stared at me, whimpering. Not what she had planned for her workday, I thought, figuring out how to kill the third guy three meters behind me. He kept firing wildly at my position, but only small splinters and dust from the uncleaned chair upholstery hit me.

I checked my watch. One minute and twenty seconds left. Time was running out. We had to get out.

"Simmons!" I shouted, not knowing where he was. "We have just over a minute until Dämmerung."

"Don't shout, you idiot," I heard Simmons from around the corner. He was crouched at the other end of the XXL table, weapon aimed down the long aisle where stray bullets flew.

"We need to get Nancy out of here and whatever's left of Lenny, too, or we'll never find out where Maddie is."
Simmons nodded.

We had less than a minute to sprint about ten meters through debris, overturned chairs, broken dishes, and a hail of bullets, each carrying someone, or half a person, depending on how you viewed Lenny.

We had to make it. I had ten bullets left in my magazine and no time to reload. We had to go.
"Forty seconds to Dämmerung."

"Okay," Simmons shouted back. "You grab Nancy with your metal arm, and I'll take what's left of Lenny. Got it?" "Let's do it!" "By the way, that was a great plan with the Wonderfries on the floor," I said, glancing around. "The cola and pickles – really creative."
Simmons looked confused. "What are you talking about? I have no idea." I frowned. "The Wonderfries and cola on the floor... That was you, right?" He shook his head. "No, man. I have no idea what you're talking about." I shook my head and chuckled.

Great, now I'm seeing things...

"On three. One, two," I grabbed Nancy by the waist and slung her over my shoulder. I heard a slight crack and moan but had no choice. With my other hand, I swung my gun forward and sprinted towards the exit. I fired in the direction I last saw the enemy, running like a berserker to our only escape. Simmons did the same, emptying his magazine down the aisle and grabbing Lenny by the opening where his face used to be. It squelched as he lifted Lenny and dragged him like a sack of wet potatoes. Bullets rained around us, but we managed to break through the door and crash outside. Simmons landed heavily, Lenny's remains sliding to a stop face down beside him.

A sharp pain shot through my leg, making the last few meters a stumbling run. I barely managed to catch Nancy as we hit the ground outside. My leg burned like fire, and Nancy screamed in pain. Simmons dragged Lenny's remains behind a nearby wall as I pulled Nancy to safety, trying to shield us from the bullets still flying through the door.

Then I felt a strong vibration from my ComUhr on my wrist.

Dämmerung had arrived.

With incredible speed, a black, 3 meter by 1 meter big drone silhouette broke through the smoke-filled sky of the Old Medical District. Dämmerung had reached its target coordinates precisely on time. This drone was a marvel of modern technology, made of matte black onyx carbon. With its aerodynamic, angular design and four silent rotors, it hovered like a predator over the diner. A large-caliber automatic rifle hung beneath, stabilized by a gyroscope that compensated for every movement. Dämmerung was equipped with high-resolution cameras and sensors, providing 360-degree surveillance and penetrating the smoke to target its enemies precisely.

„Lidar is such a great invention," I murmured as a female computer voice spoke from my ComUhr: "Dämmerung in position. Two Minutes left until retreat and refuel. Ready for action."

At that moment, three windows in the diner shattered under a hail of bullets from inside. The three shooters left inside the dinnerand the sniper form the rooftop opened fire on us. Bullets rained on my cover, and I heard Simmons curse behind the wall he had crouched just in time.

The situation couldn't be resolved any other way.

"Fire at will, Dämmerung," I shouted towards my ComUhr, and within a fraction of a second, the drone aimed its automatic rifle at the diner. A brief flicker of the targeting laser on three different points of the building and the inferno began. Its hunting instinct took over. The sound of the large-caliber gun echoed through the now almost deserted streets like thunder in a storm. Bullets tore through the diner's walls as if they were made of sand and the crumbling windows combined with rubble, sparks, fire and ash turned into an exploding inferno. The shooters inside had no chance of escaping. Two were instantly mowed down and disintegrated, while the third tried to jump out the window. He was caught in midair by a burst from the drone and was thrown back into the burning building in pieces.

The shooter on the rooftop opposite continued to fire at us, and I struggled to shield Nancy and myself behind a demolished delivery van. Bullets from the precision rifle pierced the windshield, hitting the asphalt just inches away. I shielded Nancy with my body.

It's not her time to go.

Dämmerung executed a precise maneuver, rotating on its axis and elevating several meters with a roar from the rotors. The drone targeted the rooftop shooter and took him out with a single burst, ripping him apart and slamming what was left of him against the wall behind. His rifle flew off the roof and landed somewhere in the trash riddled streets of the old Medical.

I heard a slight crackling noise coming from my wrist.

"Dämmerung here, the situation is under control. No further threats detected. Beginning retreat and refuel sequence."

I turned to Nancy. She was still breathing but unresponsive. We stepped out behind cover as I sent our position to emergency services. The drone ascended into the clouds, its rotors dispersing the smoke. The Wonder Diner was now a burning ruin, slowly collapsing. But, at least we had survived.

"Damn," Simmons said. "That was literally a last-second rescue. Great job, man." He patted me on the shoulder with his hands smeared full of Lenny's blood.

"Now we need to find out who the hell wants us dead."

"Yeah," I said, removing my right glove, limping towards the remains of Lenny leaning against the wall. I guess this would be one of these Days now…

AMITHAYUS, KOREAN DISTRICT

SEVEN.
AMITHAYUS

Amithayus Seattle, 2066 18:12 - Korean District

Neele had no problem crossing the border to the Korean District of Amithayus in exchange for her newly bought ComUhr. She stepped foot into Amithayus, the Asian district of Seattle, still slighty exhausted and panicked. The last time she had been here must have been about ten years ago. She had gone on an exploration journey through Seattle and its districts shortly after her second move and had left almost nothing
unexplored. Restlessly, she roamed many clubs and bars in various areas, always finding something new and exciting. Today, however, she was here for a different reason. She needed to meet her friend and former mentor, Dr. Alicia Yoshida. After years of disputes with her
superiors, Dr. Yoshida left the company they both worked for about two years ago.
Neele knew approximately where their meeting point was based on descriptions but had never been there since Dr. Yoshida opened a new shop two years ago.

She was about two blocks from her destination,
navigating a labyrinth of narrow alleys, crowded streets, and vibrant streetlamps. Amithayus was divided roughly into three parts: Japanese, Chinese, and Korean
populations, each reflecting their respective cultural
influences. In the Japanese-dominated part, minimalist Zen gardens and traditional teahouses were prevalent, interrupted only by Sony brand maintenance bots.
Shinto shrines alternated with futuristic skyscrapers whose exteriors mimicked traditional Japanese wood and paper

aesthetics but were made of transparent, highly flexible solar panels. The Chinese sector was dominated mainly by Huawei, which rapidly evolved from a telecommunications supplier to a leading global technology company. The ornate pagodas and glowing red lanterns were complemented by an intelligent infrastructure, with sensors, drones, and augmented reality systems monitoring everything from the buildings to the numerous markets. Who exactly was pulling the strings here remained unclear, Neele thought.

In the Korean part of Amithayus, traditional Korean craftsmanship was fused with modern manufacturing techniques under the leadership of the Samsung Group.
This was the place to be if you needed something that couldn't be found anywhere else in Seattle. The many small shops nestled into the lower floors of the Hanok houses which sold everything the heart, hand, or stomach desired.
As Neele got lost in the Chinese part's myriad scents, impressions, and colors, HELPS pinged her second newly bought ComUhr.

"Dr. Neele, you have reached your destination. Have a safe day."

Neele scanned the area. She had emerged from a small
alley and stood before an inconspicuous, old-fashioned building.
"A herb shop, okay, that's different." Neele opened the door and stepped inside.
She was overwhelmed by a multitude of different smells and impressions. It smelled of fresh grass, slightly spicy and tangy ginger and a faint medicinal scent which Neele identified as camphor. She browsed through the dark wooden shelves that reached the ceiling, looking at the antique ceramic containers covered in various characters.

Countless traditional silk paintings by different artists adorned the walls, depicting centuries-old Chinese stories in vivid colors and shapes. In the center of the room stood a large round table with a high-tech device, which Neele identified as a type of scanner. As Neele examined the device more closely, a calm, older voice spoke from the background.

"You seem to know a lot about herbs and their genetics, young ganjin." Neele turned toward the voice. She had heard the word ganjin before. Dr. Yoshida often used it, and she told her it was a short form she learned from an older couple she lived with while she was still young. It was a cuter version of gūniang, a respectful way for an older Chinese person to address a young woman. That was all that mattered.

The voice belonged to an older Chinese man, around 50 years old, who looked at her with open eyes and an alert mind. He wore a tailored Changshan, a traditional Chinese long shirt, on his upper body. The rest of his clothing was more functional and modern, with slight military influences, evident from the numerous pockets. He had a robust and respectful presence.

"Uh, yes. Hello, I mean, ni hao," Neele said, somewhat embarrassed. "I was, I think, sent here to this shop because I'm looking for..." The older man interrupted her with a small gesture and indicated she should follow him.
"Come, Dr. Neele. You are expected." Okay, she thought. She must be in the right place if this person, whom she had never seen before, knew her name. The older man, who introduced himself as Zhan Tao on the way to one of the back shelves, touched several ceramic containers in a specific sequence, causing a previously invisible door to open in the back of the shop.

He gestured for Neele to pass through, which she did.
The door closed behind her, and Neele found herself in a vast, modern, high-tech lab. The contrast between the antique-

looking shop she had just left and the overwhelming amount of technology she now faced was astonishing.

Neele could hardly believe her eyes. The lab was packed from top to bottom with the most modern equipment she had ever seen. Not even her lab was as grand and contemporary as the one she was standing in now. Machines were lined up in rows and Neele only recognized a handful.

Among them were a Hologen Sequencer which enabled three-dimensional projections of genetic material at the cellular level, a Quantum Synthesis Reactor which allowed the synthesis of biochemical compounds in an incredibly short time, and many other things Neele could only guess. She was speechless. This must be how Alice felt when she first woke up in Wonderland.

"Hello, ganjin, it's good to see you again," said a familiar voice behind her. When Neele turned around, she saw the face of her old mentor, Dr. Alicia Yoshida. She hadn't aged a bit in the past two years. She still looked like she was in her mid-30s, although she must now be somewhere in her 50s. Alicia still tied her hair in a low bun, highlighting her clear, almost white almond-shaped eyes.
She wore a typical, elegant Japanese kimono framed by a synthetic, semi-transparent flex lab coat.
She wasn't wearing a regular Lab coat or anything like the HELPS suit. Instead, she wore a high-quality titanium bracelet on her wrist which probably functioned as a communicator and discreet data access to all the technical gadgets in her lab.
Neele hugged Alicia. Finally, someone didn't mean her harm, someone she could trust. She tightened her arms around Alicia and felt a return embrace. The two women stood in the middle of the room, holding each other for almost a minute before Neele blurted out everything.
She told Alicia about arriving at the lab, the box containing her dead brother, finding herself on a completely unfamiliar floor, the data she had discovered, how HELPS had saved her life

more than once and how she eventually arrived in Amithayus at Alicia's place.

Dr. Yoshida ran her left hand through her hair and nodded as Neele continued to recount the details.
Then she guided Neele to a large table that seemed to be made entirely of glass. It stood right in the center of the lab.

"I know why you came, and I thank you for still
trusting in me and my abilities after all this time, ganjin," Dr. Yoshida said as they both stepped closer to the large glass surface.

It was a holographic projection table, similar to those Neele had used in Holster Skyway conference rooms for
presenting mundane PowerPoint slides and pie charts in three dimensions. Neele knew what to do and plugged the red cable into the designated port.
Within seconds the data HELPS had downloaded began to unfold above the table in three-dimensional images, diagrams, and texts.

The two women got to work, sifting through the roughly 650 files and folders Neele had brought.
They swiped, zoomed, read and discussed with multiple rounds of ‚Tie Guan Yin Tea 'hand-brewed by Zhan Tao.

He explained to Neele that the Oolong tea was only served on special occasions or to esteemed guests. Since both applied today, he served two rounds. The tea had a rich, floral and complex taste, improving with the second serving.

Seven hours had passed, slowly a picture
began to form before their eyes, bringing clarity to the incomplete data.

The earliest fragments they could catch were from 1986, dealing with the first major human nuclear disaster in Chornobyl. The samples collected from the irradiated firefighters were analyzed and documented, serving as a basis for early DNA manipulation.

A year later, there was a radiation accident in Goiânia, Brazil. According to a newspaper article a group of unsuspecting scrap dealers took a radiotherapy device loaded with cesium-137, leading to the irradiation of nearly 250 people. According to a text document this was the birth of Group R. Neele made a mental note of Group R, not knowing what it was but hoping to find out. Group R used this incident and the resulting data to improve radiation tolerance in genetic modifications.

Then, there was either a 24-year gap or Neele had yet to copy data for this extended period. The next nearly complete entry was dated 2011, located in Japan. An earthquake followed by a tsunami led to the meltdown and subsequent release of large amounts of radioactivity at the Fukushima nuclear power plant.

According to documents marked with a digital imprint of Project R it was the ideal scenario to study the long-term effects of radiation exposure on a large population. The research results were promising. Neele and Dr. Yoshida began to slowly piece together the puzzle. Then there was another vast time jump, filled with many scattered text fragments, numerous deeds of ownership, sales and purchase intentions and opaque contracts. The next nearly complete entry occurred almost 31 years later.

In 2042, an accident occurred in a government lab in the Japanese city of Kobe that was handling genetically modified viruses. This led to a local virus release, followed by a massive explosion that wiped out over 85% of Kobe City. According to Project R it was a deliberately planned experiment to study the effects of genetic manipulation on a dense urban population and substantiate the results of about 70 years of research.

Neele gasped as she read this. „How could anyone do such a thing? Willingly sacrifice so many people to test something and see if the research was correct?" Dr. Yoshida also couldn't explain it. What had Neele stumbled upon, she thought, swallowing hard as she read the results from Kobe, turning briefly to compose herself. The two spoke briefly and then continued at doubled speed.

They sifted through another 100 loose data fragments, but nothing else emerged that could give them any further clues. There were studies on epigenetic recombination techniques about expression patterns or quantum-genomic distortions in advanced biological functions. Neele looked questioningly at Dr. Yoshida but she just shrugged. Most documents were outside their fields and would require many more documents to explain themselves. But they didn't have them. While Neele walked away from the table, slightly frustrated to collect her thoughts, Alicia continued to browse the data.

Suddenly, she found something that caught her attention. She opened the file and looked at the content more closely. It took two minutes to understand what she was reading. She turned around and looked directly at Neele who was talking to HELPS about something Alicia couldn't hear from a distance. She looked back at the data and decided to call Neele over. "I think I've found something you need to see." Neele jumped up and ran toward the table. "What is it?" she asked, immediately recognizing what it was as she read the first line.

The document's heading, projected in large three-dimensional letters, read (2050) Snoqualmie Ridge Explosion – Start of Project Resurrection.

Seattle, 21:25 - Old Medical District

After Simmons and I had spent a good ten minutes bored studying the WonderDiner menu and finally ordering something from Nancy, I heard myself say,
"Ah, I knew she was still interested in you."

It was strange to watch myself from the third person, grimacing at every new piece of information. Had I always done that? I didn't realize my face was so flexible.

I spoke directly to Simmons, who was listening but seemed slightly distracted. Did he already know what was about to happen or had the revelation that Maddie was back thrown him off? "I asked around after your call earlier," I heard myself say, "to see if anyone knew more, and as luck would have it, someone did. And now I know, and soon you will too."

And now I did.

Lenny had called several people but only succeeded with Hiroshi Takeda. Hiroshi worked in the heart of Amithayus for one of the clan bosses named Mr. Tanaka. Some time ago, Mr. Tanaka had permitted Maddie to set up her business in an exclusive club under his
personal supervision in the heart of the Japanese quarter of Amithayus.

I heard myself say, "But first, I need to eat this WonderBread French Toast Deluxe coming my way."

Man, if Lenny had known those would be his last words. I hope to come up with something more thoughtful when I kick the bucket.

I felt something dense and metallic shoot straight through my mouth and throat and it was hard to think clearly through the pain and gurgling.

I took my hand away from what had been Lenny's head just a few minutes ago. I felt sick. The intense headache shot through my entire body. I felt just like Lenny looked—internally torn apart.

I had witnessed what happened next with my own eyes. I had no desire to feel it too. The pain I experienced from using my abilities was already intense enough.

"Simmons, I know where we need to go. And it will be anything but a walk in the park. Especially since we don't have air superiority there, and the Dämmerung and other ECLE toys won't be able to support us."

I exhaled and tried to regain control of my body, but the headache intensified. I thought about how little I wanted to go to Amithayus. I looked at Simmons, and his expression mirrored my own thoughts. "We need a plan or we won't get in there, especially not back out."

We sat on the steps of the emergency vehicles we had called and started to devise a plan. I asked the paramedics for something to wipe the pain from my mind. Nancy was being transported to the nearest hospital in one of the vehicles. At the same time, a few trained paramedics and their mini-drones worked on us, trying to patch us up as best they could.

They injected me with something that worked immediately, making me forget. After about an hour, we had a plan. At least the beginning of one.
After telling our story and showing our ECLE badges to the local head of the Old District Guardians, the better-equipped regular cops here in the Old Medical District, he nodded appreciatively. He began giving orders to his troops to clean up the area. We both looked at each other, probably thinking the same thing. "Man, what the ODG must have seen here inthe Old Medical," Simmons said as we walked toward the parking lot to our Electric Glide. I nodded, not really wanting to know.

We reached our vehicle and were amazed to find it still in its parking spot. Only a deep, about thirty-centimeter-long scratch from a sharp object on the side and an excellent new paint job on the hood with the initials of the local clan, ‚Old Medical Bastards', indicated that we had been here too long. It was time to head to the never-setting kingdom of the sun, as Amithayus was also called.

But first, we needed a quick stop at our precinct to gear up.

It took about half an hour to until we reached and then parked the car in the underground garage. Simmons went straight to the office to sort some things out, and I headed to the armory to equip us better. There were only two ways for a cop to enter Amithayus. Either you worked for one of the local gang bosses and were corrupt to the core—which, as far as I knew, neither of us was—or you had old contacts and had formerly worked undercover with someone inside Amithayus. That sounded rudimentary, like Simmons.

There was, of course, a third option, and that's what I was preparing for. I told Harold, our ECLE weapons master, where we'd be heading in about two hours, and he opened the cabinet for the big calibers without hesitation.

The third option was to look like you had absolutely nothing to lose and would clear out anyone who stood in your way. And that's how I was arming us. I emptied the weapons cabinet to the last bullet and grabbed two complete AegisFlex-Armor suits from the adjacent chamber. I slipped into one of them and pressed the three valves and the button on the side so they would hermetically seal and adjust to my body shape. It was getting serious.

Every time an ECLE officer put on the AFA suits, the news the following day would mention a massacre, a gigantic shootout, or a police operation that had utterly spiraled out of control. And that was precisely what I wanted to demonstrate with the suit. Anyone who saw it knew that anything could happen at any moment.

It was the old principle of nuclear deterrence from the Cold War, rethought and applied to the little guy.

Meanwhile, Simmons was working on reactivating his old contacts in Amithayus, hoping to get us across the district border and close to the Japanese quarter under the cover of darkness without attracting much attention. I stuffed a few thousand New Dollars into my pocket just in case.

You never knew when you might need to bribe someone to save your life.

I checked the time. Driving from our precinct to Amithayus under good traffic conditions took about an hour and a half. It was now just past 10 PM. The Amithayus district would be hermetically sealed at midnight, and no one would get in or out until seven in the morning. We had only two hours left to reach the outer border, which would be extremely tight. I decided against the car and told Simmons via ComUhr to meet me at the helipad. When I arrived, Simmons was already there, chatting with the pilot of the Holster Defense Systems Black Talon helicopter, built by Boeing and now part of the Holster empire. The Black Talon was an advanced version of the old Boeing AH-64 Apache helicopter used until the late 2040s. The new Black Talon, code-named AH-96X, was packed with technical innovations that were equally popular with the military and us. The Black Talon retained the streamlined silhouette of the Apache but was now made of 95% carbon fiber-reinforced material, reducing both radar and heat signatures to a minimum. The helicopter was powered by hybrid turbines, capable of running on conventional fuel or two electric motors for silent operations in close quarters.

It was the perfect combination of firepower and stealth you wanted when penetrating enemy lines. Politicians had recognized this too, ordering the AH-96X in large numbers. About 60% went to the Free Trade Zone of United American forces, while the remaining 40% were distributed to

various law and order keepers across the country.

Sometimes, I no longer knew what distinguished us, the ECLE, from a paramilitary task force.

The budget and equipment seemed the same to me.

With that thought, we took off into the darkness of Seattle. We had about twenty minutes of flight time and another 10–15 minutes on foot before reaching the district border. It was a tight schedule. Currently, we were just a tiny, silent-moving dot in the sky, but soon, we would play a much more significant role in the story of Amithayus. We didn't know it yet.

Seattle, 23:05 - Outside Amithayus - Japanese Quarter

Simmons and I ducked as we exited the Black Talon that had landed on one of the many Beaches surrounding Amithayus.
We where moving slowly toward the towering wall about forty meters ahead. Once we were out of range of the rotors, the Talon lifted off almost silently and disappeared within seconds.

"I've got to say, the stealth on that thing is top-notch," Simmons remarked, trying unsuccessfully to track the helicopter with his eyes. By now, Simmons had also donned his AegisFlex-Armor suit, and we moved swiftly through the shadows cast by the massive, old, and partially abandoned buildings around us.

The Border was about five Minutes away, the clock showed 23:12, so we were making good time. I felt nostalgic, when I regularly carried out semi-legal operations under the banner of the Free Trade Zone with the Emerald Strike Unit. Back then, I didn't know much about corporate-led warfare where companies directed and funded military operations directly and indirectly. It was always said to be for the good of the Free Trade Zone, but I eventually realized it was all about geopolitical power and securing interests.

And New Dollars, of course.

Simmons and I reached the barrier, marking the border
leading into Amithayus. It was enclosed by a sixty-meter-high wall, nearly impossible to scale from the outside.
We had landed far to the south and worked our way through the urban canyons to the border briskly.
So far, everything went smoothly. I scanned the sky and the wall for surveillance drones or other electronic devices that might detect us but saw nothing suspicious. An official border

crossing was bathed about two hundred meters to our left in bright light. It housed customs, security systems, automatic weapons, a few mercenaries, and an array of sensors and cameras that could biometrically scan any person within seconds. And there were a few dogs. However, I couldn't make out the breed.

They were probably not Shiba Inu waiting to lick us to death with their rough tongues.

Directly in front of us was nothing but a metal wall towering over everything around us. Hopefully, we had arrived at the right spot. Simmons activated his ComUhr and spoke into it. He signaled me to kneel, which I did. Then he took one of the three rifles he carried on his back, carefully set the other two against a wall, and pushed them into the bushes beside him. I followed suit. We didn't need our full arsenal, which was what I hoped for. A silent entry into Amithayus. I took my Sentinel Mark IV and held it in my hand. The Mark IV was explicitly designed to meet the challenging demands of Seattle's police forces. Its extensive connectivity features enabled seamless integration into the police's operational command system. It also had an integrated friend-or-foe identification system, which prevented us from accidentally shooting each other in the chaos of a firefight.

We waited in the darkness. Nearly three minutes had passed since Simmons spoke into his watch, and I began to feel that I should reattach the other two weapons probably. Waiting made me nervous. Waiting without knowing what I waited for was even worse. Then, something moved on the wall. I could clearly see a small light, slowly but surely growing larger. Someone had opened a section of the wall.

I thought there wasn't a door earlier, as Simmons signaled me to move quickly towards the opening. We ran, covering the shadows between us and the wall in less than fifteen seconds. I was exhausted. I wasn't used to so much running anymore. Simmons peered through the opening and waved me forward. It was about eighty centimeters high and seventy centimeters wide, just enough for us to squeeze through one at a time. Once we had moved from the hole in the wall, it closed seamlessly with a quiet click.

A man emerged from the darkness and approached Simmons without hesitation. I guessed him to be in his mid-thirties, but it was always tricky with Asians. I raised my Mark IV, preparing to aim at the stranger, but Simmons pressed my weapon toward the ground with his right hand and gestured with his left hand, indicating he wanted something from me. I hesitated, unsure of what he meant, until he rubbed his thumb and first two fingers together.

I understood. It clearly had paid off that I took quite a lot of new Dollars with me this morning. The new Dollar was still the best welcome gift I could think of.

I handed the stranger around two thousand of them which immediately disappeared into one of his many pockets. The stranger bowed slightly and then signaled for us to follow him. We crept and crouched through various steel-lined interior walls, likely the reinforced structure of the wall. After about five minutes, we emerged from a narrow alley into the Japanese part of Amithayus.

It was beautiful and unlike anything else in Seattle.

Strings of red and white lanterns hung over the streets, gently swaying in the wind and casting a warm glow on the cobblestones. Traditional buildings stood alongside futuristic skyscrapers that rose elegantly in contrast to traditional Japanese architecture. These modern structures were equipped with the latest pLED exterior screens, displaying advertisements for the newest services from Japanese corporations like Mitsubishi Heavy Industries, Hitachi Global, and Toshiba Robotics.

People moved through the streets wearing modern clothing and traditional kimonos. Although it was nearly midnight, they went leisurely, greeting each other respectfully and seeming to live in a peaceful coexistence of past and future. Simmons and I couldn't help but pause momentarily to take in the fascinating scene. The beauty, elegance, and tranquility of the Japanese quarter starkly contrasted with what I knew about the crime, brutality, and the dark, dangerous streets we had just traversed. It reminded me of an old Japanese proverb I had recently read in a fortune cookie. It said, "Uraomote no aru hito," meaning someone with a front and a backside. The Japanese quarter was showing its
friendly front side. The man who had just guided us through the labyrinth bowed deeply and disappeared around the corner before we could say anything.

Okay, the first part of our plan had worked. We were in before the curfew, and we hadn't shot anyone, and even better, no one had shot at us.

"Okay," I said to Simmons, who had turned to me. "How do we get to this Mr. Tanaka we're looking for?"
Simmons looked at me and replied, "First, we shoulder our weapons. Then we walk casually as if we've always been here, towards the center of the Japanese quarter. According to my informant, there is a club called Yoru no Hana, Flower of the Night, right in the center. That's where Mr. Tanaka is headquartered. And somehow, I feel like we should ring the front doorbell and ask for an audience."

"You must be joking," I shot back. "You want to ring the doorbell of one of the most notorious clan leaders here and just say hello. 'Hi, I'm Simmons; I'd like to speak to the boss. I have something to discuss with him about an old flame who might be here.'" I couldn't believe what I had just heard. That was his plan? That was a ridiculous plan. "We might as well commit Seppuku right here and now," I snapped at him. Simmons looked at me, slightly

bewildered. "That's exactly what we're going to do. Trust me, this isn't my first time in Amithayus ", he said as he shouldered his Mark IV, removed his camouflage mask, and stuffed it into his backpack.

And I did the same.

What a ridiculous idea, I thought as we both walked into the bright lights of the Japanese suburban area.

.

AMITHAYUS, MINGCHENG

EIGHT.
FORGOTTEN FACES, FORGOTTEN PLACES

Amithayus Seattle, 2066 21:12 - Dr. Yoshida's Laboratory, Mingcheng

As Neele sat at the holographic projection table staring at the floating data points dancing in the air before her she was not only contemplating the unexpected return of her brother Peet, which raised many questions, but also a strange, vague feeling that had followed her since childhood—a blurred memory of an adult woman who had saved her life in Snoqualmie Ridge, her former home.

She had suppressed the memory of the explosion 16 years ago as best as she could, but after hours of combing through hundreds of data points with Dr. Yoshida, she could no longer keep the memories at bay. The scant information about the Snoqualmie Ridge explosion, which had sparked her investigation of the data flood, slowly but steadily seeped into her consciousness. It was an exceedingly complex puzzle they had to piece together, but the fragments, albeit incomplete, lay directly before them.

Hours flew by as she and Dr. Yoshida fought through the vast amounts of documents and videos.
With each click and swipe, the chaos in Neele's head became more transparent. After about 30 more minutes of poring over numerous diagrams from top to bottom, she came across a study file with a promising name:

Quantitative Viral Dispersion Analysis for the
Examination and Optimization of Virus Spread during Nuclear Disasters.

This sounded like a result of one of the nuclear disasters they had read about hours earlier. It was unclear whether it referred to Chornobyl or Fukushima, but the term "virus spread" piqued her interest. She called Dr. Yoshida over, and together, they read the study carefully, speculating what some things might mean. Ultimately, it turned out that Chornobyl and Fukushima were large-scale field tests designed to study the spread and effectiveness of a marker completely unknown to Neele and Dr. Yoshida. The goal was to examine how the marker affected the human genome under extreme radiation exposure. Both tests, according to the study, were deemed a great success.

The two looked at each other. "What does this mean?"
Neele asked. "Why would anyone use world-altering events to conduct and test some form of genetic research?" Dr. Yoshida nodded and added, "And how could they conduct such advanced genetic research in the early '80s? According to our knowledge, genetic research was initiated in the early '50s by James Watson and Francis Crick with the discovery of the DNA double helix
structure. Still, it took at least another 40 to 50 years before the first significant success with the cloning of Dolly the sheep in the mid-'90s. The more important question is how the people of 'Group Resurrection' even knew when and where these disasters would occur.

It can't be a coincidence that we have data and documents on 70 percent of the global disasters of the last hundred years, all meticulously cataloged, analyzed, and scientifically evaluated."

Neele nodded and clicked on two more files attached to the Analysis. She read the first three lines and turned pale. Her hands began to shake, and she felt the ground lift beneath her feet. Alicia immediately noticed that Neele had discovered something significant and came over. She placed her hand on

Neele's shoulder and held her steady so she wouldn't fall. Neele read the following few lines in a panic and then turned to Alicia:

The words were hard to get out of her mouth:
"It wasn't an accident," Neele whispered.
She had found another analysis with detailed information about human genetic manipulations, but what had shocked her was the location—a lab beneath Snoqualmie Ridge. Like the entire town where she had spent the first 16 years of her life, the lab had been built for one purpose.

They were all lab rats, led through an invisible maze to see who was genetically fit and who wasn't.
"The explosion was deliberate. They wanted to see how our DNA reacted to extreme stress." Dr. Yoshida nodded, her eyes fixed on the floating text before her. "My whole life was nothing but a cruel experiment."

"And Peet..." Neele sobbed, fighting back tears. Her voice broke as she opened the following data set. It contained more background information about Snoqualmie Ridge and its inhabitants.

The first entry read: Experimental Subjects. Neele felt sick as she continued reading. The research facility beneath the small town was a covert installation used by the
Resurrection Group, under the leadership of Dr. Caldwell, for advanced experiments. "Why the hell did he do this?" she heard Alicia curse. It was the first time in 16 years since Dr. Yoshida had taken Neele as her student that she had heard her curse. "That damn arrogant bastard," Dr. Yoshida erupted. "I always knew he did things his way, but this has nothing to do with humanity anymore."

Dr. Viktor Caldwell. Neele couldn't believe it. She had spent four years researching under him at Holster Skyway. Two years with Alicia until she abruptly quit one day, and then two long years alone under his leadership. He had always made her uneasy, but she thought that was just how it was with superiors. Smile and move on quickly. Had he been using her all this time? Or worse, kept her close as a test subject? What had she been researching with him? She had never been fully involved in everything and, since Alicia left, had only been allowed to handle subprojects and minor tasks. Had her research had something to do with the Resurrection Group?

Neele had hundreds of questions she wanted to ask and answer simultaneously, but Dr. Yoshida had already somewhat regained her composure. "Here, look at this," she said, opening another file. It was an incomplete report on the expected reactions and actual results of the Snoqualmie Ridge explosion.

Neele scrolled through the file and eventually found a series of video recordings with timestamps:

August 19, 2050–7 days before the experiment

The image was grainy and poorly lit. Dr. Caldwell sat at a lab table, bathed in dim light, with isolated lights of different colors, primarily red and green, glowing in the background behind him. He spoke directly into the camera, his voice calm, though his tension was visible.

"Dr. Viktor Caldwell, Test Facility 7, Snoqualmie Ridge. Day 5692." Neele swallowed. "That was 15 years, seven months, and seven days," she calculated, and Alicia nodded. Her entire life up to that point. "Thirteen of the total two thousand seven hundred fifty-one subjects show remarkable resilience to the genetic modifications. The first effects of the marker show good compatibility with the steady increase in dosage. I am confident that we should slowly begin phase two of the tests. If everything goes according to plan, and I must say the results exceed our wildest expectations, we should be able to start the next test run in about seven to ten days."

Neele knew it had only taken seven days. She could feel it distinctly in her left Neuro-Arm, reinforced with graphene composite material. The phantom pains from her amputated left arm were still clearly felt even after
16 years. She noticed her anger rising. She opened the next recording.

August 26, 2050 - Day of the experiment

The image now had somewhat better quality.
Probably because Dr. Viktor Caldwell was no longer in his lab but on a hill somewhere near Snoqualmie Ridge, the camera was pointed toward the city, and Dr. Yoshida estimated it was about six to eight kilometers between him and the city. It was a beautiful day outside; the golden sun broke through the cloud cover. Viktor stood surrounded by several other scientists and soldiers behind a semi-transparent glass shielding. Viktor turned towards the camera and began to speak in grandiose terms:

"Dear colleagues, today is finally the day. After decades of research and planning, we render the greatest service to science today that one can imagine. Here and today, on August 26, 2050, precisely two minutes before seven, we open a new era of research and push the door to a new, better humanity miles wide."

Viktor boasted toward the camera, and one could faintly hear the applause of a small crowd. Viktor muttered something into his ComUhr and then stared intently in the direction of the city.

Precisely two minutes before seven, the ground beneath Snoqualmie Ridge began to shake, and with a bright flash, a one-kiloton tactical nuclear bomb, strategically placed for maximum efficiency, exploded under the city. The brilliant light burst from its dark vault beneath the ground at about the height of Wholemart in the city center. Concrete and steel cracked like the shell of an overripe fruit.

The explosion spread in a symmetrical, mushroom-shaped cloud that mercilessly spiraled into the sky while a fireball of dust and ash consumed everything in its path on the ground.

The scorching heat wave rolled through the streets, burning everything in its path and causing buildings to collapse and catch fire like toy houses. Glass shattered and transformed into deadly shards that whirled through the air. Cars, people, and streetlamps were swept away like leaves in the wind, engulfed by the unleashed destruction.

Amid this apocalyptic scene, the air distorted in wave-like patterns as the shockwave advanced, leveling everything in its path. Once a bustling hub of modern conveniences, the city's heart was reduced to a burning, smoking rubble field within seconds.

The golden hour had long passed and the sun could barely penetrate the chaos unleashed under the glowing sky. Where there had once been life, there was now a haunting silence, broken only by the crackling of burning ruins and the distant echo of the catastrophe that had irrevocably etched itself into the memories of the handful of survivors in the city.

Several people emerged behind the camera and shook Dr. Viktor Caldwell's hand. He turned towards the camera, visibly pleased. "The explosion," Viktor said, "was the most beautiful thing I have ever seen. And it was more necessary than we initially thought. I am sure..." He paused briefly to consider his words, then continued. "No, I know the results of today's experiment exceed our expectations."

Then, a few more people came into view and shook Viktor's hand.

Neele's heart pounded wildly. She had just witnessed the destruction of her home, the annihilation of her family, and the worst experience of her entire life from the perspective of a completely insane scientist she had worked with for years. "He knew. He knew we would die, and he did it anyway. Just like that. He killed us all for science." Neele couldn't hold it in any longer and screamed at the screen. "That damn bastard. How can he do such a thing?" Neele gripped the table, wanting to break it in two. Alisha watched in anguish.

From off-screen, she heard HELPS address her.

"Dr. Neele, your pulse and heart rate are very elevated. Please have a safe day."

Neele was about to retort with a string of expletives, telling HELPS where he could stick his safe day when she noticed Dr. Yoshida staring intently at the video material. She had paused the footage about ten frames before the end and had moved closer to the now-frozen image. She tilted her head from left to right and back again. This was something she always did when trying to remember something, a habit Neele had picked up from her.

Neele also examined the image closely, wiping tears from her face with her left arm. Dr. Yoshida pointed to one of the people standing in the frame, shaking Viktor's hand. "Do you know who that is?" she asked Neele.

"No, and I don't care who the old man in the picture is." "But you should, my ganjin.
That is Thornej A. Holster Senior, God rest his soul, the founder of Holster Skyway and the lab where we worked together." Neele was shocked. Of course.
He looked like his son, whom she had seen in the lab complex a few times, but he was much older.
How could she not have recognized him?

"What have we gotten ourselves into?" Dr. Yoshida said, and Neele couldn't help but agree. "What are the builders of modern Seattle as we know it and Dr. Viktor Caldwell
doing together in this place that was once my home?"
Neele could only say weakly from exhaustion.
Dr. Yoshida and she had been at this for hours now,
combing through the material. She desperately needed some sleep to gather her thoughts. She had the unsettling feeling that instead of piecing the fragments together, she was constantly presented with more puzzle pieces. They finally knew what had happened to her family, but why was still a complete mystery to her. She nodded to Alicia, turned, and was about to suggest that she needed to lie down when Alicia grabbed her hand, preventing her from leaving.

Neele stared at her questioningly.
"I just found another video," Alicia said, pulling Neele
closer. She relented, having no energy left to argue. All her courage and strength had suddenly left her and were now lying on the comfortable-looking bench about five meters behind her, sleeping away.

"I don't think I can handle another piece of bad news
tonight," Neele said, yawning loudly. She was dead tired and wanted nothing but to fall asleep standing up. Dr. Yoshida opened the video, and what the two of them saw on the screen

before them literally wiped all the tiredness from Neele's face instantly.

In the video were two women, one older, in her early to mid-90s, who could only stand with the help of a metal staff, and another woman, perhaps in her mid-60s, sitting in a kind of modern wheelchair. They both looked thoughtfully into the camera. The younger woman had scars on her left arm that seemed to run across her entire body, stopping only on the left side of her face. Most of her unscarred body was covered in a type of biocompatible metal. Her eyes were milky and cloudy, often seen in nearly blind people. The person appeared to be paralyzed on one side of her body.

Neele looked closer. "That's impossible," she stammered, recognizing who she was seeing. It was Alicia and her, only about 40 years older than they were now.
"This must be a fake or a manipulation," Neele stammered, and Alicia looked concerned as she played the video.

"Hello, my ganjin," said the woman, who looked like an ancient version of Alicia. "If everything has worked out as planned, you are now standing alone in front of a screen, wondering why I am speaking to you. And that's your right. It only means one thing for us both: our plan is working and we have another chance to make things right." I now hand over the word to you.
Maybe it will be easier for you to explain to yourself what you are seeing and hearing.

Neele could neither believe her eyes nor her ears as the old version, supposedly her, began to speak. "Hello you, or should I say I," she heard the old person stutter. Neele paused the video and looked at Dr. Yoshida.
"This can't be happening, can it?" she said, staring at Alicia. But she did not respond to her words. "This must be some twisted game Viktor is trying to play with us. AI voice and video

editing is so advanced now that it's no problem to digitally recreate or artificially age people." Dr. Yoshida still didn't respond. "Alicia?" Neele asked. "What's wrong?"

Before she could answer, Neele saw Zhan Tao emerge from a dark corner of the lab and quickly approached Dr. Yoshida. With three brief, different movements of his wrist, he described something to her, and Dr. Yoshida immediately wiped all files from the screen and turned it off.
She initially grabbed a memory stick she had inserted into the table and pocketed it. "We need to leave here as quickly as possible," she said, turning around.

"Zhan Tao just informed me that a small private army has assembled outside the herb shop and is probably coming to visit us. Zhan Tao said he would hold them off as long as possible to give us a head start, but he didn't know how long he could delay them."

"We have to go now," Alicia said, grabbing Neele roughly by the arm. She managed to nod to Zhan Tao, who
returned the gesture, and grab the helmet of her HELPS suit before she and Alicia stumbled through a door at the back of the lab. As the door closed and the last beam of light faded, Neele could see Zhan Tao rushing towards the entrance to meet his fate. She wished Zhan Tao good luck. He was another person she had grown fond of and would likely never see again. Just like so many times before in her life.

AMITHAYUS, JAPANESE DISTRICT

NINE.
THE FLOWER OF THE NIGHT

Amithayus, Seattle, 23:20 - Japanese District

We actually went straight to the front entrance of the Club, Yoru no Hana. It took about fifteen minutes to get there. Straight to the entrance. On foot. Just like that. In full combat gear, minus the camouflage masks. Where the smartly dressed guests were waiting, and the four bouncers guarding the entrance and four more, slimmer Japanese men with automatic weapons standing a bit off to the side. And no, we did not pass Go or collect 4000 new dollars. This was completely insane.
As soon as these human gorillas learned who we were,
there would be a massacre. Numerous innocent guests would die, and Simmons and I probably would too.

What had possessed Simmons to come up with this
ludicrous plan? With every step closer my hand
tightend around the grip of my weapon. The music grew louder, the pulsing lights brighter, and the murmur of people at the entrance rose to a constant buzz of sounds and laughter. My muscles tensed, I was scanning every little movement around me for threats. Simmons walked ahead of me as we just glided tpast the line of people wanting to get into the club.
A few guests turned to look at us; some stared and others
nodded. My ComUhr was constantly trying to translate the snippets of conversation around us into English.
"Sono fuku, meccha kakkoii ne!" and "Meccha oshare da ne!" Our outfits looked cool.
We were stylish? I stared at my ComUhr dangling from my wrist and checked if it had taken a hit during the diner shootout. But apart from a few scratches on the display, it seemed perfectly intact. Apparently, it was the year of the

revival of "tech wear" clothes that were so popular among teenagers in the early twenties of the 21st century. I remember that during my teenage years in the early forties, a Y2K revival was highly trendy. Shiny metallic fabrics, cargo pants, crop tops, and bucket hats.

It gave me the chills just thinking about it.

We reached the end of the line or the club's beginning, depending on how you looked at it. Simmons stopped and so did I. We had our two automatic rifles strapped to our backpacks and now stood, still heavily
armed before the four mountains of muscle and flesh who glared at us. Simmons tilted his head from side to side and calmly surveyed the four sumo champions who were at least two heads taller than me.

One of the four cracked his knuckles and moved toward Simmons. I loosened the safety on my Beretta Quantum X9 and slightly pulled it from its sheath. I was ready to defend our lives with everything I had, which wouldn't be much against the overwhelming odds. Nevertheless, I braced myself. Any moment now, heads would explode all around and people would fall to the ground screaming and writhing in pain. And two of those people would be us.

And probably me first.

The largest of the four giant biceps behemoths lumbered toward Simmons and stood directly in front of him with crossed arms. He expanded his chest a few extra centimeters as he straightened up; his scrutinizing gaze traveled from Simmons' shoes to his now sparse head of hair.

Simmons had lost a lot of hair in the last three or four years. A bald head would suit him. Maybe he could pass as the younger brother of the sumo standing in front of us...

Simmons stood there and looked up into the giant's eyes with a slightly tilted head. Then something happened that I hadn't expected. Simmons spoke Japanese. And fluently. With a slight American accent. But Japanese.

Where, how? And since when…

…flashed through my mind,

…which was much better than a bullet with my name on it, but…

…my ComUhr snapped me out of my thoughts as it began to translate simultaneously.
"Ne, debu-gao. Watashi no Mae ni tatsu. How dare you get in my way?" Simmons extended his hand in greeting. "Simmons, it's a pleasure to meet you. what's your name?" The mountain of flesh furrowed his brow and I think he didn't know whether to start laughing or punch him in the face. "Omae mitaina you small shit in front of me?" he said, preparing to decapitate Simmons with a single blow of his gigantic fist.

"Many people here in Amithayus may know me by another name and from another life. I was once called Onigiri."

The muscleman's face fell into incredible astonishment, and his hand stopped moving towards Simmons' head.
The muscleman wanted to open his mouth and say a few more words, but all that came through my translator was stuttering and gibberish. What I did hear clearly however was the murmur that ran through the surrounding crowd and I noticed some people cautiously stepping back a few steps.

What - was - going - on?

Who was this man with whom I had spent the last few

years drinking lousy coffee and trying to solve murder cases? Simmons ignored the tumult and spoke directly to the giant, who no longer seemed large.
"I want to speak to your boss. Mr. Tanaka. Immediately. Otherwise, there will be a blood rain, like back in the Matsubara District."

Simmons's calm was almost more terrifying than what he was saying.

That could be due to the AI translation, which recited its text very bored. Wait a minute. What did I hear?

The Matsubara District. What happened there again?
No, instead, when was that again? I remembered reading something in Simmons' files. Much of it, like almost everything else, had been redacted, but as far as I could recall, there was a bloody incident about ten years ago known as the Matsubara Massacre. As far as I could piece together, it was a Yakuza operation infiltrated by several agents to gather information on an enormous weapons deal. Something must have gone wrong, and when the local forces of the Amithayus Clean-up Team were called in, they found an extreme bloodbath.

Almost 30 Yakuza were killed. "Was that you?" I whispered to Simmons, but he didn't respond. The big guy in front of us did. He spoke something into his communicator, and a few moments later, all four mountains stepped back and cleared the way for us. The doors opened, and besides deafening techno music, a cloud of fog escaped from inside the club.
Also, a small, skinny man in a chic black suit slipped out of the dense fog and stopped before us.
He nodded to both of us and said softly:
"Welcome, Mr. Simmons. It is our pleasure that you and your friend honor us with your presence after such a long absence."

I was amazed. Simmons must have made an incredible impression to be greeted with such respect.
"Mr. Tanaka is already expecting you in the Black Hall. Please hand in your weapons at the reception.
You will receive them back after the meeting, freshly cleaned, as always. Please follow me when you are ready," the little guy said and bowed again, this time even deeper.

He must have been a contortionist in a past life, or how else could he do that with his back?

I couldn't believe it. Simmons had managed to get us through the main entrance into what was probably the best-guarded club in all of Seattle without any gunfire, and they would polish our weapons to a high shine.

It felt like a crazy dream. My hand around the Beretta Quantum relaxed slightly as I pushed it back into the holster. Everything was happening exactly as Simmons had said half an hour ago. Pure madness shot through my mind as we climbed the steps. Now, not just a few curious people were staring at us, but the whole crowd followed our every move with watchful eyes. I wondered what awaited us as the doors closed behind us.

The entrance area of the Yoru no Hana Club was simply put: Impressive. I couldn't describe it any other way.

It combined modern elegance with traditional Japanese elements, leaving an unforgettable first impression.
The massive entrance doors made of tinted glass were adorned with shimmering patterns that changed
depending on the viewing angle and lighting conditions, creating a hypnotic effect on the viewer. Past the Doors a wide illuminated path made of translucent material that glowed in different colours extended.

On either side of the entrance a row of slim statues stood representing mythological guardian figures from long ago. Above the entrance to the dance area itself hung a large holographic sign with the kanji characters for
"Flower of the Night." A light scent of incense and exotic perfumes wafted through the air, blending with the
pounding techno beats and traditional Japanese music into a unique mix. A staircase at the end of the room led down to the club's lower levels, another one up to the private rooms, including the Black Hall, where we were to meet Mr. Tanaka. A matte gold railing flanked the staircase with impressive digital artworks depicting Japanese myths in animated images hung on the walls.

The air was filled with gentle mist stemming from the heat and condensation of the writhing bodies in the back of the club. It moved in waves along the floor, giving the entrance area an almost surreal touch. A gigantic crystal chandelier, elegantly hanging from the ceiling and glowing in various colors, showed us the direct way to the reception, where we handed our weapons into the well-manicured hands of two young women. They neatly stored them in a transparent cabinet at the back of the reception, slightly out of sight of the other guests. In return, they gave each of us a small digital chip with a number. It reminded me al ot of luggage storage at an airport or train station.

The club, especially the upper floors, seemed very exclusive,which became more and more clear the higher we climbed the stairs, the fewer but more beautiful the people became. There were an awful lot of stairs we climbed.

Two floors less would have sufficed for my taste.

They could have at least installed an escalator or an elevator. How else do all these filthy, rich old geezers manage to get to their private rooms for entertainment without dropping dead right away?

I barely made it to the fifth floor, gasping for breath, and a heart attack was already knocking cheerfully on my heart chambers. One more floor, and I would collapse right here and now. Over the many years of ever-increasing office work, I had forgotten that the job was 90% endurance.

On the one hand, I meant the constant walking, going places; on the other hand, waiting around for something new to happen, which could influence the investigations another new direction. Simmons patted me on the back and nodded to me. "We're almost there," he whispered.

And I hoped he was right. "It better be," I muttered under my breath.

Otherwise, things might turn out badly for you. If I could actually catch up to him.

He was almost almost at the end of the long corridor when I finished walking up the steps. He and the skinny man in the well-tailored dark suit waited patiently for me to arrive.
I reached the two just as the door opened inward; The little man gestured with his hand and bowed deeply to indicate that we had arrived. The door closed behind us, and we were almost entirely alone in the Black Hall.

Alone was a very flexible term.

Besides Simmons and me, ten other Japanese men in even better-tailored black suits were lined up in the back of the Black Hall.

Their silent vigilance permeated the room. The Black Hall itself was the opposite of what the entrance hall and the name "Black Hall" promised.

Number one. It wasn't black. Rather bluish. And Number two, it was small, mostly plain and poorly lit. None of these fit the usual description of the word hall. Simmons and I stood in the middle of the room; Mr. Tanaka sat in a heavy black leather armchair at the other end. He was flanked on both sides by two massive statues of ancient Japanese warriors, underscoring his authority more than clearly.

The only illumination came from a faint bluish glow that bathed the room in a dim light, sharply highlighting the contours of the people present. The walls were covered in dark blue fabric that dampened sounds and created an
almost eerie silence. A sizeable polished metal table separated us from Mr. Tanaka and something that looked like a sword stand lay on it.

Or maybe it was a stand for one of those old model ships that languished in a too-small glass case.

I sympathize with the glass case. I had no idea what rich, old people did with their time these days, except maybe for murder, financial fraud and prostitution. Everyone needs a hobby. And a model wooden ship was probably the lesser evil.

Mr. Tanaka sat at the head of the table, his face hidden in the half-light. His eyes, however, gleamed clearly in the backlight, but his pupils were colorless. That was one of the signs I had learned over the years on the street. It meant that your
opponent had some implant on his retina to record conversations. He fixed us with his gaze, which permitted no contradiction.

So we had to be careful about what we could reveal and what we couldn't. We bowed to him. Then, he began to speak softly but clearly.

"Oni-giri San. It has been long since I last saw you in these halls. I can sense you have changed, not just internally but also in your demeanor. You no longer bow as deeply as you used to. But who doesn't change over such a long period? And I see you are not here alone. Just like the last time, you stood here and asked me for a favor, which I generously granted you. Have you come now to settle your katakiuchi with me?"

Settle a blood debt?

Did my ComUhr translate that correctly? A blood debt... You only do that to avenge a family member and restore your honor. So the two knew each other from before.

So, I could categorically rule out gambling debts as the cause for Simmons's warm welcome.

"I've come to see Maddie. I must... we must speak with her. It concerns a murder case that could have far-reaching consequences." Simmons now seemed more nervous.
"Possibly, even reaching Amithayus."
He bowed slightly and did not look Mr. Tanaka in the eyes.

"Maddog?" Tanaka had not moved a millimeter since we entered the room, but now I saw him lean slightly forward into the light. He raised an eyebrow.

Fuck, the eyebrow thing. That was definitely some secret signal to his bodyguards, like in Roman times when the Emperor raised his hand in the arena and pointed his thumb down.

I felt myself starting to devise a plan for taking on the five bodyguards on the right.
Unfortunately, I didn't see a vacuum cleaner drone around somewhere to save me.

Damn, it, you guys build all this electronic stuff; why aren't there any vacuum cleaner drones here?

"That's an unusual request, Oni-giri San. Not only

considering that you entered my service in
exchange for her life. No, rather considering your entire shared history. Therefore, I cannot grant this request," said Mr. Tanaka, leaning back into the darkness.

"Then I will settle my katakiuchi here and now, Tanaka San. Give me a task to settle my debt so we can be on
wo kaesu. Equal and opposite. Face to face."

Mr. Tanaka's mouth twisted into a slight smile. He had been waiting for this. He had all the cards and knew how to play them.

Maybe it was gambling debts, given how well he had played Simmons.

"So be it. I will grant you an audience with Maddie
Maddog Turner, if you settle your debt with me tonight.
Do you see this sword stand on the table?
It has been sitting there for two years, just as it is. Lonely. Empty. Kara. It has never been moved, cleaned, or touched during this time. Do you know why, Oni-giri San?"

"No, Tanaka San, I do not," Simmons replied, still slightly bowed.

Who the hell wants to touch your old wood, I thought and immediately bowed a few centimeters deeper, just in case he could read minds.

"This table and this katanakake have been in my family's possession for over 100 years. My great-grandfather gave them to my father, who passed them on to me when my time came. But it wasn't just this sword stand but also the accompanying blade. The Kami no Katana."

114

"The Sword of the Gods," my ComUhr informed me. From then on, I knew that tonight would be a very long night.

Just once I want to get home before the end of the day.

"Tell me more about the Kami no Katana," I whispered quietly, and my ComUhr seemed to find the appropriate encyclopedia article within seconds. You couldn't complain about the accuracy and truthfulness of the successor site to Wikipedia. Red White and True had been number one since it merged with Freedom Facts and The Eagle's Eye about five years ago. It became the largest and most popular participatory information platform on the free internet of the Free Trade Zone in United America.

"The Kami no Katana and its origin," my ComUhr began to whisper in the small earpiece that came with the Police Version of our ComUhr...

...During World War II in the early 20th century, Japan was characterized by deep national pride and a strong belief in the divine origin of the Emperor. At that time, a young emperor reigned who was often referred to as the...I skipped ahead...
...a child Emperor due to his youthful age.
Despite his age, he was attributed immense symbolic
significance, as it was believed that he was directly
descended from the gods.

To boost the morale and fighting spirit of the Japanese
troops, the country's leading scientists and best
Swordsmiths decided to create a weapon that would
combine both ancient craftsmanship and the most
advanced technology. This sword was meant to be a weapon and a symbol of the Emperor's indestructible power and divine protection over his subjects.

The Kami no Katana was developed under the direct

sponsorship of the Child Emperor. It was said that
The Emperor himself touched the final exemplar of this sword to imbue it with divine power. After completion, the Emperor presented the sword to Japan's bravest and noblest warrior.

After World War II ended, the Kami no Katana fell into oblivion as Japan had to give up its military ambitions and focus on rebuilding. Nonetheless, the sword remained alive in the hearts and legends of the people as a symbol of strength, honor and the unbeatable connection between tradition and progress.

Oh man, what a day. First a double murder, then a shootout with dozens of dead, and now a quest for a cursed Sword of the Gods...

...I thought as I gave my ComUhr a slight tap with my index finger to command it to be quiet.

How about meeting the love of my life tonight...

"It was stolen from my custody under the supervision of my best guards," Mr. Tanaka interrupted my thoughts.

Then they weren't your best guards.

"I executed them for their betrayal of our faith."

Great guards. Superb guards. The best of all time!

"And I will do the same to my enemies who now possess the Kami no Katana. You Onigiri San and your friend will retrieve it for me. Tonight. One of my servants will inform you of the details." And with those final words, Mr. Tanaka withdrew back into the darkness of the Black Hall. I now understood the significance of the room's name. Only certain things were discussed here that could lead to a long period of darkness. And we had unwittingly stumbled into it.

It felt like we had blindly walked into a trap set for us years ago. Simmons and I bowed, and we both walked towards the door that, as soon as he finished speaking, opened as if by magic while still facing Mr. Tanaka.

The little contortionist in the sharp suit waited for us outside. He bowed even more profoundly, if that were humanly possible until we had passed him. I was curious whether his bow was meant for us or Mr. Tanaka. But one thing I knew for sure:

I had to ask him who his tailor was. That suit was excellent.

He slid with us into another small room located two floors down. The descent didn't bother me; only what lay ahead after all this gnawed at my self-confidence. This small room was significantly brighter and unlike the Black Hall had a gigantic holographic screen in the middle of the room instead of Mr. Tanaka as a statement piece.

We sat down, and Mr. Contortionist—I was quite sure that was his real name—began to brief us on the details of our blood oath to be fulfilled tonight.

With every word he told us, the fragments in my head solidified into a clear sentence that I hadn't been able to formulate correctly since I touched Lenny.

For Simmons' sake, I hope Maddie is worth all this trouble. Whatever happened between them, she must have completely turned his head.

We would find out in the next six hours and ten minutes whether for better or for worse. We had one night to complete our mission.

Tomorrow at 7:00 AM, when the borders of Amithayus reopen for crossing, we would either walk home with heads held high or be carted out in many small pieces through one of the many trash compactors found at every corner.

Either way, we will leave Amithayus at precisely 7:00 AM tomorrow.

AMITHAYUS, MINGCHENG

TEN.
THE ECHO OF TIME

Amithayus Seattle, 2066 03:43 AM - Dr. Yoshida's Laboratory, Mingcheng

Neele and Dr. Yoshida huddled in a small hidden room at the back of the lab. Zhao Tan had protected them from the soldier's eyes, and both women held him in high regard for it. He had likely sacrificed his life for them without a moment's hesitation. As they sat there listening to the noises outside their small prison, they began discussing what they had just witnessed on the screen.

The data and recordings were incredible.
If you told someone about it, they would hardly believe it. Dr. Caldwell had knowingly, deliberately, no, willingly destroyed Neele's home which somehow was no longer her home but a laboratory, an experiment, or both... They were probably all dead. And she had survived. And maybe her brother, too? She it to be true.
And what did Thornej A. Holster Sr., God be not so merciful to his soul, have to do with it? And then those two women who actually looked like Dr. Yoshida and Neele. And what did they mean by if everything went according to their plan? Neele couldn't manage to organize the chaos in her head.

On the other hand, Dr. Yoshida had been silent for the past ten minutes, only nodding whenever Neele said something new. Alicia had the habit of focusing so intently on something that she could tune out everything else around her.
Except for essential, necessary social functions, like nodding, she would concentrate entirely on one thing. Then the next. And the next. So a few minutes passed with Neele talking and Dr. Yoshida just nodding.

Then Dr. Yoshida suddenly turned to Neele, and a flood of hypotheses and information poured out of Alicia's mind onto Neele. "I went through everything in my head again. All the catastrophes, all the little details we read.
And everything had to do with testing a marker R and
studying human genetic defects. From what I see and the data tells me, I am convinced that the explosion in Snoqualmie Ridge was the first knowingly caused explosion. All the nuclear disasters of the last 80 years or so before that had natural causes or were accidents or human error. They were exploited to study the subjects who were unintentionally harmed there.
They probably found that a tiny percentage of these people had some genetic defect. Maybe it was just one person. Patient 0 or Patient R? That would have been enough. Then, the scientists working on it were interested enough to study it repeatedly.
What exactly did they find, apart from it likely becoming more interesting to them over time. And that some point later
Dr. Caldwell came into play and called the whole thing Project Resurrection. But what struck me most about all this information, images, diagrams and videos were one particular thing."

Neele didn't know what Alicia meant. Her head was
racing, trying to understand, sort, catalog and believe all the information Alicia had just thrown at her.

It didn't really matter to her whether it was the first
knowingly caused explosion (besides all the nuclear tests by the predecessor government) or not. She had been there. In the middle of it. She had felt the heat and still felt it every day when she looked at her left arm.
"He just sacrificed us. All the people who meant something to me, all my friends were killed instantly. And for what? So that science can gain even more knowledge for itself? I don't care

about science if that's what it has to do to achieve some insight that might be useful in the future."

"Exactly," said Dr. Yoshida, holding her hand out to Neele. Neele hesitated, wanting to swallow her frustration and anger first, but then she grabbed it. Dr. Yoshida returned the firm grip and said, "The two older women in the last video we saw. I believe those are actually us in the future. And now, after thinking about it for a while, I am pretty sure I can prove it."

Neele couldn't believe it. It was impossible. Every fiber in her body resisted. It was not possible. Period.
Even the scientist in her, whom she wanted to strangle a minute ago, would rather strangle herself than believe this. The likelihood of it being a forgery, AI, manipulation, actors, makeup, and even human clones, no matter how improbable, was infinitely higher than this video being real. There were so many reasons why it couldn't be.

But there really only needed to be one relevant reason:

There was yet to be a future.
She was living right now, in the here and now.
Now.
Again now,
and now again.
What would happen in one second, five seconds, ten minutes or a year, was yet to be decided.
That was the cornerstone that made life worth living.
That held everything together.
Life happens now.
Not yesterday, not tomorrow, but precisely in the second when I think about what I will take out of the fridge for breakfast the following day.
Neele stopped her thoughts.

What was that?

A small doubt had just crept into her head.
Oh, no.
Where did you come from?
Why?
It can't be.
Stop thinking about it.

Okay, and if I now think about what I might take out of the fridge tomorrow, then do exactly that tomorrow.
Haven't I just created a future for tomorrow now?

"Oh, damn it," Neele heard herself say.

And Dr. Yoshida continued her following sentence with a bit more confidence.

Her Communicator lit up blue as she inserted the memory stick into the slot. She swiped through the multitude of data until she reached the video that, with incredible probability, showed both of them in the future.

Dr. Yoshida opened the video and paused it exactly at 00:42:00. Then, she used two fingers to enlarge the image and zoomed in on the torso of the older of the two women. She stared at it for a while, looking like she was debating with herself and finally showed the image to Neele.

The enlarged section showed the upper and lower part of the older woman's chest. She was wearing plain, slightly futuristic-looking clothes, long-sleeved, muted colors, and something that resembled a very modern lab coat. "Okay, she's wearing a lab coat, but that's not proof that it's one of us. Hundreds of thousands of people do that every day, all over the world."

Neele looked away from Alicia's Communicator and in her direction. Dr. Yoshida was standing as best she could in this small room. She had removed her overalls and was now pulling her top up under her chest.
"Do you see this?" said Alicia, pointing to a white scar that started directly under her chest and extended flat down to her navel. "This scar is the only memory I have of my mother. I was very young, maybe five and we lived in Kobe, Japan. My mother worked in one of the extensive research labs scattered throughout the city and as luck would have it, my

125

kindergarten was directly integrated into the large building where she worked.

So, it was beautiful when I was brought to her directly after kindergarten. It happened pretty often, as far as I can remember and I found it exciting to watch my mother mix various liquids, creating incredible things I did not understand.

Until one day the beautiful things she made disappeared, and it was just things. Dangerous things.

None of them were planned. Or controllable.

I still remember a thunderous chemical explosion and my mother standing protectively in front of me, wrapping her hands around my small body and pressing my head against her chest. I still remember her screams, the smell and heat. Then the pain I felt. Later, I don't know how much later, I woke up in a different place and was told this was the USA.

They had saved my life in Kobe and given me a new one in the USA. Since I was still very young and had no reason to return to Kobe, I stayed here and was integrated into a new family. They treated me like their own daughter, even though I never was. They never asked about my injury, never how it happened and I never showed it to anyone except perhaps the doctors who saved my life and now you." She looked Neele directly in the eyes.

"And those doctors were all stationed in Kobe. No one alive today knows about this scar. Since Kobe City was almost completely wiped out in 2042, there are no medical records left. "

Neele couldn't look away from her Scar. She hadn't known any of this. How could she have known? Alicia had always been a quiet, thoughtful person. Was it was because of her Childhood trauma? Had she been so kind and caring to me because she knew I had lost my family too?

Neele's eyes filled with tears again. She grabbed Alicia's hand once more.

"Do you understand what I'm trying to tell you, Neele?" said Alicia. "No, not quite yet." She sobbed.
"Look at the close-up again. Do you notice anything? Look at her top closely. Do you see the transparent areas in the fabric of her top? The skin underneath is mostly white and bleached. That's my scar. That's the same scar that reminds me of my mother every day, only 40 years older than it is today. That's no coincidence because I've never told anyone about it or shown it to anyone. The person in the video is me with one hundred percent certainty. Sometime in the future. And more importantly, the other person is you." Neele didn't know what to think. "So, we have to get out of this lab, survive this and find out what you and I have planned for our current selves in the future. And most importantly, why."

Neele was stunned. She had received so much information in the last few hours, and the most unlikely of all suddenly seemed the most realistic.
What had she gotten herself into when she walked into her lab less than 24 hours ago? She couldn't continue the thought because the fatigue was increasingly taking over. She needed to get some sleep. Right now. Just before Neele closed her eyes, she thought again about her little brother Peet and how she would have loved to go to the amusement park with him back then.
She would do anything to hold him in her arms again.

Even if it meant accepting help from herself in the
future.

What an absurd thought.

AMITHAYUS, KOREAN DISTRICT

ELEVEN.
THE WAY OF THE SWORD

Amithayus, Seattle, 01:00 AM - Korean Quarter

Simmons and I were seated in the back of one of those old-fashioned stretch limousines that had a brief resurgence in the 2030s. This particular model we were in had been completely retrofitted with an electronic ready-to-use battery set from the Far East and besides all the standard equipment one could imagine, even had a pole dance bar in the middle of the surprisingly spacious passenger area. While we double-checked our freshly polished Sentinel Mark IV automatic rifles. Mr. Snake Man, sitting on the opposite side of us gave us some final instructions in his slightly strained, louder voice.

We were on our way to the Korean Quarter of Amithayus, searching for a single Korean who were willing to have a pleasant conversation with us about a specific topic.

Where was the hiding place of the Nightshades? How could we get there in under six hours?

I could offer the guy three options: new dollars, a new chance or new teeth. I could live with all three. Whether he could too, was another question entirely.

Simmons seemed much more tense since he had spoken with Mr. Tanaka. Since we had entered the club, I noticed that he had hardly exchanged a word with me, which seemed unusual. Usually, he always had a witty remark ready, and he loved mocking my odd views or quirky ideas.

But at this moment, in this part of Seattle, on this street, in this stretch limousine reeking of cheap booze—or was that Mr. Snake Man—I didn't feel like I was sitting next to my long-time

partner but rather next to a stranger. And that didn't feel like a good omen. But we had no choice. A blood oath was a blood oath. And the time frame, dictated by Mr. Tanakas Ultimatum no matter how short was the only opportunity we had. We needed to seize it. I thought of the Serpentine family and hoped everything we would do in the next six hours would be worth it. I was doing this for one reason only.
I wanted Martin and Mona to get justice. So, there was no turning back now.

The stretch limousine slowed as we turned in a wide arc onto Neon Hangnang Street. If I had to describe this area with one word, it would be "CrazyLEDEventStreet."

It was loud, crowded, colorful and somehow dirty. Just my kind of place.

Here, I felt at home.

We stopped halfway down Hangnang Street, and Mr. Snake Man opened the doors for us from inside.
I squeezed past the pole dance bar and looked forward to finally operating in a more familiar area again. The blare of the advertising and all the other Sounds rushed into our Vehicle as we exited it.

A master butcher mostly masters masterful evening meats. Genuine with only 12% Plasticine content in the synthetic meat.

Shit. I had forgotten how loud and intrusive advertising could be in a nightlife zone. Before we could evcen leave the stretch limo, Mr. Snake Man hissed a piece of advice in our ears: "Mr. Tanaka doesn't like it when one of his subordinates fails. Otsukaresama deshita, gentlemen. You have five hours and 58 minutes left to complete your task."

He patted both of us on the back and closed the stretch limo door from inside as we were left standing together but somehow alone, among nearly 20.000 partying Koreans in a completely unknown part of Amithayus, looking for someone to help us.

What could possibly go wrong?

"I'm hungry," was the first thing Simmons had said to me in almost two hours.
"Are you kidding me?" I blurted out.

"You drag me into a club full of Yakuza, they treat you like one of their own, you have some connections with one of the top bosses of the Japanese mafia here in Amithayus and then you take a blood oath. All because of a woman you've never mentioned in the many years we've been working together and the first thing you say to me after all that is that you're hungry? Are you kidding me?"

"No, but I am really hungry and it's easier to talk while eating than out here under all these billboards, cameras and loudspeakers. So, let's go inside and get something to eat." Simmons trudged toward the nearest place that looked like it served food. At least that's what the giant, animated fried chicken on the pLED panel outside the place Simmons was heading toward said: EAT ME.

Self-sacrifice. Sounds tasty. And my stomach growled, too.

So we walked toward the BBQ Corporal Chicken under a wave of different K-pop Music blaring. Simmons' logic and that of the four-meter-tall chicken were compellingly, well logical. Maybe it was hunger driving me. I hadn't eaten in at least twenty-four hours, and as good as they were, Nancy Mitchell's mints didn't keep you complete in the long run.

I would have eaten at the Wonder Diner now if I had to.

The walk to the restaurant was short and painful for my ears and Eyes. I had never heard so many different jingles undercut with so many flashing colors in my life in such a short time. We both walked through the automated door and were hit by an explosion of even more colors and smells.

The interior of the BBQCC restaurant looked as if a bald eagle had fucked an entire herd of rainbow unicorns spreading its colors over the walls. It felt oddly patriotic and welcoming at the same time. The tables, chairs and 50% of the walls were painted or splattered in every color imaginable. The floor and ceiling were covered in black wood, serving as a stark contrast to everything else. I looked around and saw neither a kitchen nor anything resembling a counter from which to order. Apparently they had moved to order directly from the table display in the Korean Quarter. Where it came from and who delivered it, I couldn't tell. But it definitely wasn't the poor guy in the giant mascot costume. An oversized, fried chicken, grinning widely with a speech bubble saying, "Eat me!" hopped from one leg to the other on a small stage at the end of the restaurant, singing the well-known BBQCC song I had already memorized after just five minutes in the Korean Quarter.

At least these kinds of jobs hadn't been automated away yet.

Simmons and I walked all the way through the super loud restaurant and sat at one of the unoccupied tables in most far corner possivle. I stared at the display where I was supposed to order and later eat.

I couldn't read anything. Literally nothing. My ComUhr could translate conversations in real time, but it didn't have an integrated camera to translate Korean characters displayed on the table. I looked helplessly at Simmons, who returned my look with an equally bewildered expression.

Now, when speaking another foreign language would have been practical, he had no idea... great.

I randomly tapped on the screen and added something I neither recognized nor could pronounce to the cart.
A small, round, animated chicken pecked at a symbol that probably represented a new dollar bill and I dutifully
placed my wrist with my ComUhr on the table. It went *ping* and the animated chicken cheered wildly. Whatever I had ordered had just cost me fifty new dollars. From the other end of the table, I heard another *ping* and now we waited for something to eat and to talk about what had happened in the last four hours. Simmons looked around awkwardly, pretending to observe the people with us in the restaurant.

"Man, stop pretending like nothing happened and finally tell me what has been going on in the last four hours and preferably the ten years before that, too," I said impatiently, pushing a glass carafe filled with a black, thick sauce out of the way that was obstructing my view. Simmons looked at me, and his eyes twitched slightly from left to right.
I could see he was thinking and probably needed to
organize his thoughts because he undoubtedly knew much more that he couldn't, shouldn't or wouldn't tell me. I rubbed my hands over my face and felt my body slowly getting tired. I was old and several hours past my usual bedtime. Simmons hesitated for a moment, but then he seemed to have decided.

"Well," he began speaking quietly and I perked my ears.

"Maddy and I go way back. I can't tell you exactly when it started, but it was long before my time with the ECLE.

I worked as an undercover agent in Amithayus and was assigned to Maddy. Illegal weapons, biotech and stuff like that were my thing. And somehow, it was Maddie's thing, too, and then it became our thing. When you're deep into something, maybe you're just too deep into it?"

Wow, he's awful at talking about his feelings. But at least this was his way of telling me they had something going on.

"Well, that went on for a while and we were sort of a couple. I was still an undercover agent, and she was still an illegal arms dealer. But somehow, I liked her a lot. And she wanted me too. And it was all fine; I had gotten used to the role I had to play.

My Japanese improved significantly as I learned more about smuggling weapons through different Yakuza transport routes. I made new contacts, my reputation in the underworld of Amithayus grew and I could pass information to my bosses that they wouldn't have gotten without my physical involvement. And after about two years undercover, everything went wrong one evening during a mission.
It was supposed to be routine; Maddy and I went with a tiny team to Toshi, a small, tranquil and secluded park in the Matsubara district, about 20 minutes from Mr. Tanaka's club. We had done deals there several times before, and everything had always gone more or less peacefully. A bit of gun-waving was part of it to reinforce your position."

Oh shit, he was really there at the Matsubara massacre.

"Well, that evening, we encountered someone neither Maddy nor I knew and with whom we had never done business before. And this person had demands that we weren't willing to accept.
She wanted our goods and offered us our lives in exchange. She reinforced that with many Yakuza she had with her. The thing is…"

I think I don't want to know. Don't tell me you killed them all.

"Maddy gets really bad-tempered when she doesn't get her way. And if someone threatens her, she can easily overreact.

And well, one thing led to another, and yeah. We killed them all. Every single one of them. Me, crouched behind a car, slowly and precisely one after the other. At least I tried to. Maddy went into a sort of frenzy.

And then, in the end, of the six people we came with, only two were left and on the other side, no one. And the biggest problem wasn't the 30 corpses scattered in the park, but a particular corpse Maddy took out at the very end. And even for my taste, she had to much pleasure in the brutality." He paused as he said the last sentence, poured himself a glass of water from the carafes on the tables and took a big gulp, looking at me.

Yeah, and who the hell was it? Tell me. I want to know. Come on. Why do you look so weird? Oh, you're not looking at me. But behind me. What's happening behind me?

I slowly turned and looked around into the restaurant. But no matter how hard I tried, I couldn't see anything unusual.

A few middle-aged Koreans sat at their tables, chatting while stuffing something that looked suspiciously like
tomato sauce with noodles into their mouths.
Two teenagers stared at their ComUhr's and giggled. The latest song by "NeoPsy - Gangnam Legacy" blared from the speakers, and in the back a man who I would guess was in his mid-twenties, walked to the vending machines to get something to eat or drink. I turned back to Simmons who was now almost sitting on my lap, starring.

"Do you see the guy at the vending machine?" Simmons asked me as I nodded.
"Yeah, the guy is probably getting something to eat."
"Yeah, he is," Simmons interrupted me, scooting even closer. "Take a closer look at his jacket." I looked at his jacket.

A nice jacket. Black, with red embellishments around the sleeves and a logo on the back that I couldn't read or recognize.
"It's a nice jacket, Simmons. Not as nice as, say, Mr. Snake Man's suit…"
"Hebijiro," Simmons corrected me.
"Hebi, what?" I replied.
"Hebijiro. That's Mr. Snake Man's real name. Mr. Hebijiro," Simmons said and I had to suppress a grin as my ComUhr translated his name to ‚second son of a snake.'

God, I was good at giving people names based on their character.

"And what about the guy at the vending machine and his jacket?" I asked Simmons after calming down and he gave me a puzzled look.
"That jacket, especially the logo on the back combined with the red embellishments on the sleeves, is the symbol of the Nightshades. Based on the decorations on his sleeves, I can tell he's someone of lower rank, but he should still know where their hideout is. And from there, we should be able to get our hands on the Kami no Katana."
I nodded vigorously.
"Mr. Hebijiro mentioned that as we left earlier, didn't you hear?" Simmons asked me, puzzled, and I thought for a moment.

No, I was too distracted by a masterful meat maker.

"No, I somehow missed that. So, what's our plan?"

"Come with me; we'll grab him in the restaurant. There are fewer people here than out on the street, so we have a better chance of him not getting away." Simmons got up and strolled toward the Korean guy who was just pulling his hot, spicy fried chicken from the vending machine.
"Let's play a little R and R," Simmons said, turning his head to me.

"Gladly," I said, already looking forward to which part of the "Relentless and Ruthless" game I'd play today.

It was one of my favorite games. It came right after "Don't Get Angry" and every drinking game I had ever played.

The Korean guy was just about to turn around when Simmons said in a friendly way, „Hello there." He grabbed him by the neck and slammed his face into the extra hot and spicy fried chicken pieces with full force. Meanwhile, I drew my handgun and turned to our small audience for the night.

Then I yelled as loud as I could: "Excuse my friend here; he's a bit irritable, lacks sleep and is hungry too. And he really wanted the extra spicy chicken; we've traveled a long way for it, you must know, and now it says here at the vending machine that this was the last portion. So, you can understand if he's a bit upset, right? So, I would appreciate it if you all could get up and leave now. Thanks."

But to my surprise, nothing happened. Really, nothing at all. None of the five people present reacted to my speech. Not even the guy in the chicken costume standing right next to us.

I'd love to see his facial expression under that giant chicken costume.

"Uh, Simmons, they're just staring at me," I called over to him.
"Do you speak Korean?" he asked me.
"Oh," I replied. "I don't think they understand you," Simmons said, busy turning the Korean guy's face in the extra hot and extra spicy fried chicken pieces like you would with a good piece of meat to soak up the last bits of sauce from the plate.

"That makes sense." I didn't speak Korean and my watch could translate Korean for me but not output it because it was connected directly to my hearing through a negligible bone conduction earpiece. "I'm an idiot," I muttered quietly, tapping my ComUhr and asking what "get the hell out of this place, or it's going to blow" was in Korean, trying to pronounce it as convincingly as possible.

The watch spat out some gibberish, but apparently, I was a language talent because the people stood up and quickly headed for the exit after my second speech. It could also be the wild gesturing I did with the gun in my hand.
In any case, I was the Relentless part of this game.
And Simmons was Ruthless.

The man screamed in pain.

Maybe it was extra, extra super Fire Hot Chicken? As I said, I couldn't speak or read Korean.

"This is just the beginning," Simmons said coldly, pulling the now very red face of the Korean out of the very red goo and pressing him against one of the large vending
machines.

"Can you understand us?" Simmons said, and the Korean guy nodded, sniffed and squealed simultaneously. "Good, we have a few questions for you. And I think it would be to your advantage if your answers were truthful." The Korean nodded desperately while the hot red sauce dripped from his face onto the nice black jacket.

Meanwhile, I walked over to one of the tables and grabbed a glass of red powder and a carafe with the thick, black sauce from the neighboring table. "Hey, Simmons, here's a good spot, I think." Simmons understood; he grabbed the Korean by the neck and taught him to fly with two quick hand movements. The Korean flew for quite some time through the air, crashing face-first through the chairs and landing on the floor. Simmons jumped after him, picked him up, laid him on the table and lightly patted his now highly red cheeks.

"Everything alright with you? Yes. Perfect, then let's continue."

I held the two items before the Korean's tear-streaked, red-spotted face and said, "Hey, uh, say. Do you know…," I had to look closely to read the English mini-translation on the label, "Gochugaru and, uh… Samyang Hot Chicken Fire Special Sauce. Imagine you could be the first to start a new trend on social media," I said, shaking the carafe with the black liquid inside. "That would be the highlight of your life." The Korean was visibly unsure and didn't know whether to shake his head or nod, so he did both, looking very bizarre.

"Imagine how it would feel if I let this," I shook the bottle, "run into your nose and this," I pointed to the powder and looked at Simmons, who immediately had an idea.
"Oh, I would suggest the deepest opening of a human body," he said contentedly. I nodded and the Korean nodded, too, but in the opposite way to what Simmons and I were doing with our heads.
"Good, I think we have him where we want him,"
Simmons said. "It's time for you to answer some questions about the logo on your jacket and your friends, the

Nightshades. We need to borrow something from you guys tonight."

The Korean nodded and began telling us everything we wanted to know and more.

We were on schedule, with about five hours left to return the sword to its rightful owner and now we knew where to find it. So far, things have been going well. And for me, it could gladly continue this way.

AMITHAYUS, MINGCHENG

TWELVE.
THE LAST SPARK

Amithayus Seattle, 2066 05:40 AM - Dr. Yoshida's Laboratory, Mingcheng

Neele jolted awake when she felt a hand on her shoulder. She saw Alicia's face and for a split second everything was completely fine. The dream she'd just had – jumping onto a moving elevator, her little brother Peet in a kind of incubator, a massive explosion at her home and a version of herself from the future – was confusing and terrifying but fortunately just a dream. Neele looked around and realized she wasn't home. She wasn't in her comfortable, warm bed but twisted in a dark, small room, leaning against a wall with her head on Alicia's lap. She realized the truth.

"How long have I slept?" she asked, visibly confused, as she sat up. "A little over two hours. I'm sorry to wake you, but I just received a message from Zhan Tao."

He was still alive. That was the first good news since they had stormed into this little prison together. Neele cracked her shoulders and stretched further to relax her muscles. Her left arm hurt, but she knew it was just the phantom pains that made themselves known almost every morning.

"Zhan Tao just contacted me and informed me that he's created a diversion, allowing us to leave the lab in the next few minutes. We don't have much time to prepare, so get up. He should open the door any moment."

And that's what happened. A few moments after the two women had risen as much as the cramped space allowed, the automatic lock of the security door clicked and Dr. Yoshida pushed the heavy metal door of their hideout outward.

The first thing Neele could see was a glimmer of red light breaking through the darkness.

Once they stepped out of the safe room and into the interior of the lab, Neele could already hear the diversion Zhan Tao had initiated. A fierce battle must have erupted outside the herb shop-laboratory. She heard gunfire and screams, muffled explosions and plenty of automatic rifle fire staccato through the concrete walls. It was oppressive and chaotic. The stomping of heavy boots and the cries and screams of dying people turned the ordinarily silent and sterile room into a battlefield.

They slowly walked forward. The corridor they were in was bathed entirely in red emergency light, casting a menacing red glow over everything in their view. The air, usually odorless due to the filtration system, now had a biting tang of various burnt materials.

"We need to hurry," Dr. Yoshida whispered, her voice almost drowned out by the booming noise outside the lab. Neele nodded and the two proceeded slowly in a crouched position toward the exit. Suddenly, a violent explosion shook the entire building, and the floor trembled beneath their feet. Dust trickled from the ceiling and small debris and part of the wall panels crashed to the ground. Neele threw herself to the ground and covered her ears with both hands. Dr. Yoshida did the same. An ear-splitting noise poured into the lab's interior from outside. My God, Neele thought.

What have I started? And all because, less than twenty-four hours ago, I desperately pressed the elevator's stop button too early. She felt a fearful thudding inside of her, pounding irregularly against her ribs. She breathed heavily as a hand grabbed her arm and pulled her up.

"Ganjin, please get up," said a male voice and Neele

looked into the face of Zhan Tao, who had appeared out of nowhere before the two women. With a fluid motion, he helped Neele back to her feet, and they hurried toward the exit, which Neele hadn't noticed until now.
It was located to the left of the regular pressure door, separating the lab from the room filled with spices and herbs.

"I cashed in a few old favors for you Dr. Yoshida and
those favors are now fighting outside on the street against a small army that seems to come from outside Amithayus.
I can't imagine who has the financial resources and influence to smuggle a private army into Amithayus after a curfew, Without drawing much attention. But whoever it was must either have a greatly fear you or somthing you posess. So, take good care of yourself and your belongings," Zhan Tao said as he led them through the smaller exit closing it behind them.

He now guided them through the maze-like corridors of the intermediate area separating the lab complex from the rest of the herb shop. It was dark and stuffy. The air was thick with dust. They moved quickly and soon reached another pressure door, where they paused.
Zhan Tao brought his finger to his lips and listened for sounds beyond the door. They could make out the
footsteps of soldiers or militia, the sporadic crackling of radios and the clicking and loading of ammunition.
In the distance the gunfire from automatic rifles and the rumble of explosions were still audible.
It seemed they had reached a point somewhat outside the central combat zone. Yet, each audible sound underlined the gravity of the raging battle and their fragile situation.

"Ready?" Zhan Tao asked, his eyes on the two women. Neele and Dr. Yoshida nodded simultaneously and the moment he opened the door just a crack, they were hit by a shockwave from an explosion. The entire corridor vibrated from the intensity of the battle as the floor beneath their feet trembled from the force of the air that desperately wanted to penetrate the building where the three stood.

"Now!" shouted Zhan Tao as they rushed through the exit door into the roaring inferno of noise and violence. The reality of the battle raging around them hit
immediately. The noise was deafening and it was a chaotic mixture of explosions, screams, blood and the constant squealing of metal clashing against metal. Hundreds of small dust and concrete fragments swirled through the air, sparks and smoke rising in thick black clouds dispersed over the entire Chinese district of
Amithayus.

They didn't get far. About five meters beyond the door, the three threw themselves behind a row of overturned crates scattered across the forecourt. The crates were distributed randomly by the explosion that had occurred just a few seconds earlier.

Some of the crates were ablaze. Apparently, a rocket or something similar had hit the private army's ammunition supply, turning the forecourt into an inferno of flesh, blood and fire. „Holy Shit," said Neele as she surveyed the chaos. "I think we chose the wrong time to step out."
Zhan Tao agreed, spotting a group of men in the distance, quickly approaching. It looked like they were coming to inspect what had just happened to their supply depot and the rest of their comrades left behind.

"We need to hurry before they spot us," Zhan Tao said,
signaling the two women to follow him across the forecourt, through the narrow corridor and through a door shrouded in darkness.
Neele and Dr. Yoshida crouched by one of the crates

marked "Holster Defense Systems: When 'safe' isn't safe enough." Neele didn't know whether to laugh or cry, but there was no time to think about it as the soldiers approached with immense speed. They were still a little over ten meters away when Zhan Tao drew his weapon and opened fire on the group of soldiers while Dr. Yoshida and Neele began sprinting across the forecourt from their cover. "Go, we need to move," he said, firing again in the soldiers' direction before running after the two, still shooting. Two of the soldiers were knocked off their feet by the impact of the shots to their chests and were killed instantly, while the remaining ten scattered like startled rabbits. They hadn't expected their enemy to sneak up from behind. In the chaos of bullets and shouted commands, the three managed to fight their way into the corridor leading to another part of the complex.

The passage was narrow and dark and the noise of the battle was somewhat muffled here compared to the forecourt. Neele, however, noticed the soldiers' footsteps approaching even faster than before. Apparently, after a brief moment of surprise, they realized they were actually in the majority and now stormed towards the corridor entrance with automatic rifles at the ready. It could only be a few seconds before a massacre would occur in this narrow passage.

Dr. Yoshida tugged at the door, which slowly opened with a heavy creak as Neele slipped through. Zhan Tao, however, remained crouched just before the door, hiding behind an old container. He pressed his body against the outer wall, aiming his weapon down the long corridor.

But his face and gaze remained fixed on Dr. Yoshida.

He looked at her with a severe expression and said,

"Wo de lao pengyou. Sharing your knowledge and life has been a great honor and pleasure.

You must protect the young ganjin, for she carries a great responsibility. I could sense that in the short time I have known her. I will give you as much time as possible. Zhe shi gao bie, dan wo hui ji zhu ni, Dr. Yoshida."

As Zhan Tao closed the door from the outside, simultaneously HELPS translated for Neele that this was a farewell, but he would never forget her. They were on their own and had a long way to go before reaching safety. Alicia lingered at the door for a few more seconds before releasing her hand and they both began running down the next dark corridor. Behind them they heard the increasingly muffled sounds of gunfire and human screams. Alicia hoped that none of them belonged to her old friend. After advancing about a hundred meters in the dark, they reached the next pressure door, which promised them the way to freedom. They opened it and stepped into an open area filled with smoke and fire. The battle still raged around them, and the chaos and war wasn't confined to just a tiny part of the Chinese district.

It seemed most of Mincheng (民城) had now risen against the intruders from outside. Buildings around them were burning, and much of the square they now stood in was shrouded in smoke. From the rooftops, intermittent bursts of gunfire rained down into the darkness.
Molotov cocktails thrown from several corners briefly illuminated the darkness with their fiery content.

Alicia recognized a small group of people ahead of them, firing sporadically from cover toward the menacing black wall of soot and fire. She spotted an older man she knew and signaled to Neele that they were friends.
They reached the group by moving from cover to cover, careful only to run when the militia opened fire.
The older man waved to the two women, recognizing Dr. Yoshida immediately. It was Mr. Li Wei, the owner of the Moon Boat Tea House, to whom she often brought one of her new herbal creations, and they would spend hours discussing various scents and aromas.

It was unusual to see him holding an automatic rifle.
He gave a few more commands to the other armed

residents in Chinese before turning to Dr. Yoshida and Neele. "Zhan Tao has already briefed us.

No further explanation is necessary. Whoever wants to burn down our city and its inhabitants will be met with the same fire of retribution. We will get you to safety."

He turned and said, "Wo de pengyoumen, gen wo lai," to the five men and women around him, who took turns firing into the darkness. "Women bixu mashang ba tamen liang ge dai chu zhege qu." They nodded and prepared to leave.

So, the eight stormed into one of the few buildings not yet engulfed in flames and climbed the stairs until they were just below the top floor. There was a connecting
corridor linking this building to the next.

The group traversed the corridor, still firing through small openings at anything moving below that didn't look like a resident of Mincheng. Neele had to swallow at the thought.

If she weren't here with Alicia, her HELPS suit would probably makes her look more like a soldier.

She quickly dismissed the thought and followed the group through another long corridor that ended in a large hall. She had completely lost her sense of direction by now. The constant running, the screams, the gunfire, and the surrounding explosions made her a passenger on a journey whose destination she didn't know.

She and Dr. Yoshida slowly walked at the back of the group through the large hall connected to the long, elevated corridor. This hall housed many food stands and other stalls until a few hours ago until the first gunshots penetrated the night. Neele couldn't take her eyes off the unfamiliar delicacies stacked here, waiting for the slaughter outside to end and for daily life to return to the residents. Her stomach growled, and she grabbed a small item from one of the counters as they passed by, handing part of it to Alicia. The two women chewed, it tasted unusually sour, salty, and intense at the same time. When this was over, she would have to return here and find out what she had just eaten. She promised herself to pay double next time.

They continued walking and the deeper they penetrated the hall, the quieter and more surreal the sounds outside became. Now, only occasional gunshots faded into the background of their footsteps, and there had been no explosions for a few minutes.
Apparently, they had escaped the danger zone.
Neele thought of Zhan Tao, who had likely saved their
lives once again with his actions. "Hey Alicia, where did you meet Zhan Tao…" She couldn't finish her sentence as a strange noise that grew louder interrupted her thoughts. It sounded like the hissing of a snake rushing towards them. "What is that?" she heard herself say before half the group in front of her was blown off their feet by an indescribable force.

The wall on the right side and part of the hall's roof
exploded in a massive shockwave. The roof's pieces shattered upon impact with the ground into thousands of tiny fragments scattered in all directions at incredible speed. Three of their companions were crushed or maimed by flying debris within seconds, and the rest were violently thrown against or over the stalls.

Neele had shielded herself from the impact with her metal arm and only felt a minor pain on the back of her head.
She touched the spot and saw a bit of blood dripping from it.
Dr. Yoshida lay in the middle of the hall, trying to get back up.

"Are you okay?" Neele shouted toward Alicia, who
nodded weakly in her direction.

"What was that?" Neele shouted again, not directing her

question at anyone specific, not expecting an answer.

The remaining militia members struggled to their feet, running or crawling toward their injured comrades and friends. Dr. Yoshida also moved towards the wounded and dead, even though she was still a bit unsteady on her feet. Among the dead was Mr. Li Wei, who had led the group.

His body was torn into several pieces and Dr. Yoshida couldn't bear the sight. She turned away and stumbled back toward Neele. Neele, slightly hunched, leaned against one of the stalls when she saw several soldiers in black armor emerging from the thick smoke with their weapons raised. They opened fire on everyone nearby without hesitation. There was no escape.

The residents had no chance to return fire. One by one, they were taken down with a few well-placed shots to the chest and head within seconds. Neele pushed herself off the ground and leaped over the edge of the stall she had been leaning against with her last ounce of strength.

Dr. Yoshida was ready to jump over the railing, when Neele heard a loud scream of pain. She saw Alicia spin around and fall to the ground, hit by a bullet. Blood oozed from the wound in her chest. "No!" Neele screamed at the soldiers, who then began firing at her. She ducked, feeling the projectiles' vibration hitting the stall's metal exterior.

"Fuck!" she muttered as metal shards and fabric pieces flew everywhere. "What am I supposed to do?" Her thoughts raced. In front of her were four heavily armored soldiers who had killed all the group members she had been traveling with. Alicia lay bleeding on the ground a few meters away, potentially dying at any moment.

She had to do something. "Think, think, think," she said to herself.

"You don't have a weapon; it wouldn't help anyway because you don't know how to shoot. You're alone and your mentor is dying. Do something!" she shouted to herself for conviction.

Meanwhile, the soldiers kept shooting at the stall. Bullets hit the metal to her right and left. A rain of shattered food and sparks snapped her out of her thoughts. "At least they're ignoring Alicia for now. If she's still alive." The deadly rain of bullets paused briefly as she heard a familiar sounding groan behind the stall.

Neele peeked over the stall's edge and saw the four soldiers slowly approaching, reloading their weapons. They were still approaching her and Alicia.

"Shit, okay, you're doing this," she said, grabbing one of the many pans lying on the ground beside her. This is completely crazy, but you're going out there now and smashing their fucking faces with these pans. Okay. Three, two, one… She grasped the stall's top and was about to launch outward when she suddenly heard a noise like a revolving electric motor. Neele saw a large black vehicle suddenly burst through the smoke and debris where the soldiers had emerged less than a minute ago, racing toward them at incredible speed.

Startled by the same noise as Neele, the soldiers turned and tried to fire at the windshield, but the vehicle spun on its axis increasing its diameter significantly. It plowed through their line, shredding them with the sheer physical force of a six-ton car traveling at 120 kilometers per hour against several smaller objects weighing at most 100 kilos. The car spun multiple times and stopped a few meters before Dr. Yoshida.

Neele jumped out from behind the stall and rushed to Alicia. She knelt beside her, pressing her ear to Alicia's chest. She wheezed and gasped but was still alive. Neele tried to stop the blood flowing from her wound with her bare hands. She pressed as hard as she could, but it didn't help. "Alicia, please hold on!" she pleaded. Alicia looked at her in pain and slowly moved her right hand toward Neele.

She didn't hesitate and let the pan fall to the ground with a clatter.

"HELPS, can you do anything for Alicia!" Neele cried out desperately.

I'm sorry, Dr. Neele, but based on my scan of Dr. Yoshida and the calculation of blood loss from the entry and exit wound, it would be advisable to activate the emergency medical services immediately. Your personal data is
current, so your insurance will cover 86% of the incurred costs. Please have a safe day.

"Damn it, "Neele yelled at HELPS. "You're supposed to help me, not give me a lecture. "

Meanwhile, the armored vehicle's door opened, parts of a soldier slid off the hood onto the floor.

Zhan Tao slipped out the driver's door and ran as fast as he could toward Neele and Dr. Yoshida.
He knelt beside the two women. Neele stared at him as if she had seen a ghost. He was drenched in blood from head to toe. Just as Neele was about to ask if it was his blood, Zhan Tao shook his head, silencing her. She wasn't sure if the answer was for her or Alicia.

"We don't have time to talk, ganjin. Soon this place will be swarming with soldiers. Can you help me carry Alicia to the armored vehicle?" Neele nodded, and together, with great effort they carried Alicia to the black vehicle. They laid her on the back seat, and Neele sat beside her, resting her head gently on her lap. She continued pressing on the open wound with her left hand while holding Alicia's hand with her right. Alicia groaned in pain as the vehicle moved. Zhan Tao spun the car around. They were about to exit the hall through the smoke and fire-covered opening that had once been the wall and roof.

At that moment, a swarm of soldiers emerged from the dense fog, and as far as Neele could see, there were at least twenty now. They ran towards the vehicle, firing from all barrels.

"Hold on!" Zhan Tao said as he slammed the gas pedal to the floor and the black car, leaving a trail of blood, sped towards the soldiers. The Car plowed through them in a shower of sparks and bullets. Those who couldn't move out of the way in time were separated from their feet and sometimes from their arms. The others, who managed to escape in time, continued firing at the vehicle as it cut through the fog and flying debris, carving a path to freedom.

Once outside, Zhan Tao yanked the steering wheel hard to the right, smoothly turning out of the former market hall and onto a street. Bullets and shrapnel from exploding grenades flew around them, but Zhan Tao skillfully avoided anything harmful to his passengers. They sped through the burning streets of Mincheng, leaving the former complex where Dr. Alicia Yoshida and Zhan Tao had lived, researched and laughed together for two years, reluctantly but alive. Slowly but surely, the noise of the still-raging battle faded into the glowing sky behind them, and darkness enveloped the car as it smoothly guided its three passengers down the highway toward the Korean district.

Zhan Tao wasn't sure how long it would take for the soldiers to pursue them, but for now, they lived. He switched on the autopilot and turned to Dr. Yoshida. Neele held her hand and looked up at Zhan Tao. Her eyes were filled with tears. Alicia's condition was deteriorating rapidly and her now paler face indicated immense blood loss. Neele felt a slight pressure on her hand as Alicia pulled her closer with her last bit of strength.

"You have to believe," she whispered, barely audible. All the strength and grace had left her voice. "Promise me. Believe in what we discovered together. Before you came into my life sixteen years ago, I was alone. But now, we aren't anymore. It seems you have been watching over yourself for a long time. I believe in you the same way you will belive in yourself, sometime in the future, my dearest ganjin."

And with these last words, Alicia closed her eyes. Neele squeezed her hand tighter as with one last powerful twitch, the last spark of her life escaped into the dark night, illuminated only by the burning district they just left.
Neele couldn't hold back the tears nor the feeling of losing her family for the second time. But she knew Alicia was right. "I promise you." she said, lowering her head to her chest as her tears mixed with the blood on Alicia's chest. Zhan Tao placed his hand on Neele's shoulder as she sobbed. "What are we going to do now? How are we going to get out of here alive?" she asked, wiping some of her tears with her blood-smeared hand.

Zhan Tao knew precisely what they had to do. He took his communicator and dialed a number he hadn't used in a long time. It rang several times until the line connected, and a deep male voice answered. So, he was active again. Now, at least, they had a slim chance of escaping Amithayus alive.

AMITHAYUS, KOREAN PORT

THIRTEEN.
ON A KNIFE'S EDGE

Amithayus, Seattle, 03:05 AM - Korean Port

Our target location, which the Korean had so kindly, quickly and voluntarily disclosed, was about an hour outside the bustling nightlife district where we had enjoyed ourselves so much. After we had considerately and without much pressure put the Korean to sleep for the next few hours, Simmons and I took an UberFreedom taxi, which lived up to its name with its utterly autonomous driving, to within a block of our destination.
Naturally, I had to pay and since hard new dollars were king in the Free Trade Zone of Unified America, cash was still a welcome payment method, even for a robot taxi.

Poof, I was 800 new dollars lighter.

Without a further sound or even a hint of gratitude, that
I had supported the local economy; the electric vehicle trundled down the street and turned left around the corner. We arrived in the port district of the Korean sector, and in front of us lay a dark, cold-looking, artificial river that eventually, probably only a few kilometers away, emptied into Puget Sound Bay and wound through various waterways before ending in the Pacific Ocean. Many companies had discovered these waterways early on and along the different bays, a now old industry tailored to waterway transport emerged.
Our Destiantion bore the unassuming name "Han-Seong Logistics Depot." According to the local records I had studied on the way here and the vast sign hanging at the entrance, this

place officially dealt with importing, exporting, sorting and recycling electronic waste.

Yeah, right! And next the Koreans will impose a deposit on cans.

We knew something entirely different was hidden behind the building's enormous facade.
What it was, we weren't quite sure yet, but we anticipated fierce resistance, as the Nightshades weren't known for their friendly treatment of competition or intruders,
especially those from outside the walls of Amithayus.

During the ride here, I delved deeper into the structure of this Nightshade syndicate. Simmons filled some gaps in my knowledge with his past investigations and
occasional skirmishes with them in the Japanese district. What I found out was the following:

Like so many other clans worldwide but especially in the Free Trade Zone of Unified America, the Nightshade Clan was originally a small street gang founded sometime in the early '30s out of boredom and probably also Hopelessness. The first members were teenage outcasts, as usual, who grew up together in the narrow alleys of the Korean district under the harshest conditions.

The first leader of the clan to emerge from this loose
coalition was Jin-Ho Park, a charismatic, average-intelligence but all the more brutal leader who knew how to skillfully exploit his comrades' discontent and misery. His brutal honesty combined with his brutal right fist were enough to secure the loyalty of his members and a particular claim to power over a small part of the Korean district, specifically Haneul-dong, the Sky District.

The winding alleys and narrow streets provided a perfect hideout and enough retreats to steadily expand his power and network over the years.

Sometime in the early '40s, Jin-Ho Park had had enough of the narrow streets and began to expand his influence significantly. Through clever alliances with other smaller
criminal groups and many corrupt businessmen he gradually secured the most profitable smuggling routes and control posts in the Korean district.
After that and with the advice of some slightly more intelligent members, the clan began to diversify its activities extensively.

Most of the Nightshades new dollars were made through arms dealing. That's when Simmons had a first run in with them. Their second line of business was technology smuggling, followed by a venture into selling their own branded noodle soup.

"What? They created their own noodle soup alongside their other criminal activities? And why noodle soups in Boxes? "Simmons had asked me during the ride, and I replied as follows:

Jin-Ho Park, or one of his slightly more intelligent members, realized that the power of culture was significant for maintaining control and influence.
They then developed the "Black Viper Ramen" to outward project the clan's strength. The soup quickly became the Nightshades' trademark and helped solidify their presence and omnipresence through the logo and emblem used on the packaging. Many youths in the Korean and even Chinese districts felt like part of the Nightshades
themselves and their dominant history by eating the
extremely spicy soup. There was also a rumor that a special ingredient, some white sealed powder included with the

soups, sharpened the senses and boosted the consumer's energy level.

Oh shit, cocaine sold to teenagers under the disguise of noodle soup is a new sales strategy.

In the '50s, the clan became increasingly ruthless and began expanding its influence into parts of the Japanese and Chinese districts. This partially succeeded and could only be advanced through modern, mostly imported technology. They forged many informal and transactional relationships with government officials and business magnates to protect them from overly ambitious police officers like us. Over time, Jin-Ho Park withdrew more and more from public perception and leadership of the Nightshades and for several years, it had been unclear who had taken his place as the official or de facto new number one.

"Okay," Simmons said, throwing his half-eaten Black Viper Noodle Soup into the nearest trash can, which emitted a beeping sound of heartfelt gratitude.
"Thanks for the history lesson, but now it's time to look closer at the warehouse."

"Yeah, and how do we do that?" I asked him while staring at the trash can in amazement

I want one of those for my little apartment.

Simmons' eyes sparkled weakly at me or the trash can in the dark harbor light. "Observation is the keyword.
How much time do we have left to find the sword and deliver it to Mr. Tanaka?"

I checked my ComUhr, where a relentless timer slowly but steadily counted down. "A little less than 4 hours," I replied.

"Okay, no observation, we don't have time for that," Simmons replied thoughtfully. If everything went well, our return trip would take at least an hour and another twenty minutes for the stairs in the Yoru no Hana Club. So, we had two hours and thirty minutes to somehow get into the warehouse, steal the sword unnoticed, and then return to the Japanese district as quickly and quietly as possible.

"We need to find out if the warehouse has a side entrance. If there is, we'll take that. But first, let's get a clear picture of the situation and then decide how to proceed. So, I'll check out the harbor and you go up that hill and see if anything changes in the next 10 minutes or if we get any visitors. We'll meet back here and then decide. Agreed?"

I nodded and quietly moved in the shadows cast by the parked transport vehicles and trees along the roadside toward the hill. Once there, I lay on my stomach, grabbed my Sentinel Mark IV, still attached to my backpack, and checked it briefly. It was covered in some spots with a bit of spicy red sauce.

So much for cleaning it in the Club...

I wiped it with my glove and looked at the warehouse through the optical sight. I could see guards scattered across the premises. There weren't too many, which gave me a good feeling of security. I watched them walk back and forth, smoking one synth cigarette after another. Apparently, all Nightshade members were addicted to something.

Well, I must admit, they weren't the only ones.

I turned my optical sight to the right and tried to find Simmons. Our AegisFlex-Armor suits were good at blending into the darknes, and I had trouble distinguishing him from the night if he didn't move.

There, at the water's edge, something moved. He quietly moved between several cranes and crates marked Holster Defense Systems. He seemed to be undetected, and while I scanned the area through my rifle, I couldn't see any guards in his near vicinity. I stayed in my position for several minutes, observing the harbor landscape and the warehouse.
My ComUhr buzzed softly as Simmons contacted me: "Okay, so far, so good. There's a back entrance that looks pretty unguarded. I can't see any cameras or sensors. So, get your ass down here and we'll head into the warehouse. I'll hold the position until you arrive."

I got my ass down the hill and made my way back to our starting point as quickly as I could, then followed the same path Simmons had taken earlier. It took me about five minutes to catch up with Simmons. I had to admit, it was indeed pretty quiet at this warehouse. Aside from the few guards smoking and occasionally patrolling the Front of the building, I heard nothing but water lapping and the distant horn blast of a cargo ship. The air was moist, slightly salty and the smell of
heavy machine oil wafted through the surroundings.

It sounded like the perfect perfume advertisement for the few oil rig workers who still had Jobs in the Free trade Zone.

My brief excursion to the Korean district had spoiled me with ad slogans.

We reached the warehouse's side door and indeed, there were no further security measures besides a small box above the lock informing us with nine excellently cleaned numbers that we had no access to this establishment.

"No fingerprint scanner, retina or biometric eye match, not even a weight measurement system in the floor."
Simmons sounded disappointed. "Maybe it is just an old warehouse recycling old electronic waste? "

I hoped not. If that were the case, we'd be in real trouble. Because then all our options would be gone in one fell swoop, even if we only had one left. But it was still better than having none.

I nodded hopefully to Simmons as he rummaged through his backpack. Meanwhile, I looked around. In the distance I saw the lights of the cargo ship I had heard earlier, slowly approaching. It was still on the Horizon, but its powerful lights almost illuminted the sky. I estimated we had a little over three-quarters of an hour before it docked somewhere here at the harbor.

In the meantime, Simmons had pulled an electronic lock picker from his backpack and magnetically attached it to the code input device. The tiny computer began its work, sending electrical impulses that simulated pressing the
buttons in the correct order through targeted electric shocks. It took about a minute for the lock and thus the door to click open. We were in.

Simmons and I stood in the darkness of the warehouse. Our eyes had to adjust because it was even darker inside than outside. Only a faint moonlight shone through the sparse windows. I looked around and had to admit that the inside of the warehouse was overwhelming. It was a massive, open space filled from ceiling to floor with various industrial machines and containers. The floor was smooth, polished concrete, interrupted by a few yellow and red lines indicating the automated transport systems' paths through the seemingly endless aisles. Above us spanned a network of heavy steel beams, from which powerful ceiling lights hung, all off. They were covered in a thick layer of dust. No humans had worked in this part of the hall for a long time, as the little automated transport helpers didn't need extra light to see in the dark.
They were all equipped with Lidar systems and buzzed happily as we crouched past them.

Every couple of machines, a bundle of thick black cables snaked down from the ceiling, like black veins infusing the hall and its interior with its lifeblood.

To our left was a seemingly endless row of conveyor belts, each moving crates from point A to point B. Most of the crates were marked with the logo of Holster Defense Systems. Apparently, the Nightshades had something to do with packaging and transporting weapons from the forge of our godlike Lord Holster, whom I still affectionately called Jr.

I'd love to say that to his face one Day.

But the mechanical ballet didn't end there.
Many of the belts transported goods directly into large containers that looked like they were destined for overseas shipment to the crisis zones of the "Imperial Corporate Federation of Europe."

Europe. Man, that was another story that had started off so well and then completely collapsed.

Here's a quick summary:

In 2020, after leaving the EU, Britain began to exacerbate its internal tensions and social inequalities.
This led to political polarization and economic inequality, increasing social tensions. In the early 2030s, social unrest broke out in several European countries, fueled by
economic uncertainty and growing inequality.
The British government which had previously been confined to its small island, used this instability to extend its power to the entire continent.

By 2040, massive social protests and violent clashes had destabilized the political landscape of Europe, while
Britain, through economic and military interventions,

increasingly took control of key industries and resources.

In 2045, facing a deep economic recession and growing social discontent, the EU, under the leadership of the new British Empire, reformed into the Imperial Corporate Federation of Europe. This entity was led by British oligarchs and multinational corporations with different values and goals, none of which included strengthening human rights or similar nonsense.

This federation tried to solidify its control through neoliberal reforms and harsh police violence, reorganizing its police and military units under the law-and-order doctrine. There was now practically no difference between blue and camouflage helmets, evident on the now-decayed streets and railroad tracks of the countries.
Social tensions continued to escalate and in the 2050s, uprisings and revolts broke out in several major cities of the ICFE, which the British government alternately supported and brutally suppressed.

Weapons, in whatever hands, remain the most lucrative business.

British control over Europe solidified further while the standard of living for the general population rapidly declined. In the 2060s, growing social inequalities and the corporations' authoritarian rule led to a dystopian daily life for most of the now-uninsured residents of the ICFE.
The Imperial Corporate Federation of Europe was ruled by a small elite, while the general population was oppressed and exploited.

Man, we were lucky in the good old Free Trade Zone of Unified America. We were still number one.

"Stay close to me," Simmons said as we crept past the conveyor belts. We slowly moved in a crouched position along a row of shelves, reaching up to the ceiling, which started on the right side of the hall and extended at least fifty meters deep. They were loaded with goods of various sizes, shapes, and colors. Between the shelves, small automated cargo units scurried back and forth, performing their sorting and loading tasks. At the far end of the shelves was a separate zone. It was visible from our position because unlike the rest of the hall, it was flooded with light. A few huge containers clearly held precious cargo inside. The entire area was filled with cameras, sensors, and the first human workers we had seen since we entered.

These wore protective suits and every tiny movement was closely monitored by the cameras. Despite the really late hour, it was almost three in the morning, there was a bustling activity among the work drones. I could only guess what was going on, but it probably had something to do with the cargo ship that announced its presence with another loud blare of its horn. Based on its volume, I realized it was much closer than I anticipated it.

We continued to sneak, trying to stay in the shadows of the conveyor belts avoiding the cameras' and sensors' view. Our target lay somewhere beyond this mechanical labyrinth.
We relaxed a bit as we left the brightly lit part of the hall behind us. Ahead of us lay a long, poorly lit corridor with two branches at the end. Our goal was the hallway leading to the room where the Kami no Katana lay. We had no idea which room and which hallway that was. So, there was only one logical decision-making option to figure that out.

Simmons and I looked deeply into each other's eyes.
We stood at the fork that would determine the rest of our lives and, thus, our fate. There was no other way. Fate had to help us.

Rock, paper, scissors. I won the first round with Rock Against Scissors.

Rock, paper, scissors. Simmons won the second with paper against rock. Okay, now it was time. Fate had laid its divine hand upon us and would guide us in a few seconds. I felt I had to choose the left path; that was what the tingling in my veins puslating in my left hand told me.

So, with all the strength I could muster, I tore my hand from the high position into the depths of the last scissors. The air whipped around us as both our hands struck flat.

Simmons had won.

"Damn it," I said through clenched teeth.
"You're just too good at this game." My hand hurt slightly. Maybe I had overdone the smashing part. Simmons grinned, and we walked down the right hallway.

Of course, to the right. Into damnation. Now he's really sending us to our deaths.

At the end of the relatively short hallway, we came to a pressure door that was slightly ajar. Behind it was another relatively small room with poor lighting. We carefully stepped in. Several shelves were lined up in this room, filled with various things. There were some Korean Knick-knacks stored in boxes, on shelves and on velvet cushions. And then we saw it. A window gave us a view of the opposite room. There, in the middle of the room, brightly lit, surrounded by four heavily armed Nightshade members in black armor, lay the Kami no Katana behind a case made of transparent Panzerflex glass.

"Damn, we really should have taken the left path," I said to Simmons.

We both stared through the window at the case, the sword, and the guards. "Notice anything?" Simmons asked.

"Yeah," I replied curtly. "The guards don't seem to see us through the window."

"It seems to be some kind of one-way glass," Simmons added to my remark. That gave us some time to figure out how to get into the other room, past the heavily armed guards, through the Panzerflex glass, get the Kami no Katana, and get out of the room without causing too much commotion.

Honestly, we had no idea.

Draw weapons, storm into the room, shoot wildly, grab the case, and run.

I don't think that would work.

Throw a gas grenade into the room, use poor karate skills against probably experienced close-combat fighters, and get killed in the process.

One option. But a deadly one.

Turn off the electric circuit in the room, enter quietly in the dark, and take them out with a silenced handgun from 3 centimeters away, then maybe find a code card or something similar that the guards definitely, probably, hopefully had to free the Katana from its glass prison.

Another option, but it already failed at the first step because we had no idea where or if we could find and turn off the electric circuit in this building, let alone for this room.

"Fuck," Simmons blurted out loudly and I was about to respond with a "We're really in deep shit" when our little thought exercise was loudly interrupted.

"Hey, Sims," we both heard a female voice say from the direction of the door we just came in. We turned abruptly, and in front of us stood a small Asian-looking woman with short-cropped hair carrying two pistols on her belt. She was pretty and wild at the same time… and I could only ask myself one question: Who was that? And how did she know Simmons? And why did she call him Sims? I had tried that once, and he had threatened me with eternal damnation.

Who the hell was she?

Simmons answered this question before I could voice my thoughts. "M-m-m-addy… what are you doing here?"
I had never seen Simmons so baffled.

Our target person, whom we had hoped to find somehow in Mr. Tanaka's club through our blood oath and gain his favor by stealing the Kami no Katana, was standing before us. In the same building as the sword. Here, in the Korean district. Filled with a ton of Nightshades.

Oh man, they had a lot to explain.

But first, I watched as they slowly walked toward each other, and Simmons received the most brutal slap I've ever seen. Then they hugged for a long time.

An uncomfortably long time.

Alarm, it shot through my mind. ALARM. I couldn't forget the German firefighter meme I had seen long ago.

AMITHAYUS, KOREAN PORT

FOURTEEN.
THE LAST BASTION

Amithayus, Seattle, 04:47 AM - Nightshade Warehouse

Simmons, Maddy, and I...

...Okay, even ten minutes later, this still feels very weird...

...had finally moved into one of the upper rooms of the warehouse after what felt like an eternity of hugging.
It wasn't as claustrophobic here as it had been in the
Room opposite of the Kami no Katana, where the two had seen each other for the first time in nearly eight years.
Maddy was quite different from what I had imagined.

But how could I have known what she looked like?
Just a few hours ago, I didn't even know she existed.
And in between, I had been too busy avoiding bullets,
knives, or anything else that could kill me.

In any case, on our path to solving this investigation, we had skipped two steps out of nowhere. I was curious to hear what the two had to say to each other.
Simmons sat across from Maddy at a long oak table. It was filled with 3 different security monitor flimmering away, a few glasses full of brown, old looking Alcohol and our firearms. I felt out of place, mainly because I sat right in the middle between them.

Simmons began the questioning and his first question was a good opener.

"What are you doing here?"

Really subtle and right to the point.

"I could ask you and your friend the same question."

Okay, this is going to be a long night.

"We're on an assignment related to an ECLE investigation into a double murder. It brought us across Amithayus to this place," said Simmons somewhat quietly, not going into further details.

"And, did you find what you were looking for?" Maddy asked with a slightly sarcastic undertone.

"In a way, yes," Simmons replied, now quieter.

"I hate to interrupt the beating around the bush, but I don't think we have enough time for this. So..." Maddy and Simmons stared at me in surprise. I had done something wrong, though I didn't know what. I didn't care. Time to put the facts on the table so everyone knew what was happening. Then, we could see how to proceed from there.

I told her we were investigating a double murder of a middle-aged couple shot with a rare type of ammunition. Maddy listened attentively. I then told her about the diner, Lenny, and what was left of him. I didn't mention my fragment ability but instead gave a detailed account of the Dämmerung Drone and how it had saved our asses.
Maddy also found that very interesting. Moreover, we had broken into Amithayus hoping to talk to Maddy at the club, and followed a lead to the warehouse near the Kami no Katana. I didn't mention Mr. Tanaka. Both Maddy and Simmons looked at me. Then Simmons looked at Maddy, who was still looking at me. I still felt very out of place.

I could sense that she was thinking, trying to make sense of the whole story. "I have two things for you. But only because you showed up here with Sims. Without him, you'd be floating in the harbor with your belly upwards." I nodded, understanding that she was the tougher one.

"Okay. Point one. The rare ammunition. It took me a while to figure out what you were talking about. Do you both want to know why?" "The only thing we know so far is that it's scarce," said Simmons, and I agreed. "The last time I saw this ammunition was at least twenty years ago," said Maddy, lowering her voice to a whisper. She stood up and started pacing from one corner of the room to the other.

"Twenty years?" Simmons asked. "Are you sure it was such rare ammunition?"

I nodded. I had seen it and felt it. I knew what had killed me, or rather, Mona. Additionally, in the six hours we had been at the ECLE station writing the preliminary report, we had ordered a ballistic analysis of a fragment of the bullet that had pierced Monas body just before the plastinators came for packing. We had thoroughly searched the crime scene but found no other bullets. The test confirmed what I had felt. "You've read the investigation report just like I have. It came back positive to my description." Simmons nodded.

"Twenty years," Simmons repeated. "How is that possible, Maddy?" She was now leaning against a wall, observing us both with a sharp gaze. "Simple," she said. "That stuff isn't made anymore. Holster Defense Systems stopped producing those 12mm Action Express rounds when it merged with Skyway Technologies. That must have been around 2045."

"Why?" I asked, slightly furrowing my brow.
I didn't understand it yet. "Was the ammunition not effective enough?"

Maddy shook her head and came back to the table. She leaned on it with both hands and explained in more detail.

A history lesson from a weapons dealer in her hideout. I could cross that off my bucket list.

"The ammunition was more than effective. It is one of the most accurate and powerful rounds ever produced. The perfect bullet for long-range shooters and elite units. But the world of weapons and technology changes rapidly. New technologies emerge and old ones become obsolete. A good example is a company you both probably know well and is also based in Seattle."

The Boeing Corporation.

Before the merger with McDonnell Douglas, it was the star in the technology sky. Then they miscalculated and McDD took over. Old norms were thrown overboard and new structures were introduced. It was no longer the company of engineers but of spreadsheet calculators and everything that didn't yield exorbitant profits was ruthlessly cut. The same thing happened with the merger of Holster and Skyways.
It happens almost every time," Maddy said, staring at us. She was waiting to see if we had any objections. We didn't.

It's always about power, more power, and control over even more power.

"But why would someone use such scarce ammunition?" Simmons asked, now also standing up and pacing the room.

Maybe I should stand up, too?

"That's my question too. Why was someone so bent on using exactly that ammunition?" I said, and Maddy promptly responded.

"Because it can't be traced," she said. "It's so rare that no one would think to look for it. And honestly, I have no idea how you two even thought to look for it." "It was just a feeling," I replied.

A damn painful feeling.

"Okay, I'll believe you two are outstanding investigators. I know what Sims is capable of." She looked at him mischievously, and he abruptly turned and walked in the opposite direction. Maddy couldn't suppress a smile.

Oh, she was definitely the alpha in their relationship.

I tried to steer the conversation back to the main point. "That makes more sense than I thought." Maddy just nodded and kept watching Simmons.

"But why not use modern ammunition? State-of-the-art bullets. They're probably even more effective and penetrating than 20-year-old ammo," I asked into the room and received a prompt answer that I hadn't thought of the whole time.

"It's logical. Because modern ammunition is easily traceable," she said. "Every bullet has a chemical signature, essentially its own manufacturing marker. But this old ammo, which stopped prodcution shortly before the introduction of chemical numbering, has none of those features. It can't be traced. It's like driving an old classic car without a serial number. Nobody today can tell you where it came from and when it was built without first knowing what it is and then looking it up on the Internet.

"Damn." Someone went through the trouble of finding untraceable ammo just to kill someone who had nothing but debts?"

"Exactly. Whatever you two have gotten yourselves into, it's a big deal, which took a lot of new dollars to plan and execute."
"And what about the second point you wanted to address?" Simmons said as he walked back toward the table. He leaned on it with both arms and stared her straight in the face. I could see he was deep in thought.

"So. The second point is this, Sims." She had turned back to him, and the way she said "Sims" captivated even me. "I'm sorry we haven't been in contact for so long. And I'm sorry you got into so much trouble because of me. I didn't even have enough time to thank you for covering for me back in the park. And you had to take a blood oath on Mr. Tanaka because of me. For that, I want to apologize now." She walked around the table, took Simmons' face between her hands, and kissed him deeply and long. After she stopped, she slapped him hard across the face with her right hand. Simmons still had his eyes closed and stumbled in the opposite direction. "Whoa," was all I heard him say, right before he crashed to the ground. "What was that for?"

"That's for the second point," said Maddy, who now looked very angry and drew her two pistols from the holsters on her belt, pointing one at Simmons and one at me. "You two aren't just here because you got some clue about this murder case. That's bullshit. You're here for the Kami no Katana. And that can only mean one thing. You were sent by Mr. Tanaka to kill me. Me, the leader of the Nightshades."

What, what, what... what just happened? Maddy was the leader of the Nightshades? Why? How? And how did she know about Mr. Tanaka? And why did she care?

"Uh," I heard Simmons say in astonishment, and I was sure my reaction sounded similar.

"You have ten seconds to explain better, or I will scatter your brains all over this beautiful floor in my office." She raised her weapons a few more centimeters into the air and looked at us both out of the corners of her eyes.
"Simmons," I heard myself call out, and he glanced in my direction. He knew exactly what he had to do now.

"I'm sorry," he said.

Fuck, we're dead.

"I should have looked for you back then. I shouldn't have given up on you so easily. Yes, I covered for you, and yes,
I took a blood oath to Mr. Tanaka back then, which I
fulfilled tonight."

My gravestone should read: Simmons, you damn idiot.

"But that blood oath wasn't to come here and kill you.
We had no idea you were here, let alone that you were the new leader of the Nightshades. What a rise. From a small arms dealer, always striving for more.
Now you've achieved that. I last spoke to you eight years ago. And I must confess, and I'm deeply sorry, that I forgot to think about you over time. I always thought you had run away. Maybe gone to the Imperial Corporate Federation of Europe, where you can make good new pounds with weapons. But about eight hours ago, Lenny told us that you were still alive and very close by.
He said you had rented the basement of Mr. Tanaka's club, for whatever reason, to either restart or continue your arms business. Maybe to repay your debt to him.

I wanted to believe in any reason why you were still alive. That's why we went to him. And he was the one who said you were with him and that he would only let us see you if we brought him the sword.
So, I had to fulfill my blood oath. I wanted to see you again." Simmons now looked directly into Maddy's eyes.

Wow. Maybe only he will die.

"You damn idiot. No, both of you are damn idiots." Maddy was now slightly trembling. I didn't know if it was because of Simmons' emotional speech or the anticipation that she could shoot us any second now.

"We stole the damn sword from his damn club. We, the Nightshades. For a particular reason. Whoever possesses the sword has a part of the population behind them. It's a thing with religion here in Amithayus. There's always some idol to worship. For about a hundred years or so, it's the Kami no Katana and the story associated with it. And that filthy pig, Mr. Tanaka, doesn't
deserve to have the power over Amithayus in his hands or on his desk. Because he betrayed the district. He sold us all out. Every single citizen who wants to go about their business peacefully. To the damn corporations. Here in Amithayus, the last bastion in Seattle, we are still defending against outside intrusion. And for what?"

New dollars. A lot of new dollars.

"A fucking huge pile of new dollars. It's so big that he can
afford anything from now on. A private army, maybe go shopping in style. One or two new neighborhoods per evening. Oh, that sounds nice. I'll take two of those, please. And what did he have to do in return? Just break the holiest law in Amithayus."

"Let no strangers into the city. And if you do, only in pieces," Simmons and I said simultaneously.

"At least you still know that," said Maddy, still trembling but not as strongly as a minute ago. "He threw the doors wide open for the conglomerates and suits, and now they will divide our small, self-sufficient community, which has held out for so long, street by street. Building by building, apartment by apartment. We will lose everything. Our culture, our home, and our future.
In ten years, nothing here will be the same as it is now.
And I can't stand to watch that anymore.
That's why I took the top spot in the Nightshades.
That's why we stole the Kami no Katana. And now we have at least a large part of the three districts here in Amithayus behind us. And that will in due time mean war with the districts outside the wall."

"Oh man, how were we supposed to know that?" said Simmons, getting up from the floor.

Man, that slap must have really landed. It probably would have knocked my head off my body. What is that deafening noise in the background?

I was torn from my thoughts by a deafening noise and various human screams. We turned simultaneously and stared in the direction from which the metallic tearing and several extremely bright lights came. It sounded like a huge metallic object dragged across a concrete floor nearby. Before I realized what was happening outside, it was too late.

A gigantic tremor made the warehouse shake, and a deafening bang followed by a shock wave knocked us off our feet.

Concrete pieces broke from the surrounding walls, and the entire foundation of the hall trembled under the impact. The freighter, which I had noticed about an hour ago at sea, had rammed through the maritime barrier protecting the harbor and finally the warehouse. Maddy, Simmons, and I looked at each other and we all knew what had just happened.
"He's here," said Maddy as she got up from the floor.

Simmons and I knew what we had to do. We grabbed our Sentinel Mark IV and followed Maddy out of her office toward the large hall. Meanwhile, Maddy continuously barked Korean commands into her communicator as we navigated under, over, and through masses of debris and rubble from the ceiling or collapsed walls. A thick layer of dust hung in the air in the long corridor leading to the hall, and we could only see a few meters ahead of us.

"What the hell," said Simmons as we reached the edge of the hall. Almost the entire front side of the hall, where drones had been diligently loading shelves and containers just a minute ago, was now unrecognizable. Dust, debris, and the massive freightship obstructed our view. It had shattered half the wall like a piece of paper with its gigantic bow.
The occasional cries of Nightshades echoed through the hall, confused and wounded as they crawled through the remains of their workplace. The smell of burnt diesel and shattered wood from the dock hung acrid.
Mr. Tanaka had arrived and brought his latest toy: a private army.

On the front part of the ship, several containers burst open simultaneously and out of them stormed black-clad soldiers with automatic rifles at the ready. Their boots created a deep thrum that echoed through the remains of the warehouse as they jumped from the upper deck and landed on the ground below. They immediately opened fire on anything that still moved in their vicinity. They moved quickly and precisely.

They were all equipped with the latest generation Armorflex suits and helmets. Far more advanced than what we wore. Thanks to their integrated night vision devices, they had no trouble seeing in the dark, unlike us.

Damn, we should have gotten helmets instead of just camo masks.

When the soldiers on the ship's upper deck, which was slightly higher than our balcony noticed us, they opened fire. Bullets ricocheted off the debris, offering us little protection on an undefendable balcony. "Take cover. We need to get down to the Nightshades, or we don't stand a chance," said Maddy, and Simmons and I knew what that meant. We had chosen a side without being asked and now we were defending our lives against a private army of at least 200 or more soldiers, better trained, better equipped, and probably more ruthless than us. There was no chance of surviving this massacre.

If I survive this day, I will become a believer in anything. Even the Kami no Katana and the Child Emperor,
I'll believe in it. Just let us get out of here alive.

I gripped my Mark IV tightly, adjusted the sight on my visor, activated the friend-foe recognition, and got ready. We moved slowly, still under enemy fire, from cover to cover, shooting at anything not marked green on the visor. Bullets whizzed around us, and the the deafening roar of the firefight filled the warehouse.
It had transformed from a semi-legal shipment facility into a battlefield. Simmons, Maddy, and I fought through the chaos, each step forward a battle for survival.
Mr. Tanaka's soldiers were everywhere, better equipped and determined to eliminate anyone who didn't belong to them.

The Nightshades, who had survived the initial ship crash, fought with all their might to defend their positions, but they were outnumbered and killed or pushed back one by one. This did not sit well with Maddy, who yelled at us with rage in her voice to keep moving forward.

We are only three. And they are a thousand or so.

Our Plan was simple. Kill Tanaka. Get rid of the Enemy Soldiers. And not die in the meantime.
"Keep moving!" Simmons now shouted over the noise, firing another burst at a group of soldiers who had recklessly stepped out of cover. Three of the five soldiers were spun around by the impact of our Mark IV bullets, while the other two were taken out by Maddy with precise shots through their helmets. The two were a well-coordinated team. I had to keep up to avoid being the fifth wheel. Maddy charged forward, taking out another two soldiers, her pistols flashing in the dark with each swift movement she made. We slowly but steadily carved a path through the enemy lines, getting closer to where I suspected Tanaka to be. The surrounding Nightshades did their best, but the sounds from Maddy's communicator grew fewer by the minute.

They gave their best, but the soldiers' numerical superiority and vastly improved equipment did the rest. I pressed myself into every available corner avoiding bullets. I could hear pained screams and the gurgling of pierced bodies.Friend or foe was nothing I could determin. The cries of the wounded and dying merged into a loud chant of death as the hall sank into an inferno of exploding machines catching fire and Death.

We reached a row of conveyor belts ahead of us, which had transported crates marked with the Holster Defense logo. The mechanical arms of the machines were now still, unable to stoically ignore the chaos around them any longer. I took cover behind one of the belts as a massive shower of sparks rained down on me, likely from a burst of bullets that had narrowly missed my head. I fell backward in shock, tripping over my own legs, lying there like a toddler who had fallen off a swing. It took a second to regain my composure. Get up. Don't give up. React. Focus. You can do this; you were trained for it. Breathe, one step at a time. Shot to the left. Enemy down. Breathe, move forward, lookout, its Maddy. Okay, she got him. Simmons, to the right, he nods, all clear.

Good, both are still alive.

"Come on," Simmons shouted. "We need to keep moving," Maddy answered. Her Stoic commands actually helped me to focus. She took out another soldier. We fought meter by meter, machine by machine through the seemingly endless wave of soldiers.
The air was thick with rising smoke; the smell of burnt flesh, shattered hydraulic lines spilling fluids burning wooden containers filled my nostrils.

Oh, how I wish I had a helmet now.

We were trampling over masses of fallen fighters from both sides, grotesquely twisted in front of us on our way to Tanaka. At that moment, a grenade exploded to my left, shaking the ground with its shockwave.
Debris and dust rained down on me, as I jumped into cover with full force to avoid the falling pieces of the ceiling. I hit the ground hard, losing my bearings for a short while. Dust and sparks filled the surrounding air, and I couldn't see anything.
My vision was blocked entirely, and my airways
swallowed so much dust I thought I would suffocate.
I gagged and coughed my soul out, and the saliva flowing from my mouth was yellow and gray. I felt a hand on my shoulder as Simmons knelt beside me, looking into my face. I nodded slightly, and he knew I was okay.

"Reload," he said, changing his magazine, and I nodded, got up, and did the same. Maddy waved at us from behind a half-tilted container, signaling us to come immediately. We did. When we reached her, I looked into her face, and her eyes sparkled with rage and determination.

Now I understand why Simmons jumped into this adventure without hesitation.

"We need to keep moving, and we need to hurry.
Tanaka can't be far from us. By now, his soldiers must have reached the Kami no Katana. We can't let him escape with the sword. Everything we've done in the last two years would be for nothing. Amithayus would fall. We have to stop him."

And with those words, she led us deeper into the battle. Another group of soldiers, more screams, more death, everywhere, just blood and human misery.
I started feeling my old bones, and with each additional step I took in this man-made hell, I aged another year.
We killed another group of soldiers, an endless sequence of the same mechanics. Aim, pull the trigger, lower the weapon, raise the gun, turn the hip, and take a proper stance. Simmons killed one or two or maybe three more soldiers directly in front of us. I wasn't sure anymore.
On the other hand, Maddy was enjoying the adrenaline rush, shooting, kicking, and slashing her way through
hordes of armed targets. One of them...

And I swear I didn't imagine this in my delirium; she killed them with a knife and then bit a chunk out of his neck with her mouth... I'm pretty sure. Every death blends into the next so seamlessly... how long have I been fighting?

Suddenly, there was a strange metallic squealing and straining coming from above. I glanced up, ignoring the groud of soldiers doing the same thing as I noticed the front part of the freighter slowly but surely moving toward us.

"Oh shit!" I shouted toward Simmons and Maddy. „ We need to get out of here. The damn ship is breaking apart in the front. While running, I could see how the bow slowly under the immense pressure of it ramming through the Wall gave weigh to the damages it sustained.

We ran like madmen as the ship's bow separated from the rest with a hellish noise. The giant metal part cracked under its own weight, crushing everything in its path on its way downwards.
Containers and machines were shoved aside like toys and soldiers and Nightshades were either hurled through the air or crushed by the impact. The steel behemoth smashed everything in its path. Maddy grabbed my arm and pulled me along. I couldn't run anymore. My arms were so heavy.
My legs moved automatically. My fingers ached with each pull of the trigger. We ran and ran forward over debris and bodies as the rest of the ship kept coming toward us. The heat of the burning machines inside the hall and the noise were unbearable, and I felt the ground tremble under the weight of the tonnes smashing behind us.

"There, a staircase," Simmons shouted as we ran up without looking back. Just as we reached the top, the lower part got smashed as the last remnants of the Bow broke off, taking the rest of the debris, machines, and bodies with it. We had barely reached a higher level, hastily climbing the rest of the stairs.
The imminent danger was momentarily averted. Dust spread around us as our sight was blocked for the moment.

We looked at each other, and each of us checked our equipment and remaining ammunition supplies.

It looked as bad as I felt. Terrible.

Really terrible. I only had the magazine in my Mark IV and my rusted knife. I must have lost my pistol earlier during the fall.

Simmons was almost out of everything, too, but still had his pistol on him. Maddy had one more magazine for her
pistols and a knife. Physically, we were still somehow alive. I hadn't expected that when we went down those big stairs shooting. Maddy had two minor cuts on her face and a slight injury to her left arm. Simmons limped with his right leg but didn't want to admit it.
And I could barely stand on my feet, my bones aching from the exertion. Additionally, I felt a direct pain in my left hand, but upon closer inspection, I couldn't find any damage to my glove or anything else.

Probably just a cramp. Although I felt the same intense pain as when I used my abilities. What was wrong with me? It had never been this strong before.

The Dust slowly settled and from our elevated position, we could see the full extent of the destruction. Tanaka's now fully destroyed ship had turned the dark warehouse into a field of debris where nothing but chaos reigned. The area where Maddy's office had been was burning brightly, and the stairs had collapsed. Parts of the containers loaded with various goods were lying on their sides also burning. The rows of conveyor belts were still and mostly torn apart. The only part of the hall that was still relatively intact was the upper deck we were standing on, followed by the relatively small entrance area at the front of the hall.

There he is.

"Hey, I've spotted Tanaka. Left front, next to the big machine thing that was loading other stuff earlier when we came in."

Okay, that wasn't helpful.

Maddy and Simmons stared at me as if I were insane. "Straight ahead, then a little to the left, yeah exactly, and then by that big thing, where I don't know what it is."
I pointed directly at the big thing, and they saw him, too.

"That's a multi-loader machine that packs smaller crates into larger ones to be loaded into containers," Maddy
stared at me and pointed at the big thing. I nodded and smiled, which she answered with a disdainful look.

More grenades exploded below us, and another group of Nightshades lost their lives. "Hold your position," Maddy kept shouting, but she knew it was useless against the overwhelming force. Tanaka's men were now pushing
forward on both sides of the battlefield, their black armor glinting in the flickering firelight burning all over the hall.

"We need a plan to get to him without him noticing us," said Simmons. I looked around but couldn't see anything to help us get closer to Tanaka. Maddy, however, glared at us. "I've got an idea," she said, and I didn't like how she said "idea."

She can't be serious. This sounds like another crazy idea. And I've had enough of those in the last 24 hours.

And so it was. We didn't go over the plateau where we stood. Instead, we jumped through the small windows, smothered by the blazing flames.
The flexible glass that had survived the freighter's impact shattered with a satisfying crash onto the roof, and we followed a split second later. Okay, so far, the plan wasn't that crazy. But it was about to get crazier.
We ran as fast as we could along the edge of the roof, none of us daring to look down. It was assured death if we fell. As we reached the end, we stopped. From here, I could see our starting point. And the hill I had been lying on earlier.

I should have stayed up there. I'm the sniper this time, Simmons. You can have all the action. Oh, my ComUhr is making strange noises...grrscchch. Hello? Hello?

We kept running across through the dark of the night and as we reached the roof's peak, all three of us slid down toward the opposite edge. There, I saw finally saw our target. It was one of the cargo cranes usually used to load containers onto ships. The boom was at least 50 meters long. The good thing was, at its winch, hung a massive container.

She really planned to do it.

We knelt at the roof's edge, from where we could see the rest of the freighter and the mostly destroyed dock. A battle had also erupted outside the warehouse and the soldiers were pushing the Nightshades back from their positions there.

The fire from the warehouse had spread over to some of the surrounding buildings and in an hour this place would be a complete inferno of burning structures and burnt people.

Maddy had meanwhile barked more Korean commands into her Communicator and with a sudden jerk, the large cargo crane and its container started moving toward us.

It's impressive that the crane operator stayed in his cabin despite a giant freighter turning his dock, warehouse and job site into a rubble field. Maybe it was safe up there.

I tilted my head and paid my respects to the crane operator. Apparently, the other two understood my gesture because they did the same… or were more attentive than I was because the end of the container whizzed past us.

Okay, slightly miscalculated, Mr. Crane Operator.

The second attempt worked. The large container stopped at the roof's edge. Maddy and Simmons opened the heavy metal doors with a loud screech that was drowned out by the infernal noise from the warehouse battle. Meanwhile, I secured the area, watching for anyone who might have followed us onto the roof. But I couldn't see anyone. It was time to board our little surprise for Mr. Tanaka. Maddy gave more instructions to the crane operator as we climbed in and closed the doors behind us. The container began to move, and now we had nothing more to do, than to wait. And hope that her plan would work.

Maddy gave us final instructions, and we tried to hold on as best we could in the wobbly, floating heavy container we had repurposed as a battering ram. I felt we had reached the highest point of our swing, pressing my fingers into the hold ropes on the inside of the container, usually used for securing hazardous cargo.

But today, we were the hazardous cargo…

…which I quickly dismissed as I felt nauseous at the maximum speed of the crane approaching the impact point. Maddy's Communicator blared something in Korean, and she screamed at the top of her lungs:

"Hold on!" as with tremendous force the container crashed through the still-standing warehouse wall. I felt the impact and saw us all lose our Footing instantly. I didn't know which way was up or down as I crashed against each side of the container with every part of my body.

The plan had worked. The impact had pushed the
container through the wall with such force that it shattered into thousands of pieces, sending debris through the remaining room, turning the soldiers surrounding Mr. Tanaka into small

lumps of flesh. Most of the soldiers were so surprised they couldn't react before being crushed by the debris.

Only a handful of soldiers survived the debris shower.
Unfortunately for them, they faced the second part of Maddy's plan, which began with a loud click at the second peak of the swing. The mechanical claw had released, allowing the container to come down with immediate force, squashing everything in beneath it with an audible Splashing Sound.

The external impact must have been a considerable shock, but it was even more brutal inside. I hadn't recovered from the ride through the wall when the sudden release of the container snatched me from gravity for a split second before I crashed onto the makeshift ceiling with my back and all other limbs. I was genuinely glad I was wearing an Armorflex suit. When I hit the floor again shortly after, I felt so much pain. I briefly lost my sight. Everything around me spun, and I just wanted to throw up. Maddy and Simmons lay on the ground but were still moving. Good, we had somehow survived. We just had to get up, open the doors, and deal with Tanaka. I tried to get up, but my left arm burned with pain.

Shit, I probably dislocated my shoulder. The pain was extreme. My hand cramped, my head felt like it was exploding, and my shoulder did its best to bring me to the ground.

I pushed myself up with my other arm. It hurt like hell.
I could hear Simmons groaning, but he also got up.
Maddy was already on her feet when I had barely reached my knees. She was bleeding from her mouth and nose, and the two cuts on her face were now an open wound. She pushed against the doors with all her strength.
The doors sprang open, and my stomach turned once more nside out while Maddy simultaneously stormed and fell outside. I fell to my knees, watching her while Simmons limped past me. I looked around and all I could see were dead

soldiers scattered across the area. Blood splattered in all directions, a dust cloud slowly
drifting away from us. I couldn't hear anything.
Either it was tranquil around us, or my hearing was
damaged. I saw Maddy standing in the middle of the room, both pistols in her hands. She was no longer standing as upright as before the container stunt and I could clearly see she was in pain. Simmons followed slowly behind her, his ankle or his foot seemed to be wounded. He was very slow.

Out of nowhere, I saw a golden light moving toward
Maddy from above. I shouted her name, but it was too late. The Kami no Katana in Tanaka's hands sliced effortlessly through her wrists with a single movement, severing bones, tendons, and veins in Maddy's arms and cutting off her hands along with her pistols. Maddy screamed in pain, blood gushing from the stumps that held her best weapons just moments ago. She fell to her knees, howling in agony, clutching the remains of her arms to her chest.
Tanaka stood over her, his head held high, the sword balanced in one hand. He was covered in Maddy's blood from head to toe.

Simmons, who had witnessed it all, fell to the ground, screaming. It sounded like the wild cry of a dying beast. He roared all his pain at Tanaka.

I tried to get up at the edge of the container but couldn't—I could barely move. Where is my goddamn rifle?

Tanaka stood over Maddy, looking down at her face. His gaze was cold and inhuman. Finally, after what felt like an
eternity, he opened his mouth.

"Maddy Turner. I have been searching for you for eight years, and Now I have finally found you." He looked in Simmons' direction, who had stood up in the meantime. He limped like a zombie toward Tanaka.

Tanaka smiled icily, as he positioned himself behind Maddy in so that Simmons couldnt fire at him without hitting her as well. Then he turned back to Maddy.
"Thanks to your friends, I could finally locate you." He looked at her. Maddy writhed in pain, her whole body growing paler from the massive blood loss. She began to tremble.

"I have searched for you for so long, and today is the day I have the privilege of avenging my family."
He turned his head toward the sky and said, "This is the day you can finally be free, my daughter." And I realized what was happening and the rigged game we had unknowingly played since entering his club. He had used us to finally avenge his daughter's death. The whole blood oath thing was just to make Simmons find his daughter's murderer at all costs. What the Fuck.

His daughter, whom Maddy had brutally killed in Toshi Park in the Matsubara district over a minor disagreement about eight years ago. And now Simmons had to pay the price. A blood oath, he swore on his life that had saved hers many years ago. Which led to her Death now. I couldn't believe it. The Kami no Katana was just a farce to use us as bait.

Tanaka raised the sword above his head with the blade side facing down, ready to slice her at any moment.
He stared at Maddy, who looked him directly in the eyes.- despite having no strength left, she was still able to kneel.

"Tonight is the night. Tonight, you die, Akuma."
"Akuma is the right word," Maddy said, her face twisted in pain. "I am the demon from Amithayus who will put you down," with those final words, she pushed off her knees and

lunged at Tanaka. She swung her arms forward, the blood from the stumps splashing into Tanaka's face.
He was momentarily distracted, which Maddy used to throw herself at his neck, sinking her teeth into his flesh.

Tanaka screamed and brought the sword down, which with another slash, went through Maddy's shoulder, into her chest, and through her heart. He pushed it through her body while he screamed viciously as Maddy fell motionless to the ground like a dropped stone. She hit the ground with her head first, and a large, bloody chunk she had bitten from his neck rolled out of her open mouth.

Tanaka dropped the Katana in agony and fell to his knees. He raised both hands to his neck, where blood now gushed out. Maddy had done it.

She really did it.

Tanaka screamed in pain, trying to stand up again.
Blood ran over his hands onto Maddy's severed hands, which lay on the ground before him. The pistols still firmly gripped. Simmons had gotten within reach of Tanaka, but he had no eyes for him. He just stared at Maddy's body on the ground, tears streaming down his battered face.

"Oni-giri San," gurgled from Tanaka's neck. "You must…"
Simmons raised his weapon, and without looking at Tanaka, he pulled the trigger. The first bullet pierced Tanaka's forehead, and the second and all subsequent bullets in his magazine shot over Tanakas body that had already fallen to the ground motionelss.until it clicked. He hit the ground like a wet sack. Simmons kept pulling the trigger until he realized the magazine was empty.
Without any care he dropped his pistol and knelt beside Maddy. His emotions overwhelmed him, as he realized what just happened. Extending his hands, he couldn't do anything

but let his emotions run free. He screamed and cried uncontrollably, holding Maddy's face in his hands.

I dragged myself toward Simmons, grabbed him under the shoulder with my only functioning arm.
"I'm sorry for you two; she was crazy but a good person. But we have to get out of here. Now.
There are more soldiers out there. And in our state, we don't stand a chance of surviving this. Not a single one, you can barely walk, I can't move my left arm. Think.
Just for a second. Sims." The word snapped him out of his rage for a second, as he looked at me with his blood red eyes . "She would want you to survive. For both of you."

He must have know I was right. I felt him reluctantly get up. I pulled him by the arm out of the warehouse, supporting each other as we reached the street outside.
No Nightshades or soldiers were in sight, but we could still hear gunfire and distant explosions.

We had two options: Head right back into the Korean
quarter, which would become another powder keg in a few hours with the death of the Japanese Yakuza leader Tanaka and the death of the Nightshade leader. Or we could go left, along the coastline. No main routes, through the shadows of the night. Just out of range of the soldiers and the Nightshades, and then when the clock strikes 07:00, somehow, out of Amithayus.

At that moment, Simmons' ComUhr rang. It was 06:06 AM, and Simmons didn't react. After almost 30 seconds of endless polyphonic repeating of the Gangnam Legacy song, I answered his watch. It was someone named Zhan Tao who urgently needed our help. And as it turned out, we needed his too.

AMITHAYUS, KOREAN DISTRICT BORDER

FIFTEEN.
A SINGLE LIFE

Amithayus, Seattle, 2066 06:07 AM - Border Crossing

Neele nodded as Zhan Tao ended the call on his ComUhr. He held Alicia's hand for a moment longer than Neele, then they gently let go and closed her eyes. "I will never forget you," she whispered. Then she turned to Zhan Tao. "What do we do now?"

"We're heading to a rendezvous point outside the city.
There, we'll meet an old friend who can hopefully help us get out of Amithayus. But we have to be quick; things are getting worse by the minute. The entire city is becoming a powder keg, ready to explode. Also, Dr. Caldwell's army is still after us; we can't take any risks. We need to lie low for a while." Neele nodded, understanding the gravitas of what Zhan Tao was implying. They were far from safe, and their next move was crucial.

The autopilot navigated the vehicle through the narrow, war-torn streets of Mincheng. The sounds of war gradually faded, but the danger was far from over.
Zhan Tao closely watched the surroundings,
occasionally giving directions to the autopilot.
Fighting the rising panic, Neele sat silently next to Alicia, who now lay peacefully on the back seat. She had to stay strong for Alicia and for herself.

After several minutes that felt like hours, they reached the edge of Mincheng. Zhan Tao took manual control of the vehicle and turned onto a narrow side street leading to an abandoned industrial area. He stopped the car infront of an old, half-collapsed building and turned off the engine.

"Where are we?" Neele asked, looking out the car window.

"This is the old crossing between Amithayus and Seattle before a wall was built before the war forced us to shut ourselves off. Not many people in the Korean District know about this place, and only a handful of the Japanese Quarter knows the way here."

Neele nodded, got out of the vehicle, and looked around. The area was quiet; only the distant echoes of explosions and gunfire reminded them that the fight was not over.
She walked to the edge of the ruined building and peered inside. All she could see was darkness.
Behind the building, she could faintly make out the
silhouettes of Mincheng and the dim glow of lights and flickering flames coming inexorably closer.

Neele and Zhan Tao carefully lifted Alicia out of the vehicle and carried her to the small hut they had chosen as their meeting point. Zhan Tao helped her safely stow Alicia's body inside, as they lay her in the smaller second room on a old bed which was installed into the wall.

Amithayus, Seattle, 2066 06:25 AM - Abandoned Street, Korean Quarter

Simmons and I were exhausted and wounded.
I had definitely dislocated my shoulder, my left arm was burning like fire. The headache hadn't subsided since I touched Lenny, unlike during previous uses of my ability. On the contrary, with every minute that ticked away on my internal clock, the Pain grew more intense.

What's happening to me? The cramp in my arm alternated with the throbbing Pain in my head.

Simmons supported me with his body. He had a gunshot wound in his leg, so I tried to support him as best I could. We hobbled like Siamese twins, long since made obsolete by advances in biotechnology, through the maze-like alleys of the harbor district, along the coastline on our way to a meeting point given to us by someone named Zhan Tao. Simmons checked the coordinates on his ComUhr every couple of minutes.

We moved as quickly as we could through the bushes following the steep dunes seperating the sea from the land, always with the thought that Tanaka's troops were likely after us once they heard of their leader's death. Maddy was dead. But the grief and anger gave us the strength and energy to keep going.

"According to my readout, the rendezvous point is just a few clicks north of us," Simmons said.
These were the only words I had heard from him since we left the warehouse. I nodded and panted from exertion and Pain. Every movement caused sharp Pain, but I gritted my teeth and continued.

We followed the signal until we reached a small hill. We had left the narrow streets of the enclosed Harbor Industries behind and wandered through a labyrinth of rubble and debris. But nothing could stop us from leaving this godforsaken district. Nothing was left but fire, smoke, and the approaching war looming in the sky behind us. We occasionally heard dull explosions and collapsing buildings as we kept moving forward.

"We need to stop for a moment, Simmons," I said, leaning heavily against one of the few trees growing here.
I tried to catch my breath. "I don't know how much longer I can handle this with my shoulder," I said, looking at my left arm. The throbbing was getting worse.

Simmons leaned against the same tree, and the strain in his eyes told me he was also struggling with the Pain.
We stayed silent as we leaned against the only tree we could find. If we hadn't known what was happening on the horizon before us, we might have mistaken it for fireworks.
Just two old friends standing by a tree, watching a fireworks display.

> *That would be a fitting farewell for both of us.*

"We should keep going," I said to Simmons, who nodded weakly. We linked arms again and slowly made our way up the hill. It was terribly exhausting and took us twice as long as it would have if we werenr injured, but we made it. I looked back at what we were leaving behind in Amithayus. A war was brewing, one that would likely destroy everything that had been built here over the past decades. I felt sorry for the ordinary people.

"What happened to Maddy?" I heard Simmons say out of nowhere, and I felt sorry for him, too. He had found her after so long, and I could feel how much he had missed her.

"She gave her life to stop Tanaka in a way only she could," I said tensely and with a worried expression. "We should make sure her sacrifice is not forgotten."

„I will," he said with a concerned look. The only thing I could do was nod as We kept on walking. We were almost at the rendezvous point. From a distance, we saw a heavy, black vehicle approaching at high speed. Hopefully, that was Zhan Tao. It stopped directly at the hut, and then nothing happened.

we both knelt down, and thanks to our black combat suits, we were still almost invisible in the darkness. But that wouldn't be our advantage for much longer.
In a few minutes the sun would rise and if this wasn't Zhan Tao, we would have another problem to deal with. Simmons stared intently at the vehicle's lights. They burned brightly in the darkness. Then, finally, after what felt like an eternity, they went out, and an older but still very well-trained Asian man got out of the front, followed at the rear exit by a relatively young woman in a black suit which looked like very fancy laboratory gear.

"Is that him?" I asked Simmons, and he squinted his eyes. He stared into the darkness for a moment, and I noticed him slowly drawing his knife. Then he relaxed again.
"Yes, that's him. That's Zhan Tao. I haven't seen him in a long time, but his walk is unmistakable." The two went to the back of the black vehicle and opened the rear doors, and I could see them lugging a third person out of the car.
I could tell by the way the arms hung that the third Person was dead.

"Should we approach them?" I asked Simmons, but he shook his head. "We'll sit here for a few more minutes and see if anyone followed them. If it stays quiet, we'll approach."

We leaned against a hill rising from the tundra, and I watched Simmons lit his first synth cigarette in nearly ten hours. That was a sure sign that we were momentarily out of danger. He held it over to me but I declined. After Simmons finished his cigarette, he stubbed it out on the hill and peered over it.
It remained quiet around the small hut, and the vehicle hadn't moved. There wasn't any other movement on the long road that seemed to lead to nowhere, so we set off. Arm in arm, we

marched toward the hut as we saw Zhan Tao and the Girl stepping out.

Amithayus, Seattle, 2066 06:35 AM - Border Crossing

Neele was the first to spot the silhouettes of the two men approaching in dark combat suits. How had they managed to sneak up so close without her noticing? She was about to run to Zhan Tao when he raised his hand in a calming gesture. Apparently, these two were the ones they had been waiting for.

Upon closer inspection, Neele noticed how battered they looked. Their suits were torn in several places, their faces smeared with soot and blood, and one of them was limping while the other held his arm close to his body in a strange position.
"You look worse for wear. What happened to you, onigiri?" Zhan Tao asked loudly, and one of the men
replied quietly, "Hello Zhan. It's good to see you alive after all this time, even if you're covered in blood." Zhan Tao bowed slightly, and Neele did the same.
So, this was the man who was supposed to help them escape Amithayus, she thought. She went inside the hut to look for something to help with their Pain.

"HELPS, can you scan the room and tell me if there's a Medkit or something similar?"

"Of course, Dr. Neele," HELPS replied, and it felt strange to Neele that she was still being called Dr. after everything she had been through. She felt more like a lab rat in an experiment she didn't understand.

"In the cabinet, to your left, are several different Medkits for first aid, Dr. Neele. Have a safe day."

Nele rolled her eyes as HELPS mindlessly uttered the words, 'Have a safe day.' He knew perfectly well that it was likely the worst day since her brother's death. She regretted having followed Dr Caldwell's suggestion back then to have HELPS remind the user to 'have a safe day' after every interaction. As soon as she could, she would wipe it off of HELPS memory banks. She opened the cabinet door and retrieved the two aging Medkits. Most of the contents were unusable, but a few ampoules of pain-relieving liquid looked intact upon closer inspection.
There were also two functional injection devices and
various Hyposprays that she could use for wound sealing. "This should last at least a few hours," she thought as the three men entered the hut.

Simmons and I saw the young woman rummaging through a Medkit case. We also saw a sofa, which we approached and, with great effort, sat down on. Sitting after such a long time felt good, even though my arm still hurt like hell. The man who introduced himself as Zhan Tao stood nearby with his communicator on speaker. Sporadic radio messages and news from different areas came through. According to my translator, most of the Japanese Quarter was on fire.

The local Yakuza, enraged by their leader's death, were
taking out their frustration on anyone with a foreign face. Additionally, a part of a large corporate army had crossed the border and was fighting everyone who stood in their way. Many citizens and militias tried to defend their
homes, but they stood little chance as no one cared about who they were or where they came from. Everyone was killing anyone who could remotely be an enemy.

We learned from Zhan Tao that the same happened in the Chinese Quarter, but with a different private army brutally pushing through the city. We reported that another army, this time from Tanaka, was doing the same in the Korean Quarter. The remaining Nightshades were still active, but how long they could hold out was uncertain. Zhan Tao's expression darkened with every piece of bad news. Amithayus was doomed, and as far as we could tell, four people responsible for its downfall were sitting in this room.

"Five," said the young woman who introduced herself as Neele. "Dr. Neele," she said, and it reassured me a little as she approached us with the Medkit. "Over there under the tarp lies an old friend, no, a family member of mine. Her eyes jolted as she tried to not cross them with us.
„She was fatally wounded in the battle we barely escaped from, and I couldn't do anything for her." She sobbed slightly. The only thing I could do, was trying to distract her.

„Dr. Neele, please take care of Simmons. He's in pretty bad shape." She nodded, and though I was sure she intended to treat me first, she turned to Simmons and
began examining him. I heard a quiet AI voice from her suit, providing her with important medical details and
wishing her a safe day.

Zhan Tao leaned in close to Simmons and whispered something in his ear. He nodded and bit his lip as Neele applied the Hypospray to his leg wound and pulled the trigger.

What a crazy suit she had. I had never seen something like this before. As for Simmons, I had no idea if he was worse off than I was, but that was how it went with old friends.

As Simmons felt a bit better, he activated his ComUhr and sent a message directed at someone outside of Amithayus.

"Who did you call?" I asked him, and Simmons replied that Zhan Tao had secured a short corridor with roughly five minutes of airspace over the Korean area. "I just contacted one of our ECLE Black Talon pilots to pick us up, and he only agreed on the condition that he wouldn't be shot down by missiles. Zhan Tao just gave us that assurance. At least, for the No Fly Zone over the Korean District."

Amithayus was increasingly becoming a battlefield, and we had to get out as quickly as possible; otherwise, the brief corridor that meant freedom or death for us would close forever.

It wasn't unusual for me to feel short, intense phantom pains in my arm or hand after using my ability, but never with such intensity and never for so long. Since touching Lenny, my head was bursting with Pain. I hadn't said anything to Simmons. I clenched my teeth even harder, but I could no longer suppress the Pain. I yelped and grabbed my forearm with my other hand, which had also started to twitch. My body was slipping away from me. My thoughts raced. The Pain coursed through my veins like fire.

Neele looked up, approached me, and sat beside me. And with every step she took closer, it got worse.

"Shit, it looks like it hit you harder than you thought."

At that moment, I wanted to scream all my Pain at her, everything I had experienced over all those years of using my gift and my curse, everything I had seen, everything I had never mentioned to anyone. It all gathered in the palm of my hand, right at the spot where she had touched it.

And life, as I knew it, *shattered into two large fragments.*

An overwhelming flood of feelings, images, impressions, and knowledge washed over me. Her thoughts became mine, and her past, present, and future overlapped into one. I saw images of her past, of lost friends and missed opportunities. I felt happy moments and heartbreaking ones. I saw a massive explosion in **our homeland and how our brother lay dead** in the car before us, and we held him in our aching, burnt hands, unwilling to let him go. I experienced how Dr. Yoshida, the dead Asian scientist now with us in this hut, took us in like her own flesh and blood and became our mentor. I lived our entire shared life, but something about this impression was wrong. Why was I sitting in some mechanical wheelchair, and why did I have to undergo countless operations? Dr. Yoshida had saved my life, but I could barely move. Yet, I was still alive.

That was all that mattered.

I had a brilliant mind, which I knew how to use.
I experienced how, against all odds, Alicia and I went to the Skyward Tower and achieved greatness as a tentative twenty-year-old, along with her, Dr. Caldwell, and a massive team of scientists. Breakthrough after breakthrough, we managed to make the impossible possible. Dr. Caldwell gave us more and more responsibility and increasingly large projects. Even though it was sometimes long and hard, we never gave up because we knew everything we developed would ultimately improve people's lives. I was filled with so many happiness endorphones that I almost couldn't contain myself.

And then came the day that changed everything for us.
In October 2075...

    "...2075?..."

...we achieved the most significant scientific breakthrough humanity had ever reached. After decades of research, we made the impossible a reality. Through quantum entanglement and the resulting gravitational anomaly, which we precisely controlled, we transported abiotic matter like metal, aluminum, and plastics through time.

We had invented a goddamn time machine?

The first thing we tried, of course, was a coffee cup, which we sent twenty minutes into the past, of course full. And how anticlimactic it was when it just stood there, already the full twenty minutes, now almost cold on the table beside us, like it never traveled anywhere. We had invented a specific form of time travel. I was so proud of us. Think of all the good we could do with this. How much future knowledge we could send on easily understandable data carriers to every Person in every timefame. We could be improving millions of lives!

But Dr. Caldwell wanted more. He tested the machine with lab animals he had explicitly prepared for it, taking over the experiment series himself. From small mice to primates, he sent everything through time. However, the experiment failed each time, and the animals died shortly after their arrival due to their cells disintegrating. Their genes went haywire and mutated at such an extreme speed that their bodies couldn't withstand the gamma radiation. He cursed us all. With each progressing experiment, he became angrier and more malicious, retreating into himself.
He blamed everyone else for the failures, and a few months after we had created this grand success of science, he excluded us.

Dr. Yoshida and I were removed as persona non grata from all laboratory projects and lost our employment at Skyway Holster and, thus, access to our quantum entanglement technology. But Dr. Yoshida and I couldn't give up.

We had to know what Dr. Caldwell was planning, so over the years, we obtained access to his research data through friends from various labs. Piece by piece, we uncovered disturbing information. Viktor had gone insane. He was causing minor accidents at strategically essential times in human history, which were generally perceived as just that. Nuclear accidents.

Emphasis on accidents.

The results of these accidents were then studied, and over the decades, more and more data pointed to a specific
genetic marker developing in more subjects. We didn't know his end goal then, but we had to stop him.

He had thousands of human lives on his conscience.
So Dr. Yoshida and I planned to build another time machine, no matter the cost. And it cost us everything.
Dr. Yoshida sold all her patents on inventions she had
created over the decades to the highest bidding
corporations. With this money and additional investors who believed in our name and scientific skills, we secretly worked to thwart his plans.
Viktor died before us in 2089 of old age, without us ever seeing him again, but the disasters and the many deaths he had caused continued to heavily. weigh on his and our consciences.

We spent the rest of our lives rebuilding the technology we had co-invented without the original plans. By 2092, we were almost done when Dr. Yoshida also passed away.
I had my mentor with me my entire life, but now I had to complete the plan we had nurtured for over thirty years alone. It took me another whole year to get the machine running. But now it was finally time. I could put our shared plan into action.

Even though I wasn't physically capable, I had to put
everything on one card. I sent a series of information through time to a specific place and time on the second
timeline Viktor had intentionally created for his

experiments. Then I entered the machine with the only goal I had left in my mind.

I had to save myself from the explosion in Snoqualmie Ridge on August 26th at 6:58 AM. I knew I would die in the process, but I had a 75% chance that my body of metal and composite materials would give me the twenty seconds I needed. I gave the world a slight chance to prevent impending doom. My death was nothing
compared to the many lives I could save. And with that thought, I rolled into the machine, and the countdown
ticked to zero.

The bright light shining through the treetops blinded me as I broke through a cluster of branches and leaves. Nature resisted my intrusion, tearing at my skin as if sensing that I didn't belong there. With a dull thud, my 30-year journey ended in the dust stirred up by my arrival, and all I heard was a familiar repetition of notes, a faint hum that I had missed for so long. I felt my mechanical arm resisting the electrical impulses sent by my brain and detaching itself from the rest of my natural body. Using all my remaining strength, I pulled myself forward, my body sliding across the ground in a rhythmic metallic pattern. The Pain of my disintegrating flesh shot through every nerve ending. Every receptor in my brain urged me to die now. But I still had 12 seconds of life left.

Then I saw myself. I was so innocent.
Then I saw myself. **I was a monster.**

I could not comprehend. The fusion of flesh and metal made no sense to my childlike mind. Eight seconds left. I whimpered in Pain. Now or never? I heard myself call out:

"Hello, is someone there? Do you need help?"
Four seconds left! „This is it," I thought:

> "I'm sorry, but you are the one who needs help."

With the last strength I felt in my metal arm, I lunged forward, leaving the human part of my decaying body behind. The rest of me shielded my younger self and knocked her off her feet. She lay protected under me as the flash of light rose from the depths and bathed everything in white. With my last breath, I knew that all the sacrifices I had made over the years were not in vain.

"Close your eyes."

And with these final words, we both did. Two lives, merged into one in the blinding light of a man-made sun.

I screamed as Neele's hand left mine, and my whole body shook with every muscle I had. The Pain was gone. Less than five seconds had passed in our time, but my eyes were wide open, and I stared into the stunned faces around me.

Simmons yelled at Neele about what she had done. And all I did was embrace her tightly. I held her firmly in my arms, and after an initial hesitation, she returned the embrace. The others around us stared at us in even greater bewilderment.

As I slowly released the embrace, I looked into Neele's eyes with tears streaming down my soot- and blood-smeared face. She met my gaze.

I sharply inhaled and said to her, "You... you saved yourself." The realizations overwhelmed me.

Neele looked at me, confused. "What do you mean?"

"You, I don't know how else to say it, you're... or were in two timelines," I stammered. "Both start on August 26th, 2050, at 6:58 AM, but one ends in 2093, and the other... the other begins again on August 26th, 2050, at exactly 6:58 AM. You sacrificed yourself to save yourself and everyone around you."

Neele stared at him, her eyes widening as the words sank in. "That's impossible," she whispered. "What, how do you know this date, and why do you think that..."

"It's impossible for now. But in thirty years you and your mentor, Dr. Yoshida, will achieve the impossible, "or you already did.
I was so confused. "And that's precisely what you did. An alternate version of yourself saved you when you were a child. You were the one who needed help. "

Neele couldn't believe her ears. He knew Alicia's name. He knew the exact date of the explosion in Snoqualmie Ridge. And he knew that she hadn't survived it alone.

She was the one who needed help.

That was the sentence she had been trying to organize in her head all this time. Alicia's death had pushed it further to the background, but now, clearly stated, the right connections in her synapses finally clicked. She stared at the man she had never seen five minutes ago and didn't know how to explain it.

"Thank you. I finally understand." Then she hugged me, and I couldn't help but return the embrace.

Simmons, who had overheard the conversation, furrowed his brow. "What the fuck..." he said, trying to put weight on his injured leg with a pained expression. "...I know you can relive the last ten minutes of a dead person's life. However that actually works. But this... she is alive, and this was just five seconds. And you're talking about two different lives? What the fuck is going on?"

"It means we're dealing with something much bigger than we thought," I said. "I don't just feel it this time. I know it. Tanaka was just a tiny drop in the bucket. Something is happening around us that none of us, no one in Amithayus, and no one in Seattle, is aware of. But whatever it is, this young woman we just met is the key to ensuring we all survive this."

Everyone stared at me as if I had just heralded the end times. And in a way, I had. I didn't know where I got all this knowledge; I didn't know what it all meant, but I had lived it with every fiber of my being. In less than a minute, I had lived two complete lives. And both were full of Pain and suffering.

The minutes passed agonizingly slowly, and everyone in this shed tried to understand what I had just said about Neele. She lay on the sofa, looking like she was racking her brain. We waited for the Black Talon to break through the clouds and take us to safety outside the walls, but we had heard nothing from it yet. Instead, we kept hearing the approaching sound of explosions and machine-gun fire, which couldn't be more than two clicks from our position.

I wondered if the single tree we had leaned against was still standing in the other life I had experienced or if, in my reality, it had also been an illusion from a future's past.

Finally, we heard the familiar sound of the rotors approaching rapidly. Simmons and I hobbled outside while Zhan Tao and Neele carried Dr. Yoshida's body and brought it out as well.

The helicopter began its descent, and we prepared to board. Zhan Tao and Neele hoisted the body into the back of the helicopter, and then Simmons and I got in behind her. The only one who didn't come was Zhan Tao.

"I can't leave my family and friends behind. It's up to me to protect them now that Dr. Yoshida is gone." And turning to Neele, he said a single word, which she responded to with a deep bow. "Ganjin."

He spoke into his communicator and gave his men final orders to keep the corridor open for five minutes.
At all costs. At the cost of their lives. He closed the door of the Black Talon and stepped back a few paces.

The helicopter with the three of us on board took off, and we saw Zhan Tao sprint to the armored vehicle, get in, and speed off in the direction of the brightest flames in the sky.

"We made it," I said as we crossed the district boundary between Amithayus and Georgetown at cloud height.
I let myself collapse into the seat and looked at Simmons.

He stared at me questioningly. "And what do we do now?"

"Now we regroup and plan," Neele said, looking out the window at the burning neighborhood below. She seemed committed as if the past thirty minutes had awakened something in her. We had barely survived this fight. She had lost many people she loved, and behind her on the floor lay another who meant more to her than anything else. Then she turned her gaze from the window and looked at me and Simmons.

"This is far from over. It's just the beginning of a long end that we are inexorably heading towards."

OLD MEDICAL DISTRICT

SIXTEEN.
BETWEEN TWO FRONTS

Seattle, 2066 07:23 AM – Old Medical District

The Black Talon helicopter had quietly dropped us about a kilometer from our actual destination in the Old Medical District. Neele immediately noticed the state-of-the-art equipment on board, and we stocked up on weapons, ammunition, and, at Neele's suggestion, a few emergency suits from the Pacific Commonwealth. From our drop-off point, we moved on foot towards our hideout, moving as silently and quickly as possible with our gear and injuries, always careful not to draw attention to ourselves.

We knew we were still being followed, but there was no safer place than where we were headed.

We arrived at the former residence of the Serpentines—an ideal hideout where no one would expect us.
From the outside, everything was still sealed with barriers and ECLE crime scene tape, which we cautiously bypassed. After climbing six flights of stairs, I opened the unlocked door leading into the apartment's antechamber.
It had only been a day since we were last here, but the Plastinates and cleanup crew had managed to remove all evidence, the bodies, and almost all items from the apartment, packaging them neatly for further processing in one of ECLE's countless archives.

We entered the room quietly; the wooden floor still creaked. The living room and bedroom were mainly cleaned, except for minor things and bloodstains on the floorboards and walls. We told Neele this was the crime scene that initially led us to Amithayus, where we ultimately encountered her. She reacted more calmly than I had expected. She took a brief look around the apartment and asked us a couple of questions about our case, which we answered truthfully. Then, we moved on."

I noticed she was deep in thought, tuning out much of what was happening around her. Simmons lit another synth cigarette as we stood in the middle of a cleaned-up crime scene in the deserted Old Medical District, amid Seattle, in the middle of a brewing war zone, uncertain of our next steps to prevent the chaos.

All the information I had received from my brief touch with Neele was so overwhelming that I still hadn't fully comprehended it. I knew my fragment ability and had
rarely used it before joining the ECLE. In my younger years, I mainly used it occasionally to have profound conversations with the opposite sex in dark bars with lousy music and lukewarm drinks, often leading to one or more visits to their apartments. The sex afterward was intense, but the lingering pain I felt even more. After a couple of times, I had enough of it. I realized the magnitude of this ability when I applied for the not-quite-voluntary military service and later for a special forces unit.
In my first mission, a hostage rescue, I gathered the necessary information through a fragment.
By touching part of the abandoned equipment, I saw from the perspective of a freshly brewed cup of coffee how many hostage-takers there were and which door they used to a secret room. I noticed for the first time that immaterial things only left a brief, less intense imprint of pain in me after using my abilities. So, I avoided touching living people as much as possible. I ran my fingers over the scars on my arm. I still remembered all the names. But their pain had eaten its way into my own heart. The subsequent action went without complications, leading to more missions until I was severely

injured due to my own recklessness. A part of my left arm was amputated and later replaced with a metal prosthesis from Holster Defense Systems. After my demise from the special unit, the entire team was disbanded due to persistent failures, and the troops scattered. Many of my former comrades turned to the IKE, earning their keep as mercenaries, but I wanted to stay in Seattle, so I joined the ECLE for a quieter job, which unfortunately involved a lot of archival work and few field missions.

That's where I first met Simmons, who I immediately liked.

But that was all irrelevant now. I hoped Neele had a plan to help us because I still didn't understand what had happened between us.

What I did know was this: I could say with some certainty that there were, or had been, two different timelines.

I wasn't entirely sure. One of the timelines we were currently in was a branch manipulated from the first timeline. The line we were on was thus the second line. Why? I only knew parts of that. What was the actual goal of these manipulations? I didn't really know that either. Who was Dr. Viktor Caldwell, and why had he done all these terrible things? I only knew part of that. And what kind of life did Simmons and I have in the first timeline? Did we even know each other? Was I with the ECLE?

I may have died on a mission for a good cause. Or just because I was careless? Maybe Simmons was still working for Mr. Tanaka? Perhaps he and Maddy had run away somewhere?

Or the disastrous day in the park never happened.
Or they didn't know each other either.

I had so many questions that would never be answered.

We sat on the hard, dusty floor in a triangle.

Simmons had his injured leg stretched out on the floor, stroking the now sealed wound, feeling better thanks to
the irrationally large number of painkillers and Hypospray Neele had given him. Neele sat opposite us, still lost in thought. And me? I pondered things I wouldn't get
answers to. The only thing I could say for sure was that my hand had stopped twitching after touching Neele. But a small part of her pain and mine had remained. And then Simmons and Neele had reset my shoulder on the Black Talon flight. That pain was almost worse than what I felt before my amputation. This time, it wasn't phantom pain from my metal joint and amputated upper arm.

It was real, hellish pain.

As I thought about it, I stroked my joint and upper arm, and Neele woke from her thoughts. She looked at my arm, then sat up straight and explained the plan to save us, Amithayus and Seattle.
And we couldn't help but intently listen.
The plan, to put it mildly, was crazy—practically a suicide mission. But she presented it enthusiastically and packed with important details.. She had thought through every little detail countless times, and with every word from her mouth, it became clear that it might just work. But we didn't have much time; there were only three of us that had a lot to do before starting the first part of the plan.

Each of us knew that if even one aspect went wrong,
Amithayus and all of Seattle would be at the mercy of
a crazy Scientiest called Dr. Viktor Caldwell. I looked at my ComUhr. It was just after 9:00 AM. The first part of the plan would start in three hours, so I went down to the street to get us some food while the others rested.

In the morning, the Old Medical District doesn't feel as bad as it actually is...

…As I bought a row of synth dogs from a run-down stand and immediately stuffed two into my mouth. It had been over 24 hours since I had eaten; the Korean restaurant had shut down service right after our rush action, and Simmons' noodle soup had seemed suspicious even before I read the story of the Nightshades.

And much too spicy. But who knows, I didn't try it.

I strolled through the streets of the Old Medical District, trying to sort out my thoughts and all the information I
received from Neele. I sat on one of the steps leading up to an abandoned clinic and watched the few people going about their day.

It was so different here in the Old Medical. Much stranger than in Amithayus. More people greeted each other, chatted, and went about their work in Amithayus. Even though many interactions were maintained by constant vigilance of the person you were talking with. One wrong step, one wrong remark, and you could fall out of favor with the local clans.
The two faces of a person flashed through my mind. Save your own skin by offering others up. Just don't stand out negatively.

Be the whitest sheep among the white sheep.

"And here?" I asked aloud, watching an older couple arguing about something Drug releated. In the Old Medical District, it was different. Somehow, it felt more honest. Rougher. Direct. And lonely. People still feared every encounter and every spoken word. People were left alone. They withdrew and lost faith in themselves and the community. Eventually, you don't even trust yourself. The loss of humanity and the need for
cohesion stand in diagonal opposition, permeating every aspect of the streets where you survive. Everywhere, there are makeshift shelters, tent cities, and small clusters of corrugated

iron huts that barely protect from the hot daytime sun and poorly from the cool night.

"When was the last time it rained in Seattle?" I asked as I stood up, turning my gaze from all the misery and poverty.

I continued down the street on my way back to our hideout at the Serpentine House. If all the information I got from Neele was accurate, I had just pieced together a tiny fragment of the Serpentine murders in my head, even though it spanned two timelines. At least Martin Serpentine was connected to Holster Skyway. I learned from the second timeline, that he had information about Dr. Caldwell's gruesome time experiments. I didn't know what happened to the other Serpentine family— let's call them family two—but I had to assume it was similar to what happend in our timeline. "So." I had to say it aloud because it was so confusing to properly sort and articulate multi-temporal events in my brain.
"Maybe, and I'm just speculating here, Dr. Caldwell from the second timeline didn't want to repeat the same mistake as in his timeline and therefore he either gave advice to his younger Me, or did it himself. But I was quite sure that he eliminated the Serpentines from line one before the transfer of information to the younger Neele and Dr. Yoshida in my timeline occurred, with some kind of untraceable Ammunition. How he got it, I don't know. Maybe he send a pair from timeline two? Did he do it himself, or had he hired someone?"

Wow. Saying it out loud made it sound even crazier.

"Prevent an event before it happens, even though it
already did, with something that wasn't available even though it somehow was."

"You're even more messed up in the head than I am," said a short, chubby man in shabby clothes who had stood in my path intentionally. I looked at him, surprised.

I examined his entire appearance: his greasy, simple face, his jacket full of old patches, his torn, dirty jeans, and his tattered shoes with no socks.

Where did he come from?

"Give me everything you've got, or I'll cut you up," he said next, and I twisted my face into a strange grimace that was probably supposed to be a smile. Finally, I had some luck. The guy came at the right time. He pointed something at me that might have once been a pocket knife, but now looked more like a rusty piece of scrap metal.
"Uff," I pressed from my half-closed mouth. "Bad timing, wrong place, right person," I said, pulling back my trench coat with my right arm.

Polished, new standard-issue ECLE rapid-fire pistols sparkle so beautifully in the morning sun.

I saw the little man's expression shift from absolute certainty that he had chosen the right victim to fear for his meager life.
"That… uh… that wasn't meant like that. I mistook you for, uh…" he stammered. "Are you hungry?" I asked, and his face changed from sheer terror to incredulous astonishment. He probably wasn't used to being invited to eat by someone he had just threatened with death.
"Uh… yeah, kind of. I haven't had anything to eat for four days…" "Alright," I said. "You can have my two remaining synth dogs, but we need to talk about one of the patches on your jacket and the place it represents."
He nodded eagerly, and we sat on the nearest steps.
While he devoured the synth dogs with extra relish and algae mustard, I bombarded him with questions about a specific place in the Old Medical District.

The name sounded very inviting. "The Butcher's Block." Simmons would be thrilled about that.

OLD MEDICAL DISTRICT

SEVENTEEN.
COLLAPSE OF CONFORMITY

Seattle, 2066 12:15 PM – Old Medical District

"I'm supposed to go where?" Simmons asked upon learning the name of his part of the plan.
"The Butcher's Block?" He rolled his eyes. "Couldn't you find something with more class and less butchering?"

Randy had assured me that the owner of the Butcher's Block, Milo "The Knife" Kryt, was the best implant specialist in the Old Medical District.

"Randy? Who the hell is Randy?"
Before I could answer and Simmons could protest more, Neele ended our little argument. "We're doing it this way.
I rely on both of you because you know how much is at stake and will do your best. So pull yourselves together. We still have a lot to do before tonight." And with that, our argument was over. Simmons gave me a sour look, but I knew he didn't mean it.

At least, I hoped so.

In fact, further research after getting back to our hideout while we were organizing a few things we needed for our plan had reassured me about the Butcher's Block "corporate group."
Online reviews on "Stars and Gripes" were mostly positive, a rarity these days. Randy's review, with 3.5 out of 5 stars, was especially positive: "It was good, fast, and my new prints worked immediately. I would use it again."
And Willy, the chubby man with my remaining two synth dogs in his stomach, also found Milo "The Knife" Kryt competent. At

least during their last encounter, when Milo had strummed his guitar on stage with his band "Butchered Steel," prompting Willy to steal a band patch for his jacket.

What could go wrong?

So we sat on the floor again, discussing the part of the plan crucial to the main plan. Simmons had downloaded a blueprint of the Skyward Tower from the ECLE archive. Although it wasn't entirely up-to-date, Neele reported that there had been no significant renovations in the past four years at her former workplace, particularly none related to expanding the security system.
We studied the ten-year-old blueprints until Neele noticed something catapulting our plan into the second phase. After double-checking her calculations, she was
sure. Based on her results and general physics, we had a ten-second window to enter the Tower.

That would have to be enough.

We discussed the general procedure for a few more minutes and what we should do if everything went as Neele envisioned. Then, we moved on to the second part of the plan.

Neele and I had to complete our task before Simmons could start his. We had to sneak into one of the transport companies that supplied the Holster Skyward Tower daily with various chemicals. There, we needed to access one of the digital shift schedules, find a driver from the night shift, who was hopefully legally registered in Seattle under his real name, and then relay his biometric data and fingerprints to Simmons. Simmons could then begin his visit to Butcher's Block. Afterward, we, or probably just me, would visit the driver at home and neutralize him for the rest of the evening or maybe forever.

And that's what we planned as we parted ways with Simmons, who reluctantly walked towards the implant specialist. It took another hour for Neele and me to reach our destination. We had taken advantage of an UberFreedom taxi and traveled to about a block from our first target.

I declared the ride an official ECLE emergency this time, which the taxi reluctantly accepted. Neele and I had donned Urban ArmorVision suits and a complete set of operational weapons, ammunition, and communicators from the Black Talon, now lying in the Serpentines' living room. The AV suits weren't designed for combat, but rather to avoid it.

I remember playing an ancient retro game as a kid where you could camouflage yourself with a box. Were these the precursors to our suits?

The suits had become the standard infiltration tool for human operations. The major corporations had successfully sold them to various militaries and special forces, including ECLE. The suit was made of a durable, flexible fiber embedded with micro-reflectors, scattering ambient light and making it hard to spot someone.

The suits were body-hugging, with built-in tactical gear all powered by a ridiculously downsized battery that powered the system for about an hour.

Seattle, 2066, 3:27 PM – Chemical Plant 7

We approached one of the few chemical companies in Seattle that were responsible for continuously supplying the Holster Skyward Tower. It was late afternoon. The area was hectic, with lots of workers entering and leaving for their shifts. The sounds of heavy machinery echoed through the narrow street we stood on, and we had to move slowlyand in secret toward the security area of the plant.

After observing the entrance from a distance for a few minutes, I saw that two guards were manning the area.
"There are probably a few small cameras mounted here as well. That's your job, Neele." She nodded, clearly nervous. She was a young scientist visibly uncomfortable in such an environment, but she tried to mask it with some courage and a smile.

"Okay, now!" I whispered to her as we approached a small security gate as we activated our suits. Instantly, we became a strange light distortion moving toward the chemical plant. We sneaked close to the side gate, waiting for the right moment to slip inside. Our opportunity came when one of the guards left his post to light a cigarette.
We both darted through the open gate and hid behind one of the many wooden transport crates.

I had to chuckle, and for a moment, I felt the urge to use it as our cover...

Meanwhile, Neele pulled a small device from her equipment pack on her back, one of the gadgets Simmons had given her ‚ceremoniously'. He loved giving his toys away to people he did not really know. We continued sneaking through the maze of crates until we reached our target.
We moved silently on the concrete around the building, each step accompanied by a faint squelching sound from the oily film on the ground.

"In ten seconds, I'll briefly turn off the cameras; then we can move inside the building." I nodded, waiting for her to activate the device. "Three, two, one, now,"
I heard Neele say over the comms and saw the entrance camera go offline. "Quick, before they're back online."

We dashed into the dark interior of the warehouse.
After a quick look around, we reached a staircase leading to the basement. We walked down the hallway and stopped at a

small door, presumably leading to the server rooms and, thus, the digital shift schedules.

As with any semi-government building, the layout and room divisions were copied from an existing building to save costs. This one bore a striking resemblance to the ECLE building's design. I checked the digital lock on the door and attached the electronic lock picker Simmons had given me. It worked with the same precision as it did a few hours earlier. Within ten seconds, the door clicked, and it swung open.

Would'nt it be odd if a chemical company had the same security measures as the Nightshades Hideout?

We both rushed in, closing the door behind us.
It was the right room. The office was small and cluttered, with old files rotting in musty cabinets. Across the room stood several terminals, and behind a glass wall, a row of server racks filled with modern technology. A soft hum filled the room as the machines worked. Neele immediately sat at one of the terminals and began hacking the access. Her fingers flew over the keyboard while I pressed my ear to the door, ensuring we remainedundisturbed. Outside was nothing but the sounds fully automated loading machines, indicating we hadn't been discovered. After a few minutes, the terminal emitted a soft beep, confirming Neele's success.
The screen displayed a list of drivers, their shifts, and corresponding routes. We searched the database for a night-shift driver with a delivery to the Skyward Tower.

"Here, this one looks promising," Neele said, pointing to one of the names on the screen.

"John Daniels. He has a night shift delivering a large load of acetone peroxide (TATP) to the Skyward Tower. The stuff he is transporting is highly explosive when subjected to mechanical pressure and temperature changes. Plus, he lives alone on the northern edge of the Old Medical District in a rundown area that should make it easier for us to reach him unnoticed."

I nodded. "That sounds like our guy. Let's send the information to Simmons." We copied the relevant data onto a secure communication device and sent it to Simmons, who was already waiting to start his mission at the Butcher's Block. He confirmed receipt of the data with a brief thumbs-up emoji. "Almost done," Neele finally said. "Now we just need to leave here unnoticed."

"Almost done," I echoed, knowing the more challenging task lay ahead. We had completed the first part of our plan. Two more remained. We needed to delete the transport truck from the chemical plant's database and then steal the truck under the guards' noses.

"I have an idea," Neele said, typing furiously on the keyboard. She deleted the truck from today's schedule, assigning it an urgent repair appointment to be picked up from the central office in a few minutes. The directive was marked as urgent due to a technical defect in the acetone container's pump system, indicating a contamination risk. The priority level flashed red.

"Well done, Neele," I said, then read the codenames she had entered into the system for us.

"I take back the well done," I said as she grinned and stood up from the terminal chair.

"Yes, Chuck McHuge!" she giggled while I shook my head and opened the door.

We sneaked out of the office and carefully moved through the corridors back to the exit. Neele used her jammer to disable the cameras again. After leaving the building, we activated our suits, once more blending into the surroundings.

Outside, we saw the truck, which had been assigned John Daniels Profile as well as the repair directive a few minutes ago. It was lifted by a giant mechanical arm from one of the underground storage rooms. The pressure door opened, and the second part of our plan stood in front of us in all of its glory. When the mechanical arm retracted into the ground, and the pressure door underneath closed, we sprinted to the truck. We opened both doors, which were unlocked, and I sat in the driver's seat while Neele settled into the passenger seat. We removed our masks and deactivated the suits.

"Okay, Neele, we only have one shot, so let me handle the guards."

Neele nodded, and I reached up to the sun visor, catching the key card that started the truck with a single touch.
We drove around the warehouse, heading directly for the security checkpoint where the two guards had resumed their posts.

As we reached the security gate, one of the guards approached Neele's side.

Damn, I was supposed to talk to them.

Neele rolled down the window, and the guard, named John Johnston Jr., scanned one of the ID badges edge into the freight as well as the Truck itself. The other guard looked bored at the screen inside the booth. "Name and assignment?" asked John Johnston Jr., and Neele responded with a commanding tone.
"Chuck McHuge and Candy Flash from HQ over in Carpenteria. We've been here on Holiday, as we got an urgent message to pick up this truck for repairs due to a defective pump system. If we don't fix it immediately, we'll have a hell of

a mess in less than half an hour." The guard looked puzzled at Neele, who leaned out of the half-open window. She spoke with a fine texan accent.

Then he turned to his colleague, who pointed at the screen with one hand and said, "Whatever, should be fine." "It's a red alert. Let them through, Jr.," he said as the gate opened. John Johnston Jr. waved us out, and I gently maneuvered us around the corner onto the open road. The long truck was a bit different from our electric Glide emergency vehicle. I tried to navigate it as unobtrusively as possible through the streets of the Old Medical District until we reached an old warehouse on the outskirts. We parked in the shade behind the warehouse, high-fived, and walked to the front.

Two hours had passed since our last message to Simmons. Neele sent him the truck's location, to which he again replied with a short animated thumbs-up emoji.

I was slightly puzzled by Simmons' brief responses, but he was probably dozing on a cozy operating table, not wanting to be disturbed.

Neele had meanwhile called another UberFreedom taxi to take us to the last part of our plan:
John Daniels, the lone transport driver. „He will be the least of our problems tonight," I said to Neele, only to be proven wrong upon our arrival near his residence.

BLOCK 19, SETTLEMENT 5

Seattle, 2066, 7:56 PM – Block 19, Settlement 5

We stood about across the street from a medium-sized apartment block in a massive neighborhood of apartment blocks. As we stepped closer, we saw more people either arriving or leaving the gigantic party going on inside.
At first glance, I spotted around 30 people on the balconies shouting, drinking and celebrating. I looked at Neele, who stared back at me. "Damn," she said. "We're only wearing our stealth suits. That's far too conspicuous." I agreed. "We can't show up dressed like this. Oh, and so much for him living alone. A group of young adults walked over looking slightly drunk.

„What's going on tonight?" I asked them as friendly as I could.

"This is John's celebration for passing his Master of
Absolute Conformity exam. He hasn't had an accident or broken any rules or regulations in three years.
He's a real champ. So he invited everyone from work and his friends to celebrate his success tonight. By the way, how do you know him?"

"Also from work. We're his direct supervisors from HQ and wanted to congratulate him on his success," Neele replied smoothly, and the couple who had approached us and nodded in admiration.

Wow, she improvises so much better than Simmons.

I looked at the couple. What ever they where wearing, I liked it. "Yeah, am, so I have a question for you both. You're friends with John, right?" They nodded. "Okay, come here. We have a special surprise for him to celebrate his promotion." They looked at me in astonishment as I wrapped my arms around both of them, dragging them to a darker corner of the Block.

Five minutes later, we stood in somewhat tight, colourfull clothes, kindly, definitely not forcibly, lent to us by Nancy and Bill at the steps of John's Master of Absolute Conformity party.

"Are you ready?" I whispered to Neele, who looked at me and nodded. We didn't know how, but we had to isolate John from the crowd and incapacitate him for at least ten hours as quickly as possible. Or eliminate him. What ever we had to do, it needed to happen tonight.

As we entered the already open door of the Block, heavy bass waves from NeoPsy's latest song, "Gangnam Legacy," blasted through our ears.

What is it with these kids and this song?

I turned to Neele, who was slightly nodding her head. We went upstairs, and then arrived at the Appartment. The Music was blasting from the inside. As we entered, I closed the door behind me, so anyone new entering needed either a key or would have to ring the bell, thus getting our attention.

If I can hear the bell over this loud song.

I rolled my eyes, trying to spot John in the crowd. Then I realized a thing. How the hell can a simple Truck driver afford this kind of Appartment. It was a double-story, wooden floored, golden railings enclosing a giant staircase straight out the super old Titanic Movie. And this was only the upper floor we where standing on. 50 Square Meters of luxury pressed between two rooms on either side. And then, there was the downstairs part. Another hundred square meters on the lower floor, stuffed full with dancing people. We stood at the top of a railing that ran halfway around the upper floor, looking down at the crowd drinking, or whatever young people called that. I couldn't spot John in the chaos. I looked at Neele, who also shook her head. She touched the golden railing, and I could see in her facial expression that she wasn't convinced of Johns clean and mistake free image he had cultivated over the last three years.

"If we blend in with the guests, maybe we can find him and take him out unnoticed." Neele nodded as we descended the of course carpeted stairs. The deeper we went, the louder, brighter, and more noisy it became.

In front of us were at least a hundred people dancing, laughing, and snorting all sort of drugs. At the end of what, I assumed, was the living or maybe the dancing room, three more rooms branched off. One Bathroom, a single kitchen and another room with a closed door. I took the bathroom and kitchen while Neele chose the last room. We fought through the ecstatic crowd that couldn't get enough of NeoPsy.
First, I went to the kitchen. There, I saw about five middle-aged men leaning against the counter, each with a drink in hand, discussing something political and how they needed to change the world.

These are still the same topics as in my party days, decades ago.

I didn't see John among the five, so I grabbed a Coors Liberty Light beer for cover and took a sip. I shuddered internally as the warm beer slid down my throat.

How did the last two big remaining beer corporations make their best-selling brands even more disgusting...

I took another sip. Next, I headed to the bathroom for several reasons. I passed two people waiting in line who stared at me in irritation. I had no problem not achieving the Master of Absolute Conformity rank tonight, so I nodded politely, which they responded to with a pout. I opened the single door and stood before two pimped out stalls, both locked. I was irritated, to say the least. And I was baffled. In all my years as an investigator, I had never entered an apartment with two distinct, utterly over-the-top toilet stalls. Naturally, it was possible that the rich and famous had a habit of having multiple stalls for each gender—probably more for the female guests, proportional to their own increasing age. But as far as I knew, a truck driver wasn't the sort to splash out 10,000 new dollar on two mahogany toilet doors. Something really fishy was going on, and it wasn't the smell coming from one of the stalls. I knocked hard on the first door. "Hey, I gotta pee. This damn beer wants out." "Piss off, man, I'm putting on makeup." Okay, that was definitely a female voice. So, not John.

Unless he underwent gender reassignment for the occasion. Nowadays, that could be done easily and quick. But I doubt it. Conformity and all...

I moved to the second stall and pounded on the door.
"Hey, open up, man. I need to unload. Or I'll ruin John's nice hard wooden floor."
I listened and heard a female and a male giggling from the stall.

Okay, two people. One of them could be John. There were only four people in the bathroom, including me.
I could handle that. But how do I get him out unseen?

Or I could seal off the bathroom due to a major accident. Rules and all, you know. Accident risk...

I pounded on the door again, even harder.
"Leave us alone! We're fucking! Or at least, we are trying to, okay! And if you find John, tell him I didn't ruin his floor."
"Jack, what the hell. I just dolled up for you, you asshole. And you're screwing some other bitch at the party."
A furious scream emerged from the first stall.
"Oh, shit, Jill. Uh..."

I stepped back as Jill stormed out of the first stall, her lipstick smeared across her face. She pounded furiously on the second door, from which panicked cries emerged.

I slowly backed out of the bathroom, closing the door behind me. I nodded to the two waiting people, who stared at the door and then at me in shock. "Might take a while; better grab another drink."

So John wasn't downstairs. I headed toward the third room, from which Neele emerged, her face a mix of shocked emotions. "Did you find him?" I asked. She shook her head, eyes wide. "No, but what kind of sick guy is John?"
I stared at her.
"The whole room was bathed in red light. Besides a bunch of candles, there were countless Christian symbols on the walls. You know, Crucifixes, rosaries, Bibles. Whips, chains, and shackles. In the middle was an altar that doubled as a bed with restraints, on which two people lay intertwined, spanking each other with biblical verses and real world things."

That's what I suspected. To hell with the Master of Conformity.

Neele took a big gulp of my Coors Liberty Light, which she had snatched from my hand. "Ugh, this stuff is undrinkable when warm," she said, taking another big gulp.

"And is John in that room?" I asked as she handed me the empty beer. "No. I asked them. The woman said she was Maria, and the guy said he was Joseph. And yes, I know how dumb that sounds. But they said it with such conviction that I believed them." I nodded slightly in disbelief. „But John must be here somewhere."

We need to find him as quickly as possible," I said, handing the empty bottle to a guy dancing next to us, who responded with, "Nice, thanks," and started sucking on the empty bottle. I shook my head, looking at Neele as the doorbell rang.

My plan had worked. We both stared up at the door.It rang a second time, much longer than the first.
There, to the left, from the first of the two rooms upstairs, a half-naked, disheveled figure staggered out, wobbling toward the ringing. That was John. His face resembled the one we saw on the screen at his work, only with more infused drugs and bloated like crazy. I glanced at Neele, who had also focused in on John. He opened the door, and a delivery boy stood with a giant portion of Nightshade Noodles. The extra spicy version.

From then on, I had a plan.

But we had to be quick. I grabbed Neele's hand, and we ran toward the stairs. "Hey everyone, look who's here. A cool delivery boy with a Stack of Nightshade Noodles. The Extra Spicy Version!" I yelled to get everybodies attention over the loud music.

The crowd started to cheer and scream. I didn't know if they were hungry or craving more drugs. Or both. But this was our chance. I ran up the stairs with Neele in tow,
stopping in front of the delivery boy and John, who was taking a box from the top. "Hello, John," I said in the the most resounding voice I could muster, and John stopped mid-motion, looking at me with a puzzled, dopey expression.

"Uh..." he said, and I saw from his expression that he had no idea who we were, why we were wearing this tight clothes, or what we wanted from him. "Hi, uh, who are you two?" John asked, visibly confused.
"This here," I gestured toward Neele, "is my lovely colleague Candy Flash, and I'm Chuck McHuge. We came from HQ to

your party with great news and a surprise for your promotion." I saw John try to straighten up, maintaining the appearance of conformity. Behind my back, I signaled Neele to grab two of the Plastic Noodle cups from the stack and unscrew the powdery 'special sauce compartment' in the bottom. "Oh, so that's it. Yes, uh, hello. I, uh, I'm pleased that someone so high-ranking is at my party." "For a new Master of Conformity, we're happy to do a little overtime. Right, Candy?" "Always a pleasure," Neele nodded, bowing slightly as she unscrewed the cups' bottoms.

"So, John. Shall we go to a quieter room to discuss the fortunate events and your surprise?"
"Uh, sure. Of course, Mister Huge." "McHuge," I corrected him, taking his noodle box. "Lead the way, John, like a
shepherd guiding a new lamb." "Of course, this way."
He bowed slightly, focused on the noodles, and turned around, leading us to the door while remaining in a hunched position.

Internally, I was disgusted. It was so easy? A bit of God here, a bit of false rank there, and he was eating out of my hand.
Soon, hopefully literally.

While walking, I glanced at Neele, who had opened the cups and held a significant amount of cocaine in her hands. She opened the packages, and we poured them into the noodle box I had taken from John. Meanwhile, I opened the third cup and mixed the powder with the extra spicy Special sauce in as well. I took the chopsticks and stirred the powder into the sauce. Neele tossed the remaining noodle cups into the cheering crowd behind, making their way upstairs.

As we entered one of the two rooms, I saw the crowd swarm the delivery boy, ripping the cups from his hands like ravenous jackals. The poor kid. He hadn't anticipated his evening going this way.

Neele quietly closed the door behind us. Before us was a large, dark bedroom lit by candles and dim lampshades made of heavy, dark fabric, burgundy in color, barely letting light through. The little candlelight cast waving shadows on the paintings on the walls, primarily baroque landscapes, distorted gothic faces, and religious symbols cultivated over hundreds of years. A spacious balcony, partially visible through a heavy, yet translucent dark curtain at the back wall, revealed hints of the metal railing beyond.In the middle of the room stood a large bed draped in heavy burgundy velvet, its massive wooden frame intricately carved with swirling baroque patterns. The tall, ornately crafted headboard rose like a dark wave behind the bed, while thick, tasselled ropes held the velvet canopy above. Scattered across the bed were silk cushions in deep shades of red and gold, and at its foot, a heavy fur throw added a touch of opulence. Set up around the bed were three old video cameras and a lot of toys, all somehow related to Christianity and its symbolism. On the bed lay a very young woman. Perhaps a child. It was dark, and her face was turned the opposite way. I couldn't tell. She wore a short dress made of white chains, reminiscent of the Pope's clerical robe.

Upon closer inspection, the young girl appeared unconscious or dead. At the bed's foot was a small nightstand with various vials of clear liquids.

Fuck, what is this shit?

"So, Master McHuge, what's my wonderful surprise for my promotion to Conformity Master?" John asked, making me want to shove the noodles into his disgusting face.

I finally understood what "Conformity Master" meant in this context. This was a completely insane, fundamentalist Christian cult naming its member ranks after various
compliant groups. Conformity Master. Bullshit.
You're about to feel real conformity.

I approached him slowly, one arm opening wide as if inviting him into an embrace, while the other held the noodle box right before his face. „Eat, my child," I said, offering the cup. „Take this as a gift from HQ, a symbol of my affection and the body of the reborn Christ. As He shared His bread with His disciples, I now share this noodle cup with you." I paused dramatically. „And then, Sister Candy will present your promotion surprise."

John's eyes lit up. He greedily grabbed the noodles, shoveling with his bare hands portion after portion into his wide-open mouth. As he chewed and shoved, he tried to thank us. "Ets" – next portion – "a schwelly big, onor," – chomp – "dat you are emf schwisiting me," – next portion – "this evening as my honorable guest." He started choking. Neele and I bowed slightly before him, which he responded to with a more profound bow, dragging the next portion of spicy noodles across his face into his mouth. The red spicy sauce dripped from his cheeks as he chewed and swallowed, remaining in the deep bow. When he finished the entire box, he licked his lips.

He was a bootlicker of the highest order. I expected nothing less. Any second now and he should feel the Effect.

John snapped upright, and I saw the cocaine take effect. His eyes were huge, his pupils barely visible. Spit and spicy sauce dribbled from his mouth. I saw his muscles start to cramp, sweat beading on his forehead. His posture slowly collapsed from upright as he stumbled backward. His arms flailed wildly around his body, foam spilling from his mouth. His stature slowly crumpled even further backward as he tried to grab the bed with his waving hands. He crashed headfirst into the large bed and then slowly slid down it, unable to hold on due to his convulsions. His eyes darted wildly in their sockets, and he tried to force a few last words from his mouth. Neele and I slowly approached him. Then we leaned down toward him.

„Wargegsdbfsfldsfööldf." In one or the other way, we had completed our mission. The last thing I heard was a faint squeak from his mouth before his heart stopped beating.

We had killed John. It was more than we had planned, and I knew we had just opened the door to another hell. I had to tell Simmons about this. This group, of which we had only seen the tip of the iceberg, had widespread influence in Seattle and possibly beyond.

Neele looked at me with a mix of shock and understanding, and I knew I could trust her from now on. She had realized the murder was justified. We had done the wrong thing for the right reasons. Just like Simmons and Maddy years ago. We shed our disguise as Bill and Nancy donned our masks and activated the light-breaking ArmorVision suits.

Then we blended into the rays of the setting sun as we jumped off the balcony, leaving this godless place behind. In the dark bedroom lay two dead people: an unknown child on the bed and John, covered in red foam, dead on the floor. On his bare chest lay Sister Candy Flash's parting gift:

A delayed communicator, set to activate late in the night, sent its emergency signal to the OLD District Guardians. With any luck, they'd arrive in the dead of night to find the whole mess waiting for them. I could already envision the fleet of vehicles closing in on John's apartment. A fitting gift for his promotion and indeed, the beginning of the downfall of whatever John and these Masters of Conformity, or whatever they are called, had been plotting all along.

OLD MEDICAL DISTRICT

EIGHTEEN.
IMPLANTS AND INTRIGUES

Seattle, 2066, 4:30 PM - Old Medical District, Butcher's Block

Simmons was still unconvinced about his role in the plan as he separated from Neele and his partner and marched toward the implant shop in the Old Medical District. The streets were narrow and crowded with old, dilapidated buildings. Debris and junk littered the ground, and the air was thick with exhaust fumes and the stench from nearby industrial areas. Graffiti covered the walls of the buildings, and broken windows revealed abandoned interiors.

He knew he had no other choice. The plan depended on him transferring the fingerprints and access data of the
delivery man, which would appear on his communicator within the next hour, onto himself. And for that, he had to seek out Milo "The Knife" Kryt. The name of the implant technician was known to him from various files in the ECLE archive, but he couldn't put a face to it.
Most of what he had read was related to illegal operations and shady deals in different districts of Seattle.
He felt uneasy as he walked down the street, but he also knew that if anyone could forge biometric data and transfer it to another person, it was Milo. Especially now, without an appointment and in the deserted Old Medical District.

After three-quarters of an hour, he reached a dingy alley where a flickering sign pointed the way to the Butcher's Shop. Simmons turned the corner and followed the
convoluted signs also advertising various other presumably illegal businesses besides the implant shop.

There were some other small, quite patriotic shops in the narrow alley, right next to the Butcher's Shop, where he now stood lighting another synth cigarette.

Among them were Patriot Pawn & Loans – Individual Freedom on Credit, Liberty Liquor Lounge, which offered freedom in a glass, and Bald Eagle Barbershop, which promised the freedom of male hair for a hefty sum.

Simmons was no longer surprised by anything; he knew his fellow citizens loved freedom more than anything else. Simmons growled at himself as he threw the half-smoked cigarette to the ground. He looked at his ComUhr, which had just received a message with the attached data. He skimmed the message and checked the
attachment. Everything was ready for his transformation. In a few minutes, he would be John Daniels. A well-trained worker who followed the rules and didn't question anything.

He sighed loudly as he approached the Butcher's Shop.
The place looked like a cross between an old shop and a high-tech lab. Above the door hung a rusty sign that read "Butcher's Shop Solutions." An old, worn-out brass gong announced his arrival as he opened the door.
The shop's interior was dimly lit and crammed. Old, dusty technology that glowed in various colors.
Old computers and monitors flickered in the dim light.
The floor was covered with a sticky film, and the smell of chemicals and rotting flesh hung in the air. Simmons
swallowed hard to suppress his disgust.

The flickering light cast eerie shadows on the walls, and the hum of the machines created an uninviting
atmosphere. Precisely what he had expected.
Immediately, a figure emerged from the haze and
semi-darkness. That must be Milo. He was smaller than Simmons had expected, with a wiry build and a face

marked by countless healed scars. His eyes, showing slight modifications, sparkled intelligently but also dangerously. His hair was short and gray, and he wore a dirty leather apron that made him look like a butcher.
Simmons took another deep breath. If he were here in his official role as an ECLE investigator, he would have shut down the entire shop long ago. But this time he had to play along. He approached the man standing before him.

"What can I do for you?" asked the man, who had introduced himself as Milo Kryt, with a grin that looked more like a predator's than a human's. His teeth were snow-white and covered with various implants, and his canines were incredibly sharp and made of metal. He had a rough, hoarse voice.

"I have fingerprints and eye scans that I need to be implanted," Simmons said, taking a deep breath.
"And it has to be quick. Today, preferably right now."

Milo nodded slowly, as if weighing the words.
"Speed costs extra. Let's see the Data."

Simmons handed him a small chip he took from his ComUhr. Milo inserted it into one of the old computers and reviewed the data. Simmons heard occasional words coming from Milo's direction. "Interesting." "Ah, that could work." and "Yes, we'll do it that way."

Meanwhile, Simmons let his gaze wander around the room. Everywhere, there were surgical tools and vials with unknown content. In one corner of the room another customer lay on one of the two chairs resembling a reclined gynecologist's chair. A shady looking, very muscular man undergoing a grotesque body modification.
His right arm was being transformed into a metallic prosthesis twice the size of his other arm. The man had a chiseled face and short-cropped hair. Several of his facial muscles twitched

with each tiny movement of the mechanical arm, using various tools to connect tendons and veins with the metal. His eyes were cold and calculating, and it was obvious that he had been through many fights.

You can already take a seat, John Daniels," said Milo into the room without looking up from his monitors. Simmons caught the emphasis on *John Daniels* as he sat down, watching Milo prepare various devices. Among them were several vials of different-colored liquids that he didn't recognize.
There were surgical tools and various-sized blades on the aluminum tables around him everywhere. It was a
grotesque scene, but matched what he had heard about Milo.

In the meantime, Milo stood up, took a new data chip he had loaded with the processed biometric eye scans, and inserted it into the slot of a complex device that looked like a cross between a 3D printer and a microscope.
The device immediately began processing the data and projected a three-dimensional model of the iris onto a small, flickering screen.

With calm and precise movements, Milo aimed the device at a small gel-filled chamber. This chamber was
designed to shape biocompatible materials that would later serve as implants. The device began applying delicate layers of a transparent, flexible material that could
replicate the iris' exact structure and color gradients.

A soft, steady hum filled the room as the 3D bioprinter did its work. The material was extruded through a fine nozzle and immediately hardened using UV light. Layer by layer the implant took shape, accurately reproducing even the tiniest details and individual color variations.

Milo monitored the process attentively, occasionally
adjusting the settings to ensure perfect results.

After about 10 minutes, the implant was finished.
Milo carefully removed the completed piece from the chamber and placed it in a sterile solution to prepare it for the next step.

Then he picked up a fine laser. "Now, let's do the rough work first, John." He sat beside Simmons on a squeaky swivel chair and pressed Simmons' head against the headrest. Simmons hands were put into hand grips attached to the chair. It was so tight that he could hardly feel anymore. "Don't move now, or it won't work," Milo said as he fiddled with the apparatus and adjusted the wattage of the laser beam needed to burn the fingerprints onto Simmons' fingertips. Simmons gritted his teeth and held still as the pain shot through his left hand and then his right. From Simmons' position, he couldn't see much more than small puffs of smoke rising, but the smell of his skin burning in microscopic parts filled his nose immediately.
The pain induced nausea, and he felt himself becoming increasingly sick. Milo worked quickly and precisely, and the procedure was completed within minutes.
"See, it wasn't so bad," he said as he placed the laser back in its holder.

"Fuck," Simmons shouted with all his pent-up anger,
trying to subdue the intense pain with mere words.
"What kind of shit is this," was followed by
"I'll kill him when I see him later." "Yes, I hear that a lot here. But it's usually directed at me," Milo said as he stood up.

Simmons' muscles trembled as he pulled his hands out of the hand grip openings in the chair and half-sat up, staring at his fingertips. They were slightly reddened, and the whole room reeked of burnt flesh. Simmons wasn't sure if it was from him or the muscular guy in the other chair.
Milo had gone over to him and examined the progress of his procedure more closely. He nodded and bent over certain parts of the arm in the dim light. "Yes, that looks good. A few more minutes, and you can use it." The muscular man only let out a

low grunt. He had his eyes closed and endured the procedure without any further reaction of his muscles.

"And now we move on to your new eyes," Milo said, taking another device that looked like a mix of a futuristic ophthalmologist's instrument and a highly advanced surgical tool. It was enormous and consisted of many small parts, which he pulled down to him via a metal arm attached to a rail and then positioned over Simmons' head.
He slowly lowered the apparatus and attached it to Simmons' eyes, gently holding the eyelids open with cold, metallic clamps. Simmons' vision was immediately engulfed by the bright light of the apparatus. A soft hum began as the device was activated.

Milo reached for a small container that held the previously manufactured eye scans stored in a sterile solution.
He opened the container with precise, calm movements and took the delicate, transparent pieces that looked like tiny lenses with a long metal tweezer.
He placed the lenses on a special device holder, ready to apply the implants to Simmons' eyes.

"And now, hold still. The worst part is almost over,"
Milo muttered as he made fine adjustments to the device.
A soft click indicated that the device was ready, and the fine laser beam began scanning the surface of Simmons' eyes. It felt like tiny, burning needle pricks dancing across his retinas. The pain was overwhelming, seemingly
shooting through his entire body as the precise patterns of the biometric scans were prepared.

Milo slowly lowered the holder until the lenses rested on Simmons' eyes. Another laser beam began, fusing the lenses to the cornea and fixing them in the correct position. Each pulse of the laser was like a stab to the eye, and Simmons gritted his teeth to avoid screaming again. The light of the apparatus was blindingly bright, and he couldn't think of anything else but how it would feel when he finally placed his new fingertips around his partner's neck and squeezed…

He shouted again, and a surge of tears flowed uncontrollably from Simmons' eyes, burning salty on his battle wounded skin. Milo, completely unfazed, wiped the tears with a sterile cloth and collected them in one of the small vials. "That's normal," Milo said coolly, storing the liquid next to a few other vials. "By the way, John, did you know that real tear fluid fetches a high price on the black market these days? Especially when it comes from real humans and isn't synthetic." Simmons considered whether he should place his hands around Milo's neck - after all, he now had new fingerprints that couldn't be traced back to him…

Simmons felt the cold of the metal plates and the foreign body sensation of the lenses, but above all, it was the burning, stabbing pain that nearly drove him insane.
The procedure took several minutes, but it seemed like an eternity for Simmons. Finally, the humming of the device stopped, and the blinding light went out. Milo removed the apparatus and clamps, and Simmons could still feel the cold metal plates that had held his eyelids open for a few more seconds. He tried to see something, but he was
surrounded by pure darkness. So he closed his eyelids, which sent another wave of pain through his body.

"For the next two hours, you'll be blind," Milo explained, carefully rechecking the position of the lenses.
"After that, your vision will gradually return to normal." Simmons was furious but nodded. He keept his eyes closed and breathed heavily and irregularly.
The procedure was over, but the pain still echoed in his head.

At that moment, there was a massive bang, and the shop door slammed against the wall with such force that it shattered into hundreds of tiny glass and wood fragments. Several members of a local gang stormed into the small shop. They were heavily armed and wore the typical leather jackets of a gang, adorned with sharp metal spikes and colorful markings.

The leather jackets gleamed oily in the room's dim light, and the metal spikes reflected the neon colors from outside. Their faces were covered in crude, warlike tattoos, and their eyes sparkled with unbridled rage.

"There you are, you traitor!" yelled one of the gang members, a burly guy with a skull-like tattoo on his forehead, pointing at the muscular man with the metal prosthesis. "Time to kill you once and for all."

The rest of the gang members quickly spread out in the room, ensuring no one could escape. They pulled heavy shotguns, rusty knives, and improvised weapons made from metal pipes and chains from under their jackets.

"Not again," muttered Milo, grabbing a scalpel, his hand trembling slightly. "Can't you do this in another shop, like the bar around the corner?"

Simmons nearly fell as he tried to get up off the chair, still utterly blind from the eye scans. He heard the sound of footsteps and the clicking of weapons, instinctively feeling the impending danger in the air.

"What do you want from me?" he asked, trying to grasp his surroundings. "Stay out of this, asshole!" was the only response he got. "I could do that, but there's only one exit, and unfortunately, you're standing in front of it," Simmons said as he got up. "So, once again, what do you want?"

"Stay quiet, John," Milo called out, having retreated to one of the darker corners of his shop.

"The guy with the metal arm used to be one of them but then switched sides. Now they want him dead," Milo explained hastily, raising his scalpel a bit higher.

„Oh, the werent here because of him?" Simmons heard a soft clicking sound behind him, followed by several metallic squeaks The man with the metal prosthesis had risen ready for combat beside Simmons. His eyes were focused, his jaw muscles tense.
"By the way, my name is Rust," he said briefly in Simmons' direction before sprinting towards the first gang member.

"Uh, John," Simmons murmured as he heard the gang members im his direction as well. Simmons barely managed to dodge as a knife whizzed past his face and clanged against one of the aluminum tables. He felt his other senses sharpening and tried to focus on hearing.
The footsteps of the attackers, the rustling of their clothing, and the clinking of metal spikes created a chaotic
soundscape that he began to decipher.

"I can't see anything," Simmons said, pulling his weapon from under his clothes. He squeezed the trigger of his gun – and nothing happened. Simmons cursed inwardly. The ECLE weapons were equipped with fingerprint sensors that ensured they could only be used by authorized personnel. His fingerprint was no longer his own but that of John Daniels. How could he have forgotten that?

"Damn it!" he swore loudly, shaking the gun in his hand as if that would change anything. Then he threw it in the
direction where he suspected the gang members to be.
It landed with a clatter a short distance from the burly guy and lay there in the stirred-up dust.

The massive guy with the skull-like tattoo laughed derisively. "What's the matter, little man? Are your toys broken?"

He looked at the gun more closely and realized it was an official ECLE weapon. Then he pointed his shotgun at Simmons. "You're a cop, aren't you? Time to kill you, too."

The other gang members laughed and rushed at Rust and Milo. Simmons heard the sound of weapons being readied, the clicking of triggers, and the crunching of heavy boots on the floor.

Two of the gang members broke away from the primary fight and charged at Simmons. "We need to work together," he called to Rust, who was already engaged in a fierce battle with the attackers. Rust nodded and positioned himself to protect Simmons if necessary.

"Rust?" Simmons called again, and finally, Rust responded with something other than a nod. "Sorry, I forgot you're blind."

A gang member lunged at Simmons, who blindly grabbed for an object and got hold of the laser that had just been used to apply his new fingerprints. He remembered that Milo had fiddled with a power knob and instinctively turned it to maximum. Simmons activated the laser and swung it wide around him as the first attacker came close enough. A shrill scream rang out as the laser beam sliced through the attacker's arm, almost expertly severing it. The attacker's weapon, still clutched in his hand, fell, clattering to the ground. The now armless attacker stumbled backward and collapsed.

The second attacker hesitated only for a moment before charging at Simmons again. Simmons heard the swish of a blade through the air and ducked just in time to avoid a deadly strike. With a more targeted thrust, Simmons used the laser and hit the attacker in the side. He then dragged the laser forward, cutting through the man, who fell backward in two parts. The last thing Simmons heard was the attacker's groan before he heard two almost simultaneous, fleshy thuds on the floor.

Simmons heard the other attackers still fighting and grabbed blindly for one of the fallen weapons.
He found the cold metal surface of a double-barreled shotgun and picked it up. He felt its weight in his hand and held it firmly before him, ready for the next attack.

Another gang member charged at him, and Simmons could hear the footsteps and rustling of clothing.
He raised the shotgun and fired without hesitation.
A dull thud and a squishy noise, followed by a scream, told him he had hit his target. The shotgun had only two shots, and the second attacker was already on his way. Simmons turned to the second attacker and fired again. With another squishy noise and a dull thud, the attacker exploded into pieces on the floor.

Simmons heard the other attackers still fighting and grabbed a knife lying on the ground. He felt the cold blade and held it tightly.

Rust, meanwhile, fought like a berserker, his metal prosthesis flashing in the dim light of the room. He struck one attacker with the prosthesis, whose skull shattered into pieces with a loud crack. Another powerful blow and another gang member was hurled against the wall.

Milo, still holding the scalpel, dodged an attack and, with a precise swipe, cut the attacker's main artery in his arm.
The man screamed and stumbled back, blood splattering on the floor. "Why are you attacking me? I have nothing to do with this," Milo shouted, looking around hastily.

Simmons heard the steps of another attacker behind him and quickly turned around, the knife firmly in his hand. He swung it in a wide arc and felt the blade hit metallic resistance. He

instinctively ducked and heard a metallic whir pass by his head. Then he stabbed directly forward and slightly upward, hitting the opponent right in the neck. A gurgling scream filled the room as the attacker
fell heavily to the ground.

Rust took the opportunity and slammed his metal
prosthesis into the head of the following gang member he was grappling with, sending him crashing to the floor, where he lay motionless. "One more," Rust called, his voice tense.

Finally, the burly gang leader joined the fight.
He drew a long, sharp knife and charged at Simmons. Simmons heard the swish of the knife in the air and stepped back. He felt the knife graze his jacket and cut through it. He heard the gang leader's growl. "Die now, pig," he hissed as he raised his blade again.

Simmons used the brief pause to scan his surroundings.
He heard the heavy breathing and the crackling of the
leather jacket. With a quick, determined strike, he used the knife and hit the gang leader in the arm, causing him to drop his own knife. The burly guy groaned and stumbled back.

Rust grabbed him from behind and smashed his metal arm into the gang leader's face with full force.
The bones cracked under the impact, and the burly guy groaned one last time before collapsing. His face was
utterly crushed under the force of the blow.

Finally, calm returned to the Butcher's Shop. Breathing heavily and drenched in sweat, Simmons and Rust stood amidst the slain gang members. Milo, who had turned pale, wiped the sweat from his forehead and lowered the scalpel.

"You saved my life," Rust said, panting, and extended his hand to Simmons. "I owe you one."

Simmons, still blind, nodded and reached for Rust's hand. "That was damn close," he murmured, feeling the adrenaline slowly subside. "Thank you for your help."

„No problem," Rust replied with a weak smile.
„We should get out of here before more of them show up."

„You'd better leave quickly. I have a few small surgeries to perform before I can reopen my shop to new customers," Milo said, turning the sign that still hung on the shattered door from open to closed. „Oh, by the way, John. You're one lucky guy. Today's surgeries are on the house. Let's call it a *cop security discount*."

Simmons smiled slightly as he cautiously felt his way out of the bloody room. Fumbling along the ground with both hands, finally picking up his non-functioning ECLE pistol from the dust, tucking it into the holster under his tattered jacket. Rust helped him navigate the broken furniture and scattered weapons. He placed a hand on Simmons' shoulder and guided him safely through the narrow alleys of the Old Medical Distric.
Along the way, Simmons' communicator vibrated, and he received a message from Neele. Despite his still limited vision and his aching fingertips, he typed back an animated thumbs-up emoji.

Simmons' vision became a little clearer with each step, and the dim outlines of the buildings and piles of trash around him began to sharpen. Night had fallen, and only the faint light of the few functioning streetlights illuminated the paths. The sounds of distant sirens and occasional screams echoed through the alleys, but Rust and Simmons
continued on their way.

"I don't usually help cops," Rust murmured, and Simmons' muscles tensed momentarily. "But you're different. You saved my life."

Simmons nodded slightly, his vision still blurry, but he could hear the sincerity in Rust's voice. "Sometimes life brings strange allies together."

Rust laughed dryly. "Yeah, it does. I used to be with the Razors. Thought I could make a difference, make a change. But everyone is the same, no matter which gang you join. Violence, power, and betrayal within the ranks.
So I got out and tried to make it on my own."

Simmons listened attentively as they walked. "What brought you back to the Old Medical District tonight?"

Rust sighed deeply. "I didn't have my prosthesis put on voluntarily. It was a damn ambush by the Razors when they found out I wanted to leave. They cut off my arm and left me to die. I never wanted to see them again, but I had to return to get something that was mine.
Something I couldn't leave behind."

Simmons felt a pain in his chest as he thought of Maddy. "And what was that?" Rust hesitated for a moment before answering. "The most important thing of all. My self-worth. You cannot work as a mercenary for hire without a second arm" Simmons nodded understandingly. "But all I found tonight was more death – and you."

They walked silently for a while, accompanied only by the rustling of trash and the occasional squeak of rats. Finally, Rust stopped and placed a hand on Simmons' shoulder. "This is where we part ways," he said earnestly, looking at Simmons. "You saved my life. And I don't forget things like that. If you ever need my help, I owe you."

Simmons nodded, his vision almost fully restored. "Thank you, Rust. I'll remember that."

Rust nodded and disappeared into one of the dark alleys, his metal prosthesis briefly reflecting the faint light of a streetlamp before he vanished into the shadows.

The same fate that awaited Seattle, Simmons thought as he continued on his way, calling for a UberFreedom Taxi.

ABANDONED WAREHOUSE

NINETEEN.
UNDERGROUND MOVEMENTS

Seattle, 2066 21:56 - Abandoned Warehouse

Neele and I arrived at our meeting point an hour after our encounter with John Daniels. We had crept through the narrow alleys in the dark with our ArmorVision suits activated. As we moved further into the shadows of the blockhouses away from the party, we found it hard to forget what we had seen there. Eventually, we took an UberFreedom taxi for the rest of the way. We had stumbled upon something that definitely smelled like a big deal.

Damn Christian sects. Few things could throw me off balance, but religion, especially fundamentalist offshoots that claimed a higher moral authority and then did whatever they wanted, under that guise, was one such thing. I was sure we had to follow up on this. In my head, I have already prepared the entry in the ECLE database and the following case file. Simmons would surely agree that getting to the bottom of this was essential, and right once he arrived here.

It felt strange that he had only responded with animated emojis. While I was used to his brief and concise writing style, he only replied so curtly in exceptional cases.
By now, another ten minutes had passed, and he still hadn't shown up yet. I was starting to worry. Neele leaned against the transporter we had moved forward and was now parked slightly out of sight of passersby, who occasionally walked by on the opposite side of the street in the abandoned warehouse. She had rechecked everything in the last few minutes: the tank levels of the acetone peroxide – enough for our plan; the ID

badges; the tire wear; the height of the vehicle compared to the entrance height of the Skyward Tower's underground garage, concluding everything was ready.

Except for Simmons. Since then, she had leaned against the transporter, nervously looking out into the dark night, just like me.

Where was he? And what had he been doing in the Butcher's Shop? But he had confirmed that everything was going according to Neele's plan.
Then I heard a car stopping somewhere close to us. A slammed door later, someone crossed the street.

Was that Simmons? I couldn't tell for sure; it was too dark, and the dim lighting that protected us from overly curious eyes was now working against us. I put my hand on my ECLE revolver and slowly drew it. Neele had also noticed the person slowly shuffling onto our premises, creeping behind the transporter and remaining unseen. I knelt down and held my weapon at the ready.

The stranger was smoking and flicked his synth cigarette high into the air. Just as it landed with a spark, the person said,
"Hey, where are you two? My communicator says this is the meeting point."

It was Simmons. I put my weapon back in the holster.

"Don't shout like that, or do you want to alert everyone around here?" I shouted back, causing Neele to shake her head.

Simmons quickly approached us and stopped just in front of me. "Okay, I spent the whole long walk back thinking about how I'm going to strangle you. I went over every
little detail, imagining you whimpering in the dirt in front of me, my hands tightening around your neck until I

realized one thing. My damn fingers hurt so much from having the new fingerprints burned on that I'd probably hurt myself more than you. So, I'm not going to do it now. But I won't forget. Do you hear me? I'll get back to you." I smiled at him. I really missed the bickering between the both of us.

"Wow, okay, I'm sorry, Sims," I said, while putting my arm around him, guiding him towards the warehouse. I felt him slap the back of my head with his palm of the hand, and I heard a soft whimper of pain. I couldn't help but chuckle softly as we walked together towards Neele.

I knew precisely how painfully shitty finger and eye-Implantation were. That's why I volunteered for the other part of the plan.

Apparently, his evening had gone as badly as ours. I told him what we had experienced and about creating a new ECLE case file, and he agreed on all points. Then he told me about his last few hours and how he, blinded, took out an entire gang with the help of a certain Rust at the Butcher's Shop and that his ECLE gun was now useless to him. I wasn't sure who had the worst evening, so we called it a draw.

Neele had changed while I had my short argument with Sims. She handed us the disguises for the next, and probably the hardest, part of our plan. All of it was stored in an extra compartment on the inside of the Truck. She wore most of her usual suit, which she had been wearing all day, and had explained to me over the evening what it was: a prototype HELPS lab suit equipped with a somewhat—let's call it—limited AI.

Over her HELPS suit, she wore an additional layer identifying her as a member of the Pacific Commonwealth's emergency unit. This layer consisted of a distinctive black vest with light blue stripes that became visible when illuminated. The official logo of the Pacific Commonwealth, a stylized wave pattern symbolizing the coastline, was emblazoned on the front and back of the vest. Various pouches and holders hung at her side, containing multiple emergency tools and a mini-drone with cameras. A multifunctional rescue knife dangled from her belt, and her helmet, equipped with an integrated communication device and visor, was ready in her backpack.

As she explained the plan for the evening again, I put on the emergency gear over the ArmorVision suit I was already wearing. Simmons donned one of the official chemical transporter suits we found in the cab. We both understood the procedure, and just as we finished our disguises, she completed her last sentence.

"...this won't be easy, but once we're out of there, we'll have a much better chance of stopping his plan." We nodded at her as the three of us entered the transporter cab.

Simmons started the electric motor and then met our eyes one more time. "We're going to make it. Did you hear me? Get in, execute the plan, and get out as fast as possible without us getting hurt tonight." Simmons said. "Did you hear me? No solo actions, you don't separate from each other, and Neele's plan will work. We will make it," adding another point to emphasize his stance.

I wanted so much to believe that we would make it. But so many things within the plan could go wrong, so much that wasn't predictable.

I briefly thought about my last mission with the special unit, where I had become negligent due to my sense of omnipotence from my ability, losing my arm and almost all my comrades as a result. I couldn't afford to let that happen again, especially not tonight when so many more lives were at stake than just ours.

Simmons turned onto the street that lead us the highway, taking us from the Old Medical District via a few detours directly onto South Orcas Street and then straight into the heart of new Seattle, towards Downtown Beacon Hill and the immediate vicinity of the tower.

The silence in the vehicle was palpable; each of us lost in our thoughts. The streetlights passed by in a steady rhythm, casting a rhythmic play of light and shadow through the transporter's windows. It was so peacefully quiet out there, the first time in what felt like two days that the scum spreading increasingly in Seattle didn't want to massacre, slit, shoot, drown, pierce, or otherwise annihilate us.

Simmons focused on the road ahead, his hands gripping the steering wheel. I sat silently beside him in the cab, each of us nervous but also focused.
The tension was almost tangible, the silence broken only by the quiet hum of the motor and the tires' noise on the asphalt. Neele turned on her communicator, and we listened to the latest news from Amithayus during the ride.

The situation there had deteriorated further since our successful escape within the last eight hours. We had clicked through several channels, but the only ones voluntarily reporting on the situation were the patriotic Freedom Broadcast Coalition channel, a merger of the remnants of Fox News, Newsmax TV, and the OAN Network.

"Good evening, ladies and gentlemen! This is a special broadcast of the FBC News Network, live from our studio in the Pacific Commonwealth. I am your fearless news anchor, Alex Turner, and we bring you the latest heroic developments from Amithayus!"

"In the last eight hours, the situation in Amithayus has escalated to a dramatic and unavoidable climax. What started as a targeted operation to restore law and order has evolved into a glorious and vital civil war. Our brave private armies, dispatched to bring law to the lawless streets of Amithayus, are now facing a united horde of gangs and rioters who seek nothing but pure chaos."

"The battles rage in several key areas, including the entire Japanese and Korean district with its strategically important port. These districts, notorious for their criminal activities and their disgraceful support for the
insurgents, are now the scene of intense and heroic battles. Eyewitnesses report thunderous explosions and determined gunfire as our world-renowned private armies advance relentlessly to eradicate the scum once and for all."

"All border crossings to Amithayus are now entirely and rigorously closed. The Tri-state government of the
glorious Pacific Commonwealth has ordered a strict and determined lockdown of the city to prevent the spread of unrest. Military roadblocks and unwavering checkpoints have been established on all access roads.
No one is allowed to enter or leave the district to ensure no insurgent can escape."

"Our brave reporters were unfortunately unable to enter Amithayus due to strict security measures, as everything is exemplary sealed off. The information we receive is based on the heroic reports of our steadfast soldiers and security forces on the ground."

Who believed all these lies broadcast around the clock? He called the people scum. Of course, there was crime and gangs in Amithayus, but many of the people living there had initially fled from crime or civil war. And now they were in the middle of it again.

*"The situation in Amithayus is chaotic and ruthless.
Supply lines are cut off, medical facilities are overwhelmed, and essential goods are scarce. Yet, the fearless emergency forces of the Pacific Commonwealth are doing everything possible to restore order and protect the few decent citizens still living there. The constant, cowardly attacks by the insurgents severely hamper their honorable work."*

Simmons shook his head as well. He couldn't believe what was said about the residents and the oh-so-brave soldiers.

"Our glorious president of the United Free Trade Zone of America, Laura Bennett, has emphasized with iron determination and blazing patriotism that all necessary means will be used to end the conflict and restore order. 'We will not rest until this chaos is ended and peace is restored. We will hold every insurgent accountable and ensure the safety of our citizens,' she declared in a triumphant speech. With an unwavering smile, she added that even harsher measures would be considered if the situation required, so help her God."

Now it was Neele's turn to curse out the broadcaster. She ranted about how the people who had selflessly saved her life just hours ago were being vilified. And what did President Bennett meant that even harsher measures might be considered. Was she planning to escalate this into a real war? Or perhaps bomb the district? Or kill every person within the large wall? What was wrong with these people's minds?

"Meanwhile, hope is growing that the ongoing, courageous operations of the private armies and the unwavering support of the Pacific Commonwealth government will finally bring about the necessary, glorious changes. Private military corporations have increased their

presence in front of Amithayus to ensure security and fight lawlessness with all their might."

It didn't look good for Amithayus. But for us, it provided a small opportunity, the perfect moment when not everyone's eyes were on the center of Seattle as usual.
Almost all private armies stationed nearby had been moved to Amithayus. The perfect moment to create more chaos and confusion.

"The situation remains tense, and we will keep you updated on all the progress and heroic efforts. Stay with us for more patriotic updates and background reports. This was Alex Turner for FBC News Network, live from our studio in the Pacific Commonwealth."

The transporter rolled silently through Seattle's dark streets, illuminated only by the occasional streetlights and the diffuse glow of distant city lights. The closer the transporter got to the city center, the brighter the surroundings became.

As Simmons rounded another corner, the Skyway Holster Tower loomed majestically in the distance, a gigantic colossus of glass and steel that stood like a shining beacon in the dark night. The building was brightly lit from the outside, each floor illuminated by several ground-mounted lamps from all directions, piercing the night sky and shrouding the surrounding buildings in deep black.

The tower's facade was made of reflective glass, mirroring the city's light and creating the impression that the tower was built of light. High-tech laser projections displayed the Holster Corp. logo, complemented by various patriotic slogans dancing on the glass walls. Red security lights blinked at regular intervals at different heights, while cameras monitored the surroundings in all directions.

An endless row of windows stretched upward, interspersed with narrow strips of glowing neon light that highlighted the building's contours in a continuous flow. The upper floors almost disappeared into the clouds, that's how high the Skyway Holster Tower rose into the sky.

BEACON HILL

TWENTY.
BREAKDOWN

Beacon Hill Seattle, 2066 23:05 - Holster Skyward Tower

Simmons steered the transporter into a less busy side street and brought it to a stop roughly a block from the tower. He then turned to Marsh and Neele.

"This is your drop-off point," Simmons said quietly but firmly. „You'll Continue on foot; we'll meet later. Wait for my signal before you go in. Good luck, and return to our meeting point safe and sound!"

Both of them nodded, donned their helmets, and checked their equipment one last time. Everything was ready. Once they got out, there was no turning back. The plan had to work.

The two opened the transporter doors and stepped out, disappearing quietly into the darkness of the side street. Simmons watched them briefly before restarting the engine and slowly driving towards the bright light at the end of the long, straight road. The silhouette of the Skyway Holster Tower grew more prominent as he approached, and he could see the details of the lower floors and the entrance area.

The entrance was spanned by an impressive glass dome that scattered light in all directions. Guards patrolled the perimeter, and the hum of security drones was now clearly audible. Simmons took a deep breath as he approached the entrance to the underground garage.

He knew this was the beginning of the most dangerous part of their plan.

As Simmons reached the entrance to the underground garage of the Skyway Holster Tower, he paused briefly and rechecked his eyes in the transporter's rearview camera. He couldn't discern any differences and hoped Milo hadn't made any mistakes inserting the artificial implants. His fingertips tingled from the procedure, but he ignored the feeling and placed his hand on one of the two scanners at the main entrance to the extended underground garage. A short beep and another tingling sensation in his fingertips confirmed successful identification, and the heavy gate slowly opened before him, revealing the colossal underground floor of the tower.

Simmons drove the transporter inside while observing the security measures installed around the entrance, including cameras, sensors, and what looked like a gun port.
He felt a chill as he stopped at the first checkpoint.

A short, somewhat plump security guard with a massive "United Free Trade Zone of America" patch on his vest stepped out of his post and approached the vehicle. Simmons activated the automatic windows while he nodded at the man approaching.

"Delivery for the Skyward Tower and the labs," Simmons said, pointing to the ID badge on the side of the vehicle.

The guard scrutinized Simmons suspiciously and checked the data on his own device. "John Daniels, right?"

"Exactly," replied Simmons calmly. "I have to deliver important chemicals that are urgently needed. I'm a bit late due to all the uprisings in Amithayus. You must've heard about it on FBC, right, aeh… „ Simmons scanned his Name tag…
"Cletus Buckley?"

Cletus hesitated for a moment. "Yeah, I have.
„Damn insurgents. Hopefully, our president crushes them quickly so we can finally have some peace from the immigrants." Simmons nodded and flashed his best smile.

"Ac-eton-peroxide, right?" said Cletus.

"Yes, exactly. It needs to be kept cool, or it could become unstable. As far as I know, it's for weapons production to bring peace to Amithayus."

The guard nodded approvingly. "Very well," he said.
"But we had a security drill last week, and the regulations have been tightened. I need to clear this with my superior."

Simmons felt his heart race but forced himself to remain calm. "Sure, Cletus, no problem. It's your job to check everything. But listen, this stuff needs to get inside
urgently. If the temperature rises too much, we could have a big problem here."

Cletus hesitated, then took his communicator from his
greasy belt and spoke briefly with someone. Simmons couldn't make out the words, but the guard's body
language told him the situation was tense. After a short conversation, he hung up and returned.

"My superior is not thrilled about this last-minute delivery, and neither am I," said Cletus, scrutinizing Simmons again. "But I explained how urgent it is and how we free patriots need it. You can pass, but I'll be watching you."

Simmons nodded and forced a smile. "Thanks, Cletus. You've done great service to your country. I'll get this done as quickly as possible."

Cletus stepped back and opened the barrier. "Drive on, John, but be careful with the turns; it's very tight at the pump station. Almost a Labyrinth. I don't want any trouble with my boss."

Simmons closed the window and waved goodbye to Cletus. He took a deep breath as he slowly maneuvered the transporter through the narrow passages of the Holster Skyward Tower's underground garage. The vehicle's wheels rolled silently over the smooth concrete floor, the muted engine hum echoing in the eerie silence. As Cletus had said, the garage was a labyrinth of concrete pillars, loaded parking spaces, and tight passages. He reached a junction where he had to turn right. The passages became even narrower, and he had to steer the transporter precisely to avoid scraping the walls. Sweat beaded on his forehead as he maneuvered the heavy vehicle through the garage. Every millimeter counted.

He searched for the ideal spot to park the transporter, and Cletus had revealed an important detail.

The tension was palpable as he finally reached where the pump system, responsible for supplying the tower's gigantic tanks, was located.

A massive steel door equipped with multiple security features secured access to this area. Simmons stopped the transporter and got out. Moving quickly and quietly, he checked the surroundings to ensure no security forces were nearby. He opened the back compartment of the transporter, where the acetone peroxide was securely stored.

With skilled hands, he connected the transporter to the pump system. The pipes and hoses were precisely linked to ensure a smooth transfer of the chemicals. Simmons knew the pump system was the heart of the tower's supply infrastructure. It regulated the flow of water, coolants, and various chemicals into the gigantic tanks distributed throughout the building.

These tanks were essential for supplying the labs with critical chemicals. Any disruption in the system would trigger an immediate alarm and cause a chain reaction. Simmons checked his communicator one last time before starting the modification. He carefully opened the device's casing, removed the protective cover of the battery, and exposed the internal components. His fingers trembled slightly with tension as he connected to the lithium-ion battery.

He recalled the basics from his previous life in Amithayus and how dangerous these batteries could be in the right hands if mishandled. With shaky hands, he attached a conductive wire to the battery's positive and negative poles.

The next step was crucial.

He installed a small relay controlled by the communicator's timer. Once the timer expired, the relay would trigger the short circuit, causing the battery to overheat rapidly.

He looked around to ensure no one was watching him. Simmons carefully placed the modified communicator at the base of the pump system. He took a deep breath and set the timer to five minutes. That should allow him enough time to exit the building.

Simmons stood up and quickly and inconspicuously made his way toward the exit. With every step, he felt the ticking clock in his head. He knew he couldn't afford any mistakes. His eyes scanned the surroundings as he approached one of the side exits. Suddenly, he heard footsteps behind him and quickened his pace, his nerves on edge. Cletus had
followed him. "Hey, John, what were you doing back there by the tank?" he heard him call.

At that moment, Simmons heard the first wave of the plan they had set in motion come to life behind him. He glanced back

and saw from a distance the communicator beginning to spark. "Fuck," he heard himself say.
„It's too early." A loud crack and hiss filled the air as the battery overheated and burst into flames. Simmons yanked open the door he had just reached and sprinted outside, adrenaline pumping through his veins. Barely had he left the garage when the communicator exploded with a deafening bang.

The detonation was immense, shaking the ground beneath his feet, and the shockwave from the subsequent explosion threw Simmons to the ground. He felt the heat on his back and the vibrations as the pump system and the transporter's tank went up in a chain reaction.

The Holster Skyward Tower seemed to tremble as the explosion roared through the garage. Metal twisted, concrete shattered, and a massive fireball shot from the garage entrance. Smoke and debris flew in all directions, and the tower's sirens began to wail. Glass windows shattered, and people inside the building screamed in panic as the shockwave rolled through the lowest floor.

Simmons lay gasping on the ground, his ears ringing from the explosion. He struggled to his feet, feeling the aftereffects of adrenaline in his veins, and observed the chaos he had unleashed. He knew he had only seconds before the security systems switched to backup-power and the surveillance cameras returned online. Breathless and with burning lungs,
he reached a safe distance and watched the chaos unfold. People ran screaming from the building, and the entire area was illuminated by the angry lights of the alarm
system, which activated after a few seconds.

Simmons felt the adrenaline wear off and the pain in his limbs intensify. He had barely made it.
Now, it was up to the other two to complete their task.

He raised his arms, twirled them like a maniac, and ran away screaming to avoid suspicion and implement the next part of their plan as quickly as possible.

Beacon Hill, Seattle, 2066 23:15 - Holster Skyward Tower

Neele and I stood on the shadow side of the building, our steps quiet and deliberate. We moved cautiously toward the brightly lit Skyway Holster Tower that loomed ahead, casting the entire plaza in a blinding light. We had chosen the right time for our break-in, the entrance area was well-guarded, but the guards seemed more bored than vigilant at this late hour. Only a few people were still around on the plaza leading to the tower.

Neele and I took advantage of the few shadows the surroundings offered, and crept closer to the tower.

We communicated quietly as we moved past the guards. We had covered about half the distance…

…when, suddenly, a massive explosion rocked the entire area. The ground trembled beneath our feet, and we were violently thrown back several meters. "Fuck," I heard myself scream, and from Neele's direction, I heard a soft, "Have a safe day." "Damn HELPS," I heard Neele curse quietly.

Somehow, I liked HELPS. He was much more caring than Simmons.

"That was far too early." A deafening, loud boom filled the air. A huge fireball shot into the night sky, followed by a shockwave that sent dust and debris flying. The explosion came several minutes earlier than expected, and we realized that something had gone wrong. Time was running out, and we needed to hurry to seize the right moment to break into the tower. Every second we stayed on the ground could be one too many. Neele yanked me up as we sprinted toward the entrance, from which a multitude of confused, dust-covered people with bloody faces were pouring out.

The tower's lights flickered briefly before shutting off as the plaza, now filled with dust and screaming people, became overwhelmed by the aftermath of the explosion. The entire district plunged into darkness. The huge blast and the sudden darkness distracted the guards, and Neele and I slipped through the usually tightly guarded main entrance.

We ran through the lobby, pulling out our Medkits from our back slots and tossing Hyposprays and other items to random, frightened people as they panicked and tried to escape the building. Researchers and an alarming number of people in suits trying to find their way through the swirling dust ran around screaming and bleeding. The emergency system kicked in, and the safety lights started blinking again. The sprinklers activated, drenching everything in water. Electronic barriers and surveillance cameras returned online, but Neele and I had already reached the first floor unnoticed.

We started climbing the upwards and our movements were now more coordinated and determined. The building remained rumbling following the explosion, and the echoes of falling debris and creaking walls accompanied our ascent.

"Faster," Neele whispered through the internal communication system of our suits as we stormed up the stairs. She was fast, and I could only nod and follow her at a slight distance, ready to intervene if anyone recognized her.

But everyone who runs past us had only eyes for themselves. It's always me and then the rest. A good motto for the Free Trade Zone of the United States.

I counted the floors as we fought our way up. On one of the higher floors, we finally reached a point where we had to pause briefly. I was exhausted.

"What's that noise?" I heard Neele say over the intercom system, and I turned just in time to see a wall behind us collapse, filling the corridor with a cloud of dust and debris. Our way down was now blocked, so we had no choice but to keep moving upwards.

Simultaneously, we removed our masks and looked around. The air was thick with dust and smoke, and the few functioning lights flickered irregularly, casting sporadic flashes over the walls. Once orderly and clean, the floor had become a field of debris. Neele let her gaze sweep through the corridor. The glass walls of the offices were shattered, and shards of broken glass glittered on the ground in the flickering light. The walls were covered in deep cracks; in some places, large chunks of plaster and concrete had broken off, showing the steel frame of the building. Cables hung loose from the ceiling, occasionally sparking and illuminating the room with brief, bright flashes. There was a strong smell of burnt plastic and hot metal in the air, mingling with the acrid scent of chemicals drifting down from the upper floors. The sprinkler system started to mix dust and rubble into a muddy mess. There were puddles all over and the sound of water dripping was constant.

Neele noticed that some of the previously meticulously arranged desks and chairs were overturned. Papers and documents lay scattered and soaked on the floor.

A monitor hung by a single cable from the ceiling, swaying slowly as if about to fall any second now. In one of the offices, the door had been torn from its hinges, and a small fire had smoldered, filling the room with toxic smoke.

Security screens hung on the walls, showing distorted images of various in- and outside tower areas. Some were completely blacked out, while others displayed static. One screen showed a chaotic scene in the lobby, with people running in panic, some injured, others helping their colleagues or supporting them. Another screen showed a camera view outside the tower, where real rescue workers slowly approached the piled-up debris.

The floor under our feet was slippery and uneven from the falling water, and Neele and I had to walk carefully to avoid falling. She heard muffled cries and the moans of injured People through the Walls, trapped somewhere in the building. In the distance, a constant alarm siren wailed, highlighting the chaotic scene.

"We have to keep moving," I said quietly. Neele nodded as we shed our emergency suits and all unnecessary equipment. Neele was now back in her HELPS suit, donning her helmet, while I stood on a staircase on the fifth floor of the Skyward Tower in my ArmorVision suit. I activated the light refraction and gave her a few seconds of a head start, covering our backs. We felt the urgency of our mission as we navigated through the damaged floor, always on the lookout for further dangers.

The surrounding destruction was a constant reminder of the explosion's violence and the fragility of the order we aimed to disrupt. And that something went terribly wrong. On our way upwards, we used internal maintenance doors and elevators, which became accessible due to the security protocols springing into action. Neele led us through the dark and eerily silent floors as we tried to avoid crowds streaming down from the upper floors.

I felt sorry for them. Three floors below us was the end of their path. They needed to find another way, another exit. But they kept flowing downward, like a herd of pigs on their way to the slaughterhouse. Hopefully, they could escape.

The explosion had occurred several minutes ago, but the aftereffects were still evident. The tower occasionally shook, I heard the screech of metal and glass cracking, straining under the pressure. Simmons had found a particularly compelling or dumb spot to place the transporter, or we had clearly underestimated the force and explosion size of the acetone peroxide, or we had underestimated the force and explosion size of the transporter. Simmons, shit. I had completely forgotten him in all this chaos.

Hopefully, he's okay and survived the massive explosion. He surely did. It's not the first explosion we both survived in the 8 years in our Job.

We moved cautiously through narrow maintenance corridors filled with cables and pipes. The emergency lighting was only sporadically intact, and often, we groped through complete darkness, guided only by the faint light of Neele's helmet lamp. The smell of smoke and chemicals was pervasive, and our respirators struggled to filter out the worst particles.

The desperate cries of people trapped in the debris grew fainter as we ascended, and the unrelenting wail of the alarm sirens heightened the tense atmosphere.

"This way," Neele whispered, pointing to an inconspicuous maintenance door partially dislodged from its hinges.

I nodded, and we squeezed through the narrow passage, leading us to a hidden elevator shaft not intended for regular users of this floor. The elevator was out of order, but Neele noticed the access door to the maintenance elevator, which seemed to be still functional after we checked it thoroughly from the outside. We found no noticeable damage, and it appeared securely connected to the tower's inner walls. We looked at each other and decided to use it.

The buttons I pressed inside the elevator didn't respond to my touches. Meanwhile, Neele searched around and found a small box on the opposite side. She quickly opened it, then hacked into the control panel and the entire system to activate the elevator. HELPS was very helpful at that.

It took her a while to navigate through the complex inner structure of the tower's security system, but then there was a brief hiss from inside the elevator, as it slipped several centimeters downward. At the same time, the lights, and the button inside, awoke from their sleep.

"We need to be careful," Neele said as we entered the elevator and closed the door behind us. "There could be more explosions at any time, and my trust in this elevator doesn't extend beyond the distance from the back wall to the front door."

"I know," I replied, my voice sounding oddly and deliberately calm despite my inner tension. "But this is our best and probably only chance to reach our destination before we're noticed, or the tower potentially collapses."

Neele stared at me through her helmet with wide eyes. "What do you mean by the tower potentially collapsing? During my previous career in a special unit, I often dealt with what we called explosive sanitation for unwanted tenants. We usually used half of the explosive power Simmons used in the tower, and those buildings often held for a few more minutes before falling. These were usually smaller than this one. Oh, but…"

"But?" Neele said, stepping closer to me. "But I believe Simmons placed the detonation near the main tanks you told me about. The force of the explosion that knocked us off our feet on the plaza below happened at least three to four floors beneath us. It can be felt, but not as extreme as it was for both of us."

I wonder if she can handle the fact that it will be our fault if everything collapses here. First, we drag Amithayus into the abyss, and now this too.

"Tell me, will the tower collapse or not?" she said, stepping closer and looking directly into my eyes. "Probably yes. The way the walls shake with each additional tremor, the sounds, and the constant detonations of small things underground leave me no doubt. I can't tell you when and how much time we have left. Ten minutes? An hour? Ten hours? No idea. It depends on what else is stored in those tanks down there."

"And in the underground labs, storage, and manufacturing halls, many of which are operated unofficially,"

Neele added to my explanation. "Shit," she said.

"Big shit," I replied.

"Okay, let's quickly get in the elevator.

We must get up and complete the data, which I couldn't download the first time. Then we need to get out as fast as possible." I nodded and pressed the elevator button, closing the door behind us. Neele pressed the button leading to the 104th floor. I didn't understand why she chose this one, but she must have known what she was doing.

The elevator jolted and started moving slowly. We stood in silence, each of us lost in thought. Neele closed her eyes, standing in the elevator's corner, instinctively reciting the floors we were passing. She breathed a little louder than before, and I could hear HELPS advise her to stay calm and have a safe day. I wish us both that right now.

So far, the elevator kept its promise.

The minutes dragged on endlessly as the elevator took us through the floors. Just before we passed the 43rd floor, Neele opened her eyes wide and fully pounded the stop button. I heard a

loud bang, and the elevator began to sway and sink. I was overcome with panic when we felt the floor give way beneath us with a tremendous squeak of metal on metal.

Neele struck me with her hand on my shoulder and then emitted a brief cry of agony. She had struck my metal arm with her hand. I wanted to raise my hands defensively, but I think that was precisely what she wanted from me.

My attention. She got it now.

"Quick," she shouted at me. "Up there!" she yelled,

pointing to a shaft in the elevator's ceiling.

It took me a moment to realize what she wanted from me, but then I got it. Without further hesitation, I jumped and grabbed the edge of the shaft. With all the strength of my metal prosthesis, I pulled myself up through the shaft, the muscles in my synthetic arm burning with effort. As soon as I was through the shaft and out of the elevator, I reached back down and offered Neele my hand.

"Grab it, I'll pull you up!" I shouted as the elevator sank another tiny bit. Neele didn't hesitate and jumped as high as she could, grabbing my outstretched hand.

With all the strength in my metal arm, I hoisted her out of the elevator and set her beside me on the elevator's roof. I didn't let go of her arm, and without releasing her, we were now stuck on the elevator's ceiling.

I saw no further opening directly around us. The next one was about five meters above us, and there was no way I could reach that.

"Do you trust me?" I heard Neele say over the intercom as she looked at me through her HELPS helmet. I nodded. "Then do exactly what I tell you now. I did this about 24 hours ago, just in reverse order. Below us, to the left, is a small opening, a shaft. It's big enough for each of us to pass through individually. But we don't have time to discuss who goes first. So hold on to me, run as fast as you can, and swing me forward." I nodded.

"Now!" Neele shouted just as the elevator made another jolt and finally plunged into the depths. Both of us jumped simultaneously from the roof of the elevator, and I swung her forward with considerable force, allowing her to shoot through the narrow opening in the shaft first. We landed hard on the ground, one after another, and I slammed into her with all my might. She groaned in pain. Below us, we heard the crash and shattering of the falling elevator, followed by a loud impact.

Breathing heavily and with pounding hearts, we looked at each other. We had made it.

"This shaft leads us to an entrance. It's the same access I used to jump down last time," Neele whispered. I nodded.

And I was simultaneously glad I was doing this with Neele and not Simmons. We would both have been run over by some screaming person on the first floor.

We crawled along the long, narrow corridor until we reached a door blocking our way. Neele turned around and looked at me. "It's going to get extremely loud soon," she said. "It's some unknown defense mechanism active on this floor. I can mute it through my hermetically sealed HELPS suit, but I don't know if that works with the ArmorVision suit."

Unfortunately, it didn't. Quite the opposite. You could amplify ambient sounds inside the helmet, which helped you eavesdrop on people unnoticed.

"No, my suit can't do that. How bad is it in there?" I asked her, as I had never heard of such technology before. "It gets louder by the second until you can't even hear your thoughts, and then it turns into pure pain that intensifies more and more," she said. I knew what she was about to do, and I wouldn't say I liked it at all.

"I'm going in alone. I'll get the rest of the data, download it, and then come back to you, and we'll find a way through the room so we can keep moving up. Understood?" "Yes, but I can't let you go in alone…"

"Yes, you can. I can handle it. And it would be best if you didn't get hurt. You'll thank me later for only having to endure it briefly. I promise." I nodded, though I wasn't sure I was doing the right thing. "Now step back, or you'll be hit by the full blast of the sound."

Neele watched as I retreated into the darkness of the shaft. Walking backward, I looked even more ridiculous than usual.

Neele was secretly truly grateful to have met the two men in Amithayus. Besides Zhan Tao and Alicia, they were the only two she trusted as much as possible. And he had proven loyal when it came to doing the right thing at the wrong moment, which she greatly appreciated.

"HELPS, please deactivate the sounds coming inside our helmet." **"Gladly, Dr. Neele. I have done it for you. Have a safe day."** Neele pulled the door, which she knew from experience squeaked, but it didn't. Perfect, she thought as she ventured into the pitch-dark room she had entered for the first time more than two days ago, and as it turned out, it was not the last time. She closed the door behind her and looked around.

The room had changed little. She couldn't see any damage at first glance; even the machines were still running just as they had when she left the room. Excellent, she thought. Everything around us is falling apart, but here, everything seems to run as usual. Neele straightened up.

This time, she didn't want to face her fate, crouched and sneaking, but standing tall and prepared for what lay ahead. She walked softly through the room and examined the machines more closely.

The rhythm of the lights on the machines around the room had changed since the last time.

And it seemed oddly familiar to her. After a few more seconds, she realized the rhythm of a tune she had not hummed in 16 years. She felt her brother's guidance as she began to whisper the melody. As she approached the corner, she observed two of the guards who had pursued her previously lying dead on the floor in front of the immense black console. Their helmets' visors were broken, and their stun guns were pressed against their faces. Someone may have stepped in and killed them, or that they experienced a malfunction in the volume control system on their helmets and killed each other because they couldn't take it anymore.

Neele shuddered at the thought and turned her attention to the gigantic control console before her. None of the lights were active this time, so she concluded the console was still in data transfer mode as she had left it. "HELPS, please activate the UDMI port; we need to download the remaining data from the console."

She felt a slight vibration in her arm and saw the odd plug dangling from the red cable. "Alright, "she thought as HELPS wished her a safe day.

She plugged the connector into the port, and without delay, the console resumed the data download at 47%. So she stood before the dark console in this dark room. And unlike last time, she was much wiser.

She knew she was no longer alone. She had support from the two ECLE investigators in her reality. Zhan Tao and Alicia had supported her as long as they could. And then there was another reality, where there was another, her and Alicia, or had been. In any case, she knew she had a critical mission she had imposed on herself.

This other self had spent a lifetime preparing to save

herself, and now she was much closer to understanding that great task. She had to think briefly of Alicia and then Peet, who had just given her the right timing in the elevator and whom she no longer feared the second time around. She was glad to see him without fear now.

All those years before, every time she had been

overwhelmed by panic or memories of Snoqualmie Ridge, Peet's face had appeared before her, trying to calm her.

She hadn't understood that for years, only causing more panic and attempts to repress and forget everything related to him.

And now, finally, she understood it was her brain's defense mechanism to cope with traumatic events. Her brain should summon what meant the most to her, and that was her little brother Peet, whom she terribly missed. She hummed again.

"The download is complete, Dr. Neele. Have a safe day."

Neele whipped her arm around, pulling the plug, and

walked past the two corpses on the floor without looking at them. While lost in thought, the situation in the room had changed. She realized this only now, noticing that the last light source, the server's machine rhythm, had

vanished. The only light source remaining in the room was her. Her helmet illuminated the surrounding area.

She looked around and approached the door she had come through. None of the servers showed any movement. It was as if everything in the room had ceased to exist.

Had she triggered something by downloading the files? Perhaps the room had no reason to exist anymore and had shut down because of that?

"HELPS, activate all ambient sounds in my helmet again," Neele said, standing before the pressure door.

"That would be very unwise, Dr. Neele. I cannot be certain…"

"Do it. And don't call me Doctor anymore. My name is Neele. Just Neele."

—

I had been sitting in the dark for almost fifteen minutes.

With nothing around me. It was tight, I was sweating, and the explosions and tremors that shook the building became more frequent. I had my hand on the pressure door for over two minutes but didn't know what to do.

> *Why hadn't Neele come back? Had something happened to her in there? And if so, what? I had to get in there. But if she, who had been in there before and knew what to expect, had been caught… How am I supposed to handle it? Screw it. I have to help her. Okay, 3, 2, 2 1/2, 2 1/3…*

I pressed against the pressure door, and it opened with little resistance. I started to scream.

> *Oh my God, I'm going to die. DIE! Now, ahh, these pains. It's so…*

I opened my eyes and looked into Neele's face, who grinned at me. She opened the door from inside and stood directly before me without a helmet. She offered me her left hand, which I gladly took. Likewise, she pulled me out of the too-narrow shaft, and now I stood in the middle of…

> *Where am I? What is this strange room? Everything is so dark. And it's incredibly quiet. I hear nothing.*

No explosions, no people screaming, no water dripping down the elevator shaft driving me crazy, nothing. And it smells weird here. So old. And somewhat musty.

"Where are we?" I asked Neele, who shrugged in response. "Honestly, I can't tell you. Not because I don't want to, but because I don't know myself. Until a minute ago, there was a hellish noise in here, and the whole room was decorated with a pattern of blinking lights. And now, after I've

I downloaded the remaining data, but there's nothing.

No light, no noise. No movement. It's as if the room has completed its task. Moreover, the room is on the 42nd floor of the tower, which officially doesn't exist. From the incomplete records of my HELPS AI, I know there was a fire here, and the floor was sealed off."

"Okay. Then let's get out of here if there's nothing left for us to do." I suggested.

Neele nodded, and she led the way with her helmet now serving as a flashlight, illuminating the path to the only exit from this floor, which didn't exist officially.

Another elevator.

Luckily, I'm not dead. Dying by an elevator must be weird. One moment, you're in the elevator, then you hit the ground, and all your organs are forced out of your body through your feet and scattered in that tiny room. And dying by sound must be just as terrible. Almost as bad as drowning. You die from something meant to keep you alive. As my grandmother used to say, too much of anything is too much.

Neele pressed the button, and it took a few seconds before the doors opened before us. We both entered the much larger elevator than the one where we had almost died, and Neele pressed the button to close the doors.

Exactly when they closed, all the sounds broke upon us again. We heard explosions and the dull sound of crumbling concrete, and the elevator began to vibrate. Also, the sound system installed in the elevator played a rhythmic sequence of bongos and ukuleles, repeating every four beats. It immediately got on my nerves.

Neele smacked her hand on the button leading to the 104th floor. The elevator began to move. I held on to the installed metal railing as the vibrations grew more substantial. But

Neele stood calmly in the middle of the elevator, staring at the numbers, which increased faster.

60, 61, 62.

> *Something must have happened to her in that room. Her whole demeanor and expression had changed.*

"Uh, Neele? The 104th floor isn't the top, right?" I asked her while still clinging to the railing.

"No. That's where my old lab was. I need to check something before we leave here. The elevator only goes up to the 104th floor. Thereafter, it's two more floors to the roof."

"Okay," I said, unsure whether I should ask her what was so urgent that we had to risk our lives to do some sightseeing in her old lab.

Beacon Hill Seattle, 2066 23:55 - Holster Skyward Tower

Less than 30 seconds later, we arrived at the 104th floor of the Skyway Holster Tower. I had to admit, this elevator was significantly faster than the freight elevator, though the shaking was about the same. Neele exited the elevator first, and I followed her directly. The corridor before us was dark. The cold neon lights embedded everywhere in the walls and floor flickered frantically as we slowly walked on the metallic planks.

The lab we entered was in utter devastation. The pressure doors, which were supposed to keep different rooms sterile, no longer closed adequately, hanging partly off their hinges on the floor. Sparks flew from damaged cables in the ceiling and floor, and many white metallic planks were scattered across the room, exposing the cable bundles beneath them. The floor was mostly covered with debris and shards of glass, remnants of broken monitors, and other lab equipment scattered across the various lab cells. White shelves and cabinets lay toppled everywhere, their contents strewn across the floor. It looked like a bomb had gone off here.

Which, in a twisted way, it had.

The entire floor beneath us shook again, and I could hear the muffled detonation of another tank. The intervals between detonations were getting shorter. The tower was fighting its last battle with itself. "Time is running out," I shouted to Neele, but she ignored me and continued straight ahead toward a crooked pressure door. I followed her and realized this environment was utterly alien to me. I didn't know anything about this science stuff. Likewise, I only knew what Neele had shown me in the brief five seconds in which I lived two complete lives simultaneously. I didn't understand what it was about but knew it was necessary. So important that we had to risk our lives for it. "Come over here and help me open this pressure door," Neele said as she tried to push it to the right.

That I understood. Lever mechanics.

I positioned myself on the left side, and with extreme effort, we managed to shift the pressure door a few centimeters, enough for it to fall off its hinges and crash to the floor. The way was clear, except the door had stirred up a lot of dust, making it hard to breathe and see.

And all of this in a sterile lab.

Neele led the way again, and we entered what must have been her lab. It was an empty white room. Nothing about it looked inviting. How could she stand being here for so long? Day in and day out? For over four years.

After the dust settled a bit, I saw something in her lab. Amidst all the destruction, a small white box was embedded in the floor. It looked surreal next to all the technical stuff we had trudged through. It seemed perfect, like a relic from another world that didn't belong in this scene.

"Ah, the pod is still here," Neele said as she slowly approached it. "And before you ask, I saw this pod in my lab two days ago. Back then, its contents terrified me. But now I think I know what it is."

I nodded and slowly stepped out of her shadow to look closer at the container.

Neele avoided saying her dead brother's name because she was sure that whatever was in this cryostasis pod wasn't her brother. She didn't know what it was, but it wasn't Peet. She stepped closer and examined the matte surface more carefully. Her eyes scanned every corner and edge of the device. The external structures seemed intact, with no visible cracks or breaks. She behaved cautiously, avoiding direct contact, knowing a wrong move could cause irreversible damage to her or the pod. She leaned forward slightly and examined the connections and ports on the sides of the pod but found no apparent damage.

"HELPS," Neele finally said softly but firmly after walking around the pod once. "Can you scan the cryostasis pod and tell me if it's still functional?"

It took HELPS a while to respond.

"I'm sorry, Neele," replied HELPS, "but I am not authorized to access this pod."

Neele frowned. "Not authorized? What does that mean? You hacked a super-secret terminal on the 42nd floor, and now you can't access this pod? Who gave you that order?"

"The head of the lab, Dr. Viktor Caldwell, imposed this restriction," HELPS explained in a factual tone that nearly drove Neele to rage. Viktor again. "And how can we bypass it?" Neele asked, her voice revealing a mix of frustration and determination. HELPS seemed to hesitate, as if researching, before replying.

"There is a way to bypass the restrictions by manually disabling the pod's internal security mechanisms. This requires direct physical access to the control mechanisms inside the pod."

Neele seemed confused by this answer. She paced around the pod, visibly struggling.

"Is everything okay, Neele?" I asked, watching her circle the pod a second time. "No," she replied curtly before turning to me. She stepped back from the pod and looked directly into my eyes. "I can't do it. I can't touch the pod again. Last time…"

"I know," I said, having experienced it myself. The feeling was uncomfortable for me, so I could imagine how Neele felt.

"I'll do it, as long as HELPS tells me what to do," I said, nodding to Neele and approaching the cryostasis pod. "Thank you," Neele said, her face relaxing slightly. "So, HELPS tells you, and you tell me." I knelt beside her before the pod, and she did the same.

Another detonation about a hundred floors below us shook the lab again, and Neele and I both fell to the floor, hearing more things break outside the lab.

"Perfect," Neele said, and I stared at her. "HELPS just told me there's a small maintenance panel hidden here," she pointed to a tile at the lower part of the pod, "that you need to open." I tilted, staring at the fifty identical tiles lining the pod. "Here?" I asked her. "Yes, right here." "And how do I open it?" Neele furrowed her eyebrows, and I heard a faint whisper from her suit. It took HELPS a while to formulate the appropriate response. Neele pointed at the tile and looked at me. "Yes?" I asked. "Just press it," Neele replied. "Oh," I said, pressing the tile, which slid to the other side with a slight squelch.

"These are the internal components of the pod." I nodded, staring at a multitude of identical-looking circuits and wiring. I understood nothing of it. Furthermore, I could use a communicator and handle a weapon, but I had yet to learn how most technical devices worked. And I was sure most people my age were the same.

I could explain a toaster; two heating wires get hot. But this is just stuff with chips and code and more chips on top.

"Okay, HELPS says you need to disable the security now. At least, that's what I understood from his super-technical descriptions and translated into simple words," she said, pointing to the cluster of chips hidden among the wires, each smaller and seemingly more important than the next. "Okay, and how do I do that? Where, and what exactly?" I asked, shrugging.

I think we were both in the same predicament. HELPS bombarded Neele with extreme technical details, and I got only a rudimentary translation without exact instructions. "This," she pointed to a chip that looked exactly like the one to its left and the next to its right, "needs to come out." "Out," I stammered. "Okay." I looked around, trying to find something small enough to poke around the pod's microelectronics precisely without damaging the main lines or maybe the circuit board. I stood up and moved around the room. But the room was empty except for the broken items. I picked something up, staring at it, but I had no idea what it was, and Neele shook her head as well. She had also stood up and was looking around the room. We did this for another two minutes until the subsequent detonation and the building shaking snapped us out of our lethargy.

We returned to the pod, and I looked at Neele. "What about just breaking it?" I asked her, and I heard HELPS explain to something again. "Why didn't you say that right away," Neele said, interrupting HELPS immediately. She looked at me and nodded. I swung my metal arm full force into the various chips, which I didn't care about. My fingertips tingled slightly as I withdrew my arm. "Does that work," I heard myself say as I stood up.

"Yes, that works," Neele said, smiling. "HELPS, please try again."

"The lock is lifted, Neele. I will start scanning the pod."

He started the analysis immediately. After a few moments, which felt like an eternity, HELPS spoke again, with good and bad news. "The bad news is, the pod is no longer functional, but not due to our actions. There are internal damages to the cryostasis mechanisms, making them unusable."

"And what does that mean exactly?" Neele asked.

"The pod is junk," HELPS said. **"But the good news is that the subject's genetic data inside is still intact."**

BEACON HILL

TWENTY-ONE.
WAR ZONE

Beacon Hill, Seattle, 2066, 00:13 - Holster Skyward Tower

We sat tense in the Black Talon helicopter, battling through Seattle's dark clouds. The noise from the rotors and the turbulence made it almost impossible to talk. Usually, we'd try to organize our thoughts and emotions, but we told Simmons what we had experienced and discovered, and together, we marveled at the recent events — the collapse of Skyward Tower. We had detonated the transporter with the explosive charge in the tower.

However, Neele was certain the small explosion could not have brought down the 104-story tower.

After the catastrophe in New York, which led to the collapse of the WTC, all subsequent towers exceeding a certain number of floors were built to withstand explosions. Mostly up to 1000 kilograms of TNT equivalent, according to the 'Stability and Safety in High-Rise Structures Act.'

Even the roughly 400 kilograms of TNT equivalent from the fully loaded transporter with acetone peroxide wouldn't have been enough to threaten the tower's structural integrity. Simmons couldn't explain the explosion's force either, but secretly, we were glad we had at least shut down this place where so many horrific experiments had been conducted.

In one way or another, it was the right thing to do, even if it felt wrong to kill innocent people. This iconic tower, once the center of Holster Skyway and a symbol of progress and power in the Free Trade Zone of the United States, now lay in ruins.

The chaos revealed the dark truth behind Dr. Caldwell's machinations all the more clearly to everyone involved.

With HELPS' support, Neele gathered the crucial information within minutes. She extracted the data from the destroyed databases and discovered that the collapse was no accident. It was a deliberate act orchestrated by Caldwell himself to conceal his experiments from the public.

How did we know?

No one would suspect something unlawful happened in the glow of Skyward Tower, a symbol of hope, as the news broadcasts repeatedly emphasized. Then we came into play. A gang of terrorists, in this case, us three, and sometimes more, directly from Amithayus's dark underground, had attacked the golden heart of Seattle.

This news spread across all public channels right after our escape in the helicopter we were currently sitting in. The FBC, in particular, continuously spewed new rumors disguised as news.

Where there are no judges, there are many executioners. Somehow, we had played directly into Dr. Caldwell's and the Free Trade Zone's hands.

"The tower was just the beginning," I said, seeing the determined faces of Neele and Simmons. "Caldwell has something much bigger planned, and we need to find out what, when, and where it will happen." Neele joined in. "No one destroys the status symbol that made Seattle world-famous, especially not when it stands in the middle of the city. There must be a reason. I'm sure of it. Viktor knows exactly what he's doing. And I have to admit, Viktor is a brilliant man who thinks several steps ahead before taking action." We all nodded. We were dealing with a very dangerous opponent.

Just as we pondered this thought, another newscast from the FBC News Network blared over the helicopter's speakers. The familiar voice of the president boomed through the speakers, clear and penetrating, as if she were speaking directly to our souls. Her deep, serious tone even drowned out the helicopter's roar.

"Citizens of Seattle and the entire Pacific State! The time of waiting and hesitation is over. Today, we stand united as an unbeatable force to defend our freedom and crush the enemies of our great nation once and for all! Amithayus, this hotbed of terror and anarchy, will learn today what it means to challenge the power and will of a united people!"

We looked at each other as if we had been run over by a steamroller. Her voice swelled, carried by an energy that must have been electrifying to the uninvolved.

"Today, we stand here not only as defenders of our country but as advocates of freedom, justice, and the inalienable rights of every single citizen. In a few hours, our brave army, supported by the best technological achievements' humanity has ever seen, will deliver the final blow. This strike will annihilate the enemies in Amithayus and send a clear message: No one, I repeat, no one, may threaten our great nation's freedom and security!"

I exchanged worried looks with Neele and Simmons. "This must be connected to Caldwell's plan," I murmured. "Has he also got the president of the Free Trade Zone in his pocket?" I didn't believe it. He was brilliant but fundamentally just a scientist, not wealthy enough to buy everything and everyone.

How many new dollars would it cost to have the president on his side? Probably more than our tour guide in Amithayus, who brought us through the wall.

Simmons nodded in agreement. "If the army attacks Amithayus, the chaos will be perfect. Then Caldwell can complete his experiments unnoticed."

"But he must have something gigantic planned for that. The army alone isn't enough to complete a gene marker. They can only shoot people. It must be something much more terrible, heading toward a catastrophe. We're talking about another Chernobyl or Fukushima, Kobe…" Neele hesitated at the last sentence, and I finished it for her, "…or Snoqualmie Ridge."

She nodded, shaken.

The president's speech ended, and no sooner had it finished than a new voice took over the broadcast. It was none other than Thornej A. Holster Jr., the powerful CEO of Holster Skyway and one of the most influential men in the country. His deep, authoritative voice echoed through the helicopter, each word booming in our ears.

"Dear citizens, I am Thornej A. Holster Jr., and tonight I speak to you as a man of action committed to protecting our nation. Faced with the threat from Amithayus, we have decided to take extreme measures. To ensure the complete destruction of the terrorist cells and guarantee our country's safety, we have authorized the use of one of our tactical nuclear weapons. This measure may seem drastic, but it is necessary to eradicate the roots of terror once and for all and ensure that no one ever again threatens the freedom and security of our great nation. Please close your windows at the following announcement and the alarm that will alert your communicator. Thank you for your understanding, and may God be with us all."

My eyes widened in horror. "Fuck. They're all completely crazy! They want to detonate a small nuclear bomb in the middle of Amithayus." I slapped my forehead with my palm.

"That's the key to Caldwell's plan," said Neele, horrified. "The radioactive fallout will activate the genetic marker in all the people who now carry it within themselves and who are currently in Amithayus. Then, he will have enough test subjects to send over time. And the rest will die from the radiation."

Two hundred thousand flies with one swat.

"He probably has the almost-completed clones of Peet stashed somewhere there as well. He must have a lab or another research facility hidden there. Just like in Snoqualmie Ridge sixteen years ago. Only now it's the endgame." Neele turned around and put on her HELPS helmet.

"HELPS, analyze the possible effects of detonating a tactical nuclear weapon in Amithayus. Where could Caldwell place the bomb to achieve the maximum effect?"

HELPS processed the request instantly.

"Here is the answer to your request, Neele. The most likely position for maximum genetic marker spread would be the abandoned industrial area in Mincheng. The structure of the old factories and the prevailing wind patterns would optimize the spread of the marker by up to 37%."

Neele raised her head and looked at us with a determined expression. "That's our target. We must get to Mincheng, find the bomb, and deactivate it before it goes off. That's our only chance to thwart Caldwell's plan and save Amithayus."

"How much time do we have left?" asked Simmons, and Neele immediately replied with an exact time. "It's August 26, 2066, 1:32 AM. He will detonate the bomb precisely at two minutes to seven."

"How do you know that?" we asked simultaneously.

Neele hesitated for a moment before answering.

"HELPS has been comparing all the files we downloaded and looking for patterns. Based on the historical data of recorded disasters, which occurred in leap years, and information about Caldwell's previous experiments, it seems he follows a precise cycle." She exhaled and looked at us.

"You must know," said Neele, "scientifically speaking, humans have increased genetic susceptibility in leap years due to a weak radio-nuclear layer in the upper atmosphere and cosmic resonance. This layer is activated by the minimal change in Earth's rotation and tilt toward the sun, leading to increased energy release in the form of atomic and subatomic particles."

I stared at Neele incredulously, as I didn't understand a word of her scientific jargon. I understood this: "You mean all these disasters were planned to the minute and followed this cycle?"

"Yes and no," confirmed Neele, her voice firmer and more determined. "Not to the exact minute; that's technically not possible yet. However, the year, month, and same day can be determined when the layer releases the most atomic particles. Chernobyl 1986 was the first test run. Caldwell studied the genetic effects of radiation on the survivors. The Jakarta flood in 1996 was not a natural event. The Quito volcano eruption in 2000 was triggered by a deliberate detonation of a dirty bomb inside the volcano. Group R wanted to study the effects of radioactive ash on the local population. In contrast, Fukushima, as far as HELPS summarized, was not a fortunate event for the residents of the prefecture but an excellent coincidence for the scientists."

Her voice grew firmer. "All this followed the same pattern. And now Caldwell plans, precisely 16 years after Snoqualmie Ridge, in the next leap year cycle, today, August 26, 2066, at 6:58 AM, his final experiment.

The destruction of Amithayus, the completion of the gene marker experiment. But that, we will not allow."

Neele stood up in the helicopter, grabbed one of the rifles hanging in the cabinet, and handed it to me.

I understood immediately. Storm the gates. Burn everything down. Fight fire with fire. It was what I always did.

Now or never, I thought, as Simmons spun the Black Talon on its axis. Today is the day we piece all the fragments together.

Seattle, 2066, 01:45 - Arrival in Amithayus

During the flight, each of us equipped an AegisArmor suit, which was available for the entire task force in the Black Talon helicopter. Neele had fitted hers under her HELPS suit, so she was now well-armored and equipped with the best AI I knew. Simmons and I armed ourselves with semi-automatic rifles and as much ammunition as possible. Each Black Talon helicopter was also equipped with a smaller variant of the Dämmerung Drone, which hung beneath the helicopter's belly.

It was called Erwachen and was about four times smaller than a Dämmerung Drone. It only carried a small machine gun with limited ammunition and wasn't quite as agile, but it was still helpful in many situations—especially the one we were flying into.

Amithayus, once a bustling center of three different cultures, full of life and innovation, now lay before us like a devastated battlefield. The entire district behind the wall was ravaged by war and destruction. Chaos reigned everywhere; flames and smoke rose from burning buildings, and the sounds of gunfire and explosions echoed through the streets. Private armies and the regular troops of the Free Trade Zone United America were engaged in fierce battles against the coalition of the militia and the Nightshades, who fought together against the rest.

At about 6,500 feet above Amithayus, we could see the entire tragedy from above. The massive wall was breached in parts, debris covered the streets, and traces of devastation were everywhere. Abandoned and burned-out vehicles, collapsed buildings, and charred bodies lay on the main roads of the district. Hastily erected barricades meant to provide protection from enemies were broken. Small fires burned everywhere, and dense smoke clouds rose into the sky, reaching us as we crossed the wall.

The noise of the war reached us faintly in the helicopter. Explosions and gunfire echoed through the air. We saw flashes of muzzle fire in the streets and buildings as soldiers and militias moved like little plastic soldiers from one building to another. The city was a mosaic of flickering lights and shadows, each representing another scene of senseless violence and suffering.

"We're almost there!" shouted Simmons over the roar of the rotors. "Hold on tight; it's going to get bumpy!" And that's exactly what we did. Neele held both hands on the handle to her right inside the helicopter, while I sat on the left.

Suddenly, as if on command, we had to dodge several projectiles fired from the ground. I saw multiple rockets and heavy projectiles flying toward us. "Simmons!" I shouted forward, "Something's coming at us from 5 o'clock!" But he and the Black Talon had already noticed.

The infrared sensors and radar detection system had detected and analyzed the threats. The system responded immediately with the precision of a seasoned warrior. The Talon's onboard computer had been fed all the data since 1960, when a UH-1

Huey was first equipped with flares for missile defense during the Vietnam War.

A salvo of infrared flares and radar chaff launched from the sides of the helicopter. The flares ignited, creating intense heat signatures that diverted the incoming missiles. Simultaneously, the chaff deployed, creating a radar jamming field that confused the projectiles' targeting systems.

Simmons pulled back the controls, and the Talon screamed downward at full speed to evade the missiles. The G-forces pressed us into our seats as the helicopter made sharp evasive maneuvers. The metal structure of the Black Talon groaned and bent slightly under the strain. The cockpit displays flashed warnings and critical values, but Simmons remained focused.

He abruptly reduced speed and backed up the machine to shake off the missiles. The Phantom Shield system continued to work tirelessly, firing decoys and analyzing threats in real time. Suddenly, a few sparks flew on Neele's side as heavy deflected projectiles grazed the helicopter, but most missiles were diverted by the decoys and exploded at a safe distance.

A red button in the cockpit lit up, indicating the system was empty. My hands clenched the armrests as Simmons delivered the joyous news.

"Shit, hopefully, the idiots on the ground are empty too. Please, please, dear child emperor, let us arrive safely."

I clung to my seat as the projectiles ceased, and it seemed we had survived the worst.

"Hold on tight!" shouted Simmons, forcing the helicopter into a steep turn. The G-forces crushed us into our seats like an invisible hand squeezing us. My stomach churned, and I could barely breathe as the helicopter made the tight turn. The pressure was so intense it felt like my body was being pressed into the seat while my head was pulled in all directions.

Simmons' hands flew over the controls as he desperately tried to stabilize the helicopter. The cockpit displays flashed frantically, red warning lights flared, and alarms shrieked through the cabin. The altimeter jumped wildly, the speed dropped rapidly, and the helicopter's metal structure creaked under the enormous stress. The fuselage vibrated violently, and I could feel the frame groaning and bending under the strain.

"Damn it, hold on, you damn clunker!" shouted Simmons as he pushed the control stick with all his might to bring the helicopter back to a horizontal position. Sparks flew from the control flaps at the rear of the machine, and I could smell the sharp aroma of overheated electronics and burning rubber. Each of us fought against the rising panic as we battled through the aerial battlefield.

Suddenly, out of nowhere, a ground-to-air missile hit us directly in the rear. The helicopter was rocked by a massive explosion, and smoke and flames shot from the damaged engine. We immediately went into a spin, and sparks and flames flew everywhere.

"Shit! We've been hit!" screamed Simmons as he desperately tried to regain control of the helicopter. Parts of the Talon broke off, and one of the rear rotors exploded into thousands of pieces, shooting through the helicopter's exterior at insane speed. Fortunately, we were unharmed, but several hydraulic hoses and large sections of the electronics were severed. The helicopter rapidly lost altitude, and Simmons struggled to avoid a crash landing.

The artificial horizon on the display spun uncontrollably as the altimeter dropped ominously. The speed increased dangerously, and the metal structure of the Black Talon began to creak and deform under the pressure.

"We have to jump! Now!" I shouted, grabbing one of the jump modules from the helicopter cabin. Neele grabbed a jump module and an IFF transponder module, activating the Erwachen drone beneath the helicopter. The module began blinking, sending a signal to the tiny drone, which detached from the helicopter and hovered beside us, ready to provide cover fire.

"Jump!" shouted Simmons, and we didn't need to be told twice. We jumped from about ten meters into the river below. The cold water swallowed us immediately, and I felt the air rush out of my lungs upon impact as the helicopter crashed into the river and exploded. There was a massive explosion, and the shockwave pushed us several meters underwater in the opposite direction. The water had cushioned the impact and saved our lives. As we surfaced, we saw the burning wreckage of the helicopter floating in the water and slowly sinking. I gasped for air, and together we swam to the shore while the war raged around us. Neele, Simmons, and I crawled onto the land, drenched and exhausted.

"We have to keep moving," said Simmons while I vomited two liters of water onto the dry shore. I vomited my soul out of my body. The screams and explosions of the battlefield echoed through the night, and I could hear the distant rumble of fighting in the streets of Amithayus.

"Are you all okay?" asked Neele, although she looked like a plucked poodle. Her HELPS suit, worn over her armor, hung heavy and wet on her body. She shook herself. I looked at Simmons, who was slowly getting back on his feet. I was in better shape than I had been in the last twenty-four hours; I hadn't broken or dislocated anything this time.

We took a moment to gather ourselves and check our equipment. Neele was fascinated by the Erwachen drone hovering about four meters above us, making jerky movements. It detected every enemy ahead of us and targeted them with its integrated targeting system. It behaved like a small, rabid attack dog that had spotted a horde of rabbits but hadn't been given the command to hunt. I was glad it was on our side. Then we set off.

The battlefield was a chaotic mess of debris, smoke, and wandering soldiers. We had to fight our way through the decayed remains of the outer district, which shielded us from the abandoned industrial area where we suspected Dr. Caldwell and more soldiers were waiting. We stayed close together, each movement cautious and deliberate.

A few meters ahead, just before we reached a slightly larger open space, I nodded to Neele. She understood what I wanted and double-tapped the IFF transponder attached to her HELPS suit. The Erwachen drone zipped over our heads and automatically hunted down every approaching enemy. Its small machine gun rattled continuously, keeping enemy troops at bay.

A squad of soldiers appeared in front of us. They weren't Nightshades or militia. They immediately returned fire. "There's cover ahead; we need to get there!" shouted Simmons, pointing to an overturned concrete barrier forming a makeshift barricade. We dove behind it and returned fire. Bullets whizzed around us, and the sounds of gunfire and explosions filled the air.

I aimed through a small slit in the concrete, my optical sight marking the enemy in red, and squeezed the trigger of my semi-automatic rifle. The recoil jolted through my body as I took out two attackers with precise bursts. Simmons was beside me, his movements quick and deadly as he provided cover fire. Neele swiped the IFF, and the AI-assisted targeting system of the Erwachen drone shifted its focus and whizzed over our heads and the barrier.

It ascended steeply and hovered about six meters high, then began taking out our opponents one by one with precise bursts. I heard the screams of the dying soldiers and the drone's satisfied hum as it finally got to indulge its hunting instincts.

"We have to move!" I shouted, seeing reinforcements approaching. "Or we'll be overrun here!" Simmons peeked around the corner of the barrier and saw another squad of soldiers approaching. Neele looked up at the drone, which had just fired its last bullet and now made a petulant noise, indicating its time was up.

Neele looked at me, and I quickly gestured to indicate the best option. It looked like rock in rock-paper-scissors. She understood and gave the drone its final command.

It beeped twice in farewell, then rose rapidly to thirty meters and headed toward the soldiers on a direct collision course. Simmons and I fired continuously in their direction to distract them from the drone, which raced through the first three soldiers with its sharp rotors, causing a bloodbath, and then ended its service with a not-so-small explosion upon impact. With a final coordinated attack, we took out the remaining enemies and ran through the devastated terrain.

The smoke from the explosion burned my eyes, and the surrounding noise was deafening. Debris and burning vehicles lay everywhere as we approached the complex where HELPS suspected Dr. Caldwell and the tactical nuclear bomb were located.

AMITHAYUS, MILITARY COMPLEX

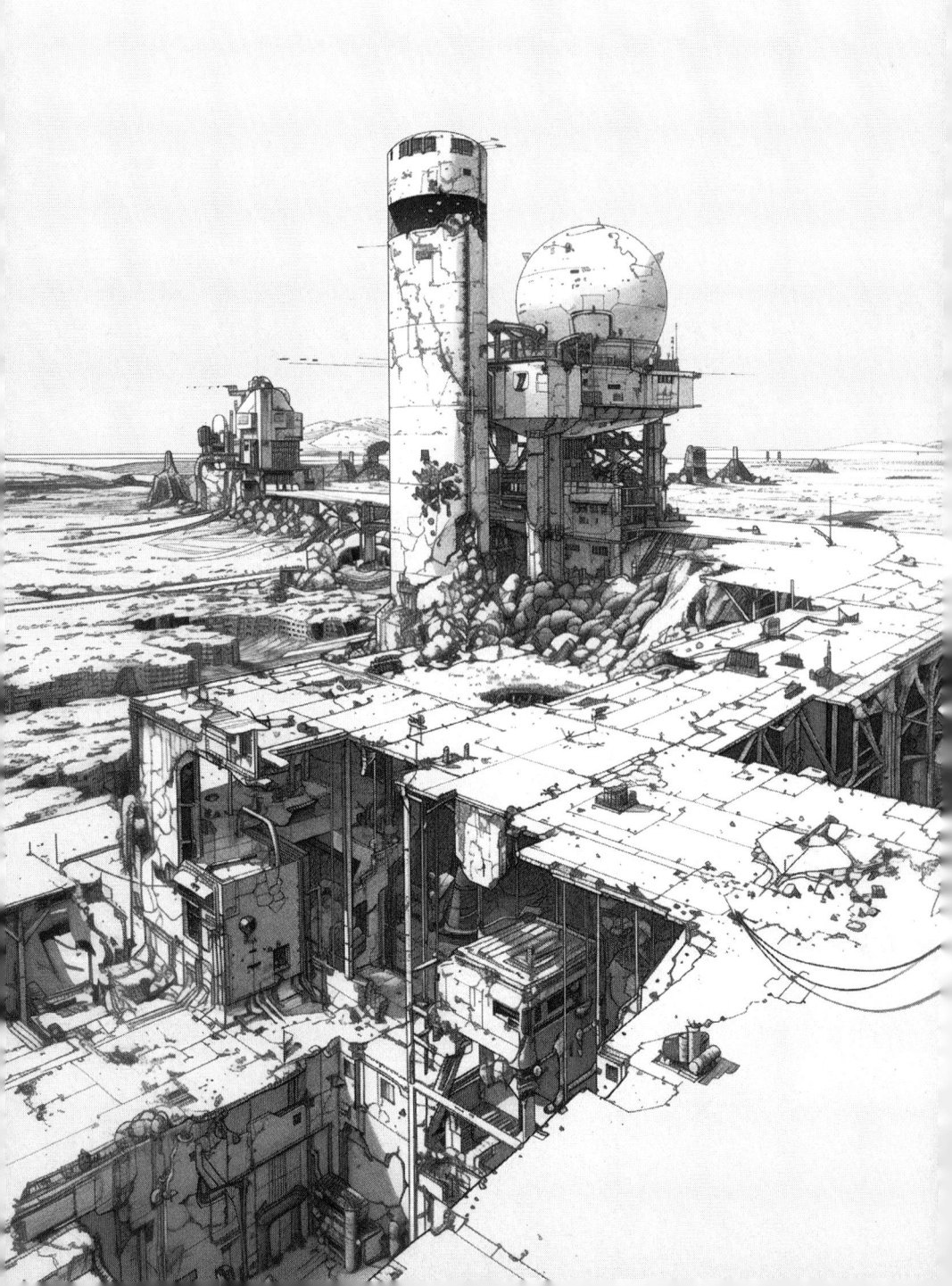

Seattle, 2066, 02:43 - Arrival at the Complex

The complex loomed dark and menacing before us. It was a large, multi-story building that must have once had industrial significance but was now just a decayed monument to the past. Weather, war, and neglect had left their marks.

The complex's outer walls were made of coarse concrete, crisscrossed with deep cracks. Large chunks had broken off in places, and metal beams jutted out of the walls like broken bones. Rust covered the iron parts, and wild plants and weeds grew in many spots, slowly claiming the building in a bizarre contest between nature and decay.

Old graffiti adorned the walls, some with political messages from earlier times like "Amithayus stays free," "Power scares the powerful," and my personal favorite, a single word: "Resistance." There were also signs of previous battles between the graffiti: bullet holes and scorch marks indicating fierce confrontations.

Several antennas and satellite dishes jutted upwards from the building's roof, apparently still in operation. Light signals flickered intermittently in the darkness, indicating that the complex was still actively used—likely by Dr. Caldwell and his people.

Next to the main building stood several smaller structures resembling abandoned warehouses and workshops. Some had collapsed, others were mere ruins. A few larger structures were reinforced with improvised barricades made of scrap, metal plates, and concrete blocks.

In the background, we spotted several large missile silos with pressure doors, and beyond that, a helicopter pad with an almost entirely black-painted helicopter. I stared at Simmons, who had also noticed the helicopter. It wasn't a serial model, as far as we knew. Simmons added that it must be one of the Night Hawk prototypes developed by Holster Defense Systems in the last two years. The fact that they were already operational and in use astonished him.

The main building's windows were mostly intact, but the few broken panes glowed dully in the weak light of the remaining streetlamps surrounding the area. Some windows were reinforced with metal grates, and others were boarded up, making the building even more inaccessible. Through some shattered windows, the building's interior glimmered, and shadows moved inside—the constant presence of Caldwell's security forces.

A heavy, new-looking steel gate marked the main entrance of the complex. It was secured with massive locks and bolts, and several armed guards in heavy armor stood in front of it. They patrolled nervously, their eyes scanning the surroundings, always on guard against intruders or overly inquisitive militias.

Neele, Simmons, and I paused as we knelt and exchanged a determined look. The lab and all the complex machinery had to be underground, indicating that the entire area was much larger than it appeared from above. This was it—the place where everything would be decided. My heart raced as I took in the scene before us. It was clear this wouldn't be an easy mission. We had to be quick, precise, and, above all, cautious.

"Are you ready?" I asked quietly, my voice barely more than a whisper in the cool night breeze. Neele and Simmons nodded resolutely.

Seattle, 2066, 03:10 - The Complex

We approached the outer walls of the complex under the cover of night and amidst the chaos of the battlefield. There, we pressed ourselves against the wall, trying to remain undetected. The cold concrete penetrated our suits, and the faint smell of smoke hung in the air. With our semi-automatic rifles at the ready, Simmons and I led the advance. Neele followed closely behind, preparing HELPS to guide us through the complex's security systems.

I signaled the others to stop with a hand gesture. We listened intently, hearing the distant rumble of explosions and the occasional crackle of radio transmissions. I pointed to a small side door guarded by two heavily armed guards. The guards wore black armored vests and helmets, pacing in a five-meter radius from the door, their fingers twitching nervously on the triggers of their weapons as I watched them through my scope. "I'll take the one on the left; you take the other," I said, and Simmons nodded, raising his weapon.

With precision and speed, honed through years of training and our bond, Simmons and I took aim at the guards. The shots broke the silence of the night, and the guards silently fell to the ground, their weapons clattering on the concrete before them.

Two down, about a hundred more to go.

Neele stepped forward and knelt at the steel door. She pulled a small device from her gear on the back of the HELPS suit. The electronic lock-picker had served us well over the past two nights. In the faint light, the device glowed blue as she connected it to the door and its electronic lock. Neele's eyes focused on the device, and after a few seconds, it clicked softly, and the door swung open.

"Okay, let's get inside and close the door behind us," I whispered, and we entered the dark, sparse corridor beyond the door. Neele closed the door behind us. The corridor was dimly lit, with flickering neon lights on the ceiling casting long shadows on the concrete walls. Faded posters with old political slogans, like "Freedom through Strength" and "Order and Progress," hung on the walls. I couldn't help but wonder who had operated this complex as a headquarters.

It could have been the Patriotic Defense Alliance, disbanded by the government in 2049, or followers of the Order of Steel Guardians, an extreme right-wing faction of the Tea Party movement that had imploded after a few years due to internal strife.

Whoever it was, I couldn't stand them.

The floor was cold and hard, and our steps echoed softly as we moved slowly and cautiously. We reacted to every tiny sound close to us, but nothing happened for several minutes.

The corridor led us deeper into the complex, past empty offices and storerooms filled with dust and decay. It was clear this place had been abandoned for a long time, but the presence of the guards indicated that something important was still happening here, even if only underground.

Neele led us to a door where we suspected the complex's security system was located. She disabled the electronic lock with the lock-picker again and carefully opened the door.

The room beyond was full of blinking monitors and control consoles that glowed blue and green in the dim light of the screens. Cables hung from the ceiling, winding across the floor like snakes. This room, where we now stood, seemed newly set up. There were few signs of decay or wear. The monitors were the latest technology. Next to one of the systems stood a regular WonderCoffee mug. I touched it lightly and felt it was still warm. "The owner can't be far," I said, and they nodded.

"I'll deactivate the security systems," she whispered, sitting at one of the consoles. Her fingers flew over the keyboard while I kept an eye on the door, and Simmons positioned himself to the right to cover the corridor with his rifle. Surveillance videos flickered on the monitors, showing different parts of the complex.

Suddenly, we heard footsteps and muffled voices approaching quickly. A group of Caldwell's elite soldiers rounded the corner, their black uniforms and armored vests gleaming in the sparse light of the monitors at the end of the long hallway. Their faces were stern and determined, and they carried an array of different, cutting-edge weapons.

Simmons and I gave them no chance to discover us first; we immediately opened fire. The first soldiers fell dead under our precise shots. Neele flinched noticeably when we started shooting. She hadn't expected so little time to complete her task.

More soldiers poured into the corridor, now firing at us, even though they could hardly see us. Bullets zipped through the air, sparking off the concrete walls and leaving bullet holes in the consoles in the middle of the room.

A fierce battle ensued. The air was filled with the loud crack of rifles and the shrill clicks of bullets ricocheting off the walls. The noise was unbearable as the hallway amplified and reflected the sounds manifold. The muzzle flashes illuminated the dark corridor in short, bright bursts. Simmons and I used our tactical skills to cover each other and keep the soldiers at bay as best we could. I felt the adrenaline coursing through my veins; each shot was precise but not always immediately lethal. Their armor was far more advanced than ours, and each hit that didn't strike the head or penetrate one of the small openings in the armor caused an injury but was survivable. We were both starting to have problems as more soldiers kept coming, firing everything they had.

Using her knowledge to open and close doors at our command while bypassing the security systems, Neele tried to stay out of the firefight. She ducked behind a console and continued working. "I need at least another minute!" she shouted over the din of battle, her voice trembling slightly with tension.

"Hurry!" I shouted back as Simmons took down another soldier. The soldier fell heavily to the ground, blood-covered, his weapon sliding out of his hands and skittering across the concrete floor toward us.

I yelled at Simmons, and we both threw one of our few flashbangs. We ducked away as they exploded just in front of the soldiers, disorienting them for several seconds. A bright light filled the corridor, and the soldiers screamed and shielded their eyes. At that moment, we charged forward; I swung my rifle into the face of one of the soldiers, hearing a loud crack as it probably broke his skull. Meanwhile, I grabbed the gun of another soldier from the ground and fired like a madman into the crowd before us. One by one, they fell in a spray of blood and inhuman sounds. Simmons finished off one of the last soldiers who had retreated with a precise shot to the upper arm, followed by a burst that shattered his helmet visor and sent him falling backward. The last shots echoed through the long corridor before a tense silence fell. We looked at each other, then stared down the long hallway. Nothing happened.

"Secure, for now," I said breathlessly, walking a few steps to the end of the hallway. I peered around the corner to ensure no more soldiers were coming. The rest of the hallway was empty. It ended at a rather large, heavy-looking metal pressure door, which bore the inscription "Central Laboratory Access."

Neele stood up and nodded in our direction. "The security systems are deactivated. We can move on, and we should. I'm sure a firefight like this won't go unnoticed."

We regrouped, checked our weapons, and moved on. We knew behind the large, heavy pressure door lay the heart of Caldwell's operations.

We went deeper into the complex. The air was stuffy and smelled of oil and sweat. Before us opened a large room divided into different honeycombs, seven in total.

Each honeycomb seemed to be its own small lab or cell, lit by cold, white fluorescent lights that barely penetrated the darkness. Scattered documents and broken equipment lay on the floor. Neele and I went left to examine one of the honeycombs while Simmons went right to check the others with his rifle ready.

The honeycombs were strange, hexagonal chambers, each about four meters wide and three meters high. The walls were made of thick, transparent plastic panels held by metal frames. Strong steel supports were embedded in the corners of the honeycombs, supporting the entire area. It almost looked like a grotesque, oversized beehive, but these cells were built for far more sinister purposes than collecting sweet nectar.

However, who knows what this mad scientist considers sweet nectar? I don't want to know.

Each honeycomb had a heavy metal door that opened like an airlock. Inside, there was various lab equipment, some broken, others sparkling like new. Metallic tables with straps and belts, obviously meant to restrain test subjects, sat in the center. Monitors hung on the walls, some still flickering with incomprehensible data and diagrams.

In the first honeycomb Neele and I entered, we found several large cages that could hold a person. The cages were empty, but the sight was still disturbing. Bloodstains and remnants of medical materials testified to the gruesome experiments conducted there.

"This is disgusting," whispered Neele, her voice trembling with horror. "Caldwell actually tortured people here."

"Yes, maybe," I replied.

"What do you mean, maybe?" she asked.

"It could have been the previous occupiers or owners of the complex. The Patriotic Defense Alliance was known for torturing their political and ideological enemies, regardless of whether they told the truth or lies."

Neele nodded silently. She knew it could only have been Caldwell. She was sure. I could see it in her expression.

I nodded silently, my gaze wandering over the oppressive scenes. We searched the honeycomb for helpful clues, while Simmons made similar discoveries on the other side. Every step echoed in the eerie silence, and the darkness in the corners felt like it was watching us.

In another honeycomb, we found medical records and data carriers that might contain important information. Neele gathered everything while I ensured no immediate threats were nearby. Simmons thoroughly checked each honeycomb, and his constant vigilance reassured me a little. I was glad he was at my side, covering our backs. I wouldn't want to be down here with anyone else but the two people I was with.

I didn't want to be down here at all, but that's another story.

One of the last honeycombs was particularly disturbing. It was full of sample containers and genetic sequencing machines. Here, Caldwell must have developed or improved further genetic markers that caused so much suffering. It was a dreadful sight, and the thought of people being used as guinea pigs here made me more than just angry. Neele looked sadly at the instruments and shook her head.

"Here, this might be important," said Neele, holding out a handful of data carriers. "We need to secure and analyze this data if we get the chance."

I nodded and took the data carriers. "Good job, Neele, you'll make a great ECLE agent someday."

She smiled slightly under her helmet, and I was glad I could distract her from the horrors of the honeycombs with this comment.

"Let's move on. We can't waste any time," said Simmons from the other end of the room. I agreed, and Neele wanted nothing more than to leave immediately.

Suddenly, we heard the sound of boots on the floor. We quickly pressed ourselves into the shadows of one of the honeycombs and watched as a group of elite soldiers crossed the room. They came from the only honeycomb that was more of a rectangle. Their eyes scanned the surroundings vigilantly, their weapons ready. It was clear they were looking for intruders— and that meant us. I didn't know if they knew who we were, but that information wouldn't be helpful to them in a few seconds. We were clearly at a tactical advantage, having spotted them without being detected.

I nodded to Simmons, and he slowly raised his weapon. The soldiers moved disciplined and cautiously in a line into the room. None of them suspected how close we were. Simmons fired the first shot, and I followed a few milliseconds later. The fight erupted around us again.

The elite soldiers were well-trained and heavily armed. But we came at them from two sides. I fired at the front half of the soldiers while Simmons targeted the rear. Bullets ricocheted off the walls, and sparks flew through the air. Neele ducked deep behind me in a corner and began communicating with HELPS. I heard her quietly trying to deactivate the security systems and grant us access to further areas.

From Neele's perspective, the world looked different through the lens of her HELPS suit. Instead of bullets and sparks, she saw only data and analyses flashing wildly across her helmet display, bathing the visual interface in bright colors as she focused on overcoming the complex's intricate security mechanisms. Her heart raced, but she knew they had no other choice. She had to find a way to open the doors while the two ECLE agents held off the attackers.

The fight intensified, and I was running out of ammunition. I had only one magazine left. Although one soldier after another fell, it seemed like an endless row of soldiers heading to the slaughter. The halls echoed with the screams of the dying and wounded soldiers as they fell one after another under the booming shots. We fought our way forward, honeycomb by honeycomb, while the advancing elite soldiers didn't give up.

"Shit, damn it, I'm almost out. Simmons," I shouted through our intercom system, and he responded with a message I didn't want to hear. He was almost out, too. We had to act immediately, or they would overwhelm us.

Then I saw our way out. The gigantic pressure door blocked our path. "Neele, can you open this door?" I asked breathlessly, trying to control my pulse.

Neele nodded. "But only if you get me there without being shot." Simmons and I looked at each other, knowing what to do. "Fries and WonderCola?" I asked, receiving only "Pickle and Synth-loaf!" as an answer.

I love this guy.

Synchronously, like two divers, we ran out of our honeycombs and fired everything we had left into the middle of the soldiers, who were confused by our sudden appearance. I leaped behind cover with all my might while Simmons ran to the other side of the room under my cover fire. Two of the soldiers fell dead. As far as I could see, there were four left. We waited several seconds, then jumped synchronously and fired everything our rifles could muster, turning the entire game around. Two more soldiers fell before us. "Two left," I shouted to Simmons, who was now in the middle behind a barricade while I was at his original position from the start of the fight. I checked my magazine and found it empty.

"Damn it, I'm out," I said, receiving only a short number in return. "One bullet."

We still had two opponents before us, but Simmons had only one bullet left. Close combat was out of the question. They would have riddled us with bullets before we got close. Knife throw? The chances of me hitting the exact spot I needed to were almost zero.

I was terrible at knife fighting.

I looked around and found nothing—no other weapon I could pick up, nothing close by. I heard the two soldiers slowly advancing on Simmons, shouting orders through their distorted communicators. I looked at Simmons, who looked at me, and then he did something really stupid.

"No, you damn idiot," I heard myself shout as he rolled out from behind cover and fired his last shot. The bullet pierced the helmet of the right soldier, who immediately fell dead. The second soldier briefly looked at his dead comrade before turning his rifle on Simmons, who had already dropped his. The soldier grinned as he aimed, knowing we were both out of bullets.

Just as he was about to pull the trigger, I heard a faint whoosh from a distance, splitting the soldier's visor, helmet, and grin into a bloody fountain. He dropped his weapon and fell backward, unmoving.

Simmons and I turned and saw Neele, her hands trembling as she held one of the soldiers' weapons. She screamed and dropped the weapon to the floor, then knelt and buried her face in her hands. We ran to her immediately. I hugged her, hearing her sob softly.

"See what he's driven me to. I just shot a man," she sobbed.

Simmons knelt beside her, hugging her as well, and said something I rarely heard from him. "I owe you my life, Neele. Thank you." She looked up at us.

Then she smiled slightly, knowing that what she had just done might have laid the foundation for saving Amithayus. She gave HELPS a command as she stood up again, causing the system to activate and the large door behind us to creak loudly as it freed itself from its constraints. Dust trickled from the ceiling as access to the complex's main area slowly opened before us.

Sweaty and gasping, we looked at each other. Now, we were finally a team. Each of us had saved each other's lives at least once. It was time to take someone else's life. And that someone was Caldwell. Dr. Viktor Caldwell.

I couldn't stand the name the first time I heard it.

CENTRAL LABORATORY

TWENTY-TWO.
FRAGMENTS

Seattle, 2066 03:30 - Central Laboratory

We crept through the dark corridors of the complex, the tension in the air almost tangible. Every step was cautious, every breath controlled. Finally, we reached the central laboratory—the heart of Caldwell's operations. The atmosphere was electric, filled with the hum of countless machines and monitors dominating the room. We paused briefly to assess the situation. There was no one else around, which was both reassuring and terrifying.

The room was overflowing with advanced technology and mysterious equipment. Monitors lined the walls, displaying various data, diagrams, and live feeds in constantly shifting rhythms. The screens flickered with a bluish light that cast an eerie glow over the room. Cables and wires ran in seemingly chaotic patterns across the floor and walls, making the room feel alive and breathing.

In the center of the lab stood a large, circular table equipped with holographic projectors. The projectors cast three-dimensional images of genetic structures, molecular models, and tactical maps into the air. The holographic displays rotated slowly, constantly updated with new information. It was as if the room were the brain of a massive, all-knowing entity.

Metallic arms and grippers hung from the ceiling above the table, resembling the tentacles of a giant mechanical kraken. These arms moved silently and precisely, picking up various samples and materials arranged in small, transparent containers. The containers were analyzed and returned by the arms. Two barely discernible silhouettes stood at the far end of the lab, shielded by a series of massive metal shelves. They worked at a large central control console, covered in countless buttons, levers, and screens. The flickering lights of the control monitors cast eerie shadows on the faces of the two figures, who seemed busy making final preparations.

"We need to find the warhead," I whispered to Simmons.
"There's just one big problem," he replied.
"And that is?"
"I have no idea where the tactical warhead is. Do you?"
Damn, he was right. None of us knew where it was, what it looked like, or how to deactivate it.

Neele nodded and checked her HELPS suit. "I'll handle the two at the control console," she said, her voice firm but with a hint of doubt in her eyes. "You two look for the warhead. When you find it, give me a signal." Simmons and I nodded. "Be careful," I said to Neele before we split up. Simmons and I moved in one direction, while Neele crept toward the two figures in the shadows.

We moved slowly and cautiously, always careful not to be detected, even though we had only seen two people in the lab. That meant nothing; someone could still jump out from any corner and attack us. At least the shelves and crates offered some cover. We knew we had to act quickly to identify, find, and defuse the warhead.

I hope Simmons knows how to do that. I have no idea.

I was snapped out of my thoughts. Suddenly, we heard a loud hum and saw a transparent sheet of vector glass being lowered around the central control station. The shimmering material blocked access to the two figures and cut off our direct path. "Damn," I whispered. "That makes things more complicated."

Neele noticed the glass lowering and crept toward a box that might control the shield. Her gaze was fixed on the two figures at the console. She knew she had to find a way to deactivate the shield to reach them. Her fingers trembled slightly as she removed the box cover and examined the microarchitecture and cables of the control unit. She tinkered with several components until they finally clicked. Hope, she thought. But nothing happened. Instead of the glass moving up, she heard something. From a distance, a faint beeping approached, and several small vacuum drones, along with their mopping variants, began their routine work.

The drones maneuvered around the massive machines, collecting the minimal dust present in the lab. Neele ducked into a shadow as she noticed one of the figures stepping out from behind the console. The person noticed the small cleaning operation. "What's this now?" she heard a familiar voice say. It was a voice she had heard earlier today. Neele continued to watch the glass barrier, and then she saw him.

Thornej A. Holster Jr. pressed his nose against the glass from the inside, watching the little drones. "Did you order this?" he said. Then Viktor's unmistakable voice followed, freezing Neele's blood. He said just one word: "No."
"Then turn it off; it's distracting me." A few seconds later, the drones stopped their work and retreated to their hiding places. Neele did the same, crawling along the wall and entering a long corridor far from the control console. She opened a communication channel to her teammates.

"I have no idea how to deactivate the shield. We can't reach it from the outside, and the shield is probably bulletproof."
"That's vector glass," Simmons said.
"Okay, the shield is too secure," Neele whispered into the communication device. "I need to find another way to reach them."

Simmons and I nodded, even though she couldn't see us. "Okay, Neele. We'll go around the lab and find another entrance. We estimate the warhead isn't in the lab," Simmons said firmly.

He could have discussed that with me beforehand. It's not easy to gamble with thousands of lives if you make a mistake.

We left as quickly as we could. There were more entrances besides the one we came through, and we chose the nearest one. It took a few minutes until we reached a pressure door leading to an outside corridor. The night was filled with the sounds of war, explosions, and gunfire echoed in the distance. We knelt and considered our next move. Simmons looked at me, and I looked at him. He whispered, "We have two options. Either we go around the lab and hope to find an entrance leading to the control room where they're standing. That's option one."

"Okay," I said, "what's the second option?"
"Imagine you're a mad scientist wanting to detonate a tactical nuclear bomb to complete a genetic test on clones. Where would you hide the warhead?"

I thought about it. It was clear. "Not near the clones. The blast force is too strong for them to physically survive a direct explosion." So, it had to be stored somewhere further away but still close enough to emit enough gamma rays onto the clones to check the results.
"Exactly," Simmons said. "Oh, come on, you had no idea. I just put it together."

"As you say," I replied. "Now we have two tiny problems."
"I understand," I said, and I radioed Neele, explaining that we briefly needed HELPS' assistance.

HELPS quickly calculated the distance of a similarly powerful tactical nuclear explosion, based on data from previous disasters, the likely protective measures for the clones, the timing of the shockwave, and potential radiation exposure. It gave us a number: two to three kilometers. Estimated, given too many variables. Then added in a friendly tone, **"Have a safe day."**

That was very kind of him. Thanks, HELPS.

So, we solved one of the two problems. The second was trickier and more of a guessing game. A 50/50 chance we were right. Our mission was to defuse the bomb. The crucial question: "Are the clones in the lab or the tactical nuclear bomb?" Simmons and I shrugged. There was only one solution. A rematch. Rock-paper-scissors. And I lost again.

"Ready?" Simmons asked, and I nodded.

We took deep breaths and sprinted off, our steps quick and quiet on the dusty ground. We had to cross the open space quickly to avoid detection. We ran like madmen through the darkness across the massive field in front of us, heading to the bunkers and silos we had seen earlier. They were about two to three kilometers from the lab, and we suspected the warhead— or multiple warheads—was stored there.

Please let it be just one. Or none.

Adrenaline pumped through our veins as we neared the first silo. Behind us, we heard the hum of a drone, but it didn't seem to notice us. We reached the silo and found a heavy metal door embedded in the ground. Simmons knelt and began examining the lock. "It's not very secure. I can crack it; give me a minute," he said, getting to work.

While Simmons worked on the lock, I kept an eye on our surroundings. The moon cast a faint light on the battlefield, and I could see the silhouettes of soldiers running in various directions in the distance. The war in Amithayus raged on, and time was running out.

Finally, the lock clicked, and the metal door sprang open. We saw a staircase leading down. "Into the abyss," Simmons said, and we quickly descended, the door closing silently behind us. The bunker was cold and damp; the air smelled of mold and old metal. I felt briefly nauseous thinking about the bacteria and organic gases down here. We proceeded cautiously, my nose wrinkling at the smell; our steps echoed softly on the concrete floor. The corridor was narrow and gloomy, dimly lit by flickering neon lights.

"And there's supposed to be a warhead hidden down here?" I whispered to Simmons, who ignored me.

As we ventured deeper into the bunker, we suddenly heard footsteps and muffled voices. We stopped and listened intently. "Straight ahead," Simmons whispered, pointing to a heavy steel door at the end of the corridor.

"At least it looks like a door that could guard something big and heavy," I replied, and we cautiously approached it. But before we reached it, the door opened, and two armed guards stepped out. We had to act fast. Simmons and I exchanged a quick, familiar look.

It was go-time.

The guards stepped out, their weapons ready, but they hadn't noticed us yet. We pressed ourselves tightly against the wall, hidden in the shadows of the dim corridor. The smell of metal and oil hung in the air; the tension was almost palpable.

Simmons took a cautious step forward, his movements smooth and precise. I followed closely, my heart pounding like a sledgehammer in my chest. It had to happen quickly, quietly, and efficiently. Then it began, literally blow-by-blow.

We had no weapons. Simmons launched himself forward with a quick, decisive move, grabbing the first guard by the collar. With another explosive motion, he rammed his fist into the guard's face with all his might. An ugly crunch echoed as the guard's nose broke, and he fell unconscious to the ground. Blood spattered on the concrete floor, and the guard's body went limp.

The second guard turned around and reflexively raised his weapon. I reacted immediately, leaping forward and grabbing his wrist, wrenching his arm aside, and striking with all my strength. My punch landed on his ribs with such force that I could hear bones crack. I struck again, hitting his cheek, feeling more bones give way under my fist. The guard staggered back, and I followed with a third blow, ramming my shoulder into his chest and slamming him against the wall. With a quick strike to the throat, Simmons finished him off. The guard collapsed silently to the ground. We were a good team.

Breathless and full of adrenaline, we looked around. The two guards were incapacitated, but we couldn't waste any time.

"Simmons, check the door," I said quietly, keeping an eye on our surroundings. Simmons knelt before the heavy steel door and began examining the lock.

"More cheap Chinese junk," he muttered, "but that's to be expected here in Amithayus," as he unpacked his tools. "I'll need about a minute."

I nodded and took up position at the corridor entrance, the dead guard's rifle at the ready, prepared for any additional guards. The seconds felt like hours, the clicking and buzzing of Simmons' tools the only sound breaking the silence. My nerves were stretched to the limit.

"Almost done," Simmons finally whispered, giving the lock a final, careful twist. A soft click sounded, and the steel door opened with a slight hiss.

"The door's open," he said, stepping aside. We hesitated briefly, watching and listening intently for any reaction from inside. More seconds passed, but nothing happened. The air was filled with an electrifying tension with every move we made.

"Be careful when we go in," I whispered. "It could still be a trap." Simmons nodded in agreement.

"I'll go first since I'm younger than you," he said determinedly, cautiously stepping into the room.

What did he mean by that…?

I followed him closely, my rifle ready, prepared for anything. The room was dark and cool, illuminated only by the faint glow of a few control lights on the walls. It was clear this bunker was used for something significant. We just needed to find out what exactly.

Seattle, 2066 03:45 - Central Laboratory

Neele walked down the corridor, her thoughts racing as she tried to piece the puzzle together. Why was Holster Skyway Inc. involved in this experiment? What benefits could they gain from it? And why Thornej A. Holster Jr.? Jr. suited him much better, she thought. What had driven him to ally with Caldwell and support these horrific experiments? Didn't he know better? Or didn't he care?

She reached a half-open door and cautiously pushed it further open. Behind it was a bright white room. It looked like one of the cells in her old lab, only much larger. The walls were covered from top to bottom with sterile white tiles. High-tech equipment hummed softly in the silence, and white cables ran through the room, ending at the floor. My old lab, only more modern, she thought. The same room where I found the first clone of Peet. She looked around, hoping to find the picture of her little brother wrapped in ThermoFlex. But the room offered nothing she wished for.

In the center were several cryostatic pods arranged in a semicircle. Her heart skipped a beat as she realized they were the same as in Skyward Tower, with the same contents: clones of Peet. Their faces were smooth and inhuman, almost robotic. They were as white as the skin of one of the geisha she had observed in Amithayus. And they looked as if they were sleeping. The sight hit her like a punch to the gut.

Then it dawned on her. She was at the heart of Dr. Caldwell's plan. These things pretending to be her brother were the result of a hundred years of pain, suffering, and madness brought about by science. Ushering in a new scientific era for humanity. She felt sick. She had heard it many times before, and now it was finally happening. And it was wrong. It wasn't a new era for humanity—it was one that Caldwell and Holster wanted to control.

Neele knew she had to act. She went to the console next to the stasis chambers and began entering commands to deactivate the chambers. Her fingers trembled slightly as she tried to input the sequences with all her knowledge.

admin_override -pass "SnoqualmieRidge"
SYSTEM: Access Denied. Code not recognized.

shutdown_sequence -id 4571 -force
SYSTEM: Override attempt detected. Access restricted.

emergency_stop -auth "DrNeele"
SYSTEM: Access Denied. Incorrect password.

halt_all_operations -key 9F2D5A
SYSTEM: Critical Error. Subsystem override failed.

deactivate_Countdown -security_bypass -level 3
SYSTEM: Authorization failed. Security protocols activated.

But the console didn't respond to any of her inputs.

disable_countdown -immediate
SYSTEM: Security breach detected. Shutting down external access.

disable_protocol -code "Peet"
SYSTEM: Error. Command sequence invalid.

terminate_operations -auth_key "XR72-KLMN"
SYSTEM: Access Denied. Invalid authorization key.

cancel_countdown -priority_high -code 89123
SYSTEM: Critical Error. Override command rejected.

SYSTEM: Security lockdown in effect. Command not executable.

Nothing worked. A red light flashed, indicating that access was denied, and the console shut itself down. The chambers were far too well secured and disconnected from the regular Holster Skyway network. She couldn't deactivate them.

Despair rose within her. "Damn," she whispered, punching the console. "There has to be a way." She looked around and suddenly heard footsteps behind her. She turned and saw Thornej A. Holster Jr. standing in the doorway. His face was tense, his eyes sparkling with curiosity. He looked directly into her eyes.

"What do you think you're doing?" he asked, his voice calm and controlled.

"If you really want to know, I'm going to destroy these clones. No one should associate my brother with these hideous experiments," Neele replied firmly, though she felt uncertain. "I won't let your plan succeed."

Holster stepped closer, his eyes fixed on her. "Ah, you must be Dr. Neele. I've heard of you. Though nothing extraordinary. You don't understand what's at stake, little one. This project will save humanity. Diseases will be cured, aging will be halted, and humanity will be elevated to a new level of evolution. You can be a small part of it under the leadership of Holster Skyway Inc. You could become something greater than you are now."

Neele couldn't believe it. What an arrogant, inhumane creature stood before her. She shook her head in disbelief. "Not this way. Not at this cost, and certainly not under the leadership of Holster Skyway or Viktor."

Holster sighed, raising a hand as if to calm her. "Viktor. Ah, yes, you could learn so much from him. Think for a moment, Neele. What we're doing here is the greatest scientific achievement in human history, and your family is a mere stepping stone, a rather insignificant coincidence in it. We could all change the future. Imagine what's possible…"

"I don't want to imagine any of that," she interrupted him with a forcefulness in her voice that left him momentarily speechless.

Holster Jr.'s voice rose at least an octave. "That's not how you treat heirs to a trillion-dollar company—"
"Shut up, boy," she interrupted him again. "It's not about science. It's not about eliminating diseases or making people's lives better. It's not even about the future. It's only about the now. The present. And how you can shape it to your advantage so the future looks how you want it to. Some government decisions you don't like? No problem. You change it in the past. Someone catches on to you? No big deal; you eliminate them in the past. Do stock prices fall? It doesn't matter; we've already sold the shares in the past. Advancing humanity. What a joke. The only thing people like you care about is personal profit, and I've seen enough of what that leads to in the real world, outside the gates of Amithayus," Neele replied, her voice trembling slightly with suppressed anger and the adrenaline coursing through her veins. She knew she had to do something, but the console wouldn't crack. Her eyes wandered around the room as she tried to distract Holster further.

"HELPS, how far are you with the stasis chambers?" she whispered into her communication device.

"Almost there, Neele. But I need a little more time; the systems are more complicated than I'm used to," HELPS responded in her ear.

"You can do it," Neele said quietly. She knew she had to find a way to hinder Holster, buying HELPS the time needed.

Holster stepped closer, his eyes blazing with anger. "Who do you think you are? You're nothing. A small scientist with a genetic defect. Nothing more. A whim of evolution. How dare you speak to me like that. To me, the son of the most incredible man who ever walked this earth. And you really think you can stop both of us? Dr. Neele. What a joke."

Neele took a deep breath and looked at him steadily. "Yes, Jr., I'm pretty sure."

That was enough. Holster Jr. exploded with rage and charged at Neele, but she only heard one question in her ear that gave her all the confidence she needed.

"Now, Neele?"
"Now, HELPS!"

The command to HELPS lowered a vector glass barrier around Holster from the ceiling. In his rage, he hadn't noticed running into the contamination marker found in every lab. He was surprised by his own stupidity, as he was thrown back by the vector glass barrier with a bloody nose and broken jaw, falling backward to the ground.

There he was, the great man with a Jr. attached to his name. Trapped in one of his own inventions. Holster Defense Systems presents unbreakable glass. Perfect for any kind of prison. Minorities are safely stored away for eternity.

"You'll pay for this! You don't understand, you piece of trash! You're destroying our future!" Holster screamed, his eyes burning with hatred. Neele thought he had a cute accent when blood was pouring from his mouth.

Neele ignored every curse spilling from his mouth and focused on HELPS. "Status?"

"I'm working on deactivating the stasis chambers. Just a few more seconds," HELPS responded calmly. While Holster continued to scream and bang against the barrier, Neele saw the control lights on the chambers begin to flicker. It's working, she thought with relief.

"Neele?"
"Yes, HELPS?"
"You should have a safe day, so please step back a few steps."

"Oh." Neele ran behind the barrier, where Thornej A. Holster continued to spit out curses and a few teeth.

Then, the first chamber began to tremble, and tiny sparks flew from the control panels attached to the cryostasis pods. The security mechanisms that HELPS had overridden caused an overload in the systems. One by one, the chambers exploded in sparks and blue, electrostatic flames. The heat filled the room, instinctively making Neele step back a few more steps.

She watched as the clones of Peet dissolved in the bright light, and though she knew none of them were the real Peet, a deep pain pierced her heart. "Peet…" she whispered. With the last flickering flame, her brother was resting in peace. She couldn't bear the thought but knew it was better for everyone. His face would have been the face that brought so much calamity to humanity. Yet all he wanted was to go to an amusement park with her and their family. She suppressed the rising tears.

At that exact moment, Dr. Caldwell entered the room, his eyes widening as he saw the chaos. "What have you done?!" he screamed, his voice trembling with rage.

Neele turned to him, her eyes burning with the anger and grief of losing her family and knowing that the man responsible now stood before her. "We destroyed your plan, Viktor. You will not create your perfect humanity."

Caldwell let out an angry growl and began typing on a console attached to his arm. "You have no idea what you've just done. But you and anyone else, no matter how many you are, will not stop me."

He pressed one last button, and a countdown began on the monitors. Then he turned and ran out of the room toward his waiting Night Hawk helicopter. The pressure door separating him from Neele closed just as she was about to rush through.

"Damn, I missed my chance," she thought. He's gotten away.

Neele knew time was running out. She looked at Holster, still trapped in the vector glass barrier, now crawling around the floor like an animal, picking up his partially golden-chromed teeth. Then she looked at the monitors. The countdown continued relentlessly.

"No matter the cost," she whispered to herself. "I will make sure the rest of your plan fails. For Alicia, and for Peet."

With one last look at the destroyed clones, she ran out of the room, determined to stop the countdown and thwart Viktor's plan.

Seattle, 2066 03:50–12:30 Minutes Until Countdown Ends

Dr. Viktor Caldwell hurried through the corridors of his newly built complex, his heart pounding with tension and hatred. The hum of the machines and the distant sounds of battle had become an all-too-close, ominous backdrop. He knew that every second counted now. Caldwell reached the exit and saw the waiting Night Hawk helicopter.

The rotor blades were spinning, creating an updraft that stirred the surrounding dust. The helicopter was his only means of escape.

He ran as fast as he could, focusing solely on survival. Internally, he boiled with hatred and contempt. These pathetic people in Amithayus meant nothing to him. Their lives were meaningless compared to his vision. The tactical nuclear bomb would erase all traces and allow him to start anew. Though the destruction of the clones had nearly ruined his plan, he would not give up. He would build another lab from scratch. Somewhere in this world, there would be someone else with the marker. He would escape and start over.

Then, the realization hit him, and he stopped in his tracks. Of course. How could he have overlooked that? Neele. She also had the genetic marker, albeit less developed than his previous test subjects. What were another sixteen years when it came to the greater good?

He was about to turn around when he heard a loud whooshing sound and saw a rocket speeding toward the helicopter from the corner of his eye. It was too late to dodge. The rocket hit the helicopter with a loud explosion, and a massive blast threw Caldwell through the air. He was slammed to the ground by the force of the detonation, his body hitting the concrete hard.

Dizzy and in pain, Caldwell tried to get up. His ears rang, and the world around him was engulfed in chaos and flames. Emerging from the ash and smoke was a figure. An older Asian man with a penetrating gaze and the composure of a seasoned warrior.

Caldwell screamed in pain. "Who are you?" His voice trembled with fury.

The Asian man remained calm as he slowly approached Caldwell, his eyes firmly fixed on him. "It doesn't matter who I am. We are the citizens of Amithayus," he said with a calm, compelling voice. "And we are here to stop you."

Caldwell gritted his teeth and struggled to stand. "You're too late," he hissed. "The countdown is running, and no one can stop it. Especially not an old wreck like you."

Zhan Tao moved closer, his movements still calm and deliberate. "The people of Amithayus have risen against every outside enemy for decades," he said, his voice like a rock in the surf. "They deserve another chance at a normal life, and we will not let you take it from them."

"What do you mean by 'we'?" Caldwell shouted as he stood up. "Ganjin and I," said Zhan Tao, looking past Caldwell.

Caldwell turned around. Behind him stood Neele, who had approached quickly, a knife in her hand. The determination in her eyes left no doubt that she was ready to do whatever it took to stop him.

A fierce fight immediately ensued. Caldwell used all his strength to fend off the two. He fought with the desperation of a man who knew he had everything to lose. But Zhan Tao and Neele were a well-coordinated team. Zhan Tao moved skillfully, blocking Caldwell's attacks with minimal arm movements, while Neele struck precisely with the knife.

Caldwell felt his strength waning. He knew he had to act immediately. He hit Zhan Tao's hand with a powerful blow, causing him to step back. Then Viktor grabbed a metal rod lying on the ground. He turned quickly towards Neele and charged at her, sweeping her off her feet with a strike from the rod. Neele screamed in pain as she hit the ground, her left leg bleeding, and she dropped the knife. She lay on the ground, and Viktor stood over her, the rod raised, ready to deliver the fatal blow.

But just as he was about to strike, Zhan Tao placed himself between him and Neele. Caldwell struck with all his might, and the rod hit Zhan Tao's head with a dull thud.
"No!" Neele screamed, rolling out of the way in pain as Zhan Tao fell silently to the ground.

But that wasn't enough. In a fit of madness and desperation, Caldwell continued to strike Zhan Tao's head repeatedly, his eyes wide with rage and hatred. The metal rod hit Zhan Tao's skull with brutal force, blood splattering, and a sickening crunch filled the air.

"Die! Die!" Caldwell screamed as he continued to strike Zhan Tao, whose body collapsed under the relentless blows. Zhan Tao's face was bloody and disfigured, yet his eyes maintained an expression of unwavering determination until the very end.

Neele screamed in horror, but she knew she had to act. With a pained expression, she grabbed Caldwell and, with all the strength in her arms, threw him backward against the rubble of the collapsed wall. Zhan Tao lay motionless on the ground, but his sacrifice had given her the time she needed. "For the people of Amithayus," she whispered, "I will finish this. For all of us." She turned and limped down one of the corridors.

She saw Caldwell getting back up from the corner of her eye. But now she had a plan. Zhan Tao's sacrifice would not be in vain. This is where it all ends. And now, she had his full attention.

Neele limped down the corridor, her body and especially her leg aching from the exertions and battles of the last hours. Her thoughts raced, but she knew she had to focus on her plan. "I mustn't waste any time," she told herself. The plan had solidified in her mind when she had given the command to detonate the cryostasis pods. She had to hurry.

Arriving at the only lab where her plan could work, she immediately began having HELPS activate various things in the room. HELPS recognized her commands and began monitoring and preparing various lab systems.

But when she was about to give the crucial command, HELPS hesitated.

"I cannot execute this command, Neele," said the mechanical voice in her head. *"The command endangers my user."*

"Damn it, HELPS, do it!" Neele shouted as she continued to work on the controls.

"The command endangers you, Neele," HELPS repeated. *"My primary objective is to protect the user."*

"That's a direct order, HELPS," Neele yelled desperately. "We have no other choice!"

"Command not executable," HELPS repeated. *"Then I can no longer guarantee you a safe day."*

"Listen, you damn, lovable machine that has saved my ass so many times," Neele shouted, her voice full of force. "If you don't do this, we all die. And by all, I mean everyone.
The people of Amithayus, the ECLE investigators, the residents of Seattle…" She paused briefly. "And me. You have to do it."

There was a long pause as HELPS processed the instruction. Then, reluctantly, the response came: *"The command will be executed at your direction."*

Behind her, she heard footsteps. Caldwell had followed her, holding a pistol, his eyes blazing with rage and hatred.
"You bitch," he screamed. "I will complete my work, no matter the cost. You, or any of your comrades, cannot stop me."

Neele slowly turned to face him, her gaze steady.
"Your work? Your work?! What have you created, Viktor? You've only followed the orders of another Viktor from the future. Created?" She laughed out loud. "You've created nothing but pain and destruction."

Caldwell's face remained cold. "You don't understand, Neele. Humanity needs someone like me, willing to make the sacrifices necessary to move us forward."

"Sacrifices?" Neele shook her head. "You talk about sacrifices, but others always have to pay the price for your visions and die."

He raised the weapon, aiming it at her.
"Enough time wasted. You die now. I can still extract the marker from your dead body, just as I did with your brother."

Neele felt a wave of anger rising within her.
"You monster," she whispered, and at that moment, she jumped to the side behind a barrier, and a shot echoed through the lab. She felt the pain as the bullet grazed her arm. She

gritted her teeth as she hit the ground hard. Her right arm had lost all function.

"You can't win, Neele," Caldwell shouted as he approached. "Give up and die already!"
"Now," Neele called out.

Caldwell fired again, but this time, the bullet missed its target. At that exact moment, HELPS activated the gamma-ray emitter, which was set up in this lab for testing purposes, and the pressure doors began to close. Caldwell realized what she was doing, and his eyes widened in shock.

"What have you done?" he screamed, raising the weapon again, but his fingers were already losing strength. The radiation began to eat away at his body from within. Neele rose with her last bit of strength and slowly approached him, her eyes full of determination.
"This is for Peet," she said softly and knocked the weapon, along with his fingers, out of what was left of his hand.
"And this is for all the others you sacrificed."

She smacked her fist into his face with everything she had left. Caldwell sank to the ground, his hand trembling as he tried to grab the weapon with his other hand, but his fingers no longer obeyed him. The radiation inexorably consumed him from within, and his face lost all form.

"You can't do this to me," he gasped before collapsing face-first to the ground with a final squelching sound.

Neele stood over him, her breathing heavy, her heart aching from the gamma rays and everything else she had survived.
"For the people of Amithayus," she whispered again. HELPS turned off the emitter, and Neele felt her body slowly recovering from the heaviness. She turned away and limped out of the lab without glancing at Viktor.

Seattle, 2066 03:53–09:30 Minutes Until Countdown Ends

"Fuck, fuck, fuck," I yelled as we ran through the narrow corridor leading to the control room. My heart pounded in my throat, and my hands shook with tension. Every step echoed in the empty, metallic hallways. We knew every second counted. Finally, we reached the room that held the fate of Amithayus in its ticking seconds.

"There it is!" Simmons shouted, pointing at the large digital display showing the countdown: 00:09:48. The timer continued mercilessly.

I tried to operate the console, but all inputs were rejected.
"Damn it!" I cursed. "It's not working. I have no idea how to disable a nuclear weapon, let alone turn on the display."

Simmons shrugged. "Me neither," he said, looking around the room in desperation. In his haste, he knocked a Black Viper noodle box off the console. It clattered to the floor, and the smell of cold, spicy sauce filled the air.

"What do we do now? We're running out of time!"

I stared at the console, feeling the weight of the situation growing heavier on my shoulders. Then it hit me.

I'm such an idiot. I had to use my Fragment Ability.

I knew there had to be a clue I had missed.
"I need to recheck the bodies. Relive the last ten minutes. There must be a clue I can find that way." I ran out of the room to the bodies of the guards we had taken down. It took two minutes to reach them.

I knelt next to the first body, tore my glove off, and placed my hand on the shoulder of the first corpse. The world around me blurred.

"Damn, it stinks in here," I heard myself say, looking around as far as I could. In front of me was a tiled wall reflecting ghastly neon light into my eyes. I tried to turn my head left and right, but all I could see from the corners of my eyes were tastelessly painted walls in yolk yellow, feeling entirely confining.

Where the hell are you right now?

I tried to tilt my head up, but I saw nothing but a white wall and the beginning of a neon light.

What are those weird noises around me?

I forced my head down with all my might; I had no time for this shit. I saw my arms hanging down. What was I holding? I couldn't tell. Just a little more…

Oh, damn. You really should've shaved, you asshole.

I snapped out of my ability and stared at Greg, the body lying before me.

I'm Sorry that you have such a small dick. But you don't need it anymore.

I ran to the second body and placed my hand on its arm. Again, the world around me blurred. But this time, I immediately recognized where I was. I was in the room with the control console. I heard myself laughing at really inappropriate jokes from Greg about the population of Amithayus.

Great, Greg has a small dick and is also a racist.

I watched myself talking to Greg, who suddenly stood up. "I need to piss, boss."
"Alright, but don't piss yourself again…" I heard myself laugh loudly and saw myself shoveling another portion of noodles down my throat.

Damn, those were really fucking spicy. Ugh, how can anyone eat such crap?

Greg had left the room. For almost two minutes, nothing happened, except I experienced more pain from the noodles while staring at the screen showing four small sections. Then I saw something on the screen, and so did Jebbediah. I saw Simmons and me sneaking down the corridor.

We looked good sneaking. Professional. Fast.

But Jebbediah had noticed. He ripped the two security keys from the console, which immediately stopped working.

Very good, very good, Jebbediah, and now show me where you hid them. Oh, come on, you can't be serious. Why does everyone do that?

I snapped back from the past and ran towards the control room.

"Simmons!" I yelled down the corridor.
"Simmons, the damn noodle box!" I shouted, exhausted.

Simmons looked at me, confused. "What?"

"The fucking bottom of the noodle box! The keys are in the bottom of the noodle box!" I grabbed the box and tore off the bottom in one swift motion. Besides a massive explosion of cocaine dispersing in the air, we found what we were looking for. Two small keys were hidden in the bottom of the box.

"Quick!" I threw one of the keys to Simmons and ran to the end of the large console.

"This is crazy," Simmons said, but he caught the key midair without hesitation. We positioned ourselves at the two locks at opposite ends of the console.
"You know what comes next," I said, and Simmons nodded. The decisive game had arrived, and I hoped we were on the same page this time.

"Rock, paper, scissors!" We turned the keys simultaneously, and the console lit up before us.

"It's working!" Simmons shouted as the countdown halted: 00:00:10. We looked at each other in disbelief as the timer stopped.

"We did it," I said, relieved. "The damn countdown is stopped."

Simmons nodded and sank to his knees, exhausted.
"We actually did it."

We had actually done it. Not just a little bit, but really, completely. The last forty-eight hours had been the wildest trip I'd ever had.

Wow, the colors in this room. **And how brightly the screen glows.**

I sniffed. Then I looked at Simmons; his entire face was covered in white powder. It looked hilarious. We both started laughing. Why, we didn't know, but it felt good. I leaned further against the console, feeling the tension slowly leave me. Simmons sank to his knees, exhausted, and breathed heavily.

The relief was palpable, but the last few minutes had taken everything from us.

Seattle, 2066 06:58 - A New Day

"We actually did it," Simmons mumbled, what felt like an eternity later, as he slowly got back up. "Amithayus is saved."

"Yes, we did," I replied, helping him up. "Let's get out of here. There's nothing more we can do."

We left the control room together and walked back through the narrow corridor. Past Greg and Jebbediah, who were now peacefully resting. Every step felt heavy and laborious, but the relief of saving the city stayed with us. The sounds of war outside seemed to be fading, and a strange calm settled over the complex and all of Amithayus.

As we left the building and stepped onto the open field, I noticed the sky in the east was slowly getting brighter.

Damn, man, how long were we in that underground bunker?

The first rays of the morning sun painted the horizon in a soft, golden light. It was a hopeful sight after all the chaos and destruction.

The wind carried the smell of smoke and burnt metal to us, along with the fresh coolness of the morning.

In the distance, we saw a figure standing before the lab complex. Neele was limping, her movements labored, but she was alive. When she saw us, she raised her hand and waved weakly.

"Neele!" I shouted, quickening my steps as much as I could. Simmons followed closely behind.

When we reached her, we saw the traces of battle on her face and in her eyes. But I could also see a glimmer of hope.

"Did you make it?" she asked, though she knew the answer. Her voice was exhausted but sounded confident.

"Yes," I replied. "Amithayus is safe."

Neele smiled weakly and nodded. "I did it too. Caldwell is done. It's over. For good."

Simmons looked at her admiringly. "That's incredible. You really did it."

"We all did," she said, placing her only good hand on my shoulder. "It's crazy, but we survived all of this shit."

We stood on a random field in the middle of nowhere as the sun slowly rose over the horizon, bathing the battlefield in warm light. It was a new day for Amithayus, and we had made it possible. The city was saved, and we had paid a high price for it. But at that moment, we knew it had all been worth it. Simmons and I sank exhausted to the ground as the tension finally left us. As we lay there, the first rays of sunlight fell on us, and we all had the same thought.

"Let's just go home," I said after soaking in the sun for five minutes. "There's still a lot to do, so much paperwork to deal with, and so much stuff to explain to our bosses. But for now, it's time for a break." Neele and Simmons nodded, and together, we set out to return to a city we had given a new future.

A future in which I was not involved. Neither of them needed to know that the relentless pain in my head would inevitably lead to my death. The clock was ticking, and there was nothing I could do about it.

EPILOGUE.
ALLIES

Carpenteria, Seattle 2067 09:21 AM - ECLE Precinct

Five months had passed since the events that changed our lives ended. After a short leave, Simmons and I were back on duty. Following a thorough investigation of all the incidents by our superiors, we were acquitted of all charges, thanks to our bosses at ECLE turning a blind eye to several issues in light of us saving the city and its inhabitants. The bills and costs incurred during our investigation were internally passed on to Holster Skyway through a US-ID promissory note.

We decided to form our own small task force for special cases. It felt good to be back at the ECLE headquarters, this time with a clearer purpose and a stronger team than ever before.

Amithayus was slowly recovering from the damage. Reconstruction was in full swing, and once the truth about the events came to light, many people outside the city walls actively contributed to the effort. As a result, the district began keeping its walls open for two extra hours each day. It became less isolated, though this was partly due to pressure from corporations gradually expanding within Amithayus. The old lab complex where Dr. Caldwell had wreaked havoc was razed to the ground, and statues of Zhan Tao, Maddy Turner, and Dr. Alicia Yoshida now stood tall in its place to honor their service and sacrifice. There was also a proposal to erect a monument for the victims of the Snoqualmie Ridge disaster, which was still hotly debated in the Senate of the Free Trade Zone of Unified America.

Though Thornej A. Holster Jr. had been arrested, his trial was set for six months later. According to his press spokesperson, the facial surgery he had to undergo and the healing of his scars were "none of the public's business" and occurred while he was away whaling. Although the chances of him actually going to prison were slim, that wasn't going to stop us from moving forward.

Simmons and I were sitting in the ECLE office, laughing about an absurd story from our past, when the door swung open and our newest team member walked in.
We greeted her warmly.

"So, how does one manage to be late on their first day?" Simmons teased good-naturedly.

Neele grinned and retorted, "Some of us have important things to do. I've been in the building for two hours already."

She pulled out a dusty file and laid it on the table. "I was in the archive and found this. That's why I'm late."

Simmons and I leaned forward, staring at the relatively thin file. The cover bore the name of a Christian sect, with traces leading back to John Daniels, the Master of Conformity.

A cold shiver ran down my spine. The date on the file was June 30, 2030—the coronation of the first gender-neutral Pope the world had ever seen.

"Looks like we have our next case," I said quietly.

The three of us stared at the file, knowing our work had only just begun.

Dear Reader,

With the last lines of this book, our shared journey comes to an end. It has been an honor and a joy to share my story with you. Every page was written with passion and dedication, hoping to touch and inspire you.

Your opinion means a lot to me. Whether you enjoyed the book or have suggestions for improvement, I want to hear from you! Your honest review on Amazon will help other readers discover this book and support me in growing and developing as an author.

Please take a moment to share your thoughts and feelings about this book. Whether it's praise or constructive criticism – every piece of feedback is valuable. Your words are the compass that guides future readers and shows me that my stories are being heard.

A little announcement:

The second book is already on its way! I look forward to sharing a new story from the same universe with you soon.

Thank you so much for your support and for participating in this journey.

With best wishes,

J. L. Litschko

Glossary

A

- **Acetone Peroxide:** A highly explosive chemical compound that plays a role in the book. It is an unstable, easily made-explosive synthesized from readily available chemicals like acetone and hydrogen peroxide.
- **Amithayus:** An exclusive neighborhood in Seattle, predominantly inhabited by Asian residents. The name means "the immeasurable life."
- **Algorithms:** Mathematical procedures used in the story to solve complex problems.
- **Antagonist:** The protagonist's adversary, creating conflicts in the story.
- **Anaphase:** A term from cell biology describing a phase of cell division where chromosomes are pulled apart.
- **Alicia Yoshida:** A brilliant scientist and a central figure in the book's plot. Dr. Yoshida is known for her groundbreaking research in biotechnology.
- **Armor Vision** Suit: A highly advanced tactical suit featured in the book. The Armor Vision suit combines the protective qualities of the Armorflex suit with enhanced visual technologies.
- **Armorflex Suit:** An advanced protective suit in the story. The Armorflex suit is made of cutting-edge materials highly resistant to physical attacks, extreme temperatures, and chemical hazards.

B

- **Beacon Hill:** A neighborhood in Seattle known for the Holster Skyward Tower.
- **Beretta Quantum x9:** A service weapon used by the main character.
- **Bio-Implants:** Artificial devices implanted in the body to enhance or replace biological functions.
- **Biocompatibility:** The ability of materials to exist in a biological system without causing harmful reactions.
- **Blockchain:** A technology used in the story for secure data storage and transmission.
- **Boeing Black Talon:** A state-of-the-art, heavily armed helicopter developed by Boeing. The Black Talon is noted for its stealth technology, high maneuverability, and impressive firepower.

C

- **Chrono-Tactile Recollection Syndrome (CTRS):** A syndrome affecting the perception of time and touch triggered by certain technologies.
- **Cyberspace:** A virtual reality where digital interactions and transactions take place.

D

- **District Border Controls:** Security measures for monitoring and controlling movement between different parts of the city.
- **Dystopia:** A fictional society characterized by oppression and injustice.
- **Dr. Viktor Caldwell:** Dr. Alicia Yoshida's respected scientist and colleague, specializing in advanced robotics and biomechanical implants. Dr. Caldwell is known for his unconventional methods and relentless research spirit.

E

- **ECLE (Emerald City Law Enforcement):** The police force where the main character works in Seattle.
- **eLetter:** An electronic message resembling a traditional letter but transmitted digitally.
- **Exoskeleton:** A wearable mechanical device that supports and enhances the user's movements.

F

- **Fragment Perception:** The main character's ability to perceive memories and emotions by touching objects or people—see CTRS.
- **Fusion Reactor:** An energy source that generates power by fusing atomic nuclei.

G

- **Graphite:** A form of carbon used in many technical applications, including bullets for firearms.
- **Genetics:** The science of genes and heredity.

H

- **HELPS Mark IV:** A protective suit for hazardous environments used by Neele, including the HELPS AI.
- **Holster Skyway Inc.:** A powerful corporate conglomerate in Seattle that is involved in various industries, including biotechnology and arms manufacturing.
- **Hologram:** A three-dimensional projection of images or data.

I

- **Implants:** Artificial devices implanted in the body to enhance or replace biological functions.
- **Informatics:** The science of processing and storing information.
- **Imperial Corporate Federation of Europe:** A powerful political and economic alliance in the book's futuristic vision, consisting of a coalition of Europe's largest corporations. This federation controls large parts of the European economy and society, often enforcing its interests through military and technological means.

J

- **Jenn:** A character involved in a relationship crisis that influences the story.
- **Joule:** A unit of energy.

K

- **Caliber:** High-caliber bullets used in deadly firearms.
- **Kinetics:** A branch of physics and engineering dealing with the movement of bodies and the forces acting on them.
- **Krokodil:** A dangerous drug that causes severe physical damage, originating from Russia.
- **Cybernetics:** The science of control and communication processes in living beings and machines.

L

- **Lenny "Corpse Mouth":** A character known for extracting secrets and valuable information from the bodies of his enemies, often working as an informant for the criminal Organizations.

M

- **Maddy "Maddog" Turner:** A fearless and battle-hardened character in the book, known for her aggressive and unpredictable nature. Maddy Turner, also known as "Maddog" earned her nickname for her wild and ruthless fighting style.
- **Main Street Pharmacy:** A rundown store in the Old Medical District, serving as a meeting point for secret gatherings.
- **Martin Serpentine:** A character whose past and fate play a significant role in the story.
- **Metaphase:** A phase of cell division where chromosomes align in the center of the cell.
- **Microchip:** A small, integrated electronic component.
- **Mincheng:** A district in Seattle known for its high population density and cultural diversity. Mincheng is a vibrant neighborhood predominantly inhabited by Chinese immigrants.
- **Milo "The Knife" Kryt:** A renowned implant specialist in the book, known for his precise and masterful work in biotechnology implants. Due to his outstanding skills and the sharp instruments he uses, he earned the nickname "The Knife."
- **Mr. Tanaka:** An influential businessman and central figure in the book. Mr. Tanaka is the head of a powerful, extensive network that includes legal and illegal businesses. He is known for his cold-bloodedness, strategic thinking, and ability to navigate society's highest circles while maintaining connections to the underworld.

N

- **Nanoflex Polymer:** A material used in the main character's gloves to protect them from perceiving fragments.
- **Neele:** A scientist in a high-tech lab confronted with mysterious events.

- **Neural Network:** A model that mimics the functioning of the human brain and is used in artificial intelligence.

O

- **Old Medical District:** A rundown area in Seattle, formerly a medical center.
- **Orcas Street:** A street in Beacon Hill known for its transformation from a residential area to an industrial complex.
- **Optics:** The science of light and its interactions with matter.

P

- **Pacific Commonwealth:** A political entity formed from the former states of Washington, Oregon, and parts of California.
- **Pastoux:** A high-quality French wine mentioned in the story.
- **Pinehill:** A safe district in Seattle where the middle class has migrated.
- **Plastinates:** Preserved human bodies or body parts used for scientific purposes.
- **Photonics:** The science and technology of generating, controlling, and detecting photons.
- **Phantom Pain:** A term used in the book to describe pain in an amputated or missing limb. This type of pain occurs when the brain continues to receive signals from
nerves that previously belonged to the missing limb.

Q

- **Quantum Entanglement:** A physical phenomenon where two or more particles become so interconnected that their states are immediately correlated regardless of distance.
- **Quantum Computer:** A computer based on the principles of quantum mechanics, capable of performing certain computations much faster than traditional computers.

R

- **Robots:** Mechanical devices often used in industry and research to automate tasks.
- **Theory of Relativity:** Einstein's theory describes space and time structure.
- **Rust:** A multifaceted character in the book, known for his expertise in mechanics and technology. Rust, whose real name is unknown, earned his nickname for his ability to revive old and rusty machines.

S

- **Seattle, 2066:** A futuristic version of the city where the book's events occur.
- **Simmons:** An experienced police officer and partner of the narrator, known for his sharp mind and dry humor.
- **Skyward Tower:** An impressive skyscraper and headquarters of Holster Skyway Inc.
- **Synth-Crocodile:** A dangerous concocted drug that causes severe physical damage.
- **Synthetics:** In the book's context, "synthetics" refers to artificially created materials, organisms, or devices designed to perform specific functions beyond the capabilities of natural substances, especially food.

T

- **Thornej A. Holster, Jr.:** Head of Holster Skyway Inc., influential in various technological industries.
- **Teleportation:** A hypothetical process of instantly moving objects or people from one place to another.

U

- **Underground Movements:** Secret organizations or groups operating covertly, often with political or criminal goals.
- **Ultrasound:** Sound waves with frequencies above the audible range, often used in medical imaging.

V

- **Virtual Reality (VR):** A computer-generated environment that immerses users in a virtual world.

Y

- **Yoru no Hana Club:** An exclusive nightclub in futuristic Seattle owned by Mr. Tanaka. The club is known for its luxurious décor and secret meetings. The name means "Flower of the Night" in Japanese.

W

- **Wonder Bread:** A brand name for white bread, symbolizing everyday habits and normalcy in the story.
- **Wi-Fi:** A wireless technology for connecting devices to the internet.

Z

- **Zhan Tao:** A significant character in the book, known for his courage and willingness to sacrifice.

Printed in Great Britain
by Amazon